FALLING FOR THE ROCKSTAR'S
DAUGHTER BOOK 3

by
WILLA DREW

Moving Words Publishing

PRAISE FOR WILLA DREW

Willa Drew's writing style blew me away.

Highly recommend this author and book without a doubt!

My first book by Willa and it won't be my last!

I look forward to reading other books by this author in the future. Because I went into this one with hope and promise, and it absolutely delivered! Now it's your turn!

This is a great story written by two clearly talented authors. The characters have been put front and centre of this book, with their story and development being what it is all about.

This is the first time I have a read a book by these authors and I enjoyed the collaboration. The book flowed well, seamlessly moving through the story.

I am glad I stumbled on this book and these authors, and I will definitely be adding them to my list of authors to keep my eye out for.

The authors did a wonderful job of writing the characters in a way that I felt connected to them right away.

PRAISE FOR FALLING FOR THE ROCKSTAR'S DAUGHTER

WE Blend slow-burned its way into my heart with a perfect mix of sweetness and tension.

Wil and El are magic. I don't usually like slow burn, but this was done right. Their chemistry is off the charts and the building of feelings each time they interact is perfect.

This books is a beautiful story to read. The romance is slow blooming and captivatingly written. I literally got lost in El and Wil's story and didn't want it to end.

This book was a must read in my books, I love how the story was told.

If you are on the fence about reading this, please read it! It is such a fun, well written read.

Entertaining right to the last page.

This story is fantastic.....and I did not want it to end. The story just flowed, even though it was a slow burn, every piece came to life.

Published by: Moving Words Publishing

www.movingwordspublishing.com

Printed in the United States of America

ISBN: 978-1-957897-25-7

First Edition: October 2024

Join the mailing list for updates and follow Willa Drew at
www.willadrew.com

If you like this book, please consider giving it a review, so others
can enjoy it as well.

CONTENTS

Characters you met in WE Blend & WE Breathe:

Melodie Vella Rockerby aka El Vella—wannabe singer-songwriter. Daughter of famous opera stars Sylvia Vella Rockerby and Mathew Vella (died in a boat accident with El present when she was 10). Only child. Her mother gave birth to her half-brother, nicknamed Pickle, in December of the previous year (in WE Breathe). El is dyslexic, has perfect pitch, plays the piano and the guitar, is an avid runner, and loves butter tarts. El has blue eyes, is 5'6" is a redhead and has shoulder-length bob with a streak of colorless hair that appeared after the father's death. In WE Breathe she turned 19 and took a job as a backup singer with the band Blatantly Subtle.

Wil Peters aka Wilhelm Peters, named after his grandfather—was studying sound engineering in Germany but switched to UCLA when he came to live in Los Angeles, plays the guitar, sings, DJs to support himself (as well as his family), was on a rowing team, constantly writes words and impressions of the world in a small black notebook he carries around. Wil is 6'3", has amber eyes and jet-black floppy hair. He turned 20 WE Blend. In WE Breathe, his father, Bill Rockerby, held a press conference to tell the world that Wil was his son. Wil got into a car accident at the end of WE Breathe, together with El's cousin, Zoe, and broke an arm and some ribs.

Bill Rockerby, aka Rocker—Wil's estranged biological father and El's stepdad (Rocker married Sylvia when El was 12). Rocker sided with his wife when she instructed El to stay away from a career in music. He is a music producer and has his own company Rocker Inc. where El worked during WE Blend and Wil worked in WE Breathe, as an intern. Rocker is 42 years old, 6'3", has amber eyes and jet-black hair. He was excited about the birth of his first baby (Pickle) with his wife and El's mother, Sylvia Vella Rockerby and shocked yet thrilled to discover he was Wil's father.

Sylvia Vella Rockerby—El's mother. She is a famous opera singer, a widow, and wife of Rocker. Pickle is her second child. She's from Norway and married Mathew Vella, who's from Malta, after they met in college in Italy studying classical singing. She is 44 years old, has blond hair and blue eyes. Her negative experience with paparazzi after her first husband's death and fame guided her decision in WE Blend to make sure El never had to go through the same. In WE Breathe El and Sylvia somewhat reconcile but still need to rebuild their relationship.

Hanna Peters—Wil's mother. She had Wil when she was 21. She's an assistant at a doctor's office. Never married. Lives in Bremen, Germany, with her father, Wilhelm Peters aka Opa aka Mr. Peters. Hanna never told Wil who his father was. She suffers from a severe case of Rheumatoid Arthritis and in WE Blend was accepted to a clinical trial program that required out-of-pocket payments she could not afford. Unknown to her, in WE Breathe Wil and Rocker made a deal to pay for her treatment. She is responding well to the program. In WE Breathe she was happy Wil was settling in LA and living with Rocker. Hanna met Sylvia and Pickle during her visit to LA for the Gala of the RA Connect Foundation Wil and Rocker created to support people like her.

Wilhelm Peters, aka Opa, aka Mr. Peters—Wil's grandfather. A retired construction worker. A widower, he helped Hanna raise Wil and became his father-figure. Mr. Peters is not good with technology. He was the one who told Wil who his real father was and concocted the plan of Wil going to America to meet Rocker to get the money for Hanna's treatment. In WE Breathe he orchestrated the deal for Wil to go back to America to live with Rocker in exchange for full payment of Hanna's experimental treatment.

Zoe Yilmaz—El's cousin. She turns 20 WE Blend. Zoe is a fashion designer and is a fan of social media. Zoe lives with her parents, Patty and Bob Yilmaz, and is El's best friend. In WE Blend, Zoe held her own fashion show where Wil and El performed. In WE Breathe, she was the passenger in the car when

Wil had his accident on the way to Death Elbow's performance that El refused to attend. Zoe fought with El at the hospital, calling El selfish. As a result, they are not on speaking terms any longer.

Mateo Ruiz Flores—Wil's friend from the Starlight Film Foundation competition who Wil lived with in WE Blend during the competition and when he goes to UCLA in the fall. Mateo is from Mexico. He is studying to be a graphic designer at UCLA, is into art, but is also a connector and is the one who got Wil his ID in WE Blend, so Wil could go to The Devil's Martini bar where he ended up playing the guitar for El's open mic competition. In WE Breathe, Mateo branched out to design merchandise for Death Elbow, the rock group that signed with Rocker Inc and that Wil is interning for.

Sven Andres—Rocker's bodyguard who becomes El's bodyguard in WE Blend after Rocker brings her back from England. Sven completed 8 years with the marines before joining Rocker's team. He loves Superman comics, attends Comi-Con dressed up as his hero and has a major sweet tooth. He is an excellent driver, works out a lot, including running with El, and has a younger half-brother Travis who often gets in trouble. In WE Breathe, he left Rocker's employment to open his own security firm.

Carlee Waters—one of the lead singers in the pop/rock band Blatantly Subtle. In WE Breathe, she handpicked El to join the band as a possible replacement. Carlee felt forced to retire from the band because she has Multiple Sclerosis and could no longer consistently perform. When she devastated El by not choosing her as the nest co-lead of Blatantly Subtle, Carlee asked El to work with her as a song writer in Los Angeles. El declined the offer.

Daniel Davison—entertainment reporter who constantly hounded El until she did a live interview with him in WE Breathe, clearing up the mystery of her father's death and outing Wil as her boyfriend.

Corbin Laceter —lead singer of the rock band, Death Elbow, discovered by Wil and Rocker and signed by Rocker Inc in WE Breathe.

Marta Nowak—Rocker's housekeeper. She's Polish, a great cook, and turned 55 during WE Blend.

Leonard Astor–famous music video director El hired in WE Blend to film her music video in England but failed to shoot any videos with.

The story so far. . .

El Vella (aka Melodie Rockerby) 18, met Wil Peters, 19 at an open mic competition at The Devil's Martini bar. Wil stepped in to play guitar when the guitarist she originally hired was drunk and El was unable to play because of her broken fingers.

In WE Blend they sang together onstage and busked at the Farmer's Market to earn extra cash, all while Wil hid the secret that his father was El's step father, the rock star Bill Rockerby, aka Rocker. Wil came to the US to get 18 years of child support from Rocker to pay for an experimental treatment for his ailing mother. Wil and El grew closer and developed feeling for each other. However, when El overheard Wil claiming to be Rocker's son and that the reason he came to LA was to get money from him, El ran away thinking Wil used her to get to Rocker.

With Sven's help, Wil sneaked into Rocker's mansion to apologize to El. Wil confessed he fell for her even though she couldn't fall for him. El stopped him with a kiss. Because she forgave him and was still angry at her parents, El decided to run away to Germany with Wil. In Bremen, when Wil arrived at his mother's doorstep with El, he introduced her as his girlfriend. No one in LA knew where they were.

WE Breathe starts with Wil & El enjoying their privacy in Bremen, writing songs, and learning to be in a relationship. While Wil and El busked at the Christmas market, the paparazzi recognized El and chased them.

On a snowy Christmas Eve Rocker turned up in Bremen to bring El home and was stunned to discover Hanna was Wil's mother. He finally recognized Wil as his son. Rocker offered Wil a deal: if Wil came back to LA, lived at his mansion and worked at Rocker Inc., then Rocker would pay Hanna's medical bills.

At the same time, El received a DM from Carlee Waters, one of the lead singers of Blatantly Subtle, a star-charting pop-rock group, with an offer to join the band as a back up singer. Although Wil thought the job was a waste of El's talent, he supported her decision. Wil landed back in Los Angeles, where he met his new stepbrother, nicknamed Pickle. El journeyed to Atlanta to train for the tour with Carlee and to meet the two other new backup singers, Yoli and Annalyn. El convinced Wil to keep their relationship a secret, fearing the backlash of the paparazzi. Rockers assigned Sven to be Wil's bodyguard.

Because El convinced her cousin Zoe to keep an eye on Wil, Zoe roped him and Mateo into helping her with her fashion show. After having spent so much time together in Germany, Wil and El struggle with the long-distance relationship. When Wil, Zoe, and Mateo travelled to Las Vegas to watch El on stage and celebrate her birthday, the reunion was sidelined because El got food poisoning.

At an LA club, during a "daddy date" with Rocker, who was trying to connect with his son, Wil convinced the up-and-coming-band, Death Elbow, to sign with Rocker Inc.

On tour, Carlee collapsed onstage. She revealed that she has multiple sclerosis and that the real reason El and Annalyn were hired was to find a replacement singer for the band. With the tour on pause, El returned home for the weekend to surprise Zoe and attended her fashion show. Wil and El sang for the guests and spent the night together.

At the family brunch the next day, Wil and Rocker were recorded changing Pickle's diapers and calling him Wil's brother. To get ahead of the gossip, the family held a press conference where Rocker announced to the world that Wil was his son. The press, including Daniel Davison, reported positively on the news.

El resumed the tour but to audition for the lead singer position she had to compose an original song and perform it for Blatantly Subtle. Wil promised to fly in and help her, but Hanna's surprise visit interrupted his plans. Alone, El put her all into the song, but was devastated when she wasn't chosen. Giving up on a career in music, El refused to return to the Rockerby mansion and moved into the pool house at Zoe's parents' place

Worried about El but on a high of his harmonious relationship with the press and rewarding internship, Wil arrived to pick El up for Death Elbow's debut event. Depressed and disillusioned in the music industry, El refused to go, instead picking a fight with Wil. At Zoe's insistence Wil left for the venue without El. Half-way to LA he turned around too quickly and crashed into oncoming traffic with Zoe in the car.

El rushed to the hospital when her mother called about Wil and Zoe. While Rocker was taken to see Wil, El checked on Zoe, who apart from a nasty gash on her forehead seemed fine. In anger and fear, Zoe pointed out how selfish El had been since returning to LA, how Wil rearranged his life to accommodate her including turning around to be with her instead of focusing on his big night. Convincing herself that she was making Wil's life worse, El picked another fight with Wil at the hospital and fled. She called the only friend she had left: Sven.

As Wil recovered in the hospital, Rocker insisted on sleeping in a chair in Wil's room. The two had a heart-to-heart and for the first time, Wil called Rocker — Dad. Wil agreed to stay in LA for at least the summer, but was concerned about El who had not returned his phone calls or texts.

Acting as Sven's receptionist, El was shocked when Carlee Waters walked through the door of Anders Investigations. Carlee explained that she hadn't picked El as the lead singer because El had the potential to be a superstar on her own, not the replacement in a band. El was stunned when Carlee asked her to work with her as a songwriter. Although El refused Carlee's offer, she listened to her advice about reconciling with Wil.

While jail-breaking Wil from the hospital despite his bruised ribs and broken arm, Zoe got an alert on her phone that El was being interviewed live with Daniel Davison

El was uncomfortable talking to Daniel Davison, the man who has plagued her with questions for years, but arranged a live interview with him where she told the world the story of her papa's boating accident and admitted that Wil, her newly discovered step-sibling was her boyfriend. Back in the location that Wil and El had busked at in the farmers' market, El performed a song she wrote about Wil to ask for his forgiveness when Wil appeared through the crowd. Happily reunited, Wil and El kissed and El asked Wil out on a date. Wil replied. "I thought you'd never ask."

For our friends,
new and old, we love you

ONE

WHAT IS THE PRICE of fame?

I click post on the new cover song my followers were asking for and prop myself against the headboard. Sven's bedroom has become my oasis over the last month and a half. Unable to resist, I scroll through the comment section from the video I posted two days ago. Although my heart glows from the encouraging words of fans, the hateful comments about me dating my stepbrother leave a bitter taste in my mouth. My fingers fly to my hair and twirl my signature colorless strand. Even all these weeks since my live interview with Daniel Davison, when I announced to the world that Wil Peters is my boyfriend, the haters leave snide remarks and send disrespectful DMs about us, not about my music.

The sound of the water stops and Wil's humming filters through the bathroom door. I should get ready too. I abandon my phone, screen down, on the bedside table and leave the guitar between it and the wall. Sven's bedroom was small for just me and my stuff, but with the addition of Wil's items that have migrated here, the only open spot is the bed. I put on a pair of jeans and a T-shirt. My hands hover over the heels from Zoe's collection, but I pick simpler sneakers instead.

I twist toward the sound of the bathroom door opening and drink in the sight of my boyfriend. Wil strikes a ridiculously overdone pose that somehow sends my heart into an allegro. His hair is styled. His right arm that's still stiff but finally out of the cast hangs at one side and adds debonair swagger to his brown fitted slacks and beige shirt. My thumb digs into the seams of my jeans and I glide my bottom lip through my teeth.

Wil's eyes shine as he crosses the room. His soft lips connect with mine. My annoyance over the post melts with the care of his touch. My head spins, but Wil pushes me gently onto the covers and his hand on my waist grounds me. He teases my mouth, asking permission for more, and when I open, he drinks me in like I'm the only thing that can quench his thirst.

My fingers slide around his neck, urging him closer. I'm quickly learning that Wil's first kiss of the day is like the sample at the chocolate shop we visited in Bremen—a sweet yet hot taste of things to come. This, here, with Wil, is my safe heaven. Unlike fame, this is worth the price.

"Hi." His low tone rumbles to my core.

A breathy "Hi" escapes my lips. Wil's hand roams from my waist along my ribs. My body tightens like the strings on a guitar. Maybe we should dump the current plan of checking out an apartment and make use of the bed we're already on. I skim my palm over Wil's broad shoulders. His liquid heat seeps into me.

The bang of the front door reminds me where and when we are. My sanity slices through the cloud of lust. Sven has clients in the office downstairs and even though it's the end of the workday for most, security firms don't keep regular hours. I turn my brain back on, sit up, and skate to the edge of the bed, out of the tempting cage of Wil's solidity.

"We need to go."

"To be continued." Wil's gaze drags over my lips and I think he's going to kiss me again. I want him to kiss me again, but he sighs and stands. "Do I look like a guy worthy of going on a date with El Vella?"

"This is not a date," I remind him.

I run my hand over Wil's chest, careful not to restart what I just put a pause on. The luxurious fabric is something that would've been in my closet last year. It screams high-end and expensive, but doesn't scream my boyfriend. This Wil is quite a departure from the guy in well-worn jeans and T-shirts who agreed to play guitar for me at The Devil's Martini. This Wil could be on the cover of GQ. My body simmers in anticipation, but the seam of his shirt bumps my greedy fingers to a stop.

"When I asked you out, I meant dinner and a movie, you know, normal boyfriend/girlfriend stuff."

Wil's thumb travels along the curve of my shoulder and my skin tingles. His palm continues down as he presses the back of my knees against the bed. "As long as I'm with you, I don't care what we do. Or where."

My cheeks are scorching, because even though we've had to be careful of his ribs and arm after the accident, we've made excellent use of this double bed. With every last ounce of restraint, I pry myself away from Wil. "I care. I promised you a date and it's happening." I straighten my T-shirt. "Today is about getting me out of Sven's bedroom for good. Once I have my own place we can spend an entire weekend in bed."

"Promise?" Wil runs his nose along my cheekbone and lightly bites the corner of my lip.

I twist out of his caress, take his hand, and drag him down the stairs. "Promise."

On the sidewalk, Wil draws me to him. I jerk away and scan the street for camera lenses.

Wil frowns. "I thought we were over this." The long rays of the oncoming sunset make his amber irises deepen to glimmering gold. "Everyone knows we're together."

"Everyone knowing we are dating doesn't call for public PDA." I separate from Wil, putting cold air between us. "We can kiss plenty more inside my new apartment. When I find one." I take Wil's hand to move him along the sidewalk. We're losing the light. "Let's go do that."

The excitement disappears off Wil's face and a muscle in his jaw ticks.

I swing our hands as we walk and try a diversion. "How was the new professor in your sound design for visual media course?"

"Fine, I guess," Wil scoffs. "Mateo was right to insist I enroll. He says hi by the way."

"Is he ready for tomorrow night?" I turn down the street that leads to The Devil's Martini, where Death Elbow will be playing.

"It's all he's talked about. He and Zoe were arguing over the merch booth. The stickers Mateo created are apparently taking space away from the T-shirts designed by Zoe."

I breathe through the ache in my chest at the mention of my cousin. Just because I haven't talked to her since the accident doesn't mean I'm not thinking about her all the time.

Wil steps closer. "She misses you."

I glance at him. "Then she should call me."

Wil sighs. "Or you could call her?"

I take a sip from our water bottle and offer it to Wil. The W&E I wrote on the bottom when we were hiding in Bremen over Christmas is still there. I point to the signature. "It's fading."

"Shall we get a new one?"

"No." I lightly slap his chest. "Don't even joke. This water bottle is the first gift you gave me. It goes with me everywhere."

We wait for the light to turn. Wil leans in. "Will you wear your blue dress tomorrow?"

"No." The walk sign flashes. "That's a bit formal for a rock concert."

He takes my hand. "Someday I'll see that dress on you."

I rest my face on the soft fabric of his coat and for a second let myself imagine a magical night where he gets to enjoy the blue dress on me at the beginning, and I get to enjoy him removing it at the end.

The further we walk from the office, the worse the street art gets. At first the murals are graphic and colorful, but the side of the corner store is covered in scrawled graffiti that's more like tagging. In the distance a car alarm cuts through the air, whining between an F and an F-sharp that makes my ears want to bleed.

Wil's fingers tighten around mine. "Are you sure this is the right street?"

"Yup." I lift my chin. The satellite image I studied this afternoon didn't show the overflowing garbage bins we're forced to step around. "It's just up here."

"El. I'm not sure this is for you."

"You're so overprotective." I drag Wil by the hand. "We'll be fine."

We turn a corner and a four-story rectangular building recently painted snow-white contrasts starkly against the brown and tan townhouses flanking it.

"This is it." I bound up the three steps to the covered portico, search for the name the landlord provided, and press a button on the entry system.

Wil twists left and right, surveying the area, and his eyes land on a woman pushing a shopping cart down an alley. He opens his mouth, but the buzzing sound of the door opening causes him to pause. He sucks in his bottom lip. "Do they just let anyone in?"

"Jon is expecting us." I push down the flutter of anticipation and hold the door for Wil.

The small lobby is cool and murky in the dwindling evening light. A cream sign with black letters states the elevator is out of order.

Wil spots the stairs. "Good thing today wasn't leg day."

I glance at his chest. Are his ribs up to a four-flight climb? "We'll take it slow."

Wil heads for the first step. "I'm fine. Let's get this over with."

Frustration bubbles beneath my skin, threatening to overflow. I follow Wil as we wind around flights, a single bulb illuminating the steps. The air gets stuffier and thicker with each floor. In contrast to the foyer and the stairwell, the hallway is brightly lit, and my eyes sting like I've stepped onto the LAX tarmac at high noon. Crisp, clean white walls are broken by deep red doors adorned with modern brass numbers and hardware.

I stop in front of number 405 and knock. The door swings open and a short, muscled man in a green leisure suit greets us. "El?" He sticks out a meaty palm. "Any trouble finding the place?" He doesn't wait for an answer. "Sorry about the elevator. It'll be fixed by the end of the month."

Parquet covers the floor of the open concept living room/kitchen area that appears smaller than the pictures I showed Wil. My harpsichord would not fit in here. But maybe it's best that Papa's gift stays in Rocker's climate-controlled mansion. Sweat drips down my back and Wil shrugs out of his coat.

"The air conditioner is currently being replaced." Jon strolls to the breakfast bar. "My partner and I bought the building at the beginning of the year and renovations take time." He nods at Wil, like only men understand the concept of installing electrical components. "Next up is the laundry room and the entry system."

We meander to the bedroom, which has a closet the size of Sven's filing cabinet. Wil pokes his nose into the bathroom, takes a cursory glance, and shakes his head.

"What?" I whisper.

"It's tiny." His breath tickles my ear. "We can't both fit in there."

"That's one strike against this place." I run my hand over his chest.

He softly captures my wrist. "Of many."

"It has potential." Like I might potentially be able to afford the rent. I can trade in my shampoo and conditioner for something from the drug store, and find another way to manage my frizzy hair. Maybe live in braids for the next few months?

The warmth has abandoned Wil's eyes, leaving them a flat yellow. "You can't be serious. This place is a du—"

I clap my hand over his mouth. "Jon will hear you." Wil licks my palm and I release him. "It's the nicest place in my price range."

"I will not have you stay here."

My back stiffens. "You sound an awful lot like Rocker right now."

"El, that's not fair. This place is not . . ." His mouth contorts.

"Not what? Good enough for you?" The words vomit out of me. I'm stunned. At me, and at him.

"Safe." His grip on me tightens. "I'd be constantly worried about you walking up those stairs—"

"The elevator will be working soon."

"And this neighborhood?"

I cross my arms. "I'm never going to find a place as nice as Rocker's. I'm not a millionaire." And won't become one any time soon. "I can't stay with Sven forever."

Wil inches forward. "You don't need a mansion. But you do need a place where you feel comfortable." His finger traces my clenched fist. "Think about it this way. If the paparazzi followed you here, they'd easily get into the building."

"Jon said he's fixing the buzzer," I protest weakly.

"I couldn't live with myself if something happened to you." Wil traces my cheek. "Please, El. Let's keep looking. I'm sure you can find a place that's safe."

I glance at the darkening sky and like the last rays of light, my willpower to resist Wil wanes. "Fine."

His arms cinch around my waist, pulling me close enough for his lips to press on my temple. "Thank you."

"But you have to break it to Sven that he's sleeping on his couch again tonight."

A soft lullaby plays as the soundtrack to my dream. The chords shift slowly up, melting into something softer, and I'm chasing the music, the melody spooling in front of me like Mormor's favorite tablecloth. Even though Sven's bed is as hard as a stone pallet, I'm comfortable and safe.

A squeak of fingers sliding on a guitar string cuts through my haze. I force my eyes open but the tune restarts and I sink back into the depths of dreams unrealized. Until it happens again.

I open my eyes and the sight before me presents a different kind of dream.

Wil.

Wil without a shirt on. His back against the headboard, guitar in hand. I float on a cloud of bliss, looking at my small piece of paradise. How lucky am I that fate brought this man to my city, to The Devil's Martini, almost a year ago?

He's balancing the headstock of a guitar in his left—uninjured—hand, awkwardly plucking notes with his still recovering right. The cast came off only days ago and from my experience breaking my fingers last year, I know it'll take him weeks of physical therapy to play like he used to.

So many great and awful things happened to bring us together. His mom falling for Rocker and getting pregnant. Wil not knowing who his father was until last year. Wil's mom getting sick. My father dying in a boating accident by my side. My mom and me meeting Rocker at the Griffith Observatory. Mr. Peters sending Wil to the US to confront Rocker. Me sneaking into The Devil's Martini for the open mic night. The guitarist I hired winding up drunk. Wil being there, offering to play the guitar, and helping me sing when I froze. Mom giving birth to Pickle. Wil and me coming back to the US from Bremen. Blatantly Subtle not choosing me as their lead singer. Rocker announcing to the world that Wil is his son. Wil's mom getting the treatment she needed. Wil and Zoe's car accident—which I know wasn't my fault but still feels like it was. Singing to millions of people live to show Wil what he means to me.

Memories stream in as Wil's music wakes them one by one. I want to cry and laugh and everything in between. My heart spins the reel of what my life has been by his side.

The El of a year ago gave up on love after Dillon's breakup text. The El of a year ago wanted to be center stage. The El of a year ago would not even imagine sleeping in a tiny shoebox of a room above Sven's office.

Today's El hasn't accomplished anything that El wanted, but today's El, today's me is happy. So happy I don't want to jinx it. No denials. No disguises. The last month and a half of being Wil's girlfriend has been the best of my life.

"I could wake up to this every day." I kiss his shoulder.

His finger slips and the off-key E echoes in my ears like feedback from a mic.

I sit up and reach out. "Let me do that."

"I thought I had an idea, but with the bum arm everything is a struggle, so it's gotten away from me." Wil runs his fingers across the scruff on his chin that tickled my inner thigh last night. "A pre-chorus, or something that leads into the chorus."

Muscle memory kicks in and my fingers find their places on the guitar. I replicate what I heard him plucking but add to the tone with my fully functioning hands.

"How do you do that?" Wil stares at me intently.

"Rocker taught me to play."

"No." He moves his fingers in the air. "Just pick up and play back the same tune I only made up a moment ago. No sheet music. Only hearing it once."

I shrug. "I don't know. I can just feel it."

"Here?" Wil traces the skin over my heart and the organ responds with an accelerated beat. "Or here?" His fingers roam across my clavicle, along my throat and cheek, settling on the edge of my hairline, by my ear. The pitter-patter of my thoughts still at his touch.

"Both?" The guitar shakes in my hands. "In my stomach as well."

"Do you have any idea how amazing you are?"

I lower my gaze. "Half as amazing as you?"

"I'm not even close."

"You—"

Wil stops my protest with a kiss and the argument is over because I'd surrender to this any day of the week. This kiss is laced with early morning tenderness, an echo of last night, a taste of what's to come. I drag him closer.

Between us the guitar wails in protest. Wil releases my lips, his eyes finding mine. "Play it again."

Never breaking eye contact, I strum his melody, repeating the notes that are now not only his, but ours. Low and soft, he whispers words that match my plucking.

> Love conquers all, the movies said
> but when I'm lonely in my bed
> I think of you

I come to the end of the portion I heard him play but I don't stop. The melody unfolds before me and I let my fingers run of their own free will. Wil keeps singing, the pupils in his amber eyes expanding like an infinite starless night. It's just his words, my melody, our souls weaving magic, and there is no feeling like it.

Singing onstage with Blatantly Subtle had the high from the crowd, the excitement of singing with musicians who were true professionals, the thrill of knowing what was next on the set list but also the uncertainty of what would happen and how we'd have to adapt. Yet something was missing. A piece of the puzzle never found its spot.

My fingers flex, my memories fade
and on this day, I can relate
I think of you

But this. This here with Wil surpasses anything I experienced during those weeks. It's him and me onstage at The Devil's Martini, busking at the farmers' market, recording our song in the studio. This makes my heart pound, my head clear yet buzzy, my stomach full of the butterflies that show up when I'm happy, not anxious. I'm floating yet tethered. Wil is my anchor.

Maybe they were right,
maybe they were wrong,
maybe I should just give up, give in and fall for . . . you

We weave the cascades of "you" between our voices, harmonizing in perfect symphony. I grin as joy radiates from me, reflecting the happiness inside.

His smile mirrors mine. We are two halves of a whole. A duet.

Maybe him and me singing together is the answer. Maybe we should—

"Damn, El." Wil cuts off the song, my breath, and my thoughts when his lips find mine.

Two

"It's exactly the same." El's gaze roams around the semi-darkness backstage at The Devil's Martini. "Even the scuffs are still on the wall."

"I doubt they've done anything since we were last here." I lead her to the green room we were never invited to use when we sang as the opening act on Saturday nights. The "HEADLINERS ONLY" sign doesn't seem as forbidding as it did almost a year ago. I open the door and walk into a wall of smells and sounds.

Corbin, the lead singer of Death Elbow, shirtless with eyeliner pencil in hand, slants away from the mirror and does a sweep of my girlfriend as if I'm not right next to her. "The infamous Melodie Rockerby. We meet at last." He drops the pencil, opens his arms wide, and advances on El.

I intercept the hug instead, slapping him on the back. "I told you she was coming this time." I wince the moment the words exit my mouth. I'm still a little bitter that she didn't want to come to the last performance of the group, but I didn't mean it that way. I'm just happy she's here. "This is Corbin Laceter." I wrap an arm around El's shoulders and kiss her on her temple. "And this is my girlfriend, El."

"El, huh. My pleasure." Corbin picks El's hand up and kisses it like the gentleman he is not. He doesn't know the names of any of his groupies and prefers it that way. He smiles at El, flirting with his eyes as if I'm not standing right there, then straightens. "I hope you enjoy the show."

Did he just flex his abs? I give Corbin a nudge. Playful but also rough enough for him to get the "get your hands off my girlfriend you wanker" message across.

"Are you going to introduce me too?" Like the golden retriever he is, Lucian bounds to us. "I'm Lucian, the bassist, and you are beautiful. The hair is even more gorgeous in-person, I've seen you in magazines since I was a kid and now I get to meet you. I still can't get over meeting so many people I've only seen on TV." Lucian bounces on his toes. "This is my brother Gideon. Our drummer."

Gideon lifts his hand in greeting and returns to braiding his hair. I'm not sure the new style will last through the set. His jet-black hair usually hangs loose to his waist and whips around as he sweats behind the drum set.

Corbin nudges Lucian aside. "This is Xander. Our guitarist."

"If I'd met your boyfriend before I met Corbin, I would've had him join our band." Xander's grass-green eyes take me in.

"Didn't you two used to play here?" Corbin holds his arms wide.

El smiles at me. "We did."

"I love the covers you've been putting out. You can play one of those. Be our opener? A little impromptu throwback?" Corbin joins Lucian and Gideon in a circle around us. "Warm the crowd up for us?"

I point to my still recovering arm. "I'm out of commission. Plus I wasn't the star of the show. El was." El still is my star. I tug her closer and nuzzle her hair with my chin.

Lucian inches closer. "Maybe El sings with us then."

"Sorry boys." El taps the spot over my heart. "I only play with this man."

Corbin laughs and returns to his reflection in the mirror.

I catch his eye. "Remember the brand team from Vatton are watching. I've placed their water bottles beside each of your instruments." The head of marketing sent over four boxes of the florescent purple canisters. "Try to remember to take a sip during your performance."

Corbin's lip curls. "Is there vodka in it?"

"Water. We'll drink after."

Corbin points his eye pencil at me. "I'll hold you to that. Play first, party after."

"Sure." I rub my hands together. "Now, let's get ready to rock this place to its foundation. El and I will be your hype team and get the crowd revved for you."

The guys roar as we slip into the hallway.

"They seem like . . ."

"Rock and roll." I tug on a strand of El's hair. "They're just pumped for the performance."

At the end of the hall, Mateo has his hands on his head like he's trying to block out sound. He shuffles back and Zoe strides into his space, her arms in the air. They are far enough away that I can't hear what they are saying, but their disagreement is clear.

"Typical." I roll my eyes and bend down to El. "Those two are arguing again."

The smile slides off El's face as she spots her cousin. "I have to go to wash my hands."

Reluctantly, I let her go. I can't make her talk to her cousin. No matter how much I want to.

Zoe spots me. "Wil. About time. Would you tell this design expert"—she air quotes the word—"that fuchsia is a violation of the dark aesthetic I've created for Death Elbow ."

Mateo shakes his head. "She wouldn't listen to me."

I wince. "Zoe, those are Vatton's hot-off-the-press signature metal water bottles. That is apparently going to be the color of the summer. I'm trying to lock down a deal."

Zoe cocks her head. "That's not my shirt you're wearing." She steps forward and tugs my belt loop. "At least it works with my pants. Wil Peters, what's going on?"

"I decided to wear something different."

"Without checking with me first?" Zoe places both her hands on her chest. "I'm hurt." Her hands fall, her left settling on her hip. "Are you going to be selfish like your girlfriend and stop talking to me next?"

"I'm not stopping talking to you. You know I love your designs." I tuck the Moderni Look shirt in. The Finnish clothing company is another potential brand deal. "This is business."

The audience screams loud enough all on their own. For a freshly signed group, Death Elbow is growing their followers faster than Dad and I anticipated. The band is all in: the daily short form videos, the Vlogs, their eagerness to go on any radio show or online interview that we can book them. The guys work hard. Concerts, press, writing session, social media—they have been on a roll. But they party hard too, which is something Dad already talked to them about.

"Thank you, The Devil's Martini. You've been the best audience, and we love you! Keep an eye on our socials for a special announcement that's coming soon." Corbin does his usual sales pitch and they exist the stage.

The boos and calls for an encore circle us. I vibrate with the energy the fans are exuding. The feeling of the crowd loving what the performers are dishing out onstage is a drug. I thought

I forgot what that feels like, but even just sitting here surrounded by the vibes brings back the longing to play, to be the crowd's focus. If El ever decides to sing again professionally, I could maybe come onstage once or twice, play for her, for old times' sake, just a gag. Just once or twice.

"Do you feel like it's last July?" El's whisper tickles my ear.

"Because one of us has an injured hand?"

She elbows my side gently. "Because we are at The Devil's Martini and the crowd is going wild."

In the shadow of the wings, I glance across the stage. "Do you miss this?"

"The audience? Yes. Singing in front of my phone is not the same."

"Thank you, Death Elbow, you've definitely been on my playlist for the last two months, and I hope you perform in front of many larger crowds." Pauline, the manager of The Devil's Martini, takes the mic off the stand and sighs. "Thank you all who came today and supported this local business that has been in the community for over fifty years." Pauline walks to the other end of the stage. "Singers such as Carlee Waters, Dasher, and El Vella had their start here during our open mic competitions. These walls have heard classical, jazz, rock, pop, country." The crowd roars in agreement.

She runs her hands reverently over the wall. "I've witnessed the last ten years, and what years have those been. I have autographs from so many singers who became staples on the radio, and some who I call friends." Pauline returns to the center of the stage and sticks the mic back on the stand. "It is with a heavy heart that I must announce The Devil's Martini will be closing its doors."

I flinch as if the news physically hit me. Stunned silence stretches around me. This is where I met El. Where we first sang together. Where I felt the magic of WE. That can't disappear. My stomach and heart switch places. The place where that began can't just cease to exist.

Beside me, El has her hand on her heart. The heart I found in this room, on that stage. The heart I can't imagine living without. I pull her closer, like the threat of The Devil's Martini closing might somehow take her away from me.

A low boo rumbles from the back. Others join until they fill the space. If the boos for the end of Death Elbow's show were loud, these boos are deafening.

Pauline dips her head. "I feel the same way. We've been searching for a buyer without success. Apparently no one wants to take this old establishment over." More boos. Pauline waves them down and gives a sad smile. "If you know anyone who wants to buy a bar, call me. I can throw in some coasters for free."

There's a sad communal chuckle from the crowd, and the buzz of Death Elbow's performance has evaporated. Around us, people murmur and shake their heads.

"In the meantime, we have a few more bands performing, so I hope you all come back and see us before we shut our doors."

El elbows me again, not so gently this time. "Maybe Rocker could buy this place. He has the money," she whispers.

Rocker Inc. definitely has the money, but it's not what they do. They deal with artists, not properties. "We can ask him. I'm not sure this is his brand."

"*You* can ask him." Her face takes on a serious quality. "He can use the venue as a launching point for the singers and bands he's promoting. Use it as a performance venue for Rocker Inc. Isn't that a great idea?"

"It's an idea." I caress her shoulder. The disappointment of no more The Devil's Martini must be weighing on her too. "But I can't promise you anything. I'm sure Pauline scoured LA and beyond before they came to the decision to close."

"I guess. Still, I can't imagine LA without The Devil's Martini. It's like Nashville without The Bluebird Cafe." El rubs her eye. "We met here."

I'm transported back to that moment, her skipping across the bar floor, her red hair hidden under that blond wig I hated. My insistence on playing guitar for her, needing to spend more time with her. Did my heart know even then that she was the one? El's lips curl like she's reliving the moment too.

"We need to save The Devil's Martini." El squeezes my arm. "I'd do anything to keep its doors open."

"Don't look at me that way. I might be richer than I've ever been, but I'm not rich enough to buy The Devil's Martini for you."

Her chest rises and falls. "We have to find someone who can."

Three

El

THE HOUSE IS THE same but different. The garage is a small corral of strollers and car seats. The toys and baby-related contraptions in the living room have multiplied since my last visit. I am a guest at my own home. Walking through the space hits me in all the wrong ways. The urge to search the kitchen for ingredients to make a salad rises. It's what I'd do if I lived here, still guided by Mom and Rocker's rules. The new independent me resists the pull. I'm not the same El from a year ago.

"We'll say hello first, then I'll pick up some clothes." Wil's hand on my lower back urges me to the gazebo by the outdoor kitchen, past the pool now surrounded by a fence.

I will away the dull ache behind my eyes. Sleep eluded me most of the night as Pauline's announcement played over and over in my head. The only person who can save The Devil's Martini waves at us from his position at the grill. With every step I take the tightrope of hope and anxiety stretches thin between my temples.

A loud shriek pierces the air, followed by Mom's lamentations. The tableau before me stops me in my tracks.

In the pool, Mom braces against the side as a woman in a Hawaiian-print swim shirt, giant sunglasses, and a trucker hat dunks Pickle under the water and lets go. I stop breathing. My knees that I thought were shaking from anticipating asking Rocker to help save the bar tremble for real. Pickle's head pops to the surface, he turns on his back, and floats. Mom catches him.

"You don't have to grab him so quickly. He's fine. Let him figure it out," the other woman instructs in a calm voice as she claps.

Pickle shrieks in what turns out to be delight and slaps the aquamarine water.

My lungs resume the expand-contract motion that I'm normally not aware of. Seeing Mom so involved with Pickle stirs both happiness and . . . not. I'm glad Mom got to have the child she and Rocker so desperately wanted. All the years of IVF finally paid off and the brother I was awaiting alongside Mom is here.

Mom's attention is no longer one thousand percent on me. That's exactly what I wanted. Why is the second thought in my head, "If she loves him so much, does it mean she loves me less?" A hollow ache resonates in my chest, a physical echo of disappointment. I don't crave Mom's stifling attention, but somehow, I do. I wish this made sense.

"This is a surprise. Should I add more meat to the grill?" Rocker hugs Wil longer than I ever let Rocker hug me. "Did your hair grow out?" Rocker examines the untrimmed sides of Wil's head. "I was beginning to forget what you look like."

Wil groans. "I'm not Pickle. I don't change that much. We can't stay long. Trying to make a movie at The Grove."

Mom emerges from the pool, Pickle attached to her hip, and swaddles them both in a pink striped towel. His swimsuit dotted with dogs, he tries to squirm free, chubby arms and legs flailing. What do you even do with a baby? They can't walk or talk. At least Pickle's no longer a drooling blob. Well, he's still drooling, but he is also smiling and reaching for my boyfriend.

"Can I take him?" Wil asks Mom.

Her face pinches as if someone's singing off-key. Reluctantly she releases Pickle and sits under the gazebo. "Finally, both of you are here."

Wil bounce-walks Pickle around all of us. Tiny fists tug on Wil's collar and I catch myself smiling.

"I can't keep him to myself," I say to Mom and Rocker. "Even if I want to."

"Pickle misses him. I miss him." Rocker watches the boys and more sadness than joy washes over his face. "Between UCLA, Death Elbow and . . ." Rocker eyes me. "I miss you too." He gives me a tight smile, then opens the grill and flips the burgers.

Mom rubs my shoulders, but her eyes follow Wil and Pickle. They have transitioned into a game of peek-a-boo that appears much more entertaining than I remember. "We miss you, El."

Mom isn't lying, but my chest tightens. I wanted to be out of this house, to chart my own life course, but there still is a part of me that wishes Mom were standing beside me, cheering me on instead of hovering over every choice I make. I tug the dress over my knees and straighten. "Do you want us to come hang out more often so Pickle," I roll my eyes, "can spend more time with Wil?"

"Pickle would love to spend time with you too." Rocker sets the utensils down and sits next to Mom. "How was the concert last night?" He drapes his arm over her shoulder and kisses the hair over her ear. "Death Elbow are lucky, getting to perform at The Devil's Martini before it's gone. Another LA institution closing its doors. It reminds me of how old I am."

I square my shoulders and flatten my hands on my lap. "You could change that." My throat is dry but I push through. "Buy the place. Renovate it and showcase artists from your label, have them perform there."

"Me? Running a bar and concert venue?" Rocker flicks at a nonexistent speck on his dark jeans. "I'd like to expand, produce more music, open more locations doing what we already do well at Rocker Inc., not figure out a brand-new business that clearly couldn't make ends meet." He pushes a strand of hair behind my mother's ear.

"That's a lot of work," says Mom. "And a labor of love more than profit, at least for a while."

Rocker folds his hands. "I'm not the person to do that job."

Mom gives a slight bow of her head in agreement.

Disappointment swirls, making me feel all mixed up inside. Rocker is my greatest hope for saving the place. I thought Mom would be on my side. That if I asked for help, they'd support me. "You don't have to do the work. I'm sure there are people you can hire." I grasp at straws. "I could be part of the project."

Rocker's gaze meets mine, and the hope there makes the chaos in my ribcage double. He curves forward. "Us working together again? Tempting." He strokes the stubble on his chin, then shakes his head. "It's not a sound investment."

"If you want to come back and work for Rocker Inc., you know the door is always open," Mom says.

I drop my gaze to my hands. Rocker Inc. was never my dream. I glance at Wil, who's giggling at, or is it with, Pickle. "No, that's Wil's thing, not mine." I want to tell Rocker the bar is worth saving. It's the place Wil and I sang together first, it has sentimental value, and when it closes, that will be erased. But he doesn't know Sven snuck me out night after night to sing there, and today isn't the day to spill secrets. We just got back to normal, or at least a new normal. I play with the colorless strand of my hair and wish I could lie. "I might want to do something with music, but I don't know what."

Wil spins on the lawn with Pickle, twirling until he collapses, carefully letting Pickle fall with him to the grass by the bar. Their giggles reach us all the way on the couch.

"I'm going to make a cocktail, would you like one?" Mom pecks Rocker.

Rocker returns to the grill. "I'll have whatever you're having."

"One for you too?" Mom asks me.

"I'll help." I join her at the bar. Maybe I can talk her into helping me. If Mom wants to purchase The Devil's Martini, Rocker will do anything she wants.

"We have limes, so a margarita?" Mom takes out the ingredients and four glasses and stares at them.

"About The Devil's Martini."

"Can we please not talk about that bar again?" Mom shakes her head. "I'm not a bartender, nor your grandmother, but I can wing a margarita." Generous pours of tequila go first.

Quiet frustration builds its pressure behind my eyes. Fronting Blatantly Subtle, saving The Devil's Martini. Anything I dream about seems to fall out of my reach. My efforts don't matter. I focus on Mom's hands splashing more alcohol into the glass. "Mormor would tell you to use the jigger."

"When Mormor is here, she can use all the jiggers she wants." Mom squeezes in some limes and adds a tiny splash of agave syrup, gives each a quick stir, drops in ice, and decorates the glasses with lime wheels.

"Mormor is coming? When?" And am I the last person to hear about it?

Mom glances at Wil and Pickle. "I don't want to go to Norway this summer so she's coming to us." Mom sighs. "Her first time in Los Angeles. She hasn't been on a plane in ten years so Bill is sending the jet to pick her up over the Memorial Day weekend." Mom takes a sip and winces. "I'll take this one to Bill."

I gingerly try the drink. Definitely heavy on the tequila, light on the sweet, and missing the salt. Maybe it will silence the cacophony of distress in my gut. I take one gulp. My throat burns and I push my more-tequila-than-margarita away.

Wil plops on the barstool next to me and situates Pickle on his lap. "I see there's one for me too."

I start to warn him when Pickle lunges for Wil's glass, and my boyfriend swivels it out of reach. "I don't think you're old enough for this." Wil settles it on the bar. "But as soon as you are, I'll take you to my favorite bar in Bremen." He talks as if the kid understands.

Pickle ignores Wil's warnings and reaches for the glass so abruptly he almost falls off Wil's knees.

"You can't reach for things that aren't safe for you." Will jerks upright and holds the baby tightly as they bounce-walk away.

I abandon the cocktail on the bar and trail alongside Wil. The feeling of being a guest around here grows. Would they have told me about Mormor coming if it didn't come up today?

Pickle tugs on the collar of Wil's shirt and jams it into his mouth, where two teeth and a lot of drool glisten in the sun. I search for a sense of connection with the baby, like Wil has, but I come up empty. Is there something wrong with me?

I reach to remove Wil's shirt out of the baby's mouth, but Wil takes a large blue ring out of his pocket and does a switcheroo. "He's teething," says Wil, as if he's a proud father.

"You love this little guy, don't you?"

"I do." Wil rubs his nose against Pickle's and smiles break across both their faces. "I love him so much." Wil's gaze lifts to mine and the word hangs between us.

Love.

Wil is full of love. He loves Hanna and Mr. Peters. Of course he loves Pickle, but I don't think I've ever heard him say it out loud. I definitely haven't heard those words directed at me. Not that I have said them to him either, even though without a shadow of a doubt I know I love Wil. With Dillon, I was desperate to love someone, to be in love. With Wil I resisted giving this cocky guy my heart, but day by day, note by note, word by word, he snuck into my life, my head, and my heart.

The sun beats down and a bead of perspiration trickles along the back of my neck. It would be so easy to tell Wil how I feel. The tension grows and my tongue yearns to say the three words. "I—"

A wail similar to a broken car alarm pierces the space between us, a perfect C-sharp. With the full volume of his little lungs, Pickle bawls, tears welling in his amber eyes as he flails in Wil's arms, the rubber ring on the grass between our feet. Wil pats his pocket and mutters under his breath, "I should've brought two."

I bend and pick up the ring covered in grass and dirt. "Um. Should I go wash this?"

I doubt Wil can hear me over Pickle's crying. I didn't think he could get any louder, but the little guy proves me wrong. I resist plugging my ears with my fingers. Wil's bouncing grows more pronounced and he starts to sing.

His voice is low, aimed at the half-brother we share. The melody and words create a rhythm that matches the bouncing movements. Like magic, Pickle shudders once and quiets, his stare intent on Wil's moving lips. I watch them too. The song grows louder.

> Love conquers all, the movies said
> but when I'm lonely in my bed
> I think of you

I recognize the words and the melody. The sketch of the song we started working on a couple of days ago sounds like something that can become a real composition. Pickle's eyes are shining brightly, his mouth is smiling, and his hand is back on Wil's collar, tugging for more every time Wil tries to stop.

It's nothing new for me to be entranced with Wil's singing. It's been that way since the moment we met. I guess I've finally found something my half-brother and I have in common. "He likes our song."

Wil maintains the melody, singing his answer. "I sing to him before bed."

I'm envious of the baby in Wil's arms. I want him to sing to me before bed. We've visited two more apartments this morning. One was a shoebox and the other was out of my price range. I have to find a place soon. Sven needs his bed back.

Wil's phone rings and stops his singing. It's been going off so much recently that I've composed an accompaniment for its melody in my head.

"Hel—" A stream of words I can hear but not understand pours from the phone. "Slow down, they did what?" The voice on the other side of the line grows louder and more desperate. Wil glances at me. "I need a minute. Could you hold him?" Wil passes Pickle over and leaves me and my baby brother staring at each other with suspicion.

Pickle's hand tentatively reaches for me. My sundress doesn't have a collar, so after a timid slap on my bare shoulder he reaches up and finds the white streak of my hair. I wait for him to tug. He doesn't. Instead, he stares at it like something shiny and new. He makes tiny grunts while his chest rises and falls.

I scrutinize him, half anticipating that he'll start the wailing again and I won't be able to stop it, and half curious. I search for any similarities. He has Wil's and Rocker's amber eyes, that's obvious. His nose is too tiny to be anything like mine or Mom's. There's a picture on Mormor's wall in the library of Zoe and me as babies. I had just been born and Zoe was propped against me like we were sisters. It must be a trick of the afternoon sunlight, but I swear I see Zoe's expression. The way she studies a new fabric, her face concentrating like Pickle's does now.

In an instant, the look is gone. Pickle yawns and droops into me. His soft cheek rests on my collarbone, my hair still in his hand. My breaths soften. I try to imitate the bouncy walk Wil performed and cruise around the pool fence back to the bar so I can exchange the baby for the burger Rocker is taking off the grill.

Four

Wil

"Someone needs to fix this," the manager of The Stand, the venue Death Elbow is scheduled to play tonight, shouts into my ear. In the background the wail of a guitar cuts into his words. ". . . how we do business."

I glance across the patio where Dad is unloading burgers off the grill, a wide smile on his face as he jokes with Sylvia, and I speed-walk away. What was El going to say? How is it that one minute I was basking in the warmth of an afternoon off, and now I'm pulled into a Death Elbow vortex? I pinch my wrist. I can deal with broken woofers and smashed beer bottles, but Corbin drunk before the performance . . . I grind my teeth.

"I expected better from a band represented by Rocker Inc."

My chest tightens, causing my ribs to sting. I attempt to stuff my other hand in my pocket but the bones that were just freed from the cast protest. I let it swing uselessly.

This is my fault. Dad put his trust in me and I can't let him down. I should have been there with Death Elbow, making sure everything went smoothly. Instead I chose viewing apartments with my girlfriend and visiting my family. The phone is hot and my palm slippery with sweat. My paycheck depends on Death Elbow's success. Vatton won't put their precious water bottles in the hands of a group that doesn't actually get onstage.

"They brought in their own and now they're sloshed in the green room. They broke the couch by apparently launching themselves on it. The room smells worse than the bar."

"It's completely unacceptable." I try to sound both stern and placating. "I accept full responsibly and apologize on behalf of the band. Of course we'll pay for any damages." By we, I mean me. I hope my bank account, which is finally in the black for the first time in forever, can take the hit. If Dad decides to drop Death Elbow because of this stunt, I'd have to start over, and I know the guys are good. They can go all the way. Sell albums. Sell stadiums. I can see their success in the dollar bills flooding their accounts. And mine. I clench my fist.

The guy on the other end of the line lets out a puff of air and it sounds like a train barreling through a station. "Look, kid. I get it. Bands like to live a rock and roll lifestyle. I've been there, got the T-shirts to prove it. But they need to wait until after the performance for the antics. Getting wasted before the show just isn't professional."

"It won't happen again." I bite the inside of my cheek.

"I doubt they'll be sober before they're due onstage unless someone gets over here and feeds them coffee, supervises them. And it won't be me."

My fingers protest my grip on the phone. What the heck do I do now? I unclench my fist. "How long until they get onstage?"

"An hour and a half. I'm pulling them from the meet-and-greet portion with the VIP's and reporters." The manager's voice fades, like he's holding the phone from his mouth. El catches my glance and studies my face like it's a road map. He returns to the line. "I suggest you get here quick and get them into singing shape before my boss gets wind of this."

"I'll be right there," I grind out. "Thanks. Send me a bill for the damages. You have my email."

"Go through the side alley and give your name to security at the back door. They'll let you in." The line goes dead.

I pocket my phone, close my eyes for a breath, and work on unclenching my jaw.

A peel of baby giggles comes from the patio and I'm back in action. I circle around the pool, keeping far away from Dad, tap on El's arm, and tug her away.

The sunlight catches her brilliant eyes. Why isn't my job 9–5? Other kids my age are partying on the beach and snuggling under blankets with their girlfriends. I'm stuck with sobering up a drunk band and making sure they perform as the opening act. I caress the line of El's cheek, and the knot in my neck unwinds. Damn, how can she be so beautiful? Did I tell her that today? I tuck a strand of hair behind her ear and allow myself another second of just looking at her. "This dress is amazing on you."

Her forehead creases. "That bad?"

"Can't I compliment my hot and talented girlfriend?"

"Anytime." She reaches up and runs her thumb along my bottom lip. I shiver. She checks over her shoulder for any bystanders and leans in. "But I can tell something's not right. Talk to me."

We abandon the patio and hide in the shade of a palm tree.

"Death Elbow . . . Corbin. . . they screwed up." I tell her what happened and I sound as angry as I feel. The emotions I was holding back with the venue's manager spill like venom. "Which means I screwed up." I drum the fingers of my uninjured hand on my pants and catch a peel of laughter from Sylvia and Dad fawning over Pickle. If I'd been at the venue this wouldn't be happening. I need to be more on top of this. This isn't busking on the street for tips. "I need to go."

El follows my gaze and crosses her arms. "Can't someone else deal with it?"

I step deeper into the shadow of the flower-covered fence with the gate that leads to the beach. "It's my responsibility."

El's fingers slip into mine and the thudding in my temples dulls. "Everything will be fine."

I want to smile at her words. I want them to be true. I will make them true. I kiss the top of her head. "I'll text you once I know what's up."

Her fingers grip my bicep. "Oh no you won't." Her eyes dart to the laughing trio. "Rocker said no to saving The Devil's Martini and Mom was no help. I need you to ask him."

I stare at the brilliant blue sky. "I can't ask him for a favor when I'm failing to take care of the group that's my responsibility."

"I thought you agreed that saving The Devil's Martini is important."

"So is making sure Death Elbow performs tonight."

El places her hands on her hips. "If I didn't know better, I'd think you want to spend time with Death Elbow more than with me."

Heat blazes up my spine. "Never." My hands find her waist and draw her in closer, like I never want to let her go. The scent of her shampoo mixes with the florals of the early evening. "In case you haven't noticed, I've been practically living at Sven's place. Dad thinks I only come home for clean clothes."

A wrinkle forms in El's forehead. "You don't have to stay over every night. You should spend time here with Pickle and Rocker."

The panic drains from my veins and I give her a little shake. "I only want to be where you are." I kiss her forehead. "Give me a few hours to clear this up and when I'm back maybe we can still talk to Dad."

She lifts her chin. I know that move. I love that move. She's about to challenge me and if I didn't have to go rescue my mess of a band, I'd pick her up, find a place with a locking door, and use her stubbornness for good.

I open my mouth to protest but her hand is on my lips. She stands on tiptoes and brings her nose to mine. "I only want to be where you are too."

My resolve crumbles. I don't want to tear her away from her family when they are starting to mend fences, but I also don't have it in me to say no to her when she's looking at me this way. When she's touching me. I kiss her palm and she lets go.

We stare at each other, suddenly playing who blinks first. She crosses her arms again. I shake my head in capitulation.

"Fine." I'm a fool. A head-over-heels-in-love fool. It's impossible to resist her.

El's ear-to-ear grin takes my breath away.

"Can I drive?" She bats her eyelashes like she's a cartoon character.

I pull the fob to my SUV out of my pocket and toss it to her. "I can't say no to you."

The street is blocked to accommodate extra parking for the event, and the single lanes in each direction are jammed with cars searching for spots and dropping people off. We could've parked and walked there faster, but the tinted windows of the car are the only protection I can provide El right now. The vehicles ahead inch forward. El's gaze is focused on the bumper-to bumper traffic, her fingers wrapped tight around the wheel. I recline against the headrest. Dad gave me this mini-tank to replace the car I totaled in the accident.

I reach over the console and put my palm on El's knee. Panic circles in my throat. There's no Sven to shield us from the crowd. This should've been great exposure for Death Elbow, but now I have to hope the aspirins, coffee, eggs, and oatmeal from Blend will sober them up enough to avoid splashing their faces on all the gossip sites.

Death Elbow's first release blares from the car beside us. Trepidation singes the lining of my stomach. How many fans are here to see the band perform tonight as the opening act? Disappointing them is not an option.

El turns into the gate by The Stand. A few flashbulbs go off and El stiffens in the driver's seat.

"You could wait in the car."

"Nope. Everything will be fine." She straightens her shoulders, parks the car in one of the two empty reserved spots, and jumps out.

I grab the coffees and food with my good arm.

"Let's get them onstage," says El.

We stick close to the wall as we sneak between the cars parked by the venue. El's not hiding our relationship anymore, but there's no need to draw attention. My mission is to get Death

Elbow to perform with as little fuss as possible and find a way to smooth this over.

We round the corner into an alley between the venue and a twenty-four-hour laundromat. I don't see the door the manager mentioned and pick up my pace.

El tugs on my shirt. Tingles crawl up my spine at the sight of her fingers teasing the ends of the white streak in her hair. I follow her gaze to the end of the alley where a man is standing, staring.

"Where's the side door?" she whispers.

A bright light illuminates her face.

"Damn it." I step in front of El. "The door must be on the other side." El's hand in mine, we jog down the alley, past the man and the rat-tat-tat-tat of his camera, the darkened night interrupted by strobing flashes.

We spill onto the street but the cameraman acts like a beacon and more paparazzi are scuttling our way.

"It's El Vella!" one shouts.

"And Rocker's son."

Shouts of "El, when did you first know you liked Wil?" "What does Rocker think of his kids dating?" and "Wil, look here. Who are you wearing tonight?" assault our ears as I push past the crowd. A sense of apprehension creates a crater in me. I walked El right into this rat's nest. A woman shoves her phone in our faces. "Are you singing tonight?"

Between the flashes and the reporters jostling me, I lose all sense of direction and resort to pushing through them. It's no use. They swarm us and I can't find the door. I shove the coffee and food at one of the paparazzi, tuck El into my side, spin us around, and track back down the alley. The circus follows and I'm jostled against the wall, jamming my injured ribs into hard brick.

"Wil!" El elbows us some space, her hands gripping my face. "Are you okay?"

I nod.

"We need to run." She doesn't wait for my answer, just grips my hand and hauls me out of the alley. I hold my other hand up to shield us from the blinding flashes. It barely works as they slither between parked cars, setting off alarms. The blue Range Rover SUV towers over the other cars. I push El in front of me and face the reporters. "We're not answering questions today." I try to casually stave them off, give El a chance to get in, but they press in, one cameraman climbing on the trunk of the car beside us, his camera snapping away. "You can reach out to my publicist for interview requests." Harper's words come out of my mouth on autopilot. I back into the open passenger door and jump in.

Reporters pound on the windows, camera lenses pressed against the glass as El backs up. "Get away from the car," she shouts but her voice is drowned by their feverish questions.

"El, why did you quit Blatantly Subtle?"

"Look over here."

"Are your covers autotuned?"

El lays on the horn and finally the questions stop. Most of the paparazzi step far enough away that she maneuvers us onto the road. "Why did I think this would end? That telling my story will be enough?"

"Are you and Carlee Waters in a fight?" One reporter jogs along with the car.

"Get out of the way," El shouts and guns the gas, jerking into traffic. "Remind me to not trust any reporters ever again." The muscles on her jaw tick faster than my heartbeats. Anger and fear come off her in waves. Her lips quiver but her grip on the wheel tightens.

I should've persuaded her to stay at Dad's house and wait for me there. I should've thought this through and known the paparazzi would discover us, hound us the moment they recognized who we are.

"When will they leave me alone?" she cries as the car gains speed, and soon none of the paparazzi can keep up.

I want the car to stop, to pull El into my chest and whisper into her hair that everything will be fine. I reach over the console as the Bluetooth announces, "Incoming call from Manager at The Stand."

I pinch the bridge of my nose and answer.

"Where are you?" the venue manager screams through the car's speakers.

"I—"

"Don't tell me, I don't care. Even if you're at the door it's too late."

The relentless pounding that intensifies in my temples might as well be the rhythmic drumbeat of my despair. "Give me—"

"Corbin vomited on the monitor sound board. Your band isn't coming back here. My boss wants them gone. And you can forget using us for rehearsal space."

"We couldn't get inside," I say. El careens up the ramp to the highway, the blue glow of the dashboard's lights illuminating a tear running down her cheek. I slam my fist into my thigh. I have to fix this. "How can I change his mind? Maybe a tour of Rocker Inc.?"

"Too late, kid. They are banned. For life." A door slams in the background. "I'm calling a taxi and shoving them into it. You can thank me later." The line goes dead.

I tip my head up and rake the roof of the cabin to stave off the liquid threatening to spill. I made everything worse. How am I going to tell Dad? Harper's going to have a public relations nightmare on her hands. I don't know which I dread worst—the articles they'll write about Death Elbow not performing, or the pictures of El and me practically running over the paparazzi.

The streetlamps whip by. I gently touch El's shoulder. "I think we lost them. Maybe we could slow down?"

"Right." El sucks in air. "I can do that." The car matches the pace of the others around us. "What are you going to do?"

"Them not performing there is one thing. But the rehearsals . . ." I set my elbow on my knees and drop my head into my hands. Finding a space willing to squeeze Death Elbow in for rehearsals is going to take me days. Maybe weeks. "If they don't rehearse, they won't be ready. I can keep them in the studio for a while, but that's not a solution." My heart slams into my chest.

Everything is not fine.

FIVE

THE LIGHT IN SVEN'S office is still on when Wil walks me into the reception area of Ander's Investigations. My skin itches where the flashbulbs of the paparazzi cameras imprinted on me, like a temporary tattoo. Hopefully a long shower and hard scrub will wash away the residue.

Wil tightens his grip on my hand. "I'm sorry, El."

"Not your fault." I shake my head. If I let him go on his own, he might've salvaged Death Elbow's performance. I squeeze Wil's hand back. We would've avoided new photos that are bound to restart the frenzy over whether the two of us should be dating. "I insisted on going with you."

"I thought you were sleeping at Mr. Rockerby's tonight." Sven walks out of his office with a familiar scowl on his face. Except these days it's accompanied by bags under his eyes. "What time is it?"

Wil pulls me closer. "After ten."

Guilt layers over the adrenaline and unease. Sven's been working long hours getting his security company up off the ground, and sleeping on the couch because I'm living in his place isn't helping.

Sven checks his watch. "That late?"

"If you need the bedroom, we can drive back to Malibu." Does Sven have a girl here? I shake my head. I'm projecting. Must be a client. Odd to be working so late but Sven doesn't really keep 9–5 hours. Kinda like Rocker. Kinda like Wil too.

"Stay," Sven says to us then peers back into his office. "Let's finish tomorrow," he says to someone inside.

I go to the coffee machine, find the beans, and pour grounds into the top.

Sven stands in the doorway, watching my every move. "Bit late for coffee?"

"It's decaf, and I need to drown the paparazzi's' questions in something. I don't have any hard liquor upstairs." I pour water into the carafe.

"Paparazzi?"

"My own fault." An ache pulses behind my eyes. Why did I think I would suddenly be invincible to their jabs? Leaving Mom's place was a rash idea. I should've stayed and tried to persuade Rocker to save The Devil's Martini. A tear runs out of the corner of my eye and I dab at it. The last thing I want is for Sven to worry more about me.

"What's wrong?" Sven hovers like a pushy big brother.

"Rocker won't save The Devil's Martini."

"Our The Devil's Martini?" says a voice behind my back. I turn and nearly drop my mug at the sight of Carlee walking out of Sven's office, a computer bag over her shoulder. "The bar you and I got our starts at?"

She says you and I as if we were singing there together at the same time, not years apart. "Didn't realize you were here."

"Sven is helping me assess security elements for the house I recently rented." Sven shuffles his feet as Carlee joins us by the coffee maker. "Why does the bar need saving?"

I recount Pauline's speech, trying to make my voice not wobble. Wil's finger skims my skin and I slouch into his touch, even though what I really want is for his forehead to press against mine. I clear my throat. "I asked Rocker to buy it."

"Didn't know he was interested in performance spaces." Carlee edges closer, her eyes growing sharper as she examines me.

"He's not." I catch another silent tear before it falls from my lashes. Wil's fingers stop their caress, settling at my nape. I sniffle. "We can't let The Devil's Martini disappear. So many great acts have launched there." I twist to count the drops of brown liquid splashing into the coffee pot. Carlee's stare brushes my skin. Her offer to work with her, to write songs with her sits in the silence surrounding us.

I thought I wanted to get back onstage, but after tonight . . . I scratch my forearm. A shiver runs through me. I don't want to let go of The Devil's Martini. A voice thrums at the base of my skull, insisting this is important. I square my shoulders and face Carlee.

Her gaze darts to me. "It would be a shame to lose such an influential part of the music landscape."

"I guess sometimes things change. We have to let go." Wil's words burn in my ears.

"I'm not so sure." Carlee gives Sven a raised eyebrow. "What would your security assessment for the bar be?"

Sven sets his feet hip-width apart, folds his huge biceps across his chest, and stares out the window. I know Sven is smart, but watching his brain work in real-time is more mesmerizing than watching the stars.

He glances at the ceiling. "I haven't been there in at least six months, but unless they've done major updates, you're in for a brand-new security system. A rotating roster of three full-time and two part-time security guards, new locks, probably some bulletproof glass, if you plan to invite anyone who is . . . shall we say, controversial. The back lot could do with some improvements, but the gated entrance is a bonus regarding keeping unwanted threats like the paparazzi out of the way. Good for artists coming and going." He glances at me. "We'd have to implement a key-card system for the employees—"

"So, a total overhaul." Carlee rubs her forehead. "Still, that's not as bad as some of the other places. It's a possibility."

"Better than the last two we visited. I'm no promoter, but it has good street appeal. One of the reasons it's survived this long."

Carlee taps her computer case with a manicured nail. "I'd have to get my lawyers involved. Make sure there aren't any liens or other entanglements I'd be getting myself into."

"I'll make some calls, check there's no underground element putting pressure on the place."

"Having someplace turnkey with an established reputation would be better than starting from scratch." The corner of Carlee's lips twitch. "I do have history there. Could be a fresh start for both of us."

My neck creaks from the crosstalk, my pulse ticking. I understand all the words, but I don't get the meaning. The coffee machine hisses like it's having trouble keeping up as well.

"You're looking to purchase a venue?" Wil's expression is all business, like when he was reminding Death Elbow about the water bottles.

"I'm interested in finding a place where the artists I will be working with can perform. A real space rather than my home studio. There's nothing like being onstage." Carlee avoids my gaze this time. "Sven and I have scouted out old theaters and cafes, but The Devil's Martini is more authentic. Plus, I could use it as a rehearsal venue during the day and rent it out for events."

"That was El's idea as well." Wil's eyes wander briefly to mine.

"El is a smart woman." Carlee stares at me.

I pour myself a cup of coffee. The bitter black liquid tempers the small sliver of hope. Maybe The Devil's Martini is not lost. Just maybe.

"A bar with an existing liquor license has advantages. More profitable than a coffee shop," Sven offers.

"Cocktails do bring in the money. When Blatantly Subtle first started out, some of our gigs were paid as skim off the drink haul. That's where our song *Champagne Dreams* came from." Carlee picks a cup and pours herself a coffee as well. "This could work."

I grip my mug with both hands. "You're going to buy The Devil's Martini?"

"I'm thinking about it." She settles against the counter, mug in hand. There's a glint in her eye that makes my skin tingle. "It hinges on one key factor."

"What?" I bite. "For them to agree?"

"I don't think that will be a problem. I'll make them an offer they can't refuse." She stares at me over the rim of her mug. "No. My only condition is finding someone to help run the place."

I stare back at her.

"I mean it'd have to be someone who knows a little something about music. That's a given." She holds the cup up to her lips, not drinking. "Someone with an ear for talent. Maybe with perfect pitch?"

My skin prickles. I let the thought of working with Carlee to save the bar I love roll around in my mind. Nothing against Sven, but I'm tired of answering phones and booking appointments. I picture myself playing Pauline's role, working with the bands. A flicker of hope ignites within me.

"Someone who could help me bring in a crowd." Carlee watches me, "Say, by performing onstage a few nights a month."

The "onstage" part snuffs the flicker in my body. Lights flash before my eyes and the nasty questions hurled tonight shout in my brain. When I said I'd do anything to save The Devil's Martini, I didn't mean *that*.

I lift my chin. "I can give you the contact information of the temp agency Sven has been working with."

"No," Sven sputters, "Not them."

Carlee takes another slow sip of her coffee and my hand flies to my hair. She can't be serious.

"What do you say, El?"

She *is* serious. The tips of my fingers have gone numb. The implications of being onstage file through me like the click, click, click of the cameras tonight. I set the mug down, coffee sloshing over the side. Ignoring a tugging sensation below my right rib, I shake my head.

Wil leans in and whispers in my ear, "Are you okay?"

I glare at him. Doesn't he get it? Twenty minutes ago, the paparazzi were chasing us for a sound bite. If I get back onstage it's like inviting them into my life, stepping into the spotlight again. They'll never leave me alone. I'll have to move back into Mom and Rocker's place just for the twenty-four-hour security measures.

Sven picks up a napkin and wipes the coffee that sloshed out on the counter. "It's a good offer."

I knead my wrist. "What if I don't want to sing?"

Carlee regards me like I've just suggested juggling as my new career. "How about you be my right-hand woman?" Carlee folds her arms across her chest. "I need someone to help run errands, make sure I have the right food, get me to my doctor's appointments."

I blink at Carlee. I've never seen her so casually mention her condition. I didn't know for weeks while singing backup that she had multiple sclerosis. Aside from the press release stating the reason she was retiring from Blatantly Subtle, she's refused to comment.

Carlee tilts her head and sips her coffee. Her new offer hangs between us and my skin doesn't crawl with angst. More like a tingle of anticipation runs across my forearms.

Be Carlee's assistant.

I gnaw my lip. Carlee gave me a chance with Blatantly Subtle. Maybe I should give her a chance. My lungs constrict. I've seen what MS can do when she takes on too much. She truly needs help. "So, not working at The Devil's Martini."

"Well, if I buy the bar, it will be my priority. You'll have to stay on with me until the reopening. I'll be there a lot, thus naturally so will you. I'll need you to audition people, book talent, and help with the general management of the contractors. Once the venue is renovated and officially open we can re-evaluate. We'll have to play it by ear." Carlee raises one shoulder, seemingly pleased with her pun.

Wil pushes my hair off my face. "You did say we need to save The Devil's Martini. If Carlee buys the place because you agree to work for her, technically you'll have a hand in saving the place. Think of it as a charitable donation."

A vile laugh bubbles from me. "I can't afford a charitable donation. I need enough money to pay rent, buy food and gas, and hopefully have enough for an occasional trip to a nail salon." I glance at Sven. "And to move out of Sven's apartment."

"Maybe I can help with some of that too." Carlee perches on the couch. "I'll pay you a salary of course. But this isn't a 9–5 job. I'll need you around after-hours. I'm moving into a new place soon. What if—"

"Carlee, I really don't think I'm the right fit for this jo—"

She lifts her hand, but it wavers, and she sets it back down. "I can trust you, El. And there isn't an agency in the world providing that. With you, whatever I do, say, or go through with my health, those stories will not be sold to the paparazzi. Such loyalty is worth more to me than you'll ever know."

I swallow. I do know though. She and I discussed this while on tour. How hard it is in our world to let people into your inner circle. I loved being part of her world.

Carlee watches me. "I trust you. Do you trust me?"

I nod.

"So help me. Move in with me."

I open my mouth to protest.

"You'll still have time off." She glances at Wil. "I won't suck up all your days. But you'll have a place to stay, rent-free. Bigger than this. No offense Sven."

"None taken," Sven scoffs.

I open my mouth again but she continues.

"The salary is not as substantial as what I'd pay, say, a songwriter on staff, but it will be competitive with the rates assistants get in LA. I'm only renting until I can find something permanent." She rubs her hands together. "This could be perfect. I'm searching for a live-in housekeeper so I won't be alone in the house. You can keep me company until that position is filled."

I could keep her safe, and she can be my ticket out of Sven's place. This does sound like it might be the perfect solution. I glance at Sven. His face is blank, but I know he needs his apartment back. His bed back. I really can't stay here. Going back to Zoe's pool house isn't an option and I'm not living with Mom and Rocker. I lift my chin. "What's the catch?"

"No catch." Carlee crosses her legs.

"And if you can't purchase The Devil's Martini?"

"I'd still love to hire you. In any capacity, but I understand if you'd be less eager to take the deal."

"Give us a minute." Wil urges me to the end of the counter, creating what little private space he can. "You don't have to do this, but it sounds pretty great." Excitement is written all over his face.

I fiddle with the hem of my sundress. "You think I should?"

The pads of his fingers trace the line of my jaw. "I think you should do what feels right. I'm on your side. Always."

Tension seeps out of my limbs. Wil isn't pushing me—he's with me. I nibble on my lower lip. "Can't beat the rent."

A smile blooms on Wil's face.

"I can save more for a down payment on a better place."

Wil's eyes twinkle. "One with a working elevator?"

"Picky, picky."

"When it comes to you, I only ever want the best."

I want the best for him too. I squeeze his forearm and turn to Carlee. "You won't be disappointed if I don't sing onstage?"

Carlee's shoulders slump. "I will. It's a waste of your talent. But I won't make it a condition of your employment."

"Then you have yourself an assistant." I drop my shoulders from their tense position by my ears. "Let's save The Devil's Martini."

Carlee claps and Wil smiles. Sven uncrosses his arms.

"But." I hold up a finger.

Their elation freezes.

"I'm not leaving until I find a decent assistant for Sven."

Six

Wil

THE BLINDS ON THE solitary window of Sven's bedroom have gaps around the sides. I know this because as soon as the sun hits the east-facing façade of the building, the room fills with enough light to wake me from the soundest of sleeps. My room at Dad's house, which is technically a guest bedroom though everyone calls it Wil's room now, has proper darkening blinds that make even high noon appear like the middle of the night.

But even with the built-in alarm clock of the sunrise, spending almost every night here over the last three weeks has been worth the lack of sleep, because I have the only thing I really need. I nuzzle into El, who burrows deeper into the covers. With a month of physical therapy after my cast was removed, I finally have full dexterity. And one of the best ways to use it is to touch my girlfriend. I trace El's ribcage.

"Morning," I say.

A soft sigh escapes her lips and I long to capture it with my mouth. Instead, I pepper her neck with barely-there kisses, working my way along her back, over the thin strap of the tank top she wore to bed, and down her bicep. My efforts to rouse her go unrewarded as she mumbles and turns on her side.

I pry myself away from El.

I'd rather spend this morning with my girlfriend, but every minute of my day is scheduled: meeting with Death Elbow and Harper, finishing my music theory assignment before it's due tomorrow, and carrying the boxes and suitcase El already packed down the stairs so she is ready for the move to Carlee's place tomorrow.

El's officially on Carlee's payroll.

Sven gets his place back and I get to see my girlfriend reenter the music world.

I'd prefer her in the limelight over backstage, but I get why she doesn't want to deal with what fame brings. Singing and songwriting is her calling, what she was put on this Earth to do. I knew that the first time we sang together, the times we recorded music together. The spell that she puts on me and every member of the audience is almost tangible. She belongs onstage, but I can't push her.

My girl does things her way.

One of the many things I love about her.

A buzz begins at the base of my skull. El's soft breaths, the determination on her face even in her sleep, copper waves across my pillow; a picture I could be happy with every morning. Whatever she's dreaming of, I'd like all her dreams to become a reality.

I reach for my little black book. Of course it's not on the nightstand. I throw back the covers, sneak out of bed, and rummage in the front pocket of my jeans. My ribs are healed and I'm thrilled to be writing with my right hand again. Little black book and pencil in tow, I scurry back to bed and scrawl the words that need to get out of my brain.

Going once, going twice

It's in my head, it's in your eyes.

I put on paper the adoration that's been permeating through my cells after every glance, every touch, every kiss. My heart composes the lyrics that belong to El, just as it always does.

Your voice, my guitar in the dark, an honor

Our moans a rapid beat I can't refute

When they said in the movies that love conquers all, I thought that meant something ridiculous and pathetic. These days I can relate. What I feel for this sleeping girl is movie mate-rial. I'm totally and completely whipped, but happy. So happy

I'm scared. I have the girl who I have more feelings for than I can express in words, who my mum and Opa love, who is my best friend, who I want to spoil rotten. And yet. I'm afraid I'll open my eyes and it'll disappear.

Sometimes the unexpected is what you were waiting for

even if none of it is what you've ever thought possible before

My fingers cramp from the effort. I can't write any more, but I'm wide awake. With the thoughts and emotions circling my head, falling asleep again isn't an option. Between finding a new assistant for Sven, helping Carlee with the plans for The Devil's Martini, recording new covers, packing, and spending every night with me, El's had little sleep.

I sneak out of bed, put on the new traveler pants, hide my black book in my back pocket, and wear the shirt with a tiny Moderni Look logo. Both are soft after Marta ran them through the washer for me. El tucks her hand under the pillow. I tug a baseball cap on and close the door as quietly as I can. Breakfast first, then off to Rocker Inc. Morning runs to Blend have become a familiar routine.

The final weekend morning of May in LA hints at the heat of the upcoming day. The streets of this commercial part of town are quiet with only an occasional car passing an occasional pedestrian. I smell coffee shops and exhaust as my feet carry me to the familiar coffee cup design on the front door. Two trays of to-go coffees in hand, I head to the office.

The conference room on the third floor of Rocker Inc. reeks of a morning after a rager back in the frat house at UCLA. Alcohol and sweat mixed with coffee. Xander, Lucian, and Gideon perk up at our entrance and a third scent hits me. Something sweet.

"Have you been smoking in here?" I close the door behind me.

"Not me." Corbin snatches up an unclaimed cup of coffee from one of the trays I set on the table.

"I had to burn some candles." Harper points to a trio of tealights on the windowsill.

"The smell was getting ripe."

I offer Harper a smile. I've never seen her in casual wear and the matching hot pink yoga pants and top remind me it's Sunday. She's here on her time off as well. "Thank you for rounding up the guys."

Rocker Inc.'s public relations maven rolls her eyes. "I didn't even need to carry anyone in."

"We left the party before midnight because someone schedule a nine a.m. meeting on a Sunday." Xander sits in a chair at the head of the table, his thick brown boots propped on another. If his stare was a taser, Corbin would be flailing on the floor by now. "He's the one who stayed and came straight here."

Gideon drums his fingers on the table. "The only one." His knee bounces so high he hits the conference table.

Corbin chucks his unfinished cup into the trash can as if it's a basketball hoop and jumps up and down when it makes it in without splattering. "And he scores," he shouts. "The crowd goes wild."

"Sit." I push Xanders feet off the chair and shove Corbin into it.

"Yes, Dad." Corbin sits but even in this seat, inside Rocker Inc., I can't quite trust him.

The candle scent gets stuck in my throat and I try to breathe through my mouth. I settle my palms on the table and glare at the lead singer. "Three radio shows canceled interviews with you over the last month. And last night you were drunk all over social media again."

The band looks at Corbin and they nod like they're in an old-school heavy metal band.

Harper clears her throat. "Yes, he messed up the most, but you all played a role."

My turn to nod. "Being in a band is not an individual sport. You have to take each other into consideration and take care of each other, or this is not going to work."

Harper looks at the screen of her laptop. "The story hasn't caught much traction so far, fortunately." Harper closes the lid. "Some starlet married her bodyguard in Vegas yesterday. Officiated by an Elvis impersonator. That story is in the limelight."

The knot in my chest loosens.

"You might've gotten lucky this time but I need you focused on rehearsals, interviews, being a band, not being rock stars." I survey the group.

Lucian and Gideon exchange glances while Xander shifts in his seat.

Corbin even has the sense to look down, his shoulders stiff. "Maybe if we had a real place to practice."

"I'm working on it." I hope El can come through for me.

Harper snaps her fingers. "All this can go away in a blink of any eye. Then you'll be back to being a garage band that performs at bowling alleys and gets paid in beer." She crosses her arms. "What we need is something to tweak your image. Less rock and more pop. Make you more approachable. Do you have any songs that didn't make it to the album that are upbeat and fun? Something to soften the edge? Radio-friendly?"

"We haven't exactly been writing," Corbin snickers.

The smell in the room is getting to me. I snuff out the candles and open the window. Cool morning air trickles into the room.

Harper joins me by the window. "You helped El with her songs, right? Can you write one for these guys?"

My fingers skim the cover of my black notebook in my pocket. "I have notes, partial verses, not full songs."

"Wil, we need something. Anything."

The only actual song I've been working on is the one with El. It has a melody and lyrics, not complete, but there's at least something. I shake my head. No, I can't give this band our song. I run my teeth over my lower lip. Some songs you write to give away, some songs you write for others. The song with El is for us. Only for us.

The furrow on Harper's brow deepens. I pull out my black book and flip through the pages. Harper peers over my shoulder. The few lines I wrote about found family went nowhere, the stanza on butter tarts was me fooling around. I skim through a few more pages and land on the lyrics I finished writing this morning in bed.

"What about that?" Harper taps the page covered in my handwriting. "It looks complete."

"This is only a rough draft." My insides cramp. The words I wrote this morning were honest, about El. Two components that can lead to a good song. The sentences poured out of me, generating energy, not draining me.

"Can you work on it with the guys?"

I exhale. I never even considered showing it to anyone. Playing it for EL? Sure. See if she'd find the right notes to make my lyrics shine. Something tugs at the spot under my breastbone at the thought of someone else singing this song. Using my words. I rub away the pain.

"We're game if you are," says Xander.

Corbin, Xander, Lucian, and Gideon watch me, like I know what I'm doing and not winging this whole music business thing. The band needs this, and I need the band to succeed. I can sacrifice this one song. My palm presses against the dull ache that won't fade. My nostrils fill with the mix of herbal candle and LA air. I pinch the bridge of my nose. It's not like I'm going to record the song myself. I'm not in a band, not a performer. What else am I going to do with these words?

I nod to the door and place my index finger as a placeholder in my little black book. "Let's find an empty studio."

Getting lunch for everyone was the best excuse I could make to get out of the studio. My lyrics came alive with the melody and treatment Death Elbow came up with over the last hour. Maybe Harper is onto something. This might actually work.

The phone in my back pocket comes to life. Did El wake up? I unlock the screen to a picture of Mum at the charity gala. For once the old ache of distress about her health doesn't coat me. The program is working and Mum has never been better.

"Did I wake you?" Mum's eyes are narrowed in the tight frame of her eyebrows.

I pan the camera to show her the building and the street around me. "On my way to grab more coffee and lunch."

"Well, I'm sorry to ruin your day, but Opa is in the hospital."

I stop. "Is it his back?"

"No." Mom rolls her lips. "He tried to take down a wall in the kitchen and ended up electrocuting himself. According to him, he thought it was a good idea to renovate. Wanted to surprise me when I got home from the treatment center."

Mum's kitchen is older than me, but Opa could've told me what he was doing on our last call. "How bad is it?" My throat constricts. Opa is sixty-seven and apart from his back and his hearing, he's been in good health.

"The doctor said that he was lucky but I'm going to cut my stay short and go home—"

"No." I run my hand through my hair. "You can't split in the middle of a session." I scan the empty streets as if they can offer a solution. "I'll hop on a plane and I'll be there by tomorrow morning."

"Wil, you can't—"

"I can and I am."

"But your school. Your work."

"It's a long weekend over here and I just spent my whole Sunday morning with Death Elbow." The song might do the trick. Time to see if today's conversation and the hours of media training Harper will run them through this afternoon help them behave like adults. "I'm coming."

The lines of worry around her mouth relax. "I don't know what I'd do without you."

"You don't need to know. You have me." I wink at the screen.

I pace the small waiting room of Sven's office, El following like a tail. "You did the right thing calling me. What did the doctor say?" Dad's whisper is rough.

"He'll be fine. His heart is doing well. They are treating his burns now and there doesn't seem to be any damage to internal organs, but they insist he should not be doing any electrical work on his own, or any heavy construction work for that matter."

"So he just needs to rest for a bit."

"Opa doesn't know what rest is." I spin on my heel. "They are releasing him tomorrow and even if I fly there for the week, once I'm gone he'll be there by himself and I don't know what else he'll decide to fix."

"Your grandfather is not a child. But he's stubborn."

"I won't let Mum cancel her treatment." I glance at El.

She nods in agreement.

"Hanna needs to focus on her health." Dad's footsteps punctuate every syllable. We're both pacing it seems. "What if we send your grandfather to a resort? I hear Mallorca is great this time of the year."

I snort. "Opa doesn't do resorts. He doesn't do leisure. He works, or makes other people work. The only time he's ever not working is when he's hanging out with Mum or me."

"That's a good idea. Hanna can't stay there. You can't stay there. But your grandfather can come here." I stare at the phone. He can't be serious. Dad keeps talking. "We have plenty of space. Sylvia's mother will be staying with us for the summer, but she can stay in El's room."

"I'm not sure I can get Opa on a plane." I meet El's eyes and her face pinches. "The last time he was on one was before I was born. He said it was like he was a sardine flying in a tin can."

"How about a private jet?" Dad's keyboard clacks. "I just sent mine to Norway to pick up Sylvia's mother. I'll get the pilot to swing by Bremen and bring all three of you to LA."

"Hold on." I press mute. "That means I can't help you move tomorrow." I sag against the edge of the counter.

El hugs herself. "Everything but the final suitcase is packed. I can do it on my own."

"Or I can ask Mateo."

"I'm fairly positive Sven will help." She offers me a sly grin. "He's anxious to get me out of here."

I tip forward and kiss her cheek. "His loss." I unmute the phone. "Even if I could get Opa to agree to come to LA"—I glance at El to make sure she really is okay with the idea, and she motions me to go on—"which I highly doubt, he wants the renovations done before Mum's back. Having this ready for her is a big deal."

"What if we sweeten the deal?" A door creaks on the line. "What if I cover the renovations for the entire house? We'll hire a project manager. Your grandfather can supervise from here.

Everything will be done, not just the kitchen. That way he has nowhere to live and is forced to come stay with us. All he needs to do is hang out with his grandson for several weeks."

A full-house renovation for Mum. El nods like it's a great idea. Opa would love the chance to spend Dad's money. This might just work. "Thank you for helping."

"Thank you for letting me know what you need."

The commercial flights to Bremen seem to take days, but the car ride from the airport to Mum's is much easier than the train-bus combo El and I trekked when she first came here before Christmas. Faster too. My key still works in the door but I have to jiggle the handle to get it open.

The house is dark but I see a construction site gone wrong: the wall that separated the kitchen and living room is only partially there. The cabinets and the oven unit that was on it lie in the middle of the floor. The drywall is gone and a colorful spaghetti of electrical wiring and exhaust vent piping glares at me.

Did this room shrink while I was away? Dad's place, with its wide granite island that seats six, feels like what a normal kitchen should be, not this tiny, tired space. There's a piece of molding missing from underneath the microwave, the door to the panty is slightly ajar, and the table I ate a million cookies at is covered in dust. I push up the switch for the light over the sink, but it won't turn on.

"It's on the fritz." Opa nudges me away from the malfunctioning item.

"Opa." I pull my grandfather into a hug, sucking in the scent of his aftershave. "You scared me."

Strong arms squeeze me then push me away. "I'm fine." He steps to a chair and slumps onto it. "I've been doing construction for over fifty years and I was dumb enough to touch that wire unprotected." He lifts his bandaged fingers. "I'm better than that."

I kneel in front of him and examine his hand, then his face. He's paler than usual, but not to a concerning degree. "A little California sun and some football on Dad's big screen and you'll be good as new in no time."

Convincing Opa that since the kitchen wasn't operational, maybe the whole house could do with a renovation, takes more out of me than negotiating the contract with Vatton. When Opa balks at the cost, I spin a tale of Dad owing eighteen years of backpay for child support and what an improvement a renovated house would be to Mum's quality of life when she comes home. I use the Mum card like butter, slathering it on every idea. Opa and I even walk through the house imagining the improvements, like the dishwasher and new railing for the front door that will make Mum's life easier.

Packing Opa's bag takes less than an hour and we even have time to drink a cup of tea. During the entire ride to the airport,

Opa explains the options for flooring and his eyes light up at the idea of double ovens. We smile as we imagine Mum's reaction to the whole-house renovation. Dad's plan seems to be exactly what Opa needed.

The private security line and passport control take minutes. I hand Opa's luggage over to the flight attendants.

"No line again?" Opa stops in front of the stairs leading to the jet.

"It's just us. It's a private plane," I say for at least the third time.

"Flying across the ocean for three people? Waste. What a waste." Opa takes the steps and his trim figure disappears through the door.

My phone buzzes and a text from Harper stops me with my foot on the first step.

> Harper: I sent the demo of the song to ten radio stations and they all said they'll play it once it's cut.

The song, my song, will be on the radio? Well, technically only the lyrics are mine, and I will have production credits, but even with the song for *Indigo* I didn't have as much of me in a piece of music as there will be in this song. I clutch the phone. My heart beats so loudly it quiets the sounds of the airport around me.

Harper: Also, Moderni Look can meet tomorrow morning to discuss a possible contract. Are you available?

My fingers fly over the keyboard.

Me: Set it up. I'll be there.

A trickle of adrenaline hits my bloodstream. Death Elbow messed up the rehearsal space and some performance opportunities, but it seems like increased media attention is what gets the brand opportunities rolling in. Or should I thank Mateo and Zoe for improving the way the band looks? I bound up the stairs and enter the cabin, ready to claim the couch so I can have a movie marathon for the entire flight.

"You are not serious." A blond woman who's definitely older than Mum, but doesn't look like anyone's grandma, says to Opa in a voice that would fit a queen.

"I'd like to sit with my grandson. I'm not sure what is ridiculous about that."

She sets an elaborate cocktail on the table in front of her and waves her arms at the empty plane. "And you can. You can sit anywhere you want."

"But those are couches, not seats." A red flush is creeping up Opa's throat.

I've seen that before on the construction site—two seconds before he's about to blow up. I step forward. "You can sit on the couch with me." There are two couches along either side of the plane and we could each have one, but if sitting with me gets him more comfortable . . .

"I'm not flying on a couch." Opa turns and heads for the exit. "I don't know why I even agreed to this trip."

I hurry to block the door. "Because you want to spend time with your favorite grandson."

"Only grandson."

"Explains why you have a stick up your bum." The queenly lady, who I know must be El's grandmother but my brain refuses to assign a label of grandma to, chimes in.

Opa's eyes narrow and he crosses his arms over his chest. "If anyone has sticks up their bum it's you. You're on a plane." He scans her from head to toe. "Why do you have a cocktail and look like you're going to a fancy ball?"

"If you think this is a compliment, you need to dust off your skills." She adjusts a sparkling broach on the collar of her velvet jacket. "I take pride in my appearance no matter where I go."

"Dressed to impress? Who are you trying to impress on this plane? The pilot? It's definitely not working on me."

"I'm trying to impress myself." She turns to the flight attendant who is entering the cabin. "This man just insulted me. Can he be escorted off the premises?"

The flight attendant smiles at me in confusion.

"I'm not being escorted off." Opa stomps like a three-year-old who's being threatened with a time out. "I'm flying to LA with Wil. In a normal seat." He jabs a finger at the single seat across from the one El's grandmother is towering over like it's her throne.

I try to direct Opa to the couch, away from El's grandmother. "You'll like the couch. It has seatbelts just like a regular seat. But more comfortable."

Opa digs in his heels. "Why can't she sit on the couch?"

"I'm Wil." I extend my hand to El's grandmother.

"Estelle." She picks up the cocktail and takes a sip while scanning me from head to toe. "El has told me a lot about you."

"All good things, I hope." I give her my most charming smile and she reciprocates. I turn to Opa. "You can sit on the couch with me or across the table from Estelle."

"No," Opa and Estelle say in unison.

"You, young man, can sit across from me though. They have all the ingredients here for an old fashioned. I have already told the attendants I prefer to make my own." The face that was cold to Opa blooms into a smile as Estelle pulls me into the seat on the other side of her. "Stay with me. Tell me everything about how El is really doing."

I'd love to get to know Estelle better, but I need Opa on the couch, buckled and distracted.

"How about you start that cocktail and I'll join you after we take off?"

Estelle releases my hand and waves us to the couch. Opa slouches next to me and I show him how the built-in TV works. This day—or two?—has been endless, and we haven't even taken off yet.

Seven

Sven in the driver's seat feels too familiar. At least it's not Rocker's Rolls Royce. The truck is packed with my things to move to Carlee's. I had a bedroom with a walk-in closet the size of Sven's apartment at Rocker's. How is it that I now only need a couple of suitcases and a few boxes to pack my life? I pull up the moving list in my notes app and check again. The feeling that I left something lingers. "Are you sure you remembered the box I set on the desk?"

"Sure." Sven keeps his eyes on the road to Malibu. He changes lanes and slows to take a familiar off-ramp to Pacific Coast Highway.

"Are you sure you're going to the right place?"

"I am." Sven reaches for his bottle, one of the florescent purple Vatton samples Wil gave him, and takes a long sip.

I return to my phone and switch to a different, longer list. "By the time Gretchen clocked out on Friday, she seemed to be getting the lay of the land. At least she knows how to book your consultations and order coffee and filters. I created a list of to-dos, but need to add fixing the sticky door to the office bathroom. I promised I'd check in on her next week if I get a minute before work."

"Don't stress." Sven's finger taps the steering wheel. "If Gretchen isn't a good fit, Zoe can help."

I consider protesting but clamp my teeth and concentrate at the next item on my list. The letters dance and sway so I close my eyes. "I saw the jacket of the suit she's designing for you hanging in your office." The light blue linen my cousin selected is almost the exact shade of Sven's irises. I gotta give it to her, she has an eye for these things. Like me, Zoe has always known what she wanted to do in life. Unlike me, nothing will stop her dreams of becoming a fashion designer.

"She has to alter the pants." He shifts in his seat. "Too tight."

"Maybe you should ease up on leg days?"

"Gretchen asked for next Friday off for her granddaughter's preschool graduation." Sven ignores my jab.

"I thought she was going to come in on the weekend instead." I tap the side of my phone. In the last three weeks I interviewed six candidates for my replacement. The moment Gretchen walked in the door, I knew she was a perfect fit.

My phone pings. An alert about another story on Daniel Davison's website. A phantom pain in my gut has me firmly setting my teeth. The headline reads, "El Vella Rumored to Be Drunk Before Performance: Banned from Venue," accompanied by a photo of Wil and me from the night we went to pick up Death Elbow. The gossipmonger had been quiet since my exclusive interview with him two months ago, but I guess the truce is over. More proof that I do not need to draw attention to myself.

A text pops up over the article.

> Wil: We're about to take off. Wish me luck.

> Me: It can't be that bad.

I adjust my sunglasses. I was excited to introduce Mormor to Wil but now I have to wait until tonight to get my grandmother's opinion.

> Wil: I need peace negotiation lessons.

Me: I can teach you. My negotiation with Carlee to let Death Elbow rehearse at The Devil's Martini went off without a hitch.

Wil: And I'll never stop thanking you for that. You are the best girlfriend ever.

A smile takes over my lips.

Wil: Can't wait to see pics of Carlee's mansion.

Wil: And your new bedroom.

Wil: And your new bed.

My stomach does that thing it always does when Wil is being cocky. Every now and again I even manage to send him back something flirty.

Me: I can't wait to try out my new bed.

Wil: Am I invited?

Me: Always.

"She knows how the computer works?"

Sven's question pulls me from my Wil-bed induced coma.

"She has years of experience managing a private investigator's office in San Fransisco but had to quit to move to LA and help out with her granddaughter. So yes, she knows how the computer works."

I glance at my friend. Mirrored shades hide his eyes and as usual his chin is rigid, but I can see a tiny muscle in his jaw ticking. Is this about me leaving the office? I know I hurt his feelings when I went on tour with Blatantly Subtle and didn't keep in touch. I'm not making the same mistake again.

"You know that if she works out, you'll be hiring all of my future employees."

"I'll be happy to do so." I lay my phone on my lap. "For a consulting fee."

"Oh, so now you've got a better job, no more friend discount for me."

I punch him in the arm. Which must feel like a feather's tap against his bulging bicep. "You'll always get the *family* discount." I emphasize family. "Besides, I have to work off all the cupcakes of yours I ate."

Sven scratches his nose. "More like the other way around. I still owe you money from when you paid my bail last fall."

"Get serious." I wave a hand. "You've paid me back a million times over. You don't owe me anything."

"Don't you want to finally make that music video with Mr. Mustard?"

"Astor," I correct. "Leonard Astor. And I'm not interested in a video." Artists who don't tour or plaster their faces and music on every social media and streaming channel don't make money, and I'm not getting back on any stage.

The truck turns onto a street lined with palm trees I know better than the back of my own hand. If I roll down the window, the scent of the ocean will fill my nose. Up ahead a man with a long-lensed camera slung around his neck rests against the hood of a car. Paparazzi. I shiver and I twist in my seat.

"Sven. What is this? I told you and Wil and everyone who'll listen that I'm not moving back in with Mom and Rocker." My entire body tenses, every muscle coiling in protest. "I am an adult. You can't do this to me."

Sven captures one of my flying hands and holds it down on the seat. "I always listen." The truck whizzes past the entrance gates of the mansion I've lived in since I was twelve. The cameraman pays no notice to us and the tension in my spine eases. Sven stops in front of the shiny steel slats of the gate right beside my parents' place. I straighten.

"What are we doing at Asher Menken's parents' house?"

Sven clicks something on his phone and the metal gate glides open. "Welcome to your new home."

I gape as he drives along the wide circular driveway that leads to a white stone mansion that always reminds me of the museum we toured when visiting my cousin Bailey in NYC. Two marble columns flank each side of a dark maroon door, the brass lion's head knocker glinting in the sun. The truck comes to a halt in front of the gleaming white walkway reminiscent of a red carpet made of snow. I hang my head. "Sven Anders, did you know that Carlee rented this house?"

Sven shrugs.

"And you never thought to mention this?"

"You never asked."

"Ahhh." I groan into the ceiling of his truck. "I can't with you."

"Good thing I'm no longer your problem." Sven hops out and I get out too. "Carlee is." We walk to the back and Sven opens the latch. "Are we doing this or are you moving back to my place?"

"I'm not moving back with you." I stomp over and yank out one of my suitcases. I'm not prepared for the weight and almost drop it. "Enjoy your bed."

The whole point of not moving back to Rocker's mansion was to be independent. To make my own way in life so I didn't have to rely on my family for support or listen to why they think I'm messing up. Technically, I'm doing just that. With this job I'll have my own money, be gainfully employed, and live in my own mansion. Well, not my own, but I live in a mansion that is not where my parents are. That's progress.

With a slow and low, "I will," Sven stacks two boxes on top of each other and leads the way to the front door. I trail, rolling my possessions up the walkway.

Inside, the house is modern like Rocker and Mom's but more open and airy. It has long expanses of wood and the side that faces the beach is floor-to-ceiling glass that I have no way of escaping. The ocean stretches before me: a menacing creature, whispering its curses with the waves.

I hear the click-clack of Carlee's shoes on wood, like the drumstick countdown to a song, before I see her. In her white linen jumpsuit without a stich of makeup, she could be closer to my nineteen than thirty. Her blond hair is swept to the side with a lotus clip. "Is that everything?"

"It is." I position my suitcases against the wall and Sven places the boxes on a long wide glass table. He looks at me. I look at him. He raises an eyebrow and my lungs constrict. Sven has been central to my world. My confidant and protector. The big brother I never had. Family. I stand closer. Before he turns I crush myself against his burly chest for a little too long. "I'll see you at The Devil's Martini, right?"

Large hands grasp my arms, and my personal Superman gently escapes my hug. "Can't get rid of me that easily."

"Thank you." I blink away the moisture forming in the corner of my eyes. "Thank you for everything."

His nods. "Anytime." His gaze lands on Carlee. "We'll talk soon."

My heart pinches as I close the door behind him.

"You'll see him plenty." Carlee nudges my shoulder. My stuff that was a mountain in Sven's bedroom is not even a tiny island in this large foyer. "Let me show you the place." She twirls her hands in the air.

I grab the handle of one of the suitcases.

"Leave everything here until you choose your room."

I rock on my heels.

Carlee's carefree smile dims. "Anything wrong?"

Apart from me not knowing this place is next door to my family? I keep that to myself. It's not like she picked a house with me in mind. I find my voice. "Are there any bedrooms that face away from the ocean?"

"One." Carlee heads toward the side of the house that would face Rocker's place.

We walk down a long hallway past three rooms, all with windows that highlight the sparkling ocean, until we turn right into a smaller room that has a daybed, a chest of drawers, and a bedside table. "I think this is a spare room for overflow guests, but it's way too small. The room I had in mind for you is much better, with a balcony you can sip your coffee on in the morning and watch the runners on the beach."

I walk to the curtains and pull them aside. A familiar window I usually saw from the inside is across the fence. My old room. Close yet separate. My shoulders relax. "This one will be perfect."

"Are you sure?"

I nod.

"In that case, the next stop on the tour is my idea of paradise." Carlee heads in the opposite direction. Once past the kitchen she opens the wall of sliding glass to the entertainment area, with a clear partition separating the deck from the ocean behind it. A resort-like bar and lounge area to the left surrounds the infinity pool that stretches along the beach. Waves crash against the white sand. The blue ocean wooshes behind the transparent divider, merging with an equally blue sky.

My heart accelerates. I turn my back to all the water and watch Carlee's face. "Why did you move from Atlanta to Malibu?"

"This view is hard to beat." Her voice is quiet, like she's speaking in church. "Besides. I needed a fresh start. A new chapter." Carlee stares at the panorama behind me.

Guilt creeps across my spine. The image of Carlee beside me onstage, unable to sing the words to the song that made her famous, needing my help to keep her upright while she was in the midst of an MS flare-up, Beau sweeping her offstage, her limp and barely responsive lying on the couch backstage. Carlee's condition forced her into early retirement. Unlike me, stepping away because I'm . . . I shake my head.

Carlee catches my eye. "I guess it's new chapters for both of us."

EIGHT

I FORCE OPEN MY eyelids, which feel like sandpaper, and instead of sun peaking though the gap in the blinds of Sven's bedroom, I stare at a pale yellow wall. I blink. Nope, still a blank wall. I roll over and practically squash a sleeping El.

Right.

I'm in her room at Carlee's place. After a twelve-hour plane ride where the inside temperature was colder than the outside, and then getting Opa settled into Dad's place, I slipped out to kiss El. One kiss was not enough and we ended up christening her new bed. Which I'm not sure is an improvement over Sven's. Sure it's softer, but it's also smaller. I wriggle onto my back, then my side, and drink in the sight of my sleeping girlfriend.

Her soft pink lips part slightly like she's about to spill a secret.

I lightly trace the freckles on the bridge of her nose and it twitches beneath my touch. How can a nose be sexy? I lean forward to kiss it. El moves and her nose goes into my mouth while something hard rams into my groin.

My vision swims, black spots appearing, intense pain radiating through my body, and my internal organs surge upward. I howl and bunch into a ball.

"Wil?"

El's hand on my bicep usually calms me but it barely makes a dent in the searing waves of anguish. My teeth and toes hurt and I squeeze my eyes closed to keep from vomiting. I open my mouth but can't speak.

"Shit." She shifts on the bed.

The movement bounces me and a new spasm of pain sets off. A pitiful moan leaks from me. "Don't"—I gasp for breath—"move."

"I'm so sorry." El's words are muffled and I crack open an eye. Her hand is clamped over her mouth, her eyes wide, and her shoulders shake.

"Are you laughing?" I rasp.

Her head swings back and forth, but tiny spurts of laughter escape between her fingers. "I'm so sorry." She sucks in her cheeks. "You startled me."

"Same here."

"What can I do?" She reaches for me but stops. "Can I touch you?"

My internal organs feel shuffled, like the words of a song rearranged for a choral performance. I wheeze through the pain, "Not yet."

"Ice? Should I get ice?"

The thought of cold down there makes me flex and a new level of hell racks me. "No," speeds out of me.

"I have to do something." She slips to the edge of the bed, jostling the mattress again, and I can't think straight. "Water. Let me get you some water."

"Please." I don't really want anything but she's so desperate to help.

I don't dare to move even a finger. After an eon, my muscles unlock and I can breathe normally. Anticipating the worst, I move my hand, but the pain doesn't rip a hole in me. I ease myself up to sit with my back against the headboard. My lower half throbs but most of my senses return.

"Water?" El stands a foot away from the bed, holding the glass for me.

"Put it on the table," I say, and pat the mattress beside me. "Sit with me."

"Are you sure?"

"Absolutely." I hold out an arm, inviting her to join me. She gingerly climbs onto the bed. I grit my teeth but can manage the pain now. I pull her to my chest and run my fingers through her hair. My heart rate settles. "There wasn't a room with a bigger bed?"

"Ocean views." El's hand hovers like she doesn't know where to touch me.

I grasp her fingers and pull them to my lips. If only my kisses could take away her pain. But if anyone has a right to fear the water, after losing her father in a boating accident, my girlfriend does. I tuck our joined hands under my chin, glad her father made her wear a life jacket.

We breathe in sync and I close my eyes. With the comfort of El pressed against me, the world gets a little hazy, and I don't want to move for a different reason. She begins to hum. Her fingers flutter like she's playing the chords on her guitar. I add the words of the verse.

Bow of your spine, my palm on yours
Your tears seep into my pores
I think of you

We come to the end of what we've worked out and stop. El's thumb drags across my palm. "Not the best way to start our day."

"I disagree. Any day I wake up with you is a good day." I kiss the top of her head. "And sing with you."

"We could find a stall in the market and do a little busking."

My heartbeat stamps out yes, yes, yes. Last summer, I lived for those hot, sunny days at the farmers' market when I got to see El and make music with her. Here in the dim light, with El tucked into me, singing together feels like a possibility.

The prospect shimmers before me and I can almost smell the gyro stand across from our favorite spot, hear the clink of coins dropping into my guitar case.

Except I need to get the money for Mum. The reminder bursts my bubble. Back then we made barely enough to buy gyros, never mind taking El on a proper date. Now I can do that but still don't have enough to afford a safe place for El to live.

Not enough.

El moving in with Carlee was better than her taking a crappy apartment in a dodgy neighborhood. With Sven, El was safe and I didn't have to fret. Carlee has security and understands the risks with the paparazzi. El living next door to Dad's mansion is a bonus. Splitting my time between Dad and El will be easier, and El can be around her family too.

I disconnect myself from the girl who makes my world shine and cup her cheek. "I'd love to spend the rest of the day with you, but you have a new job to get to." I avoid El's gaze. "And I need to get back to Dad's. I have a call with the Finnish company that sent over those shirts they want the band to wear. Plus it's Opa's first morning at the house and I better be there before he's up."

"You'll get that contract. I know you will. And I can't wait to see Mr. Peters. Bringing him here was the right move. I'll make sure to give you that lesson on negotiations." She pecks my cheek. "Go. Be awesome."

I defy gravity as I exit her room.

Weaving between the beds of orange, yellow, and pink flowers, I sprint across Carlee's gravel walkway that separates the pool from the fence to Dad's property and tug at the rusty latch that holds the white wooden planks closed. The gate creaks from disuse. An overgrown vine from the Menken's garden spills over the top and trails down to the sandy pathway between the properties that leads to the beach. I open the mint green door in the fence across the path and run over the recently watered lawn to Dad's house, hoping everyone is still asleep.

I'm wrong. As I slip into the kitchen, the room is brightly lit. Pickle is strapped into his highchair, flanked by Opa on one side and Dad on the other.

"Why are you wearing the same outfit?" Opa asks me and glares at Dad. "Aren't you paying him enough to buy some decent clothes?"

My solar plexus tightens. "I slept at El's place." I kiss the crown of black hair on Pickle's head.

Opa spins to Dad. "You let him sleep with El?"

Dad almost chokes on his coffee.

"Opa. I'm almost twenty-one. If I want to spend the night with my girlfriend, it's my business," I say.

My grandfather mutters into his mug but I don't take the bait.

Dad turns to me. "Are we driving into the office together today?"

I alter my course and steer toward the coffeemaker, snagging a cup on the way. "Can't. I have a conference call with that potential endorsement."

"Vatton?"

"No. Moderni Look. It's a Finnish clothing company trying to carve a sliver out of the US market. The brand deal is a good one." I fill the mug. "They're offering five percent while Death Elbow are on tour if I convince the whole band to wear them at all press conferences."

"Five percent?" Opa crosses his arms. "Of what?"

"Gross sales of the US market for a three-month period."

"Why would they do that?"

"They want the exposure a hot band can provide. People like to buy what celebrities wear."

Dad finishes feeding Pickle, whose little hands wrap around Dad's thumbs. "Harper's on the call, correct?"

"Yes, she set it up." I check my watch. "We're meeting in ten."

Dad taps his fingers on the countertop. "How's El? The picture of you two in yesterday's news wasn't particularly flattering."

I sigh. Pictures from the night we picked up Death Elbow are still being used for stories. One from Daniel Davison's site yesterday was particularly nasty.

"Why would the press want pictures of you and El?" Opa stares at me.

"Wil is my son. That comes with heightened interest from gossip rags." Dad wipes cereal from Pickle's ear. "They might approach you as well." Dad glances at Opa. "Maybe Mr. Peters should meet with Harper for some media training."

Opa scoffs. "I do *not* need training."

I move closer to Opa. "It might be helpful. They can be pretty sneaky. A few pretended to be classmates of mine just to get an inside scoop."

With no more food forthcoming, Pickle stuffs his own fingers in his mouth and whimpers. Pickle and Opa have remarkably similar grumpy expressions, like Pickle is attempting to imitate my grandfather.

"I don't need training because I'm not planning on talking with anyone I don't already know in LA. That's too many people already." Opa drains his cup and reaches for a refill.

"Still, it wouldn't hurt. Just in case." From the freezer, Dad retrieves one of the push pop feeders that Marta fills with her homemade avocado smoothie mix. Pickle laughs like this is the best half-hour of comedy in his life.

Opa stares at the frozen green mash. "You are not giving that to the baby."

Pickle does a gimme-gimme gesture with his chubby hands.

"Avocado is good for him. Frozen like this, it also helps with his teething," says Dad.

"What's wrong with rubbing a little schnapps on his gums?" Opa scratches his nose. "I did that with Wil and he turned out great."

Dad gawks, as if Opa suggested giving Pickle crack cocaine. "Sylvia and I are trying a more natural approach."

"Schnapps is natural. I made it myself."

"Giving alcohol to babies is something the American Academy of Pediatrics of California prohibits." Dad fusses with the tufts of hair on Pickle's head. "Both the baby-led weaning books and the online seminar I took on the importance of homemade baby food agreed it's important to promote healthy gut bacteria as they get less breast milk. Avocados contain monosaturated fatty acids similar to breast milk and can help with brain development and energy."

Pickle smiles at his dad, the expression of trust plain for all to see.

Opa huffs. "Wil didn't eat any avocados as a baby and his brain is plenty developed."

"I know I wasn't there to feed Wil avocados, throw a ball with him, take him to the doctors. I know I missed out on his childhood, but I'm here for him now." Dad's usually cheerful demeanor is gone. His face is drawn, and he watches Opa with a challenge in his eyes. "Had he been here with me, he would have had everything my money could buy him."

"I wouldn't have let you raise my grandson here without me." Opa squares his shoulders. "I was the only father he had."

Pickle's no longer giggling. He hiccups and his face scrunches.

"You did a great job. But you are not his father," Dad snaps.

Opa's nostril's flare. He's a bull readying for an attack.

"Opa." I slam down my coffee cup and step forward. "I need your help." Dad and Opa both turn to me. I focus on Opa. "Can you come with me to The Devil's Martini today? Meet the band? Give me some advice on how to handle them?" Advice is the last thing I need from Opa in this situation, but better he talks my ear off than continue verbal sparring with Dad.

Opa slaps a hand on my shoulder. "Anything for you."

I avoid glancing at Dad. He doesn't deserve this treatment from Opa. If Mum were here she'd be upset at her father and defending Dad.

"Let me change first." Opa bustles out of the kitchen, coffee cup in hand.

I finally face Dad. "I'm sorry about him."

Dad plucks Pickle out of the highchair and tucks the baby into his chest. I'm not sure who's getting comfort from whom. "I did want to be there for you."

"I know."

My phone chirps.

Harper: We're all on the conference line. Are you still able to make it?

Shit. The endorsement deal. "Dad, it's work." I run out of the kitchen.

Nine

EL

THE DEVIL'S MARTINI AT night seemed like a well-worn guitar, all worn wood and a frayed shoulder strap. During the harsh light of day it looks like the guitar is a prop, nothing more than cardboard glued together, ready to fall apart if you try to play it. When Carlee asked me to make a list of the things I think need to be updated or replaced, I thought it would be a quick task. Two hours in and I'm starting to feel that tearing the whole thing down and starting from scratch would be faster.

"Anyone here?" a voice shouts from the back door I left propped open to let in a little fresh air and release the clouds of dust I overturned as I opened the tall chest holding the different light gels.

"By the bar," I answer.

Corbin saunters in. The rest of Death Elbow file behind with yawning mouths that might suggest it's six in the morning, not almost two in the afternoon.

"Our savior." Corbin stretches and his already cropped shirt exposes most of his midriff. Tattoos scroll along the side of his ribs and wrap around his back.

I eyeball the door, expecting Wil to come last, but my boyfriend doesn't appear.

Corbin plops into a chair, his long legs blocking the path to the stage. "Wil texted that he'll be late. Some meeting."

I unearth my phone and check the missed messages.

> Wil: Running late. Show the guys around. <3

Corbin eyes the bar. "Can we get a drink?"

"The venue does not provide food or beverages until we open." Carlee comes out of her office, Sven behind her. "That's not for another four hours."

Corbin stands, brushes his knuckles on his shirt, and offers Carlee a hand. "You're even more beautiful in-person." The corner of his lip lifts.

Carlee jams her thumbs into the loops of her stonewashed jeans. "I would also advise you that if you decide to smoke, use drugs, or break my property, I will not hesitate to call the police on you and will evict you no matter how much Rocker Inc. is paying to rent this as your new rehearsal space."

I cringe.

Sven crosses his arms behind Carlee and Corbin's grin dims. He holds up both palms. "Right. Sure. Got it. Must be on our best behavior."

"Not sure that your best behavior is good enough." Carlee lifts her chin. "I've been in this business for over ten years and let me give you one piece of advice: no matter how talented you might be, if you behave like assholes, you will not have a career."

Corbin snickers. "We're a rock band."

"And hopefully professionals, so people keep wanting to come see you. Because believe me," she glares at Corbin, "if you can't book places for your fans to see you because your reputation precedes you, those fans will dry up faster than spilled ice in the desert."

Corbin squints at her, but the other band members pale a little. "Appreciate the advice," Lucian pipes up. "We'll keep the partying outside the club."

Carlee's face changes from stern teacher to girl-next-door. "El, please, let me know if they don't comply with any of the stipulations in their contract. I do not tolerate incompetence."

I gulp but nod. Her manicured fingernail taps on the tablet in her hand. "After you finish setting them up, come back to the office to discuss the needed upgrades." She waves at the band, spins, and struts back to her office like she's leaving a sold-out stadium wanting more.

Sven surveys each of the guys, a stony expression on his face. "I'll be back." The table wobbles as he strides past the band and marches out the back door.

"I'm so scared." With a cocky smile on his face, Corbin shakes dramatically.

"You should be. He's ex-navy." I guide them backstage. "If you cause me or Carlee any trouble, Sven can snap your neck within seconds."

"And Rocker Inc. will sue him within seconds. My neck is about to make them a lot of money."

"I think Rocker cares about me more than the money." The second I say the words, I know they are true. Even though he didn't help with The Devil's Martini when I asked, he has always treated me like his own daughter, and to Rocker, family is everything.

Corbin picks up a microphone and turns it on. "Let's test the acoustics here." Each member filters into place, Gideon taps out a hi-hat, and my diaphragm expands as if I'm about to sing.

I step to the edge of the stage, like my body is the compass and the stage is True North. I dig my heels in. My brain shouts in distress, reminds me of the attention, the press, the flashlights, the negatives that come with being front and center for everyone to judge, to create stories I can't refute or change. The stage might feel like the place to be, but I shouldn't be here. I choose the peace of privacy over the price the stage demands.

Xander plays an F chord and the ever-so-slightly wrong pitch slices through my brain.

I reach for the offending tuner peg. "Your second string is too tight."

He scrunches his face like he's smelling something rotten. "Sounds good to me."

"May I?"

"Whatever." He releases the guitar, leaving it hanging by the strap. I turn the second peg a fraction to the left.

"Try that."

He strums the chord again. "Hmm." He tries a few more chords. "You know your shit." His eyes slide to my hair. "Perks of being a rock star's daughter."

"Stepdaughter," Corbin interjects, practically breathing down our necks. "Our boss's stepdaughter." He gives Xander a light shove. "Let's start with *Going Once*."

I step around the boys, but Corbin grabs my wrist. "I need an audience for this one."

"No thanks. I have work to do."

Corbin cocks his head. "Don't you want to tell your grand-kids you were serenaded by Death Elbow?"

"I'm good." I inch backward.

Behind me, Xander kicks in with some low slow chords that don't sound like Death Elbow's usual grunge rock. Corbin winks at me and the drums start next. He lifts his mic and his hooded yet electric eyes root me to the spot.

Going once, going twice
It's in my head, it's in your eyes.

His voice has the gravel that makes it instantly recognizable on the radio. When bracketed by the instruments, the rough tone crawls along my skin, leaving goosebumps in its wake. He's good. I knew Death Elbow was a hit when I heard them here during the concert, but there's something about this song that resonates on a different level.

Corbin's hips sway to the beat and he snakes backward, pulling me along by my wrist. I'm the planet sucked into in the orbit of a star, unable to escape. At center stage he raises my arm over my head and twirls me.

> Crying lips, words pierce
> Chased you away when I was a goner
> Without you my soul is stuck on mute

After I complete my 360, I somehow end up closer to Corbin, our chests nearly touching. He lets go of my wrist, his finger inching along my arm and throat to rest under my jaw. My skin tingles at the combination of his touch and his words. He lifts my chin so I'm forced to stare into his murky hazel eyes. They widen and his mouth quirks up.

> Always sweet yet fierce
> Your voice, my guitar in the dark, an honor
> Our moans spell out the truth we can't refute

Lucian strums the final outro and Corbin bends forward like he might kiss me. I turn my head away, so not interested, and my gaze lands on Wil. It's only been hours since I've seen him but my heart leaps at the sight of him, like it wants to catapult off this stage and land in his lap.

Straight black pants and a button-down pull his overall appearance into the business casual he's been adopting since he started working for Rocker, but his unshaven cheeks and messy hair underline the tiredness of jetlag painted on his face. His lips are pressed together. His hard glare makes my insides churn.

"Wil?" I say.

"Hey, man. Didn't see you there." Corbin steps back and runs his fingers through his shaggy hair. "El here was being sweet, helping us warm up."

Wil storms forward. "My girlfriend is too sweet sometimes." He jumps onstage and greets me with a kiss that would've knocked me off my feet if both his arms weren't around me.

There are whistles and hoots from the band members behind me, but I'm lost in the world of Wil's embrace. A little voice somewhere in the back of my head worries that Carlee might see us, that this is not appropriate, but as his tongue slips into my mouth, I can't find it in me to care. My fingers try to get access to his skin, but unlike his T-shirts, what he's wearing is tucked in and I'm locked out. I settle for my palm against his cheek.

I suck in his small moan, wrestle my lips from his, and smile into our kiss. "You're here."

"Things went sideways at home." There's a tightness around Wil's eyes. "Warning: Opa is here."

"The baseboard is missing in this spot as well." Mr. Peters points a foot away from me at a gap that stretches between the stage and the wood floor of the venue. "It's the same issue by the back door."

Dazed and confused, I lick the taste of Wil's minty kiss away and track down my tablet. Baseboards were not on the "Issues to Address" list. "I guess we'll have to redo the baseboards."

"Redo? All this?" He holds out his arms wide. "Not necessary. You can match the style to your existing ones, paint them all the same color, and no one would ever know there was a gap." Mr. Peters steps on the stairs that lead from the stage to the audience. The second one squeaks under his weight. "Oh, not good." He bounces on the step, and it practically groans. "Probably the joists. Easy fix."

Wil raises an eyebrow. "Maybe Opa can help with some of the repairs?" There's a pleading look in his eyes. "Keep him busy?" Wil nuzzles my ear. "Please. He's driving Dad around the bend. We almost had World War III in the kitchen this morning."

I've seen Rocker upset, disappointed, frustrated even, but never actually angry. I lower my voice. "I'll speak to Carlee. She can't refuse free labor."

"Now you've marked your territory, think you can move?" Corbin sticks his elbow between Wil and me. "You're on our stage. We need to rehearse."

Hands entwined, Wil and I exit the stage, and I give Mr. Peters a side hug. "Got time to help me go over this place for deficiencies?"

Mr. Peters grins, a sight that should be cataloged because it's as rare as a full solar eclipse. "I've got all the time in the world."

Wil kisses me on the cheek and glances at his buzzing phone, lost to the latest email or crisis. I show Mr. Peters around the bar. He shakes tables, rattles chairs back and forth, and finds things out of order I never would have considered.

"A caulking gun is all I need to fix this."

My brain, already struggling with translating the words and construction jargon he's been throwing at me, fizzes. My form of dyslexia has always made it hard for me to break down the phonetic sounds of unfamiliar words.

I pass the tablet to Mr. Peters. "Could you type that for me?"

With one finger, Wil's grandpa adds caulking gun to the list, then caulk, then other things as he pokes and prods the walls. We're in the little alcove where Wil and I spent so many nights waiting to go onstage when there's banging on the front door. I know I have the CLOSED sign on it.

"I'll be right back." I leave Mr. Peters on his knees, tablet in hand, inspecting the well-worn wooden slats, and check who's knocking.

When I see Zoe's hazel eyes on the other side of the glass door, my neck stiffens like an overtight string. Mormor is next to her, reading the flyer Mateo created that advertises The Devil's Martini's new management and the Grand Reopening, as well as the note that we are open during construction. I consider shrinking back into the shadows, but I can't pretend they didn't see me, so unlock the door instead.

This is the second time Zoe and I have seen each other since I sat in her hospital room on the night of the accident. My gaze flies to her hairline, searching for a scar to mark the gash on her forehead. New bangs hide the spot. My cousin hates bangs. I ball my hands into fists to resist brushing the bangs of to the side. The sharp ping between my ribs at the loss of my best friend hurts more than slamming the door on my fingers.

"Why are those people taking photos of us?" Mormor sails into The Devil's Martini, her floral perfume trailing behind her like an invisible train.

"It's the paparazzi. They're trying to get a pic of Wil and El." Zoe's voice is flat. Very un-Zoe-like. As she steps out of the sunlight, her gaze catches on mine. Her words about how selfish I was around Wil, that not everything revolves around me, ring in my ears, burned into my memory of the night of the car accident.

Mormor fluffs her hair and dips to peer around the closed sign. "Will I be in the papers?" She shrugs and doles out air kisses along my cheeks. "I thought we'd come get you for lunch."

I wait for Zoe to say something. To talk to me. If she says hi, I'll say it back. She juts out her chin, cruises by me, and heads to the table where Wil is typing on his phone.

So much for making peace. I relock the door and nearly bump into Mormor. Like a statue, she's frozen in front of the bar tucked into the left corner of the open floor area.

"Is this supposed to be a nineteen-seventies throwback bar?" She wrinkles her nose. "Do you even have a decent vermouth back there?"

"They haven't done an inventory of the alcohol yet. The bartenders don't get here until four. It's not a priority."

Mormor swings opens the access panel, letting herself behind the bar, and runs a finger along the middle shelf. She regards her dusty digit. "Suitable drinks are always a priority." She snatches a bottle covered in grime. "I've never seen something this sad calling itself a bar and I've been to many hole-in-the wall locations." The bottle lands on the bar top, not back in the place it's obviously sat for months, if not years. "How do you expect to make money on this?"

"People come here for the music, not the food and drinks." Carlee reappears with Mr. Peters. "Look who I found pulling up tiles in front of my office."

"That woman again." Wil's grandfather's whisper carries.

Mormor's fingers tap the bar, her gaze intent on Mr. Peters. "Are you following me?"

"I was here first, so if anyone is following anyone, it's you."

Mormor's arms cross. "I most certainly am not. I'm here to take my granddaughters to lunch." Her expression softens as it lands on Carlee. "Assuming you can spare her for an hour or two."

"Mormor." Even I cringe at the whine in my voice. "It's my first day. I've only been here three hours. I can't go to lunch."

"You have to eat."

"Carlee and I had a late breakfast at her house. I'm working different hours now."

I nibble on my lower lip. Of course, I'd like to spend time with my grandmother but I promised Carlee I would help make The Devil's Martini the best it can be. I can't walk out on the first day.

"How about I test your bar and make you some cocktails." Mormor places her palms on the bar.

"Can you make mocktails too?" Carlee takes a seat at the bar.

I introduce Carlee. "This is my grandmother. If they gave out Grammys for mixology, she'd have a shelf of them."

"My favorite one is with papaya juice. Let me see if you have any." Mormor opens the under-the-counter fridge. "In fact, if you like, I could make a list of alcoholic and non-alcoholic drinks you could add to your menu to switch it up. So people come for cocktails as well as music?"

Carlee's eyes shine brighter. "That sounds fantastic." She sneaks a notebook to Mormor. "Write down the ingredients and I'll have them brought in. That way you could come by in a few days. I'd love to try some out."

Mormor bounces on her heels. "I'll start with the classics and then give you some signature drink suggestions. Maybe music-based? Or I can play with the devil theme?"

"Or both." Carlee winks at me. "It's settled then. You tell El what you need, and we'll schedule a mixology session."

"So, what?" Zoe's voice reaches from behind me. "Mormor is working here too?"

Carlee spins her way. "Do you want a job?"

Ten

"NONE OF THE LATE shows have returned my calls." Dressed in a pink suit, Harper puts down her tablet, interlaces her fingers, and regards Dad and me. "It's not looking good."

On the opposite side of the black polished table, Dad drums a single finger. A quick glance at me and he says, "Still?"

I cross my feet to stop myself from tapping my shoes on the floor and set my elbows on the armrest of my chair. The unease in my gut spreads tendrils around my ribcage. Our goal of getting more exposure for Death Elbow to align with the album launch fizzled after fans complained online about them being a no-show the night the paparazzi swarmed El and me. We have a couple of months to go, but the last month has felt like we're at a standstill. "Fallout from the concert they missed?"

"Possibly." Harper examines the awards placards on the walls. "It could be timing. Summer blockbusters are in the middle of press junkets so they are mostly booked right now."

"I want Death Elbow on something national, mainstream." Dad pushes off his chair and rounds the table. "Let's put out more feelers." He walks behind me and sets both hands on the back of my chair. "I'm willing to fly the group to New York or Miami."

I twist to face him. "What about Europe?"

"Smart." Dad cocks an eyebrow at me. "Maybe overseas isn't as fussed about their antics." He turns back to Harper. "See if you can set anything up. In the meantime, any Fourth of July lineups we can get them into?"

Harper shakes her head. "But I have them opening for Blatantly Subtle at the Greek Theatre end of this month. They haven't called to cancel yet."

"Yet" hangs in the air. I tap my phone to see the hour.

Dad checks his watch like he can find more time to save Death Elbow's reputation.

"Anything else?" Harper stands. "I've got my work cut out for me."

The implication that my screwup is hampering Death Elbow's launch hits me in the middle of my chest. "I should go too." I pocket my phone. "Want to get to the bar before the band." And maybe get a moment to kiss my girlfriend. Between my final exams in the mornings, days at Rocker Inc., and El's nights at The Devil's Martini, we barely have time to sleep together, never mind do normal couple stuff. Once the endorsement deals are signed and Death Elbow's album is launched, I'll have the time and money to take El out on a proper date that doesn't involve raiding Marta's leftovers at two a.m.

"Actually." The crinkles around Dad's eyes bloom.

Dodger Stadium is packed with baseball cap-wearing fans sweating in the midafternoon sun. I twirl the signed baseball the batter autographed for Dad, which apparently is part of the first pitch ceremony.

"The popcorn here is the best." Dad takes a plastic cup of beer and a blue carton from the spread that could feed ten.

The buffet is laden with salads, entrees, and desserts that might belong in a five-star restaurant rather than a sporting arena. With my plate loaded with anything that looks familiar and a drink, I follow Dad out of the suite to the narrow table built into the divider behind the stadium seats. The suite is to the right of home plate and could probably fit twenty people. With just Dad and me, it feels even more wasteful and decadent.

"I thought baseball games are all about hot dogs and peanuts." I take a bite of the mac-and cheese.

"Still is. I can get you some if you want."

I shake my head. "There's plenty of food here."

"Too much actually." Dad picks up his phone and texts someone. He points to the packed crowd below. "We could try and go incognito, sit with the general crowd, get you the experience of baseball I had as a child."

"Maybe next time." I sip on my soda. El warned me that Dad loves his surprises. While spending time with him is always a blast, I need to review Vatton's latest contract changes before the end of the day.

"I missed a lot of your firsts. I thought at least we could share this one," says Dad. "We should celebrate the end of class too. Maybe have a few of your friends over to the house."

The leather of my chair squeaks as I settle my drink in the holder attached to the seat. "Mateo has an end-of-term party planned for Saturday." Which I hope to drop by after El's finished work. If we aren't too exhausted.

"Right. Good." Dad drums his fingers on his thigh.

I watch a man on the mound in the middle of the diamond toward home plate. Nothing happens and the squatting player wearing the same-colored uniform catches the ball. No one claps, so maybe it was a practice throw.

"Do you like it here?" Dad asks.

The man throws another ball and again nothing happens. I scan the crowd for some sense of what's going on. "The stadium seems nice."

"I mean LA. Rocker Inc. UCLA. Our home."

Our home. Although I feel more and more at home in Sylvia's and Dad's Malibu mansion, I spend most of my time in El's tiny room in the mansion next door. El is my home.

"It's very . . ." I search for a word to describe the feeling of warped reality the days in LA have been like. "Sometimes it feels like I'm in a dream. Or a movie. Like I'm an impostor playing this role and will be soon discovered and booted out."

Dad spears some salad with his fork. "Impostor syndrome. I still have it to this day. I wish I could tell you it's something you grow out of, but there is always something new to give you a different flavor. More fame. Less fame. More awards. Less awards. More money . . . you get it."

I nod as I crunch the particularly crispy pizza crust.

"But." Dad turns to me, scanning my face. "Do you think you want to stay here permanently?"

I wipe my lips with a napkin. "I think I can see a life here. Finish Uni. Work with you behind the scenes of the music world."

"You are a hard worker."

"That's what you pay me the big bucks for." My salary as Death Elbow's intern isn't what's bringing in the majority of the money. Yet. My leg bounces as I think of the contract I'm not reviewing.

"Big bucks they may not be, but it's just the beginning." He balls up his napkin. "I mean it, Wil. I'm impressed. After El hated working for Rocker Inc., I wasn't expecting much enthusiasm from you. But you have potential as a producer. Your instincts are on point. Your advice is sound. The song you helped Death Elbow with, *Going Once*, is exactly the kind of a vibe that'll warm the album, the give-me-soul to the don't-give-a-damn on the rest of the tracks. Perfect for the radio too. You've picked up so much in less than six months of working with me, I'm excited about what you can become."

The can feels heavy in my hand. Should I tell Dad that I wrote the song for El? Or should I tell El first that I wrote the song for her, that the lyrics are my love letter, the declaration I should make. I will make. I just need to get my shit in order. Get the brand deals done. Have the money to take her some place special, buy her a present that isn't a handmade bracelet. Show her how much she means to me. I'll tell El. I'll tell Dad. But not today.

I open my mouth and cram in another portion of pizza. This is about Rocker Inc.'s success, not just mine.

"I love music." That's the truth. When El and I sing together I feel more energized than any other part of the day. I wash that thought away with another swig of soda. "And I love the flexibility of having enough time to go to school in the morning." Even if there aren't quite enough hours in the day.

There's a knock on the door and two men come in. They start packing up the food into individual containers. Dad gets up and starts signing a few of them. He hands the pen back. "Take them to the 500 level and give them out for free."

Dad takes his place by me again and notices my stare. "What? We weren't going to eat all that. Shouldn't go to waste." He hands me a container of popcorn. "I saved the good stuff."

The crowd claps and the team in white heads off the field. On the scoreboard a big zero lights up under the one. I recline in my seat.

The ping of Dad's phone breaks our silence. "Well, this is good." Dad taps to open the message. "Dillon has a friend who's a booking agent. He says he can connect Harper and possibly get them in front of some music shows in England."

"Who's Dillon?" I ask.

"Eldest son of one of my bandmates. He and El were pretty close for a while."

Now the name rings a bell. The asshole who moved to London without telling her and dumped her over text.

Dad puffs his cheeks. "I think he thought he'd manage El's music career one day."

"Sorry?"

"Yeah, he's a good kid, but got in way over his head." Dad scratches his jaw. "Have you considered producing for El?"

Everything I do is for El. I pull down the cap of my new hat to block the sun. "She refuses to talk about putting out any new music."

The smiles drops off Dad's face. "There was a time when that girl would do almost anything to get on a stage." He sighs. "She has the right to be anxious. Being out there onstage, spilling your guts in songs, showing the world your worries and your joys is scary. And then there's the paparazzi." The crowd claps but Dad pays no attention. "Being behind the scenes is so much safer. After the initial frenzy over you being my son and that you and El are dating dies off, you won't have to worry for your safety or have cameras shoved into your face every time you decide to go on a date. Trust me, I'd love to have the money but not worry about the simple act of changing my son's diapers becoming the day's hottest news. Sometimes I wish I had the option to sit with you and Pickle in a normal seat in this stadium instead of this box."

"But you love performing."

Dad's eyes shine in the sun. "I do. Those minutes before you step onstage, the electricity in the air of thousands of people brimming with excitement, anticipation. Never knowing how the night will go. Being surrounded by people who get you, trust you. The ad-lib moments. That spark when you find the perfect chord or word then playing it live. The thrill of slipping into the music, living in the song."

I never seriously considered being onstage in front of crowds, but the way Dad speaks about songwriting and performing plucks a hidden string inside me. My blood hums. I hear Dad but in my head I'm onstage in a packed room as the crowd chants "WE, WE, WE." El stands beside me, a light sheen of perspiration coating her grinning face as she belts out a high G that brings the audience to its feet. She's electric. Performing with her has always been the time when I felt most alive. Most myself. My fingers grip the can like a microphone, ready to sing now.

"There's nothing quite like it." Dad laughs.

"El loves performing too."

"But it's a grueling lifestyle. Rocker Inc. is more stable."

A tiny thing inside me gets squashed. Not a dream or a wish even, but that "maybe" that I experienced when El and I were WE, singing at The Devil's Martini or busking at the farmers' market. I drain my drink.

Dad takes a sip from his beer. "El just turned nineteen in January, she has all the time in the world to figure out what she wants to do in her life. Not everyone knows what they want at such a young age."

"You did."

"And you do." The air of pride in his expression makes my chest ache. Dad turns back to the game. "But that's not the average."

"She is not average."

"That's not what I meant—"

"When she decides to sing again, really sing, I will cheer her on, no matter what you and Sylvia think about it." I hope he hears the challenge in my voice. "I hope that doesn't change things between us."

Dad swishes the remaining beer in his cup. "El is . . ." He sighs. "It's an impossible choice. I'll always have Sylvia's back. But I think my wife is changing her stance. In the end all we want to do is to take care of you. To make sure our kids are provided for. Happy. That this world doesn't break you." Dad holds my gaze. "All we want is for you to suffer less than we did."

Eleven

"Stop. Stop. Stop." Corbin jams the mic into the holder on its stand and the sensitive receptors revolt at the sudden movement, sending reverb through the empty space. I grit my teeth. I'm used to musical instruments and equipment reacting to the harsh movements of musicians, but this is the third time in an hour Corbin has stopped the song.

Xander throws up his hands. "What's your problem now?"

"My problem is you don't know what you're doing." Corbin gets in Xander's face. "You rush the transition in the second line of the verse. I'm not an auctioneer. I can't say the words that quickly."

"I played it exactly as it's written." Xander jabs the sheet music on the screen of the tablet before him.

"It's not about the notes written. You need to listen to what's going on onstage. I'm singing at the fastest speed I can. Can't you hear my rhythm?" Corbin shouts.

"I can slow the down beats." Lucian moves between the two men. "Maybe that'll help."

Wil taps against his leg under the table. He pushes pause on the session recording.

My wrist is aching from the repetitive clicks as I sort emails. Potential bands go into one folder, bills go into another, much larger one. I never considered how hard the leap from lead singer in a band to owner of his company must have been when Rocker started Rocker Inc.

Under the table, I slip my fingers between Wil's marching ones and the tapping stops. His shoulders slowly relax. He arches my way. "Corbin and Xander have been at each other's throats all afternoon."

Onstage, Gideon counts in the band. "One. Two. Three," leaving the last beat silent. Corbin belts the opening line of the pre-chorus, "Going once, going twice. It's in my head, it's in your eyes."

The song they've been rehearsing is catchy and more pop than rock. The words full of imagery are a bit of a departure from their usual fare but I know Wil is working on giving the band a more marketable sound. As he puts it, "The fans show up for steak, but we want to give them something for dessert they didn't expect or know they wanted."

I can't keep my toe from tapping, the conventional 4/4 timing easy to follow. I hum along, getting into the tune, mouthing the words I've heard umpteen times today. "It's in my head, it's in your eyes."

"Xander." Corbin screeches. "I swear you're doing it on purpose."

Wil pops up from the table. "Okay." He walks to the edge of the stage. "I think it's time we take a break. Maybe get some lunch."

"Or a drink." Corbin kicks the mic stand.

Phone in hand, Wil paces. "I'll order from that Thai place we had last week. Any requests?"

The boards creak as Corbin stomps across the stage, sets the guitar on a table by the drums, and murmurs, "Xander needs to get his head out of his ass," as he disappears into the left wing.

Xander wrenches the guitar strap from around his neck. "I can't with him."

Lucian settles his bass into its holder and glances at his brother. Gideon shrugs.

Wil rolls his eyes. "Children."

Lucian squeezes Xander's shoulder. "Let's get some air."

Gideon follows the two band members out.

"Should I get enough for Carlee?" Wil nods toward the office where she's been cooped up all day.

I shake my head. "She's trying out a new diet and this week it's smoothies. We brought in a blender this morning." I indicate the machine on the corner of the bar.

"You want those shrimp spring rolls you love?"

I offer him a playful grin. "You know me so well."

Wil taps away on his phone, and I can't get Death Elbow's song out of my head. Corbin wasn't wrong, there is something missing. I run the melody through from the beginning, my fingers moving at one-two-three-four. Just like Corbin, I get stuck at the second line. I start again, humming to myself.

"Is it the lyrics?" Wil's staring at me. "Do I . . . I mean, do we need to change the words?"

I rise from my chair and cross to him, brushing hair off his forehead. "Quite the opposite. The words are inspired. I love the line 'It's in my head, it's in your eyes.' Can't get it out of my head."

Wil's lips twitch like my praise of his band's song means the world. But just as quickly, it falls again. "But something's missing."

"It's too . . ." I search for the right word to describe the feeling of lack that drains the momentum.

"Clean." Wil interprets my meaning instantly.

"Exactly. It needs more playfulness."

"Maybe I add a keyboard track to create contrast?"

I hum the bars leading up to the chorus. The part of my soul that resonates with melodies takes over and I let go, surrendering to the tune. I add a bit of room between the end of the first verse and the beginning of the second chorus, allowing for the vibe to get more infectious. I sing the chorus line, and instead of running straight into the second verse, I repeat the chorus.

Wil blinks. "Do that again."

"Doubling makes it catchier and there's the play with the words."

He picks up the last line of the first verse.

> Spent nights awake, my heart a tumbleweed
>> Going once, going twice
>> It's in my head, it's in your eyes.
>> Going once, going twice
>> It's in my head, it's in your eyes.
>> Crying lips, words pierce
>> Chased you away when I was a goner
>> Without you my soul is stuck on mute

By repeating the chorus twice, the second verse doesn't feel as rushed. I nod and smile. Wil's tone is different from Corbin's. More velvet and less steel. It creeps under my skin, enters my blood stream, and nestles next to my heart. My nerves respond, caught in the magic of those words sung to me, like he's telling me a story. My story.

The air between us heats and I'm lost in a pair of liquid gold eyes that see only me. I'm drawn to him like a moth to a flame and his fingers caress my wrist, wrapping around it and drawing my hand to his chest.

There is nothing in this world but Wil, me, and music. I'm light and airy and only he tethers me to the ground.

He reaches the final chorus, and out of instinct I echo his words. That shade of delay surges the song into something new. Something living and no longer sterile.

> Going once, going twice/ Going once, going twice
> It's in my head, it's in your eyes./ It's in my head, it's in your eyes.

Under my palm, I can feel his heart pounding.

We sing.

WE sing.

My pulse quickens as I chase his words. It's a game of cat and mouse: him leading, me following. He reaches the end of the chorus and instead of the next verse, I switch the order again. Now I'm leading, inviting him to follow.

Wil accepts the invitation without hesitation. I slow to let him catch me, our verses colliding in unison on the last few words. I float. The room falls into silence. Our chests rise and fall in unison as we catch our breath.

"You could record demos for us." Corbin returns us to reality.

Wil drops my hand and steps back. "I'm not a singer."

My heart glitches at his words.

"In that case"—Corbin picks up the mic—"let the professional take over."

Wil's gaze falls to the floor. "Good idea."

No. Bad idea. "I should get back to work." I move to follow Wil to our table.

"You can't leave me hanging." Corbin stalks toward me. "I only heard the last bit. Run through your version again."

My hand flies to my hair. "Wil, were you still recording? Just play it back." My heart sings at the possibility there is a recording of our voices.

Wil glances at the screen of his phone. "I paused it." His eyes meet mine. "Could you sing it again?" His gaze drifts to Corbin. "With him?"

My soul screams no. "If you want me to."

He points the camera on his phone at us. "It's recording. Take it from 'Saw you first, heard second.'"

I jump at the sound of Corbin's voice so close. He's crouching by the edge of the stage, eyes on me. When he launches into the verse, his gruff baritone adds a harsh tinge to the words that coated my skin when Wil sang them.

The alternative arrangement plays through my head again. I show him how to double up on the second chorus and when Corbin inches closer on the third chorus, our mouths separated only by the microphone, I hear myself weaving the echoes I came up with.

Corbin's eyes widen and the corner of his mouth quirks when I insert my twist. This time it's a different game of cat and mouse, more angst than fun. He doubles down and even though the result sounds like we've rehearsed this before, and the song works the same, it feels different. Like I'm eating store-bought pie instead of homemade. The rightness of our tones contrasting and matching is there, but the magic I felt with Wil is lacking. It's off, just like Xander's guitar the first day they played. It's not wrong but I can tell the difference. It's not how I'd want it performed.

We wind down to the end of the song. Our voices meld on the final words but the playfulness is less tender and more showing-off.

Applause erupts from the side. I turn to find Carlee by the bar, slow clapping. "Wow. I came out here for lunch but got a show. That was fantastic."

My gaze sneaks to Wil, seeking his approval. His fingers fly over the screen of his phone, his attention elsewhere. I chew on my freshly painted nails.

Corbin whispers into my ear. "I see what he sees in you."

I shiver. I mentally beg Wil to look up, but he's distracted by his phone.

Corbin stands. "This girl can sing."

"Oh, I know." Carlee nods. "On tour, El sang *Give Us a Chance* better than I did."

My head snaps up. Is she serious? "I didn't know you felt that way."

Carlee shrugs. "It's the truth. I felt like Dolly Parton must have the first time she heard Whitney sing *I Will Always Love You*. Sometimes a song belongs to a person, no matter who wrote it and loves performing it."

"I want El to perform this one with us." Corbin points at the drum with Death Elbow painted on in sharp black letters.

I back away from the stage, like it can lure me in with its scuffed floorboards. "Not happening. I don't sing anymore."

"Bullshit." Corbin's eyebrow hikes up. "I just heard you sing. You made the song better."

"What's going on?" Xander walks onstage, Lucian and Gideon in tow.

"El here fixed our song."

I hold up a hand. "Not just me. Wil was the inspiration." I turn for support and he's there beside me. My nerves quiet at his hand on my hip. "I just . . . helped."

"Let's hear this fix," Gideon says.

Wil taps his phone and the song plays again. Much to my dismay, I hear what Carlee means. The song works with Corbin and me, just different to how it sounded with Wil.

The recording ends and the boys nod their heads.

"Having someone to brainstorm with, to riff off is sometimes key," Carlee says. "Beau and I workshopped songs all the time. Like you and Corbin, Beau and I had different styles. Those different perspectives elevated our songs. Five diamond albums don't lie."

I slip my arm around Wil's waist, the room swimming before me. "It wouldn't work like that with Corbin and me." I glance at Wil, expecting confirmation, but he's distracted by a message on his screen. "He's not . . . right for me." I address Carlee. "I told you I don't sing anymore."

"What's holding you back? It's not your voice or your stage presence."

"It's the scrutiny that comes with it. I love singing but it's not worth the price of being a public person."

"I can't help you there." Carlee's face falls. "Every job has its risks. Firefighters risk their lives to save others but that's what they love doing. You need to decide what you want more. To hide or to be center stage."

"Maybe you just record it with us? Doesn't mean you have to sing onstage." Lucian gives me an encouraging nod.

If it's only in the studio, I don't have to perform live with the band. They can use an audio track while on tour. Or find someone else for the vocals, using my version as a template. That might work.

I study Wil for some signal on his thoughts, some reassurance he wants this for the band. For the song. I'd do this for him. "Just a recording?" I prod. "With Death Elbow?"

"You can try it." Wil tugs me closer, and I want to melt into him. "If you don't like it, we don't have to use it."

I swallow my disappointment. I'd rather be singing with Wil. Homemade pies have always been my favorite.

Twelve

THE RENOVATED GREEN ROOM of The Devil's Martini gleams with fresh paint and new mirrors along the counter lining one of the walls.

"Are you sure this is good enough for wherever you're taking me?"

El's pleated skirt gives me an excellent view of her runner's thighs and the cropped top is cute. My girlfriend is beautiful in any outfit. Without Zoe's advice, I've now been given the role of El's fashion adviser. I might've persuaded Moderni Look that I'm a trendsetter but dressing me for success has been Zoe's department. I haven't told El's cousin about the endorsement opportunities yet. She doesn't need to know until they are real. "Are you almost ready?"

"Almost." El applies another layer of lip gloss and hangs her bag across her body.

I lean in for a kiss, but she sets her palm on my chest and points to her lips. "Lip gloss."

"You'll taste even sweeter." I nip at the side of her neck, inhaling the scent of home I can't get enough of. El's body yields.

My fingers dive into the shorter bob she styled into waves and pull her closer. I take my time stamping her skin with tender pecks, working my way along her jaw until I claim her mouth. Without any resistance she answers my kiss, tugging me flush to her by my belt loops. I kiss El so thoroughly that the lip gloss disappears. Orange with a hint of vanilla. I'll buy her cartons of this stuff if I get to kiss her more. The disappointment of the morning leeches away with each stroke of her tongue and a roll of her hips. I'm made new again, ready to concentrate on her for the rest of the evening.

I prop El against the wall of the green room and set my thigh between hers, desperate to be as close as possible while we remain fully clothed.

She frees her mouth from mine and licks her naked lips. "No more lip gloss."

"I love this look on you." I drag a finger over El's slightly puffy mouth and peck the spot I just touched. "I've been waiting to do this all day."

She smiles coyly, pushes us away from the wall, and tugs down her skirt. "I've been listening to the worst sets all day. My ears hate me. Note to self: demos have very little to do with the live performances. If I knew how far off tune some of the singers would get, I would've never invited them to audition. The idea Pauline had with an open mic makes a lot more sense now."

I tuck in the tails of my shirt that are somehow out. "Are you going to reinstate that?

"I've been working on the presentation Carlee asked for. I think it's a good plan. Instead of spending my time listening to mediocre bands and some rather talentless sets, I can make an entertaining event where patrons can vote, like a reality show. They get in for free, and we make money selling bar nibbles and alcohol."

"Is Estelle still pitching Carlee her fancy cocktails?"

El adjusts the strap of her shoe. "Rocker ordered every ingredient Mormor requested, and she's been creating drinks for Mom to taste test."

"About tasting. You will love what I have planned for us tonight." Last year El wowed me with her homemade tacos. The Mexican coastal cuisine restaurant Mateo got me reservations for has one Michelin-star and a gated parking lot that he assured me should help avoid the paparazzi.

"Are you going to tell me now?"

"What kind of a surprise would that be?"

"Let's go then." El tugs me out of the green room and into Sven's chest.

"The alarm system is ready." Sven gives El a folded card. "Here's the code. Don't give it to anyone without my approval."

"No construction workers will get their hands on the codes, I promise." El crosses her heart.

"You have fifteen seconds to lock up after setting it." Sven tilts his head. "Where are you going?"

I tap him on the bicep. "Don't worry. She'll be safe."

The photographers camped outside The Devil's Martini jeer and catcall. Their cameras snap trying to catch El and me as we depart, but we dive into the back seat of the car I arranged without incident and the driver speeds us away.

El scrutinizes the label behind my collar. "Is this another Moderni Look shirt?"

I set my hand over hers. "Yeah." I lift her fingers and kiss the inside of her wrist. "We finally signed a trial contract for three months to see if they get a boost in sales, and if it goes well, we'll re-up for a year."

El disentangles from my grip. "I do not see Corbin wearing this." She runs her finger along the embroidered pattern over the pockets. "But maybe we should take it off so I can inspect the stitching." Her palm skims along my chest and over my shoulder. "How long until we get to the restaurant?"

"Actually." I reluctantly remove her hand. "We're making a stop before our date."

She widens her eyes. "What are you up to?"

The cabin of the car darkens as we pull into an underground garage. The driver punches in the code I gave him earlier and the security door opens. "I promised Mateo I'd make a decision on the merch samples or we won't be able to order bulk quantities in time for Death Elbow's concert at the Greek."

El's eyebrows scrunch. "Can't you do it after our date?"

I massage circles into the top of her hand. "It's going to take fifteen minutes. Tops." El starts to move away. "And you can tell me what you like. Maybe see if Mateo can design something for The Devil Martini's reopening too. Merch is a great revenue stream for venues." El continues to move away. "Please." I tug her closer. "Mateo got us the restaurant reservation. I promised him I'll stop by."

Her shoulders slump. "Fine."

I breathe out. "Have I told you that you're the best girlfriend ever?" I get one more kiss in as we park.

We take one of the three silver-toned elevators to the sixteenth floor. The doors open to a brightly lit hallway with freshly painted casing around each apartment door.

"Since when does Mateo live in such a fancy place?" asks El.

"He's house sitting for a 'friend' for the summer. He keeps bragging how there's a private gym even Sven would approve of on the second floor, complete with a half-mile loop around it for runners and a pool with lap lanes." I slip an arm around El's waist. It's impossible not to touch her. "Plus they have a coffee shop, juice bar, and dry cleaner in the lobby, all only for residents." I search for the number Mateo gave me, counting each door.

Up ahead the hall ends at apartment five. I tap the video doorbell button.

Mateo swings the door open. "The power couple. Welcome to my temporary abode." He opens the door wider to let us in.

"This is nice." El swivels her head as she walks in.

Early evening light from the tall windows lends pinkish hues to the light wooden floors that run the length of the room. A peek around the corner offers a view of a shiny fridge. The living room and kitchen are devoid of furniture.

"Are they redecorating?" I point at the empty walls.

"He moved to a larger pad, but until he finds someone to sublease it to, it's mine." Mateo leads us to the room on the left. "I have a blow-up mattress here. And the smaller room off the living room is where the merch samples are."

We return into the kitchen.

"A gas range?" El touches the knobs on the six-burner stove and runs her fingers along the powerful hood, then opens the giant refrigerator. "Beer and takeout containers."

"I have tequila, rum, and vodka if you want to pregame." He opens one of the cabinets.

"Not today." El stands before the window over the sink. The fading sunlight lights her skin and hair, reminding me of a sprite in a fairytale Mum used to read to me.

"I'll go get the merch samples then." Mateo disappears down the hall.

"This is beautiful." She opens the cabinets that go all the way to the ceiling.

I grasp her waist and pull her close. "You are beautiful."

El makes a show of dragging her nail along the buttons on my shirt, stopping at the belt buckle. "For a moment I was imagining that this is my place." She pushes her finger into my waistband.

I cock an eyebrow. Heat flares like tiny lighters where her body comes in contact with mine. "Oh yeah?"

She stands on tiptoes and puts her mouth next to mine. "You'd be my most frequent guest."

"Would you have a bigger bed?" I breathe into her ear. The tips of her hair tangle in the stubble I'm keeping longer because she likes the feel of it on her skin.

"California king." Her finger plays with the button on my pants.

"I'm sold." Blood rushes from my head to where her hand is. The counters are a perfectly usable surface.

Her lips brush the corner of my mouth. I press the advantage, intent on turning this into a proper kiss, but she pulls away. Her gaze meets mine. "How much do you think the rent is?"

"He'd probably sublet to you for less than he's paying until his lease is over." Mateo's voice is better than a cold shower. I loosen my grip on El.

He opens a box and takes out a stack of T-shirts. "But then you'd have to pay the full price." Mateo says a number that's three times the budget El was working with. "Are you still in the market for an apartment?"

El shakes her head. "I'm staying with Carlee now. But even if I wanted to have a place of my own, places like this are out of my price range."

"Would you want to live here?" The brand deals might not be fun, but they are basically free money. Money I can spend on El. "If you still want a place of your own, I can help with rent. The least I can do to pay you back for all the overnights I'd be spending here." I caress her cheek with my nose. I've taken care of Mum and Opa for years. I know how to be the responsible one. "You don't need to worry about money."

"I've heard that before." She steps away. "I have my own paycheck now and I won't to go back to living off the work of others." El wraps her arms around her. "This place is beautiful, but I'll stay where I am until I can afford my own apartment."

It's not just beautiful. This is the first place I've seen with her that I can imagine El living in. In fact, this apartment is perfect and safe, with underground parking and security. She wouldn't even have to go outside to run or get coffee. A paparazzi-free zone.

"Let me know if you change your mind." Mateo finishes laying Death Elbow branded T-shirts, bobbleheads, stickers, hats, hoodies, sweatshirts, and socks on the island. "Let's make some decisions."

We dive into the items, discussing pros and cons. My phone buzzes. I ignore it.

"What's the price point on this one?" I ask.

Mateo inspects the tag inside the T-shirt. "$5.15 each. The branding is free. Courtesy of my friends and family discount."

My phone buzzes again. And again. "Damn," I mutter under my breath.

El avoids looking at me. "You should take it."

I yank the phone from my pocket. My temples ache as I flex my jaw at the caller ID. "Harper."

Harper knows I'm off tonight. Stopping by to make a decision on this merch was annoying enough. The ringtone blasts again. El nods, encouraging me to answer.

I jab the button as if that can vent the frustration coursing through my veins. "Yes."

"Wil." Harper's voice is tight. "I know you said tonight was your night off, but I need your help."

I recline against the counter. "What's Corbin done now?" I know he's the one about to ruin my night with El.

"It's Vatton. They're thinking of pulling the offer."

"You've got to be kidding me." I kick the cabinet with the heel of my boot. Why can't I get a break?

"Wil?" Distress is evident in Harper's tone. "They're leaving tomorrow morning. The only chance to talk to them in-person is tonight."

"For real?" If I lose this contract, the clothing company won't renew theirs, and all the other brands that were orbiting will smell the rot.

"Should I call Rocker?" asks Harper.

"No." I head to the door of the apartment. "Text me their location. I'll be there soon."

"You're leaving?" Mateo's eyebrows raise.

I recap the Vatton mess. "I have no choice."

"I guess I'll help Mateo pick the merch." El's voice is flat. "And add Vatton to my ruin-our-date bingo card."

"You can still have dinner." I reach for her hand. "Why don't you ask—"

"Don't say Zoe." El crosses her arms.

"I was going to say Mateo."

"Sorry, this hunk is spoken for tonight." Mateo lifts his hands then raises an eyebrow at El. "And you need to talk to Zoe at some point. This fight has gone on long enough."

El's jaw is rigid. "She knows how to get in touch."

I groan, open the door, and hold out my hand. "You two are so alike."

"What does that mean?" She comes closer but doesn't take my hand.

I place my palm on the small of her back and lead her to the elevators. "You both are beautiful, determined women."

"Nice try." She traces the stitching on my shirt. "You know that even if Vatton falls through, you are still doing an amazing job at Rocker Inc."

"They're not going to fall through." I kiss her temple. She lets me. A corner of my lip inches up.

Thirteen

My mother's formal living room seems to be the only room that bears no trace of baby stuff. I stop by my harpsichord that I haven't played in months. The pastoral scene on the lid is an old friend that used to bring me peace. A bittersweet ache radiates from my heart to my fingers. Maybe I play one song? The antique clock chimes five times. Shoulders squared, I turn my back to what used to be my security blanket and march up the hallway to my old room. I'm here to visit Mormor on my day off, not revisit my past.

I tap on the door. "Are you decent?"

"That depends, but come on in." I enter to see Mormor in a black cocktail dress, the cap sleeves hanging loosely on her shoulders. She half turns. "I've been trying for ten minutes to get this zipper up. Could you?"

I make quick work of fixing her dress. "You look nice."

She runs her hands down the silky material, smoothing nonexistent wrinkles. "Stunning enough to make the men on this sunset cruise drool?"

"You'll be the envy of every woman on the boat."

"Exactly what I was going for." Mormor sits in front of the makeup table Mom had sent from France and opens her make-up kit.

I flop onto my old bed and stare at the ceiling dotted with the stars Mom and Rocker bought me at the Griffith Observatory gift shop after I moved into this room. The tourist attraction has been a good luck charm. Where Mom met Rocker. Where Wil first kissed me.

I snap a picture of the stars on my ceiling and text Wil.

Me: The stars are still here.

Sadness binds to my ribs when I don't see an immediate reply. He's probably in the middle of dragging Corbin onto the stage. In two weeks it'll be me and Death Elbow, not onstage, just in the recording booth. I wish I had said no, but it's too late to go back on my word. They need my help. I'm doing it for the music. I place my phone on the bedside table and sit on a chair next to Mormor.

When I'm in Norway, Mormor and I have our routine, but having her in LA is like a twisted fairytale. The character you're used to seeing in one setting suddenly appears in a different story and you don't know what to do with them.

"Always be kind to your skin." Mormor pats foundation into her chin. "Is Wil kind?"

"Very." One of the many qualities that made me want to be more than friends with the cocky German.

"Good." Mormor spritzes her favorite perfume and my room smells like summer in Norway. "Never underestimate the value of kindness. A man can be handsome, and brave, and smart, but if he isn't kind, those other traits come with an edge."

I watch her reflection in the mirror. "Was Morfar kind?"

"Your grandfather was a good man. The strong, silent type. Devoted to his family, provided everything we needed, and kept us safe and secure." She dabs something under her eyes. "I couldn't have asked for a better father for my children."

She says all the right words but the tone and hard set of her jaw betrays more than she thinks. My mind races. Does my inability to lie come from Mormor?

The semi-smile on Mormor's lips is tender. "Are you sure you don't want to come with us?"

"I'm sure. Wil is taking me out for ice cream and a movie instead. He should be here any minute." I hide the anxious feeling sliding down my throat. "Not a fan of boats and water, remember?"

"I could never forget, my dear." Mormor tucks a loose curl back into place. "But with your mom and the baby, I have barely seen you. I won't be here forever you know."

"Mormor!" My pulse quickens. She's only sixty-three and spry at that. Unless she's not telling me something. "Don't say such things."

"What? I have to return home to Norway at some point."

My heartbeat returns to normal. Talking to her is more of a workout than running on a treadmill on an incline.

"Promise me we can have a day out soon, maybe see some of these famous Los Angeles sites I've read about." The tips of Mormor's mouth perk up. "I only want to spend more time with you."

Hanging out with Mormor used to be one of my favorite things every summer. "Are you not having fun in LA?"

"Of course I am. Aside from that insufferable Mr. Peters." Mormor arches an eyebrow.

"Mormor." I shake my head.

"I'm sorry." The mascara wand in Mormor's hand glides over her eyelashes. "I know he's Wil's grandfather, but it's a good thing Wil didn't seem to get any of his traits."

"Mr. Peters is a great man." I scrape the side of my index finger where the nail polish is separating already. "Once you get to know him."

She stares at me horrified, like when she ate the Stuffatt tal-Fenek I made and then found out it had rabbit meat in the stew. "I am not planning on getting to know him." Mormor recaps the mascara. "Wil, on the other hand . . ."

Anxiety spins a web of goosebumps across my chest. I want Mormor to fall for Wil just as I did, but I don't want her to pretend. Mormor isn't one to sugarcoat things. She's always been the one to tell me the truth, whether good or bad. I keep as calm as I can and give my grandmother a tight-lipped smile.

"Wil's delightful. He has manners." She gives me a cheeky grin. "And he's nice to look at."

"Mormor," I whine. Maybe I don't want her to like him.

"His mother did a good job." She shrugs. "Like your mother did with you."

"Mom is a good mom."

"She is, but she is still a ghost of her former self." Mormor picks up a tube of lipstick. The red crème outlines her lips and Mormor goes from grandmother to glammother with a few strokes of color. "No matter how much I try to take her out, to have girl time on the beach or to go shopping, or a museum, she refuses. I'm worried she's so absorbed with Pickle that she doesn't remember who she is anymore."

I peel the polish off part of another nail. "Mom spent so long trying to have a child with Rocker." For years I reassured her she should try another round of IVF. "He's sort of a miracle."

"I didn't think you were that into your half-brother."

"He's growing on me."

"All done," says Mormor, resembling a perfectly aged version of Audrey Hepburn with silver locks. She pats my cheek. "Now,

I think it's time for you to try some of my most recent cocktail ideas." She steps into kitten heels while I do up the straps of my platforms. "I promised everyone an aperitif or two before the limo gets here." The tips of Mormor's mouth perk up. "Make sure to tell your mother she looks beautiful."

My phone buzzes and I read the text.

> Wil: Corbin is still not here. I'll text you when we're done.

I bury my disappointment and inhale the tangy scent of freshly cut grass. That's at least an hour before he gets here. I open the movie app and check for later shows. Doesn't mean this date is canceled. Just delayed. I grasp the phone a bit too hard. Everything will be fine.

"I call this one Snack on the Beach." Mormor hands me a glass garnished with a collection of fruit wedges and cherries that could be an edible bouquet if served without the drink. "Tell me what you think." She motions for me to try.

I find the straw and taste the cocktail. Sweet and tart and definitely alcoholic. Mormor loves her drinks. There's a hint of something. "Is there mint in it?"

"Rosemary. To offset the sweetness." Mormor picks an identical cocktail up and clicks it to mine. "To a fun summer."

"It's really good." I take another sip.

"I'm experimenting with California flavors. Going local." She lowers her glasses and gives me a stern look. "Do you think Carlee will approve?"

With the straw still in my mouth I shrug.

Mr. Peters strides across the patio, a small blue cloth in his hands. "This fell out of the pocket."

At least I think that man is Wil's grandfather. It's hard to tell as his typical worn jeans and loose T-shirts have been replaced by a trim black suit and pale blue shirt. Cleaned-up Mr. Peters is a sight to behold. I'm amazed by the similarity between him and Wil with this transformed effect.

"It's a pocket square." Mormor steps from behind the bar and snatches the material. "It can be boring and straight, or you can have a little pizzazz." She quickly folds the material and it makes two sharp points out of his jacket pocket, a pop of blue against the dark suit. "Like this."

Mr. Peters glares at Mormor's creation. "Useless thing." He catches my gaze. "What do you think, El?"

"You look very handsome," I say.

Mormor scans Mr. Peters. "You look well for someone your age."

"Our age." Mr. Peters isn't as tall as Wil and he is on the slender side, but with mostly white hair and slate eyes, he could be anywhere from early to late sixties.

Mormor twirls the straw in her cocktail. "By now you should have learned not to ask women about their age."

"I wasn't asking." He shrugs. "I was stating an obvious fact."

"The only obvious thing here is that this is the first thing I've seen you in that actually fits." Mormor waves her hand in a circle around Mr. Peter's torso. "El, you should introduce him to Zoe and personal style."

My heart speeds up. I haven't exactly told Mormor that Zoe and I aren't on speaking terms. I keep sipping the cocktail, because talking seems like an awful idea and everyone knows I can't tell a lie.

"You really like the drink then?" Mormor watches the rapidly disappearing liquid in my glass. "Do you think Carlee will like it?"

"If I could have one of these, I might tell you what I think." Carlee joins us by the bar. Today she's in a pale-pink loose sundress that flows to her sandal-clad feet. Her blond hair is swept into a messy bun and she appears more yummy mummy than pop-star diva. "But I am not drinking alcohol at the moment."

"Are you pregnant?" Mr. Peters's eyes fall to Carlee's very trim stomach.

"Another question you don't ask women," Mormor snaps. She places a delicate hand on Carlee's forearm. "I have something new for you to try. So good you won't even notice there's not a drop of alcohol in it."

Mr. Peters huffs. "Do you still want me to refinish the bar shelves?" He takes a Heineken out of the under-the counter fridge.

"If we are having a new cocktail menu, an updated bar only makes sense," says Carlee.

Mormor's eyes shine with excitement. Mr. Peters nods.

Carlee points at my glass that is now officially just a fruit bowl. "Can I have one of those?"

Mormor grins. "Virgin Snack on the Beach coming up." A glass similar to mine lands on the bar and she busies herself mixing the drink.

"One for me too, Mor." Mom sidles up to the bar and clutches a beaded purse that complements her burnt-yellow dress. With her hair styled in a French twist, she reminds me of her nights on tour, the moments just before her concerts when it was just the two of us before she went onstage. The buzz of anticipation in the air. Except right now, she lacks the confidence I admired then. "Glad you decided to join us, Carlee."

Carlee hums and gives Mormor a thumbs-up. "Taking time off is exactly what the doctor ordered."

Everyone chuckles, but I know there's more truth than joke behind Carlee's words. She's been running herself ragged. She may show a brave front to others, but I see her barely getting out of bed every day.

Rocker jogs out of the house, staring at his phone. Breathless, he alternates his focus between Mom and Mormor. He passes the phone to Mom.

Her face turns sallow. "It's impossible to find another babysitter on such short notice." Mom's voice is tight when she passes the phone back to him.

"Can't El watch Pickle?" Mr. Peters pulls on the cuffs of his shirt. Everyone turns and stares at him. "What? Pickle is her brother too."

Mom's gaze cuts to me. Ocean breeze blows loose tendrils across her face. The expertly applied makeup does not fool me. She's been cooped up here since Pickle's birth, marking his every milestone, counting his new teeth, not venturing anywhere he couldn't come. The ache in my heart is stronger than the uneasiness in my head. The last thing I want is to be on my own with the baby, but Mom needs this night out of the house more than I need a date with Wil.

I lift my chin. "I can watch him. Wil is coming here as soon as he's done at the Greek."

"See. El can babysit." Rocker waves at the side of the house with the nursery and their bedroom. "Pickle is down for his afternoon nap." He glances at his watch. "He was exhausted from his swim lesson. He'll sleep until seven. Wil is sure to be here by then." Rocker traces the line of Mom's jaw. "Nothing to worry about."

"I don't want anyone to miss the cruise, but what if something happens?" says Mom.

"We haven't had a night out in six months." Rocker puts his mouth to Mom's ear. "It's time." His words are meant for only her but I can't help but overhear. He caresses her cheek.

"You look so beautiful." Mormor rounds the outdoor bar and pats Mom's arm. I don't remember the last time I saw Mom this dressed up. "It'd be a shame to waste all this effort."

"You do look fabulous, Sylvia," says Carlee. "So does Estelle." My grandma fluffs her hair. "Even Mr. Peters."

"I think I should stay here." Mom finds me across the semi-circle of people around her.

I push off the counter. "Like Rocker says, Pickle'll be asleep for another hour and a half and Wil and I can hang out here, have a picnic in the media room. It'll give me a chance to cook something. Guaranteed paparazzi-free meal for a change." I try my best to sound confident. Nonchalant. Despite my stomach revolting at the thought of staying home alone with a baby even for a little bit, I straighten my spine. I'll prove Zoe wrong. I'm not selfish. I can take one for the team. For Mom.

"Right. It's settled." Rocker spins Mom around and hands me the device. "Here's the baby monitor. There're bottles of formula in the fridge." Panic must be spreading on my face because he quickly adds, "Wil knows where the bottle warmer is when it's time. Tell him Marta restocked the diapers." He slips his arm around Mom's waist. "We'll be home around ten."

Mormor makes a "come on" motion with her hands to Mr. Peters and follows Rocker across the lawn to the garage.

Mom halts, and like the cars of a train my family grinds to a stop. She takes in the patio, her glance landing on me. "Text me if anything happens. Anything."

I nod but read Rocker's lips behind her: "Call me first." I motion for them to leave. "Go. Have fun."

In the silence of the back yard, the baby monitor crackles with a sigh. I stare at the black-and-white screen and see Pickle's hand move. Wil better be here soon.

FOURTEEN

My breathing has gone into overdrive. I knew I should have insisted on picking Corbin up. I stab out "ETA?" and turn to Xander. "Do you know where he went?"

Lucian glances up from his tablet. "He said something about going to Manhattan Beach to catch a wave."

"He surfs?" That beach is at least half an hour away. It'll take an hour to drive there and get back to the Greek.

Xander scoffs. "The girl he met last night does. He'll have a new obsession next week."

I squeeze the empty Vatton bottle in my hand. Why do I feel like a babysitter? Pickle gets into less trouble when I watch him, and he likes to stick his fingers in questionable places. Even after spending a night last week reassuring the Vatton reps that Death

Elbow isn't going to tarnish the image of their brand, the deal is on shaky ground. Tomorrow's concert is supposed to bring Death Elbow back to positive reviews and win Vatton over.

I tamp down my fury and concentrate on what I can control. "Call me the minute he shows up. I'm going to talk to the stage manager."

With every step I take down the hall, grips and crew dip out of my way like I'm a clumsy intruder. I keep my gait slow and steady but my heart is jackrabbiting against my ribs. If Death Elbow doesn't do the blocking and sound check, we'll have a max of fifteen minutes before the show tomorrow. I wipe the sweat off my forehead. They can't mess up again. I can't. Vatton will pull the contract and I'll have to explain to Dad and Harper why I am unable to get the group to perform.

"Don't tell me he's still not here." Pauline taps a pen against her clipboard at the door to the stage. "Harper swore I wouldn't have a disaster on my hands. That Death Elbow is past the rockstar antics."

"They are. We just need a bit more time. Any chance you can give us the next slot?"

Pauline presses the button of her walkie talkie. "Did you say She Should Smile More are here already?"

A muffled "yes" crackles through the line.

Pauline turns back to me. "Some musicians take this seriously and arrive early. You shouldn't teach your group the bad habit that almost booted you out of The Devil's Martini."

One time I was late. "Can we switch then?"

She nods. "But if he's not here by then, Death Elbow is doing the sound check. Find someone to sub for Corbin. Or you play the guitar. You sing."

I open my mouth to spill my usual line. To deny. To divert. To lie. But I don't have to and an intense wave of relief washes away my reservations. "Got it." I can't keep the grin off my face.

Pauline pins me with a stare and I temper my excitement.

"Right." She scribbles something on the page before her. "Might be fun seeing you sing again." Her gaze meets mine. "Don't tell anyone, but the nights WE performed at The Devil's Martini were my favorite. The way you had the audience wrapped up in the music you and El sang made me want to get back onstage myself."

I cough out a strangled laugh and shake my head, unable to form words.

Pauline presses a finger to her earpiece. "Okay folks. Send She Should Smile More out. Death Elbow will go after them." She winks at me. "Break a leg."

In my back pocket my phone buzzes and my heart ticks up with the hope it's Corbin.

It's not.

> Mum: New test results today. I'm still improving.

The concern of Corbin forgotten, my fingers fly over the screen.

> Me: Want to videochat?

A request for a video call from Mum appears. I slip into the nearest bathroom, accept, and see Mum's face smiling on the screen.

"You had a haircut." Mum's eyes go up, down, left, and right, and I wish she caught me at a better time when I haven't been pulling out my hair in frustration.

I squint at the tiny video of me in the corner and comb through the longer hair on top, attempting to turn it from manic band babysitter to the effortless chic messiness of the salon. "Dad's hairdresser suggested I try shorter sides."

Mum lowers her gaze. "You call Bill Dad now?"

I massage my temple. "Is that okay with you?"

"More than." A shy smile touches Mum's lips. "I've always wanted him to know you. For you to have a dad and not just Opa filling in the role."

"Opa did a great job."

"That he did." Mum's gaze is back on me. "How's he doing? Settling in?"

I wince. If I say he's great, she'll be able to spot the lie. Opa is rarely happy unless he's tackling a project.

"He likes drinking Dad's ale."

A tiny laugh comes from Mum. "Have him call me." Something catches her attention and she gives a short nod. "I have to go do some laps around the grounds before dinner." She sends me a kiss. "I love you. Talk soon." Without waiting for my response, she's gone.

"Love you too," I murmur to the blank screen. Mum, Opa, and now Pickle are the only people with whom these three words come without overthinking. Calling Rocker Dad was something that happened naturally, but I can't imagine saying I love you to him. At least not yet.

I fling open the door and find three men staring at me. "Corbin still not here?" I search their blank faces. "Okay." I rub my hands together. "We're next. That's the best I could do."

"We can't go on without a lead singer." Lucian ogles me as I cross the hall to our green room and roll up my sleeves.

I pluck Corbin's guitar out of its case and sling the strap over my shoulder. It bounces against my hip as if greeting an old friend. "I'll do it." My pulse quickens.

Xander frowns like I stole his presents. "I thought you don't sing."

"For all your sake let's hope I still can." I slap him on the back as I head for the exit.

The backstage is a hive of people dressed in black taping cords to the floor, moving boxes, and lining up equipment for tomorrow's show. As I get closer, the shouts and claps from the spectators grow louder.

I step out in front of the small group of people who're not even a tenth of the crowd that'll be here tomorrow night. I set one foot on the stage. Then another. We take our places, Xander and I up front. I stand to his right, just like I used to with El. Gideon bounces behind us, his drumsticks clacking together in the beat slower than my heartrate.

The spotlight finds me like I'm a god about to ascend my throne. It flicks off then on. There's a solitary woot from the waiting audience. As if that's the cue, three spotlights flood the stage and swing until they find the band members around me. The audience and backstage chatter dulls to a hushed murmur. My skin absorbs the untethered energy, every pour soaking it in like the desert water after a drought. Blood pounds in my ears and my fingers tingle.

I step up to the microphone, hands in the air. "We'll be running our set through but there might be interruptions and adjustments, so we hope you come tomorrow to see the actual show."

I pluck at the strings of Corbin's guitar. The strap presses against my shirt like a lover's caress. The neck is longer than mine and the bumps and notches from thousands of hours of heavy use are different, but that familiar fizz of excitement thrums at the base of my spine. I strum a few chords of *Going Once*, adjust the tuning peg, and strum again. The instrument vibrates in my hand like it's lulling me into playing it. Corbin is a lucky guy, getting to play this onstage.

Gideon matches the rhythm, pushing the crowd to clap faster and faster. Xander riffs his guitar in an ascending scale ending in a long guitar wail.

Like gripping the steering wheel of Opa's old sedan, the fingers of my left hand settle into the familiar spot to play a C major chord. I reposition the pick between my thumb and forefinger of my right hand and press against the first string. Anticipation mixes with nerves into a cocktail of a heady high I haven't felt in far too long. What will tonight hold? I can't wait to find out. To be in the driver's seat, rather than in the back row, watching.

A hand clamps my shoulder. "Man, didn't think I'd make it." Corbin pulls on the guitar strap.

His guitar strap.

My heart sputters, like a car running out of gas while speeding down the freeway.

Corbin tugs on the guitar. "Wil, I got it." I can't seem to let go. "Wil?"

I release the guitar. Corbin flashes his stellar grin and steps in front of me, blocking the spotlight, and grabs the mic. The gears grinding in my head drown whatever he says to the audience. I can see the people in the front row, their attention focused on the lead singer.

On Corbin.

A rogue spotlight hits my eyes, transporting me to a different evening, where I was blinded by the headlights of oncoming traffic. I fumble my way to the side of the stage, plunging into the darkness. My breath screeches to a halt like when the steering wheel cracked my damaged ribs. I cling to one of the lighting ladders, trying to find my bearings.

"Well that was disappointing. I was hoping he wouldn't show." Pauline loops her arm through mine, grounding me to where I am.

Not on the road.

Not on the stage.

In the wings of the Greek, where I'm safe.

Opening chords of *Going Once* fill my ears.

I remind myself to breathe as I shake off the panic attack and roll down the sleeves of my shirt, slowly buttoning the cuffs. My pulse slows. Everything will be fine. "It worked out for the best. Singing is his dream, not mine."

The lie sits like concrete in my mouth.

FIFTEEN

I GRIT MY TEETH. I've been pacing the driveway for half an hour. The baby monitor comes to life every ten minutes because Pickle keeps moving. Not much, but I jump every time.

My stomach drops. That's cutting it close to when Pickle is supposed to wake up. This isn't what my evening was supposed to be like. I was looking forward to time with my boyfriend, not babysitting. Wil's face fills my screen on the second ring.

"Pickle moved again," I whisper into the phone in case the baby monitor works both ways.

A horn honks on Wil's end. "That's how he sleeps." His voice is low and irritated. "You'll know when he's awake."

"Are you upset I agreed to babysit him?"

"I'm not upset." He tries for an encouraging smile. "At least your mom gets to have fun instead of being stuck in traffic." Wil glances up. "I'm not going to mess up our next date."

I groan. "Maybe we should just give up on dates?"

"We are not giving up on dates."

A squawk emits from the baby monitor and I jump. "Wil? Pickle just made a noise."

"It's fine. He mumbles in his sleep sometimes."

"This doesn't sound like"—A piercing wail interrupts—"mumbling. Listen." I hold the monitor to my phone and cringe at the obviously crying baby. "What do I do?"

"Just pat his back. He'll go right back to sleep."

With a scowl at the cloudless sky, I turn and head for the front door. "Hold on."

I run down the hallway, into the part of the house I rarely go, and pause outside the nursery I helped Mom pick the furniture for just a year ago.

The screaming resumes both from the monitor and through the door. I fling it open and see Pickle kicking his feet in the air like he's in a kickboxing lesson with Sven. "Hey there." I hesitantly approach the crib and put the monitor on the changing table. The wailing pauses as our eyes meet.

"Is he okay?" Wil asks.

Pickle answers him with a deafening off-key C-sharp shriek.

Since I can't pat his back like Wil suggested, I tap his belly, which only makes him howl louder. "No. I mean he seems fine." I hover the phone over the crib so Wil can see the baby. "But he won't stop crying."

"Pick him up." Wil's voice is low and soothing. Not sure if that's for my or Pickle's benefit.

I glare at Wil. "This was not part of the deal." Pickle continues his assault on my ears. "Fine." I prop my phone on the changing table beside the monitor and rub my hands together. "Don't I have to support his head or something?"

"He's past that stage. Pretend he's a loaf of bread."

I glare at Wil. "Bread doesn't try to kick you."

Pickle bellows to remind me that he is the priority. I lean over the crib, cradle my arms under the squirming body, and lift. He tries to roll and I almost drop him. Red-laced amber eyes blink at me. Pickle delivers a series of kicks that would cause me to step away if I weren't the only adult in this house. A little slower this time, I put my hands under his armpits and hoist him up. His legs still and he watches me like I'm an intruder.

We stare at each other.

His lower lip quivers.

"Now what?" I ask Wil without taking my eyes off the baby.

"Hug him to your chest," says Wil.

Hug him? I don't do hugs. The lip trembling increases and I tuck the baby into my chest. No crying. My shoulders relax.

"See. You got—"

Pickle yowls, most likely damaging my hearing permanently.

Wil's face grows larger on the screen. "Try walking around and bouncing him like you did at the barbecue."

I take a turn around the room, my hand cupping Pickle's bottom to secure him in place. "His butt is squishy."

"Probably needs a diaper change."

My insides scrunch as if a rubber band is wrapped tightly around my vital organs. "No. Nope." I walk toward the changing table with my phone. "Can't he wait until you get here?" Wil's mouth twitches and I shake my head, continuing my bounce. "Don't laugh at me. I've never changed a diaper in my life."

"You learned to play the harpsichord at age six. I think you can master wiping a baby's bottom."

"Please Wil." I bounce in place in front of Wil's face on the screen, as if he can reach through it and do the dirty job for me. "Don't make me do this."

Pity appears in a tight line between his eyebrows. "You can wait, but that's likely why he's crying. Once he's dry, he'll probably go back to sleep."

I eye the stack of diapers sitting on the edge of the changing table beside my phone. "Promise?"

Wil nods.

Pickle takes the wailing up a notch.

"Fine." I give my little trumpet another bounce, hoping it'll lower his volume. "How do I do this?"

"Place him on the table on his back."

I follow Wil's instructions, lay Pickle down, and unsnap his "I Can't Wait To Rock 'n' Roll!" onesie, freeing his legs. The obviously soggy diaper hangs off Pickle, who squirms and continues to cry. "He won't stay still."

"Keep one hand on his tummy at all times and pull the sticky green tabs on each side to open the diaper. Then you take his feet in one hand, lift them and slide the diaper from under him."

"I only have two hands." Pickle kicks my stomach and I bear the pain to keep one of my hands on him. "This is impossible."

"El, you can do this."

I take a deep breath and rip at the tabs on each side of the diaper. It falls open. I catch Pickle's feet and lift his butt high enough to move the diaper from under him.

"Make sure to take one of the little cloth caps that are stacked on the side." Wil draws a triangle in the air.

"Little caps?" I search for something that matches his description when a stream of liquid jettisons into the air. I let go of Pickle's legs. "Wil, he's—"

"Yeah, that's what the little hats are for."

I grab a diaper to shield myself against the flood of urine soaking my shirt. Behind the diapers is a stack of weird cone contraptions that remind me of the party hats Zoe and I had for our dolls' tea parties. "This thing?" I hold it to the screen for Wil." He nods and I gingerly place the cloth hat over Pickle's privates. A wet spot forms on the cloth underneath him, leaking into the bottom of his onesie. At least I'm no longer being drenched. "It worked."

When I think my brother might be finished, I peek under the cone thingy. Pickle hiccups and my shoulders relax. Maybe the threat is over. "He's out of pee, I think. But the onesie is now soaked."

"There are fresh ones in the drawer on the left-hand side." Wil walks me through the twenty-step process of using the wipes, wrestling Pickle out of his clothes, and donning a diaper.

Despite his incessant squirming, I manage to snap Pickle's "Daddy's Little Star" onesie without any additional incidents. "There. You're changed." I glance at the video version of Wil. "Can he go back to sleep now?"

Wil doesn't answer and I spin to the screen. "Wil?"

"Damn it." His eyebrows knit together. "It's the Vatton rep. I gotta take this."

"No. You can't abandon me."

"Try singing to him."

"I don't know any kid songs."

But it's useless because Wil hung up on us.

Pickle eyes me like he is saying "do something or I'm going to cry." I pick him up and the lip of doom trembles. I walk to the crib and the wailing that'll haunt me in my worst nightmares starts again. I tuck him into me. "No. You're dry. Why aren't you happy?"

Every time I separate him from my chest, the crying machine whirs to life and now Pickle's face is red. I'm tempted to wail along with him. Tears of frustration cloud my vision. I bounce him around the room. "Please, baby. Stop crying."

His fingers grasp the collar of my T-shirt and the weeping changes into a series of strained whines.

I roll my eyes. "Okay, Okay."

Wil said to sing, so I'll sing. I lower the baby to my hip and launch into *Mary Had A Little Lamb*.

Pickle's wails compete with my voice. My head is pounding and I need to change my top. Maybe the smell is grossing him out as much as it does me. We bounce-walk to my old room and I switch to *Twinkle, Twinkle, Little Star* but Pickle's cries drown out the sound of the song.

In my walk-in closet I grab the first shirt that isn't covered in sparkles. With Pickle on the bed, the howling continuing, I strip out of the urine soaked top and into the clean one. "There, now we've both had a change of clothing."

Pickle whimpers and kicks his feet and his hands, rolls to his tummy, and then to his back squirming dangerously close to the edge of the bed. Back into my arms he goes.

I didn't think he could cry louder, but Pickle proves me wrong.

Tears simmer beneath my frustration as I pace the room, each step a weary testament to my desperation. Rocker said he might be hungry. Pickle stuck to my side, I clamor to the kitchen, yank open the fridge door, and retrieve a baby bottle. I tip the nozzle into the baby's mouth and the crying subsides. I rest my chin on his head. "Thank goodness."

My joy is short-lived. Pickle coughs and swats at the bottle like it's sour. Could it be sour? I tip my head back and hold the nipple over my mouth, waiting for the formula to drip down. Nothing happens. Is it broken? I plop the bottle on the counter and thank the weeks of living with a splint on my hand because my skill set now includes opening a bottle with one hand. I pour the white liquid into my mouth.

It's sweet. But cold. Rocker did mention a bottle warmer. Without Wil to give me directions, I scan the counter for a machine or something that could warm bottles. Nothing. I open cupboards and come up empty. "Oh, Pickle. I don't know where it is. Can't you drink it cold?"

Pickle's scream seems to insist he can't. I reach for the cap and the bottle slips from my hand and rolls under the cabinet.

"Really?" Every cell of mine is shaking. I can't feed him floor formula. I want to kick and scream alongside Pickle, but I find another bottle in the fridge.

I grab a glass from the shelf, fill it, and put the contents in the microwave for thirty seconds. "Hold on. This will warm it up." I circle the kitchen island, bouncing Pickle and singing one of Rocker's songs.

The baby's face scrunches and I think I'm onto something. Then the wailing starts again.

The microwave beeps and the glass is warm. I transfer the formula into the bottle. "Just another minute," I sing. But my newly earned skills do not transfer to screwing a cap on a baby bottle so I lose my grip and milk spills across the counter. "Really? Really!"

Pickle fusses, kicking me in the sides. I can't think. I can't breathe. My brain is splitting in two and I just want some silence. I should never have agreed to do this. I'm a failure. I can't even comfort my own brother. Half-brother. Whatever.

"What do you want?" I beg the baby for an answer.

His mouth yawns wider and wails. I swear he says, "Willlllll-lll."

"I want Wil here too." I abandon the formula-soaked kitchen and head for the harpsichord in the living room. I tap on the G key. Pickle wails another Wiilllll. Playing the harpsichord isn't going to work so I sit onto the hard cushion of Mom's baroque couch. "Wil would know what to do. He's the baby whisperer. He's always good with words."

Maybe Pickle is a words guy, like Wil. In my last-ditch effort, I sing the first line of the song Wil and I have been playing around with over the last months.

Love conquers all, the movies said

but when I'm lonely in my bed

I think of you

Pickle hiccups and just as I think he's winding up for another epic scream I launch into the second part of the verse.

> My fingers flex, my memories fade
> and on this day, I can relate
> I think of you

My brother's bottom lip wobbles, but no sound comes out.

Is this actually working?

With fingers crossed, I keep singing the unfinished song, repeating the chorus more times than I should. His eyes study me like I hung the moon. He blinks as I whisper-sing the chorus yet again. Pickle's eyes begin to droop.

This is working.

My muscles relax. I sink into the couch and stop singing.

Pickle's head jerks back and his hand smacks my mouth.

No. No. No. No more crying.

I start the song over again.

Like magic, Pickle settles, his ear against my cheek, like he's trying to get closer to the music.

Afraid to move, I stay on the couch, singing Wil's words over and over.

Sixteen

LA TRAFFIC FINALLY BEHIND me, I'm almost at the mansion. I close the calendar app on my phone as the front gate opens.

On the phone the Vatton rep drones on. "That's reassuring. We'll send over the paperwork for signatures."

My brain and my gut war, the first happy to have the deal with Vatton back on the table, which means ten percent will go to me, and the latter twisted because I have no idea what's going on with El and Pickle. I unbuckle my seatbelt. "I'll let Harper know."

The car doesn't even stop before I'm out and running. El's not standing in the driveway so that has to be a good sign.

When I enter, the house is quiet.

Too quiet.

Maybe Pickle wore himself out.

Maybe El took him outside for a walk in a stroller like Marta does.

The kitchen seems like a milk monster threw up. A baby bottle sits in a puddle of formula. The counter has a milk lake in the middle. Cupboards and drawers hang open.

"El?" I shout-whisper. If Pickle has settled, I don't want to disturb him. I tiptoe across the tile floors. "El. Where are you?"

On the way past the formal living room, I spot a head of red hair. I creep by El's harpsichord and my frantic worry dies down at the sight of El on the couch, Pickle resting on her leather and lace halter top. Both are sound asleep, Pickle's hand curled around El's finger. I exhale.

El's fine.

Pickle's fine.

Everyone's fine.

My chest buzzes. There's a circle of drool on El's shoulder. I probably shouldn't but I snap a picture of this priceless moment. I knew she could do this.

Without touching El, I pick up Pickle. He stretches like he might wake up, but I sing *Going Once*, bouncing in rhythm with the catchy chorus, and he settles into the crook of my neck.

This song has what it takes to be a hit. The tingle between my ribs is the same as I had with El's *Don't Give Me Comfort*. There's a rightness to it, like the words just exist and all I had to do was pluck them out of the air. Corbin can't quite get the variation in the chorus I hear for the song, but when El comes to record, we'll get there. I'll have my second producing credit, Rocker Inc. will have another gold record for the wall, and I'll make Dad proud.

The scene in the nursery is worse than the kitchen. The normally tidy stack of diapers is strewn around the room like popcorn from an exploding bag. Pee cups dot the alphabet rug and a soaked onesie sits in the middle like the outline of a body at a crime scene.

Pickle settles into his crib and I repeat the verse, adjusting "Devil winds brings promise" for "Devil winds, they beckoned" as I toss diapers into the container to avoid stepping on them. Santa Ana winds will always remind me of last September, celebrating my twentieth birthday here at the mansion, hiding who I was from El. Am I still hiding? The words for another verse itch in the back of my brain as I walk down the hall. I slip into my room, retrieve the little black book and my pen, and settle onto the couch beside El.

Saw you first, heard second

Beneath the lies of our first impressions

I hid the truth when you chose to confess.

The black scrawl materializes the words from my head onto the page. This tweaked first verse feels truer. A reflection of how we met. How her voice mesmerized me. How not telling her why I was in LA was the dumbest thing I've ever done. I could've lost her.

Bloody hell.

I should tell her now. It's not like me writing lyrics is a secret. I told Corbin this song was inspired by El, yet could be any girl. But that was a lie. This song is not only about El, it's *for* El. It's my way of telling her the things I can't quite say out loud yet. I am a goner.

The desire to read these words to El, to witness her reaction to the news that these are my words, begs me to wake her. But I don't have the heart to disturb her. The small creases that have so often marred her forehead are gone. Instead, I rewrite the verse over and over. El shifts and her head finds my shoulder. I gently kiss the top of her head and switch the word tender for sweet. It fits better. It's more her.

El opens her eyes and I scooch to kiss her. Her eyes grow wide as she sits up. "Where's Pickle?" I can hear the panic in her voice.

"I moved him to his crib." I brush the hair off El's forehead. "Nothing happened to him."

"But it could." El catapults off the couch. "You just hung up on me and left me again, this time with a baby."

"You were doing great and it was Vatton. I just got them back on track. I can't ignore their calls."

"Since when is this deal so important to you?"

"Since it gets me cold hard cash monthly for a year. Money to pay for Mum's renovations. On taking you to Michelin-star restaurants. Money to live our lives like we want to."

"All I hear is money, money, money. Money seems to be the only thing that you care about these days."

"These days? I've always cared about money. That's why I came to the US in the first place. That's why I was busking with you." I sit up straight. "That's why I agreed to return to LA and work for Dad. How is this a surprise?"

"I guess I shouldn't be surprised. I just thought that now that you and Rocker, that it's official, you have enough money."

"There's never enough money. And that's Dad's money, not mine. You of all people should understand."

"I thought I did. But maybe I don't. Not abusing Rocker's money I get, but you lived without money before."

"That's how I know how hard that life is. And I don't want that for Mum, for Opa, for you. If I can make enough money, you all can be happy."

"What about you?" She crosses her arms. "Are you happy?"

I want to tell her that as long as I'm with her, I'm the happiest, but the words stay inside my head. I reach for El's hand.

Somewhere a door slams.

No. Not now.

"Wil. El? Is everyone okay?" Dad's voice cuts through the haze of my indignation.

Beside me, El stiffens. "We're here." She pushes off the couch and heads into the kitchen.

"Oh, thank goodness. Neither of you was answering your phones. I saw on the cameras that he was up and crying, and probably hungry." Sylvia scrutinizes El's funky shirt and stern face. "Is Pickle safe?"

"He's fine." I throw my thumb over my shoulder. "He's in his"—Sylvia brushes by me before I finish the last word—"room."

I turn to Dad. "Where's everyone else?"

"Mr. Peters and Estelle are on the boat with Carlee." Dad sighs in defeat. "We dropped them off after Sylvia insisted we come back." He slumps on the couch. "Maybe next time will go better."

"Maybe Mom needs help." El walks around the room, collecting her phone and bag. "Maybe she should talk to someone outside the family."

"El, she just had a baby," says Dad. "You know how long it took us . . ."

El puts up a staying hand, her eyes ablaze. "This isn't *just*. I've seen her this way before, because I was the center of her laser-focused attention. She wouldn't go anywhere without me. I traveled the world with her after Papa's death because she was convinced that only by her side could I be safe. This is not new. Not just. Not because he's a baby. Mom needs help—again. And I understand that you didn't want to contradict her about the best way to raise me, but Pickle is your son too." Her chest pumps in and out, and I rise to stand beside her. "You are as responsible for his well-being as Mom is. Don't let her old patterns build another golden cage for another child. I might not know how to change his diaper, but I do care about Pickle. I'm not perfect, but I'm working on overcoming my fears and I have to speak up. I want my brother to have a better life." Her voice cracks. "I care."

I know she does. Dad knows too. And Sylvia. El's always cared. I squeeze her palm in support.

Dad drops his head into his hands. His shoulders shake in silent tears. "What am I going to do? Tell her she's a bad mother? She isn't. She's too good—and I know that's the issue. But I don't want to hurt her. She's already worried, so much. I thought with the latest gadgets, if she can still see the baby from the cameras even when we are out, she would be able to take some time away from him."

"Maybe instead of throwing your money at the problem, talk to her. Explain that you are concerned for her and for Pickle. Tell her what's going on in your head. Be honest." She flicks her eyes to me then back to Dad. "I can give you the name and number of the therapist she used to see after Papa died. Maybe you both go."

"Do you think she'd go?" Dad drags his tear-stained eyes back to El.

"You won't know if you don't ask."

"What if she says no?"

"What if she says yes?"

Dad pushes himself from the couch. "Text me the info." He takes a cleansing breath. "And thank you. I keep forgetting that you're all grown up." He wipes the moisture off his lashes. "I'll do better."

Beside me, El turns beet red. "Good. Both Pickle and Mom need you."

"Right. I'll go check on them." Dad leaves us alone.

"I should get going," says El.

I follow her. "I'll walk you home."

She won't look at me. "We should call it a night."

"El." Her name hangs between us.

"I'll text you tomorrow." She disappears down the stairs and I stand alone in the middle of the kitchen, questioning everything.

SEVENTEEN

Me: I'm sorry.

El: You said that already.

I glance at her in the rearview mirror of the SUV as our car takes another turn up to the Griffith Observatory.

Me: Taking you here was supposed to be my way of apologizing for messing up our last date.

SWe pass the parking lot of the Greek Theatre and my guilt resurfaces. My phone pings again. Texting is not how this conversation should happen. I'd much rather talk to El, but with Opa and Estelle in the second row of the SUV and El in the third, I can't even have a normal discussion with her.

> El: I couldn't say no to Mormor. She specifically asked to come here. And you said you booked a private tour in front of her and your grandfather. How were they to know it was a date?

> Me: You don't need to explain that. I'm fine with them tagging along if you are. I'll just have to come up with a better way to apologize.

> El: The best way is to not ditch me again when work calls.

I clench the grab handle as my driver speeds up the hill. At least we're almost to the top. I can pull her aside and say all this when she can hear my words and see my face instead of the letters on the screen.

> Me: I won't. I promise. I'll turn my phone off on our next date.

El: I will too. All I want is to spend time with you.

Me: I'll make that happen. You have my word.

I catch her eyeroll in the mirror, but by the curl of her mouth I know I have a stay of execution. For now. I'm not going to screw this up again.

Thirty minutes before the start of the tour, the driver drops us in front of the Griffith Observatory, feet away from the spot Nick and Sarah filmed El's *Don't Give Me Comfort* video. The spot where the on-camera kiss for El's video turned into a real one, as my body took over and I couldn't deny my attraction to her anymore.

"My late wife, Sidra, and I used to have date nights at the Olbers Planetarium in Bremen." Opa offers his hand to help Estelle out of the car.

I do the same for El. "I didn't know that. You never talk about Oma."

Opa clears his throat. "She was the love of my life."

"I know how losing that feels," Estelle whispers.

"Gone too soon." Opa holds his chin high. "Like her name, she truly was a goddess worthy of the stars."

"Estelle is Latin for star. My husband and I named our firstborn Nova because she was a supernova in our life. Her daughter was supposed to be named Halley, like the comet, but her ex-husband never liked the name and put Bailey on the birth certificate." Mormor holds onto Opa's arm and tugs him forward. "You did promise to tell me about the Astronomers Monument. Visiting the Oschin Planetarium was on my bucket list. It's reportedly the best in the world." Estelle addresses El. "Thank you for letting us tag along."

"I read that every show is narrated live." Opa pulls up his phone. "The first one is at 1:45. We could do the tour and then the show, plenty of time, right?"

"And we can have pictures taken by the Hollywood sign." Estelle prods him toward the lawn with the statue.

I rest my palm on the small of El's back and hold her next to me. "This was supposed to be the best date ever. Just the two of us."

Estelle and Opa joining us was not what I planned for the day. But Dad hoped that with Estelle and Opa out of the house he could spend an afternoon with Sylvia, well and Pickle, and broach the subject of therapy. So when El suggested we bring the grandparents on our date, I caved.

"They are family. That's what counts." El slips her arm around my waist. "We'll still spend the afternoon together. As long as you don't have to rush anywhere. No Death Elbow emergency. No brand deals to save."

My shoulders fall. "I'm not answering my phone until the tour is done. Or until we get back. Or until tomorrow morning. Tell me what you want me to do and it's done."

"The best thing you can do is be here. With me." She steps out of my reach and twirls on the sidewalk, arms outstretched. "At this beautiful place."

"You're right." At least we are together. Even if we have chaperones.

I drink in the panoramic view of LA and El's smile. Her eyes are hidden behind sunglasses, and the hat she's wearing today covers up her signature white streak, but her smile is on full display, dazzling as ever. "This might be the first time I've ever been here during daylight."

The white building runs low and flat behind her, its three dark domes hinting at the treasures inside. El loves the stars. Maybe one day I can take us somewhere with less light pollution to see the actual night sky, but today the observatory is as close as I could get to a romantic gesture.

"And I was worried the paparazzi might crash our privacy." I walk alongside El toward the banister that separates us from LA sprawling below. "Didn't have Opa and your grandmother on *my* bingo card for reasons this date would go sideways."

El chuckles. "It does feel like I've spent less time alone with you since we became Hollywood-official than when we were just friends."

"We were never just friends." I thread my fingers through hers.

"You told me you didn't do the girlfriend thing."

El's hand feels light and relaxed, like her tone. Relief floods my veins to my heart. "I hadn't met you."

She adjusts the brim of her hat. "I thought you couldn't stand me at first. Only made the deal to perform with me for money."

"You captivated me the moment I laid eyes on you at The Devil's Martini, before I realized who you are. I tried to ignore the pull, but singing with you week after week, learning what drives you, what scares you, what gets your music flowing, I fell for you more and more." I pull her to the exact spot from the video. "It wasn't an instant fall, but a gradual slow descent."

The chilly wind at this height fans her hair across her heart-shaped face like it did the night of the video shoot. Then I was worried she might be cold. In the afternoon sun, a different chill covers me. "But the night we shot your video, when I kissed you here." I reach to put the strand behind her ear. "I thought you would read how much I wanted to touch you, see the restraint it took me not to do what I wanted with your mouth. Sometimes I convinced myself that I was imagining the attraction."

"I didn't know. I thought you were doing what Sarah and Nick asked. We were such fools. I should've just told you I liked you. Or kissed you. Or both. We spent so many months not kissing and instead wondering what if we were imagining this thing between us." El's lips stretch wide. "Sort of like in *Going Once*? What's in my head is in your eyes. That doubt at the beginning of a relationship: do you like me or am I imagining it?"

My heart stutters at the softly sung lyrics. That's exactly what I meant when I wrote the song. I should just tell her I wrote it.

That the words are mine. That the words are about her. That so many things I've been doing are about her. That I love her.

"El—"

"Don't move." She holds me in place with her finger on my shoulder. "Stand here."

My heart jumps into my throat. Did I curse us? Has she spotted a camera lens trained on us? I expect her to move away but instead she removes her hat and her sunglasses. "There's something else we can do in the daylight here."

"Are we taking a picture?" I let out a breath.

El shakes her head, grabs my shirt, and stands on her tiptoes. Her lips take my mouth hostage.

"Mine," they say as she presses closer into my chest and kisses me like we are not in the middle of an open space surrounded by tourists, but in the privacy of an apartment of our own. I stiffen and set my hand on her arm to halt her enthusiasm.

As if to challenge me, her tongue darts out to meet my teeth. El grips my shoulder, then runs her fingers over the muscles in my back. Heat rushes over every part she touches. She takes a step closer, plastering her hips against mine. Her hair surrounds us. A smattering of anxiety prickles below my collarbone. Or is it abandon? She deepens the kiss and I slip my fingers through the hair at her nape, capitulating to her demand.

Every part of me tangles with her, every touch of her fingertips, graze of her teeth, every breath we share mounts my internal pressure. The yearning inflates my lungs and heart, spreading my ribs from inside out. I'm so filled with love for this girl, I can float away with her in tow. Unable to care what rating this kiss is escalating to, I dip my other hand down to her waist.

With a muffled groan, El separates her lips from mine, and I should have more air but I'm short of breath without her mouth on mine. I'm dizzy and gasping. Her kisses are the kind of mouth-to-mouth I might need permanently to survive.

"Done," she whispers into the space between us with pride and finality.

I am not done.

I will never be done with her.

"El." My whisper is hoarse.

"I've dreamed of doing this since the day of the shoot." El straightens the collar she was crumpling seconds ago. "Grabbing your shirt and kissing you in front of everyone. For real, not because Nick and Sarah put us up to it. Showing you that I wanted more than your friendship. I wanted your everything."

"You have my everything." I bend to touch my forehead to hers. I've waited for a perfect moment but every moment, no matter how messy or hard or fun or unpredictable, is perfect in its own way. Right now is a moment with my girlfriend when I can tell her exactly what she means to me, what I think when I look at her and when I think about her. Not in some song. My lungs burn with the air I'm holding in. Now is the moment. I cup her face. "You know that I love you, right?"

Her nose touches mine as she nods. "I do."

"I really love you, El," I say louder. I want her to know that I mean it. That this is not a joke. I tried to show her many times but saying the words twice doesn't seem to be enough. "I love you so much."

"I know." Her cheeks grow pink. "Do you know?"

"What?" I think I know. The pangs of inner turmoil migrate from my throat to my head. I know, but I still want to hear her say it. To me. Out loud.

Her hand splays across my chest, over my heart. "I love you too." Her lips brush mine as she murmurs what I've known for a while. Hearing her say the words unlocks a new bottomless compartment in my heart ready to collect more days, weeks, years with the love of my life.

I cup El's cheek with my palm and stare at her. "I love you not just because you are beautiful and talented, or because I can never imagine not wanting to talk to you or be around you." I can't stop. "I love you because I want to carry your troubles for you when you can't, and I know you'll do the same for me. I love you because I'm not afraid to tell you the good stuff either." My temples pulse. "I love you because you are the center of my universe, of my wants, of my plans. I belong by your side, and I need you by mine: morning, noon, and night." My love for her already feels bigger than anything and it's just the beginning. "Whatever connection we have spans oceans, and tours, and fights, and attention from the media."

The corners of El's eyes turn up in sync with the corners of her mouth. I need it back on mine, but even though we aren't within earshot of anyone, we are in the middle of a public sidewalk visible to the people milling about. More in the open than when we walk down LA streets. We're lucky no one is taking pictures of us already. My gaze flits between delight in the sparkling blue of her eyes and her growing grin. I clench my jaw, holding the last shreds of my restraint. El's bottom lip glides through her teeth and the world around us blurs.

Screw propriety.

I brush my thumb over the tiny indent on her lower lip.

Screw tourists.

I ignore the alarm bells that remind me of where we are. Kissing my girlfriend shouldn't be a secret thing. I'm hers and the world can do . . . whatever it wants with that fact. I raise El's chin and bend down to continue what she interrupted.

"Where are we meeting the guide?" Opa's question stops me from restarting the kiss. Every cell screams but I close my eyes and regain control. Be responsible.

The chatter of people increases in volume and the observatory clicks back into my awareness as I blink at my grandfather. Opa gestures with his thumb behind him. "There's a guy by the monument pointing his phone at you two. Is he a paparazzo?"

I twist to study the person Opa's talking about. The tall guy with a beard and mustache matches the photo of the guide I received earlier. "He's our guide."

Opa rubs his palms together like he's getting ready for his first coffee of the day. "What are we waiting for? Let's go."

I redirect my attention to El's lips. "To be continued somewhere," I peck her mouth, "Opa can't interrupt us again?"

"An actual date where it's just the two of us would be nice." She puts her hat and sunglasses back on.

"Prepare to be surprised."

Eighteen

Wil: You know I love you, right?

I've seen this text every day during the week since our tour of the Griffith Observatory and I don't think it'll ever get old.

Me: I love you too.

I pocket my phone and try to school my face into something that's not an ear-to-ear grin.

"There's that look again." Carlee sits in the makeup chair by the bar that's mid-refinishing. Today her foundation is so thick even Daniel Davison wouldn't suspect she woke up resembling a ghost.

The makeup artist finishes dabbing Carlee's lips and turns to me. "Are you next?"

I back away and detach two new microphones off the stands on the stage. "Nope. I won't be on camera today."

"Are you sure?" Carlee removes the tissues that were protecting the collar of her peach chiffon blouse. "You're part of this. My right-hand woman, remember? You should get the credit."

I tuck my hair behind my ears. "I'm more of a silent contributor."

I place the microphones into their holders and the red light blinks on, indicating they are charging. Some artists, like me, prefer to grip the microphone when they sing. The image of Wil's face close to mine, our voices mixing, blooms in my mind. I sigh and choose two state-of-the-art sleek headsets from the rack in the equipment room.

Some artists, like Dasher, like to have their hands free during a performance. We're lucky he agreed to help promote The Devil's Martini even though he's only in LA for one day before he's off to Tahiti for the Fourth of July long weekend to shoot a video.

"Got 'em." I place the headsets on the stool at center stage and head toward Carlee. "I think we're ready."

The makeup artist snaps her steel box shut. "I'm all done then."

"Thanks, Felicia." Carlee eases off the stool. "I'll see you again on the sixth?"

"You're in my calendar." She leans to air kiss Carlee's cheek. "I can't wait to read the article."

I unlock the door for Felicia and find the man I loathe waiting, one foot resting against the brick wall outside, his sandy brown hair trimmed to perfection.

"Well, hello El Vella." Daniel Davison straightens. "Or is it back to Melodie Rockerby now that you don't sing anymore?"

I want to yell at him, smack him for posting those horrible and untrue stories about me, but he's here to create buzz for The Devil's Martini reopening. Carlee needs this to go well. I need it to go well. So at least there's no gossip about me in the interview. "El. It'll always be El." I hold the door open for him.

"Will your boyfriend be joining us?" Daniel's smile makes me wish today was my day off.

"He's at his office. I don't know if you've heard, but he's working with the next hot band." Might as well milk this opportunity and see if I can help Wil and Death Elbow. "You might want to check them out."

Daniel weaves between the red leather booths still wrapped in plastic to where Carlee sits at a bistro table we've set in front of the stage, the new The Devil's Martini logo Mateo designed propped up on a canvas behind her. Daniel stops a foot from Carlee and clasps his hands before him. "Don't you look fabulous."

"Did my hair just for you." Carlee doesn't get up from the chair. This is part of the plan. We're not sure if it's a symptom or the new drug she's taking, but her left leg keeps going numb at random moments, so the idea is to keep her seated as much as possible.

"My photographer is running late, but when she gets here, she's going to eat you up with a spoon."

There's a tap at the back door and I hurry to get out of the room. On the other side waits a tall, slender Black man who stands out more in-person than on his album covers. He's flanked by two bulky white men in wraparound shades dressed in head-to-toe black.

"Dasher." I open the door. "It's an honor to meet you."

He holds his palms together and dips his head. "And you. Carlee sings your praises." He winks.

A giggle bubbles up at his compliment. I've watched countless hours of this man singing, attempting to recreate his style for the covers I post online. My heartbeat rams in my temples but I stop myself from jumping in excitement.

Dasher joins Carlee, Daniel, and Daniel's phone that's recording every word we say from the center of the table. I hang back with the bodyguards, offering water which they refuse, their eyes glued to Dasher as they hover by the bar. Daniel asks Dasher about his latest collaboration, his plans to go on tour, and his upcoming sixth studio album. Not once does Daniel glance my way.

I blow a breath through my nose. I got it. I'm fine. This is fine. Nothing is wrong. My plan to fade into the background is working.

Daniel clears his throat. "So, Dasher, why was it important to hold this interview here? At The Devil's Martini?"

Dasher glances at Carlee. "Because I want to support my friend. Carlee is saving an important part of musical history here, keeping The Devil's Martini open. It's a brave choice. This land is valuable and I'm sure some developer would have demolished this place and put up condos. But Carlee knows the value of giving emerging artists a place to learn and perform. To grow." He taps the scuffed up floorboards beneath him. "We both got our start in this very room."

"Yes. We were just babies then." Carlee turns on the charm.

"If I hadn't won the open mic night here, I would have given up on my music career. I was this close to quitting." Dasher pinches two fingers together until there is a small gap between them.

Daniel inches forward. "Really, why?"

Dasher waves a hand. "Oh, who can remember now. It's water under the bridge. All I know is this place helped me and I don't forget my debts."

"Does that include singing here again?" Carlee wiggles her eyebrows at him. "There's a microphone onstage and we happen to have the backing track of your latest album cued and ready to go."

Dasher glances at me and nods. "I'll sing. If El sings with me."

All eyes turn my way. My skin prickles and I grip my fingers to keep them from diving into my hair. This was not part of the deal. I look at Carlee. Did she plan this? We had an agreement. I thought she understood. Fear blankets me in prickles. Her eyes widen and her head shakes so subtly, I'm not sure I'm not seeing things.

"I know you know my songs. I've seen the covers."

He's seen my videos? My head spins.

Dasher rises and climbs on the stage "What do you say, El?"

I squeeze my hands and glance at Daniel Davison. How do I get out of this? It's not like I haven't sung on this stage before. I did it with Wil and Death Elbow. The stage is not my enemy—it's the device sitting on the table. I step forward. "I'll sing if Daniel turns off his recording."

Daniel's eyebrows furrow. "My fans would love a Dasher and El Vella collab exclusive."

"Well, it's not happening today. I'll sing for you and Carlee." I turn to the bodyguards. "And you guys. But no recording us." I meet Daniel's eyes. "Do we understand each other?"

He drums his thumbs on the table, sighs, then picks up his phone. He taps on the screen and holds it up for all to see he has turned off the recording. "Happy?"

I hold myself back from skipping onto the stage. Dasher and I both don microphones and he points to the guitar. "Shall we do it old school? Acoustic guitar, no backing track."

I take the guitar and hang it across my body.

Dasher grins at me. "Do you know *Nobody's Baby*?"

I strum the opening notes to prove I do.

"Let's do it."

I dive into the intro and sing the lyrics in the low, sultry tone they are meant for. When I finish the first verse, Dasher steps closer, singing to me. He's good, of course, driving the song along. But he doesn't affect me like Wil does. As the chorus approaches we launch into the famous lines, our voices mixing together. He harmonizes with my lead, riffing a new rendition of the repeated chorus. Daniel and Carlee both cheer and even the bodyguards in the back whistle.

Far too quickly the song comes to an end. I point to my singing partner. "Dasher, everyone." Four pairs of hands clap, Daniel and Carlee on their feet.

My unease swells as Carlee places a hand on the table to steady herself. I move to jump off the stage to catch her, but Dasher beats me too it, scooping Carlee into a bear hug. "I love the acoustics in this place." He pulls back to smile at her. "I'm glad you are keeping so much of the original stuff."

I don't know if he saw what I did, but I'm grateful for the distraction. If Daniel Davison noticed Carlee's wobble, he doesn't let on. "Can I turn the recorder back on?"

There's a part of me that regrets putting down the guitar, leaving the stage. My blood screams to continue, to play another song, and another. Even to this small audience.

Carlee settles into her chair, Dasher at her side, and the interview starts again. This time Daniel asks Carlee questions about the bar, about her vision. The closest he comes to talking about her illness is when he asks if she'll be singing at the Grand Reopening.

"As you know, Daniel, I'm retired." She places a hand on Dasher's. "Maybe we can convince Dasher to come back for a repeat performance?"

He raises her knuckles to his lips. "I'll clear my calendar."

The photographer arrives and she takes snap after snap of the trio talking and laughing, of the stage, and of Dasher and Carlee sitting in front of the new sign.

Everyone says their goodbyes and I close the door behind the men. The bar is quiet and I can breathe fully again.

Carlee holds her head. "How did I do?"

I touch her shoulder. "You were amazing. You had Daniel eating out of the palm of your hand. You'll have to teach me your ways, oh wise one."

This earns me a weak smile. "Years of growing a thick skin and throwing them exclusives helps. Still, living my life is the most important thing. I try not to let them dictate it. These days I have to slow down and reinvent myself. But you are young and talented. You can't divert your future because you are afraid of the gossip rags." She stands and grabs the table.

I throw my arm around her waist. "I'm calling your driver. You need to go home and rest. And we're calling your doctor for a follow-up. I'll clean up here and lock up." Carlee doesn't resist and allows me to walk her to the car.

I pull my phone from my pocket and turn Do Not Disturb off.

An onslaught of buzzes vibrate my fingers as the flood of messages, notification, and . . . a voicemail? Who leaves voicemails? I open the app, my mind conjuring scenarios of Mormor or Mr. Peters getting hurt, because even Mom and Rocker don't use voicemail anymore. The number is familiar but not one I need to program into my phone, because I used to answer it. I punch the button to listen.

"My office," Sven grunts. A squeal that could belong to a small dog, or child, or woman in distress peals in the background. "As soon as you can."

I play the cryptic message again. Did I miss the first part? The same seven words. A quick scan of my missed texts and none are from Sven. The hairs on my forearms stand. Sven is not someone who'd call me like that unless there's an emergency. I hit reply and hold my breath. I count the rings. After eight the automated recording kicks in. Gretchen's calm voice requests I leave a message.

This is not good.

I text Sven's personal phone but don't get a reply.

That's it.

I grab my bag, punch a string of numbers into the new alarm system, and run out of the bar. If the man I think of as Superman has an emergency, it really must be dire.

A closed sign hangs on the entrance to Ander's Investigations. I thank Sven's insistence on me keeping a copy of the key, just in case. Which at that time I interpreted as his insurance that I can come back in case Gretchen doesn't work out. I tap 911 on my phone and hold my finger over the call button as I unlock the door and make sure to close it very quietly behind me.

Christina Aguilera's *Reflection* from the original *Mulan* soundtrack blasts loud enough to conceal the door slamming shut.

Maybe Sven isn't here.

Or being held captive by a Disney-loving stalker?

My progress down the hall grinds to a stop at the sound of a man's voice echoing the chorus.

Disney-obsessed stalker it is.

The singing continues as I inch to the door of the office and my chin might as well hit the floor.

I thought nothing would ever top seeing Sven in his Superman costume at Comic-Con. This sight is better and worse.

In the middle of the office floor, Sven, his shoulders hunched, sits cross-legged on the comforter that usually covers his bed. The sleeves of his good white shirt are rolled up to the elbows, revealing thick forearms.

But it's not just him. A small girl who might be younger than me when Papa had his accident kneels in front of Sven. With her head cocked to the side, dark hair curtains her face. Her tiny hands hold his paw, of which three fingernails are sporting the red color I think might be the polish from the set Zoe kept here.

I blink. Did I walk into another dimension?

Sven's voice quiets.

The girl pauses her artistic endeavor. "Don't stop. You can't be a real princess if you don't sing. It's a rule."

The snort that comes out of me startles the girl enough that the brush skims off Sven's nail and red streaks up to his knuckle. "Jiminy Cricket," exclaims the girl. "Who's that?"

Sven's body stays still but his sharp gaze lands on me. The tightness in his jaw and around his eyes are his trademark "I'm ready to spring into action the second I spot danger" expression. At the sight of me his shoulders relax.

Eyes wide, she examines me. "Is she going to be Ariel?" The girl sets the brush on the piece of printer paper the nail polish bottle is sitting on next to a scattering of highlighters and skips over to me. Her Mary Janes make a clopping sound on the floor. I stare closer. Those are not *her* Mary Janes. The shoes are several sizes too large. So is the shirt she's wearing more like a dress. The rose-colored, pleated silk material is one of the spare outfits Zoe stored in the downstairs closet.

I smile. "And what's your name?"

"I'm Poppy." She curtsies. "But today I'm Princess Rapunzel." She shuffles to my old desk and picks up something. When she turns, her head is covered in blond hair. My wig. The long tresses that reached my hips when I was performing with Wil almost touch the floor on her small frame. "But Sven doesn't know how to braid hair." Her big eyes peer up at me, briming with hope. "Do you?"

I step into the room. "Sure. My cousins and I used to braid each other's."

She takes my hand and leads me to the comforter. Sven hovers like he wants to run away but has to protect the girl at all costs. I eyeball him with a "What's going on?" expression as I settle onto the floor.

"Poppy's Gretchen's granddaughter." Sven starts to cross his arms but must remember he has wet polish on his nails and lets his hands fall to his sides.

"Sveny promised to take good care of me." She beams at him like the sun revolves around the big guy.

I snicker. "Sveny huh?"

Poppy bounces in front of me and I adjust my old wig so it sits properly on her head. It reminds me of the times Wil used the same move as an excuse to touch me before he admitted he had feelings for me. I pat the spot before me. "Hold still please."

She does and I separate the rather matted strands into three even parts and start weaving them.

"Sit, Sveny." Poppy radiates delight as she pats the spot in front of her.

My ex-bodyguard turned security expert, who I've seen tackle three-hundred-pound superfans without hesitation, sits cross-legged and holds out his hand. My heart pitter-patters at the splatters of polish, most of which manage to cover his nails.

"One more coat." Poppy globs on more. "When I asked Sveny what princess he wanted to be, he didn't know. I said Mulan, because she is a warrior and can fight and can protect us from bad people, so that must be the right princess for him. But he doesn't sing very well." She twists to me, the wig sliding. "Do you sing?"

"I do."

"I thought I might want to be a singer too, but I've decided to be a princess." Poppy's head bobs and weaves as she talks and I struggle to keep hold of the braid. "I get to sing, and dance, and wear pretty dresses, and fight villains, and kiss frogs. I think as a job it has a lot more opportunities."

I nod and hold my lips tight not to burst out into laughter. Sven narrows his eyes at me. The playlist moves from *Reflections* to the theme song from *Frozen* as I get to the middle of the disastrous braid I'm working on.

The entry door bangs and "I'm here" echoes in the hallway. The laughter that is still rumbling in my chest gives way to anxiety.

"Zoe?"

My cousin fills the doorway, her sky-blue, off-the-shoulder jumpsuit swishing as she walks carrying multiple bags. Her grin waivers when her gaze lands on me.

"Another princess!" Poppy jumps up and skips over to Zoe. "You're dressed like Jasmine."

"I've always pictured myself more of a Cinderella." Zoe flips her brown hair over her shoulder.

"But she is blond and has blue eyes and you don't."

"True. However we both love fashion and making dresses, so I think that's more important than what color my hair is." Zoe adjusts her bangs, flattening them against her forehead. "You must be Poppy."

Zoe knows her name? The muscles in my neck constrict and I wriggle closer to Sven and grumble, "You called Zoe?"

"I needed help." He scowls. "You didn't answer."

Poppy and Zoe are digging through the shopping bags. Zoe triumphantly pulls out a sleeve of plastic tiaras and rips the packaging. She places one of them onto her own head and strikes a pose. "Voilà."

"Did you bring more?" Poppy peeks into the bag.

"Enough for everyone." Zoe's gaze flicks to me.

Poppy pulls Zoe to the bedcover on the floor, takes a tiara, and places it on Sven's head. His short blond buzz doesn't have enough hair for the accessory to grab onto. If he were to breathe heavily, it would topple off. Sven doesn't move a muscle.

Zoe completes our little circle, filling the gap beside me. She hides her smile with her fingers. "He's very handsome."

Sven scowls.

I join the glee with Poppy and Zoe. Until I remember I'm not talking to my cousin.

Poppy puts a tiara on her head. Their three crowned heads form a perfect picture for this ridiculous event. I'm the odd one out. With Zoe here, Sven doesn't need me. I move to stand. "I think I should go."

"No." Poppy scrunches her eyebrows. "You promised to sing for us."

"I . . ." I search for a plausible excuse.

Zoe unwraps a set of teacups and saucers that could belong in the castle from *Beauty and the Beast*. She shakes her head. "She doesn't have time for us." Zoe produces a container with tiny multicolored cupcakes. "I also brought these. There's chocolate, caramel, mango, and strawberry."

Poppy hops and claps, and her wig slides, dangerously close to falling off. She catches it with both hands. "Strawberry please." Her body crushes against my side. "You can pick two if you want."

Something in me must have broken, because I can't say no. Even though the same room with Zoe is the last place I want to be, I don't want to ruin this little girl's tea party. I settle back into my spot. "Caramel please." I glance at my cousin. "And chocolate."

Nineteen

Across the conference table from the Vatton representatives, I fiddle with the cufflinks Zoe had custom-made for me. Silver squares are engraved with the new RA Connect Foundation logo. If I can't wear her designs, I can at least keep this with me as a reminder that five percent of the profits from this deal will go to the Foundation Dad and I started. The money aims to help other people with rheumatoid arthritis avoid suffering like Mum has. The only other people on the Rocker Inc. side of the room are Death Elbow.

Today the band comes across as polished in an about-to-rock way. The smudged eyeliner around Corbin's eyes is a fashion statement for once, not a sign of a sleepless night. The shirt from Moderni Look is Corbin's homage to the business part of his outfit. His leather pants and the custom Doc Martens boots that rival Dad's are all front-man energy. Xander, Lucian, and Gideon are wearing versions of the same shirts, but each with a different spin that makes the reserved style appear more fashion-forward. With the Moderni Look contract in place, if the partnership with Vatton goes through today, the band and I will get richer, and I can be a contributor to the foundation, not just the founder.

Once I sign, the high-end water bottle on the table will be my constant companion. My hand shakes. It's just a prop I'll have to carry. The security of the money is worth the price. "And the signing bonus will be transferred to our account by end of day tomorrow?"

"As agreed. With quarterly payments after that for the duration of the contract." The lawyer from Vatton gives me a pen similar to one I saw behind a glass case in the paper shop in Bremen and could never afford. I'm certain they'd have no issue giving it to me at a mere suggestion.

The pen is heavy in my hand. The decision is heavier. This deal changes everything. Our legal team went through this with a fine-tooth comb. Harper reviewed it. Dad approved this.

I square my shoulders, scrawl Wilhelm Peters on the signature line, and push the document away. The rep finalizes with her signature and we shake hands. Deal done. "I guess it's official."

"Don't forget your bottles." The rep hands each band member a fluorescent purple cylinder as they file out of the room. I take two, say goodbye, and trail them.

In the elevator, Lucian uncaps his and takes a sip. "Do I need to actually drink from this?"

"As long as you hold it in your hand, you're fulfilling your obligation." I dangle one off the tip of my index finger. "There are reporters out front so make sure its visible on your way out." The doors open to the first floor. "I have a car waiting for you."

This isn't a performance per se, but it's a spectacle Death Elbow is being paid for.

Harper and Opa stride out of the same room we held the press conference in when Dad announced to the world I was his son. Opa scratches his head. "So I don't smile when they take the picture?"

"Correct." Harper gives him an encouraging smile. "Your goal is to pretend they are not there so they take a photo and move on. If you engage, they'll ask more questions, and unless it's a paid or a scheduled engagement, the best policy is to ignore."

Opa sees me and his scrunched eyebrows relax. "Is it lunchtime?"

"I'm ready if you are." I glance at Harper who gives me a thumbs-up. I offer Opa one of the Vatton bottles. "We're going to exit first. Let the paparazzi get their pictures and warm them up. Then, when they come out," I gesture to the band, "they'll distract the paps from following us."

Harper holds Death Elbow aside, arranging them in order of who will exit first. Opa and I walk out to the sunlight-drenched sidewalk in front of Rocker Inc. A few reporters call my name and the cameras click but it's a subdued commotion, nothing like the near-mobbing El and I had outside The Stand the night we tried to rescue Death Elbow. I saunter down the sidewalk, Opa by my side, and a couple of photographers follow. They are quickly distracted when the chatter by the door grows into the cacophony of a full orchestra tuning their instruments. Death Elbow has left the building.

"I can't believe that worked." Opa glances behind us. "All that just to get pictures of this fancy bottle?"

"That's the goal." I take the familiar path to the farmers' market: lots of lunch options and easy to stay unnoticed. "For the next six months, the band and I can't be seen with any other bottles."

"Even if you don't drink from it?"

"Exactly." The flower stand marks the entrance to the market. The smell of kettle corn wafts around us. "This is not about what's inside. It's about people seeing celebrities with the product."

Opa's head swivels as we cruise by the stands of fruit and produce. He picks up an avocado and squeezes it. "And what do you get out of it?"

"Money." Pins prick in the hollow below my throat. The spot where El and I started busking is two stalls away. Last summer this was one of my favorite places, my chance to see her outside of The Devil's Martini, to laugh at her silly hats, to practice our songs. When she agreed to do it with me, my bank account was hovering around zero most days of the week. A violin starts playing a cover of a popular song from that direction. No more busking for me. No more singing. I unscrew the cap on the Vatton bottle. "It's a solid reliable stream of revenue for the band, Rocker Inc., my charity, and for me. Enough money to put some away in case you or Mum need something."

"Is this a job you want?" Opa moves over to the stand with local honey and frowns at the bear-shaped bottle. "Would Pickle like this toy?"

I take the honey out of his hands and set it back in a row of its brothers. "It's not a toy. And he can't have honey until he's at least one."

A woman in the avocado stall points her phone at me. I steer Opa to the next booth with pickled cucumbers, tomatoes, cabbage, radishes, and even watermelon.

The woman abandons all caution and walks as closely as possible, filming me. El had the right idea with her hats. I should have brought one. I take a swig from the Vatton bottle. At least I can call this work and not an invasion of my private lunchtime with my grandfather.

Opa snickers and chooses the largest jar. "How about this? Pickles for Pickle?" He breaks into laughter at his own joke.

"No," I say harshly. Opa frowns at me and I flick my gaze to the woman who's following us.

"Will she make money from that video?"

"Maybe." I move us along at a less leisurely pace. "I don't know how long the press is going to be interested in me. I'm a celebrity for now. This is my chance to cash in, get paid for being Rocker's long-lost son." At the next booth, a balloon artist has a small circle of children around him who do not care at all about me, but several of their adults give me a side-glance. Maybe it's not about me. Maybe I'm just dressed too nicely for lunchtime at a farmers' market. "Isn't that what you sent me to LA for? Money to help Mum?"

"I didn't expect you to stay here." Opa tosses a glance over his shoulder and his face sours. "The plan was meet the rock star, get money, come home."

I smile. "I didn't expect to fall for the rock star's daughter." We're finally in the center of the market. The spot Sven found El and me busking at is empty. I don't have a guitar nor a microphone, but a confusing feeling tugs me into the spot that'll forever be named as ours in my head. "We used to perform right here." I lift my chin and hum *Don't Give Me Comfort* under my breath. "I'm not going anywhere without El."

Opa grasps my bicep. "I'm not telling you to." The sides of his mouth hitch up. "I like the girl. She's a keeper, but LA?"

The chattering people around us are as colorful and loud as the market itself. I used to fit in here. Now I stick out like a sore thumb. But at Rocker Inc., I fit. "LA grows on you."

"Some parts I like. The weather hasn't been too bad. The pool in the backyard is convenient. And the food Marta prepares is almost as good as your mother's." Next to a stall selling handmade pottery, he looks at me with a mixture of concern and resolve. "Other parts I'm not so sure. This band you're palling around with, for example."

"I'm not palling around with them." I tug on the collar of my shirt. "I'm working with them."

"Right. Working. They remind me of your father when he was young. The papers were full of stories of him at parties, with drugs. Getting girls pregnant." Opa's gaze falls to the ground. "It's not how I raised you."

I stop in front of the gyro place. "You do know a lot of that was made up by the press." Amidst the chatter of vendors and the shouts of orders from the stalls, I lower my voice. "Dad wasn't a saint, but he regretted that part of his life. That's why he tried to protect El from it."

"And who will protect you?" Opa says firmly.

Having Opa here has been disruptive, but also therapeutic. Drinking coffee with him in the mornings. Watching him splash in the pool with Pickle. Listening to him bicker with Estelle over how to restore the bar at The Devil's Martini. I clasp my hand over his and give him a side hug. "You don't have to go back. You can stay longer."

"The house renovations are done." He steps away. "Hanna comes home today." He inspects the four-item menu like it's the Rosetta Stone. "I don't need to squat on Rocker's property anymore."

We place our orders and stand to the side.

"Didn't you promise Carlee to help with the floors?"

Opa rocks on his heels. "I'll get that started this week. Won't have time to refinish the bar top for Estelle though. Plus, the steps need shoring in. Carlee still has no one lined up to fix the baseboards. Did you see the benches in the wings off the stage? I know no one but the musicians see them, but those need sanding and revarnishing."

That list doesn't sound like something Opa wants to run away from. It sounds like a list of reasons for him to stay. Calm fills my lungs. Opa wants to stay.

"The Grand Reopening is a month from now." I tap my tongue on my teeth and act on my suspicion. "We can invite Mom here for it, show her what you've done at The Devil's Martini, take her around LA, celebrate my birthday in September, then you two can fly home together."

"Maybe."

"If you don't want to stay at Dad's, I know of a great apartment Mateo is housesitting. Five minutes from here. It has two bedrooms. One for you and the other for Mum. I thought it was perfect for two people."

Our number is called and Opa comes back with two warm wraps covered in aluminum foil. "Being useful makes me feel like myself again." He hands one to me. "I can't get paid on my visa here, but Carlee said she'll donate to Hanna's charity to thank me for the work." Opa takes a bite and chews slowly. "But only if Hanna is okay with this plan."

"Let's call Mum." I push the videocall button and wait, but she doesn't pick up. "She's probably still en route."

The violinist plays a version of our song *Orange* and I suppress my grin at the memory of El dancing with the crowd to the peppy tune.

"If I do stay, I could help you." Opa draws me back to the present. "What do you need for the new apartment of yours?"

"It's not ours."

But I can see us living together there someday. Cooking in that kitchen El loved so much. I take a sip of water from my purple bottle. There's a slight metallic aftertaste. The woman that was filming us is nowhere in sight, but I don't want to discuss this in the open. In the shade of the trees, the spot I often ate at after our busking performances appears empty. I drag Opa over and we sit. Around us the market bustles, creating a soundtrack of shouts, claps, laughter, and an occasional ringtone.

I take a giant mouthful of the wrap. Should I tell Opa the real reason El refused to consider the place? I swallow the perfect combo of rotisserie lamb, veggies, and soft pita, and go for it. "I suggested El rent the place, but she said no."

"She doesn't like it?" Opa angles his torso so I become his view instead of the market.

"She loved the place but not the price tag." I take another bite, convincing myself that sharing with Opa is not a betrayal of El's trust. I tap the toe of my shoe on the leg of the bench. "The place is out of her price range and she won't let me help."

A wry smile graces Opa's lips.

"What?" I cock an eyebrow at him. "It's important to her. To be . . . independent."

He shakes his head. "Not that. I applaud her desire to stand on her own two feet. It takes courage." He crinkles the aluminum foil around his food. "I had the same issue with my Sidra, your Oma, when we moved in together. The thing we learned the hard way is relationships don't operate like that. They're not always an even fifty-fifty partnership."

"Isn't that the goal?" My voice rises in disbelief. "We each contribute equally?"

"We don't always have a half to give." Opa shrugs. "True partners work together to keep the relationship thriving."

I stare at him.

"Think of it this way: some days I came home and your Oma had a rough day taking care of Hanna. We were both exhausted, but I had a bit more energy." He squints into the sun. "I was at sixty percent so I made dinner, meaning she could nap with Hanna. Other days, she was at eighty percent and she cooked a roast. And on the days when neither of us had the energy we would bundle Hanna up, go to the pub, and desert the chores."

"El loves to cook, but I don't think our relationship will be like your and Oma's."

"This isn't about food." Opa waves a hand. "I'm making a point." He faces me. "The goal is about finding a balance. It's the balance of shifting and sharing the load each time life takes you through twists and turns. There will be a time when you'll take on the load, and others when she'll hold the partnership together, handle things you can't."

I munch and consider Opa's words. "I never thought of it that way."

"Years of wisdom over here." Opa throws his wrapper in a trash can with a flourish of a basketball player. "Now. Are you going to show me this amazing apartment?"

I stuff the final piece of my gyro into my mouth and throw the wrapper into the trash. "You want to see the place?"

"I'd love to tell you my opinion on it." He stands and stretches.

That's my Opa. I grin as I text Mateo to confirm it's okay to drop by. When he pings me back with the entry code, I steer Opa to the building I can imagine as El's long-term residence.

During the day the living room is bright and airy. I love it even more. I can see El and me drinking coffee here.

"No one above you?" Opa knocks on the walls, flips the light switches off and off, and peers into every room.

Opa keeps talking like it's already our apartment and I stop correcting him. "Top floor. There's a private roof deck residents can reserve, but no one lives above." I hold the door to the primary bedroom. "Check out the view from here."

Opa whistles low. "Too bad you can't cut a skylight into the ceiling like we did in Hanna's room."

Both of us stare at the ceiling.

"El would love that." My phone buzzes. "It's Mum. Her ears must be burning." I slide the receiver icon to answer the video call.

"Why didn't you tell me?" Mum's smiling but there are tears in her eyes.

"Surprise," Opa and I shout in unison.

"A whole-house renovation?" Mum sobs. "After getting pregnant with you, this is the best surprise of my life."

Opa slaps me on my back smiling at the screen. "Do you like the open kitchen?"

The screen shakes as she turns it around to display the new floorplan Opa and I worked on. Her voice is nasal, but strong. "I didn't even think of doing that. Everything is so spacious now."

"Did you see the dishwasher?" My matching smile fights for space in the smaller rectangle on my phone.

The screen swivels back to her grinning face. "No more washing dishes by hand. I'll feel spoiled." She wipes tears off her cheeks. "How did we afford it?"

I glance at Opa. I want to be truthful with Mum for once. "Opa started the ball rolling, then Dad chipped in. With the deal I signed today and my salary, you don't have to worry about money ever again."

"Wil. We talked about this. You don't have to worry about me anymore. I'll be able to return to work in the fall." Her lips press together. "Still, I don't know how to thank you for this."

"Stay healthy."

Her lower lip trembles. "How did I get so lucky?"

"Good genes." Opa points to himself.

Mum's head tilts. "Where are you?"

"About that." I elbow Opa to speak. "How would you like to spend the summer in LA?"

TWENTY

AFTER EIGHT RENDITIONS OF Ariel's song, I think I'll be singing it in my dreams or nightmares tonight, drinking a tub of invisible tea. Poppy hands me my wig. "You promise to come by the next time I'm with Sveny?"

Based on Sven's bedraggled look, I don't think there's going to be a next time, but I say yes.

"Can you watch the phones while I drop her off at her house?"

I say yes again.

Once Sven and Poppy leave, the bed cover with the red nail polish slashes, empty cupcake wrappers, and plastic tiaras gives the impression even more that a Disney-obsessed serial killer has been here. I collect the polish and do my best to ignore Zoe, who's haphazardly shoving the non-trash items back into the bags they came from.I wait for her to say something. Not an apology, but a truce offering. A line I can grab onto and pull us closer, because no matter how much hearing what Zoe really thought of me hurt, I miss my best friend. I miss her more than I've allowed myself to admit.

I text Wil.

> Me: Zoe's here.

> Wil: At the bar?

> Me: No. I'm at Sven's. And he had his nails painted.

> Wil: Pic or it didn't happen.

> Me: I'll take it when he's back.

I shove the phone into my bag and glance at Zoe's back as she hangs her skirt in Sven's closet.

Without Disney music blasting from the speakers, the silence stretches and fills every crevice of Sven's office. I clench my jaw and command myself to stop hoping for a reconciliation. I screw the top back onto the nail polish and stalk into the bathroom. The tiara is still on my head and I place it, the wig, and the bottle into the storage cabinet next to Sven's collection of hats, sunglasses, and other surveillance junk.

The door creaks open and I spin around to find Zoe.

"Oh," she crosses her arms. "I thought you'd gone."

I slam the cabinet door closed. "I have as much right to be here as you do. Maybe more."

Zoe steps into the bathroom. "Sven called me."

"Only after he couldn't get in touch with me." The irritation I've been holding onto for months takes charge of my mouth.

"Oh, I see, I'm not allowed to be friends with Sven. Is it the same for Wil? Is that why he's avoiding me?"

"Whatever." I brush past her and push on the handle of the door. It doesn't move. I jiggle it again.

"Move over." Zoe squeezes past me.

I gesture at the handle. "It's jammed again. Gretchen was supposed to get this fixed."

Zoe pulls but the door doesn't budge. "Call Sven, ask him to come back and open it."

"You call him. You're the one who has your phone on you constantly."

"Posting content with my outfits is part of my job, but I don't usually bring my phone to the bathroom unless I need to take mirror selfies." She gestures to the wall above the sink. "Look at this mirror, I told Sven he needs to put in a decent one. No one in their right mind would take a selfie here." Zoe juts out a hip. "You call him."

My hand skims my back pocket and I cringe. "I don't have my phone on me. It's in my bag."

Zoe throws her hands in the air. "Great. Another mess you've gotten us into."

"I didn't do this." I slap my palm on the door. Then I do it again and again, like I can use my frustration to get us out of here.

Beside me, a set of social-media-worthy nails splay against the wood. "Can we maybe break the door?"

"Neither of us is Sven." I rest my head against the wall.

"Couldn't agree more."

"The window?" I push off the door to the other side of the room, climb onto the lid of the toilet, and peer through the rectangle of glass above it. With a shove, I open the window and try to pull myself to it. It's too high. "Help me."

Zoe snorts, but latches onto my legs and lifts. I manage to get my shoulders through and I hang with half my body out the window. Far below, the alleyway is empty. No one to hear us if we shout for help. Even if we manage to climb out of it, the drop is sure to cause broken limbs. And between Wil and me we've had enough of those this year.

Zoe glares at me. "Are you going to squeeze out of it and abandon me? Again?"

I lower myself back onto the lid. "I did not abandon you." I fist my hands into balls.

"What would you call your selfish attitude then?" Zoe studies her nails.

My blood boils. I run at the door, kicking at it. Moisture blurs my vision. This isn't fair. Zoe is calm and collected while I'm falling apart. I suck in air and turn to face her. "You think you're so smart?"

Her head jerks up. "Am I wrong?"

I stomp forward. "Actually you are. If I were so selfish I would have stayed and lived off Mom and Rocker's money. Instead, I tried to make my own way with a music career."

"Which I supported."

I ignore her declaration. "I tried my best with Blatantly Subtle and when they rejected me, it hurt." My voice cracks and I swallow to remove the frog. "I'm allowed to be upset. That does not make me selfish."

She taps on her chest. "I know. That's why I suggested you stay in *my* pool house, so you had time to regroup. Again, I was there for you."

"The car accident wasn't my fault," I bellow.

Zoe matches my volume. "This isn't about faults." She pushes off the wall. "That night, I was scared. After the crash Wil wouldn't wake up. I thought he . . . the world was spinning," she touches her forehead, "and I couldn't tell if he was breathing. The paramedics had to cut off the door to get him out."

Bile rises in my throat and I prop against the wall for support. Wil was so lucky he only injured his arm and fractured some ribs.

Chest heaving, Zoe stares at the ceiling. "They took him away and I didn't know what was happening. All those paparazzi were snapping photos." She sniffs. "I was all alone."

My chest hurts. I was so focused on Wil that night. I'm accustomed to Zoe being strong, I didn't stop to think about the effect the accident had on her. "I didn't—"

"No. You were too busy thinking about yourself." Zoe waves a hand at me. "Selfish."

The word grates against my heart. "No. I was scared. I hadn't seen Wil at all. You seemed fine."

"Well I wasn't fine." Her confession hangs in the air between us. "I lay in that hospital bed alone hoping for someone who cared about me to arrive."

I step toward her. "I do care."

"When you got there," Zoe stares at the ceiling, "you acted like I didn't matter. I got mad. For weeks Wil, Rocker, Aunt Sylvia, Sven, everyone was obsessed with making you whole. I would have killed for someone to care about me like that. But you just pushed them away."

My heart cracks. I can keep denying it, but I don't want to anymore. "I thought I was standing up for myself and what I wanted." The truth bleeds out of me. "I thought I was being more like you." Zoe's gaze flicks to mine then away and she crosses her arms. "You are always so strong and confident. I'm . . . jealous of that. Wonder sometimes how you can stand to be around me."

Zoe grunts and backs into the wall, turning her face from me.

"Especially that night, I thought I'd failed. Again. I'd hit rock bottom, lost my music, fought with Wil." The dread of those silent days when the notes wouldn't speak to me seeps into my mind . "The one person I could rely on."

A tear trickles down Zoe's cheek.

"Besides you." I pull at my ear. "I didn't mean to hurt you. You're right, I was selfish, wrapped up in my own head." I scuff my shoe against the tile floor. "I'm trying to do better."

"You seem happier." Zoe says through her teeth.

"I am. Working with Carlee is better than answering phones for Sven. And the music came back. I'm writing with Wil and singing. I just sang a duet with Dasher."

Zoe's gaze snaps to mine. "Really? We've always loved him."

I press my hands to my chest. "He's even better live. He's performing at The Devil's Martini in three weeks. You have to be there."

"I'll add it to my calendar when we get out of here."

My lips curve, but I force them down. "I can send you a reminder. I do that now. And PowerPoint presentations. And pay bills. These months at The Devil's Martini taught me a lot."

"I almost talked to you again when I came over that day with Mormor."

"Why didn't you?"

Zoe cocks an eyebrow. "I was jealous. I was there for Mormor, but all she wanted to do is see you."

"It wasn't about me." I hold up a hand. "Really. She's in LA for Mom. She's worried about her. We all are. I even agreed to babysit Pickle so she could get out of the house for once."

Zoe gawks. "You? Looked after Pickle?"

I lift my chin. "Changed his diaper and everything. Did you know they put little hats on his . . ." I wave at my lower region, "to stop him from peeing on you?"

Zoe's forehead wrinkles. "Hats?"

"Yeah." I adjust the hem of my shirt. "They have little airplanes on them."

The tips of Zoe's lips curve. "Why? Shouldn't they have whales instead?"

I shrug. "No idea. They seemed useless to me. I got drenched. And he wouldn't stop crying. Remember the cat you tried to rescue that turned out to be in labor?" She nods. "Pickle made her wails sound like whispers."

Zoe's shoulders shake. "That boy does have a pair of lungs on him."

Our gazes meet.

I step forward. "The point is, I'm trying to show the people I love that I care. That I'm there for them too. Like they are for me."

Zoe dips her head.

"I missed you." I embrace my cousin.

Zoe tightens the embrace. "Life sucks without my best friend."

"There's no one I'd rather be trapped in a bathroom with."

We sit on the rug in front of the sink and she tells me about her ventures to get her design business going, and what her brother has been up to, and how she's planning to use the money Mormor gifted her. I recount my failed dates with Wil, his brand deals, and the progress at The Devil's Martini as Zoe carefully paints my nails to match Sven's. We are stuck between the sink and the toilet, but I'm transported to the days and nights we've spent gossiping in Mormor's living room in Norway.

The door groans open. "What are you two doing in here?" Sven points his red fingernails at us.

"Remembering how to be friends," says Zoe.

TWENTY-ONE

THE PATIO DOOR SWEEPS open quieter than the pianissimo at the end of Chopin's *Prelude in E Minor (Op. 28 No. 4)*. The glass partition exposes the ocean stretching ahead still busy the day after the Fourth of July parties. Surfers in wetsuits dot the rolling waves. With Carlee's acai strawberry breakfast bowl in one hand and a banana almond butter smoothie in the other, I find her sipping a matcha latte by the infinity pool.

"You're not supposed to be drinking caffeine." I balance Carlee's food on the side table by her lounger. "The new meds, remember?"

Carlee winces. "I needed a pick-me-up."

Excessive fatigue is one of the warning signs the doctor told me to watch for. "Are you feeling worse?" I perch on the edge of the lounger beside her.

"Yes, but it's not just my health." She offers me her tablet. "Davison's article was published this morning."

I glance down at a photo of Dasher and Carlee laughing. "It's a great picture." My mind scrambles the letters of the headline and I have to run a finger under it to get them to settle.

"Dasher Vows to Save Ex-Blatantly Subtle Lead's New Venture"

Annoyance splatters across my head like a bucket of ice water. "Oh. I see."

"Is that all I'll ever be? That girl who once was the lead in a band, until the younger, prettier version replaced her?" I recognize the emotion in Carlee's voice.

I set aside the tablet, no need to read the article which I'm pretty sure centers on Dasher's new album and not the revamped venue. The headline is clickbait. "For years headlines referred to me as the late Matthew Vella's daughter until they switched it to the rock star's stepdaughter. Now I'm the girl who's dating her stepbrother."

"I should've known that you of all people would understand." Carlee's red-rimmed eyes turn to me. "Why are we reduced to the relationships in our lives? I worked my ass off in this business. Yes, Beau was my collaborator. My bandmate." She massages her elbow. "My friend." Her gaze falls to her hands and she doesn't speak for a moment. Then her chin lifts. "But he didn't carry me. We were partners. We both had a huge hand in the music the band produced. I'm as responsible for Blatantly Subtle's success as he is. Just because I quit the band doesn't mean my talent died."

"You are incredibly talented. I wanted to be you, remember?" I scoot closer. Her chin dips. "Still do. If I had half your strength, nothing would stop me."

Her hand snatches my wrist. "You are phenomenal El. Never mind the pitch-perfect once-in-a-generation voice. Your melodies make people feel . . . everything. It's like you have the ability to translate the human experience into something understood with only eight notes." Her fingers tighten. "When you performed with Dasher, he was beyond impressed. And that man is a spectacular singer."

My neck tenses as I both bask in the praise and shrink away from it. "Wow, can you be my publicist?"

"No, but I can hire you one." The intensity of her gaze crackles along my skin. "It's why I wanted you to work for me. With me. Why you can't give up. You can't deny the world your combination of music and heart. You have to get back on the stage."

I tug my wrist. "I can't."

She holds tighter. "You can. Think about what you are saying no to. Think about the music." Carlee twists to face me. "I've lost the ability to perform and I've been so angry about it for months. I don't know what to dream of. This disease has robbed me of the one thing I was good at. The love of my life.

And no matter how hard I want to fight it, there is no cure. But you—there's nothing stopping you from singing."

I pick up the tablet. "Except them. The relentless prying into every moment off the stage." I shake my head. "I can sing for myself, with Wil, but not in public. Not where the paparazzi will hound me, make up stories in the pursuit of money."

Carlee slumps back in her chair. "Except we all need money. I need patrons to visit my bar. You in the lineup for the Grand Reopening would draw them in."

"Carlee, you can't ask that of me."

She sighs. "I know. But something big must happen or this whole experiment is going to fail."

"It won't fail." I watch her hand quake on her lap. "I believe in us. You have to as well."

She closes her eyes. "I'm so tired."

The ocean spray dots the beach beneath us in white specks. A seagull screeches as it flies too close to the glass divider. Even though I don't like the view, Carlee loves it.

"Listen, why don't you take today off. Enjoy the ocean. Lounge by the pool. I can schedule you a massage. We're still waiting for the sanders for the floors so there's not much to do at the bar. I'll handle things. You rest."

"No." She moves to stand. "It's my responsibility . . ."

I gently press on her shoulder. "I'm your right-hand woman, remember. You hired me to help you. At the bar, and with your health. Let me do my job." She hesitates and I rise. "Be kind to yourself."

Her agreement is slight but I call a ride share and leave the mansion before she can change her mind.

Traffic is light today and the driver drops me in the back parking lot of The Devil's Martini as I'm finishing my own smoothie. I take out the key and halt. The doorframe is splintered.

Slivers of wood lie on the ground and the door hangs open an inch. Ice fills my veins. I scan the area, but today there are no paparazzi or passersby in sight. I walk along the back wall, away from the door. Going inside feels unsafe. Staying out here feels unsafe too. I should've taken Carlee's car. What am I supposed to do now? Sven's training didn't cover potential break-ins. I make it to the sidewalk in front of the building and stand under the nearest tree. Far enough away from the front door that my heart rate slows.

With shaking hands I call Wil. I close my eyes. Please, answer. Please answer.

"Hey, now is not a good—"

"I think someone broke into The Devil's Martini."

"Where are you? Are you safe?" I hear shuffling in the background. "Are they still there?"

The air in my lungs vibrates. "I don't know. I didn't go in. The back door was damaged and hanging open." I press my palm against my forehead. "Wil I—"

"Go to Blend and wait for me there."

The café is not busy this time of day. I order a tea and sit in the corner, staring at the cup, my stomach in too many knots to actually drink anything. Did I not press the alarm buttons in the right order when I rushed to help Sven? Did I forget to press the star key? The air conditioning must be too high because goosebumps pebble my skin. Should I consider sitting outside? A gang of people crowd by the window. I turn away and grasp at my colorless strand for comfort and reassurance. But there's no doubt it was my fault. I was the last one in the building. If the alarm worked, we would've heard from the company that installed it, or the police. How could I be so careless?

Wil bursts through the door and his eyes rake over me. A cord snaps and my hands shake. He crouches by my chair and clamps me in a vise of his embrace.

I bury my face in the crook of his shoulder. "I can't remember if I put the alarm on when I ran out yesterday to help Sven," I muffle into his shirt. Against my ear his heart is racing faster than when I run on the treadmill.

"I don't give a damn about the alarm." His hands bracket my face and he kisses me hard and fast. Then pecks at my forehead and searches my eyes. "I need you to be safe."

"Is she okay?" Zoe tumbles into the coffee shop, holding red-bottomed high heels in her hand. She spots me and puffs her cheeks. "Thank goodness. You can't go scaring me, I just got you back." She cruises by Wil who refuses to let go, sits on the chair next to me, and rubs my back like she's done countless time before. Having her by my side again makes all the difference. My shoulders drop and the loop of worry about The Devil's Martini and guilt over letting the break-in happen quiets.

Zoe's sets her heels on the floor. "I was at Rocker Inc. when you called." She brushes her bangs out of her eyes and glances at the board with the day's specials. "Did they add kombuchas to the menu?"

Wil shakes his head and turns to me. "Are you sure you're not hurt?"

With Zoe and Wil here, the idea I might have overreacted seeps in. "Nothing happened to me, but the door was damaged. I might not have turned on the alarm when I left. Or maybe I didn't close the door properly? We need to go check."

"I texted Sven, he'll meet us there." Zoe fastens her shoes. "No running, though. I don't want to break these."

Sven's truck veers into the parking lot as we walk in. He exits without closing his door. "Are you okay?"

Tears clog my throat. Sven also dropped everything to be here. For me. I nod, failing to hold back the moisture.

"Good." He turns to the door. "Wait until I come out. If I'm not out in five or you hear something, call 911."

For the second time , I tap in 911 on my phone, my finger hovering over the call button. We stand in silence, punctuated by the thumps of my heart and Wil tapping on his leg. Sven reappears and holds the door open. "All clear." He leads us into the bar where cords lay scattered across the floor like a pile of snakes.

"No." I run to the side of the stage and phantom roaring spreads in my ears. The wall is empty. "They stole the headsets."

I turn to where the new microphones should be. "And the mics."

"Doesn't seem like they got much further," says Sven. "They must have grabbed the first easy thing to carry and split."

I point to the new alarm system. "I got your voicemail, and I just ran out. I'm sorry."

"If anyone is at fault it's me." Sven's palm engulfs my upper arm. "You came to help me. I've got this."

Wil's phone rings. "No, she's fine." I glance at him. He mouths "Mateo" as he listens. "We think they just stole some audio equipment."

I pace back and forth. "What am I going to do? We have two bands coming in tonight and no mics."

"I'm sure Rocker can lend you some." Zoe walks around the main room, touching the new leather booths and the unfinished surface of the bar.

"Those are studio mics. Not the same. These have dual-engine transducer technology," I say.

"Hold on, I'll ask." Wil holds the phone away from his ear. "Mateo says he has some Shure's at his place."

I snag the phone. "Are they KSM9's?"

"Um." Mateo sighs on the other end. "No, a Nexadyne 8/S and two KSM11's. Oh, there's a KSM32. Will that do?"

"I don't know. Can you bring them all?"

"I'll be right over," Mateo says into my ear and hangs up.

I should call Carlee and let her know, but she's already not feeling well. If I call her with the bad news, I at least need to have good news too. I walk around the club, making sure nothing else is missing. The cabinets under the bar hang open and one of the shelves hangs loose. The small selection of hard liquor is gone. The beer keg is missing. My breaths come in staccato, flooding my lungs. Alcohol. That's probably why they broke in. At least the bar wasn't fully stocked yet, or we would've lost even more money.

Wil and Sven inspect the damaged back door.

"What's wrong?" Zoe sits on the bar stool. "Um, aside from the obvious."

"I don't know if I should call Carlee." I peel the cuticle on my thumb. "Obviously I will tell her. But she was so pale this morning and kinda down. Honestly, I don't know what the stress might do."

Zoe cocks her head. "El, I know you can't lie, but sometimes it's okay to not tell the truth right away, for a good cause. Think about it this way. Is telling Carlee right now going to make a difference?"

"No. Sven is filing the police report. And handling the equipment, making sure everything is ready for the shows is what she pays me for."

"Then I say wait." Zoe pops off the stool. "Go to her with a plan to fix things. Soften the blow. Rather than reacting in the moment."

I twist my hair. "I guess there's no harm in waiting."

"There is harm, however, in your boyfriend not telling me he's wearing some other designer's shirts." She pouts. "He paired this new company's inferior products with one of my suits and I just about died. Paisley and stripes, El." She smacks her forehead. "Paisley."

"Yeah." I wince. "I barely recognize him these days. All he talks about is these brand deals. Says they are cash cows."

Zoe snorts. "He sounds like Dillon."

My face must show my dread because Zoe grabs my hand. "Wil is so not Dillon. That asshole definitely wears paisley on the reg." I try to smile. "Seriously, El. Wil is right. There is big money in endorsements. One picture of the right celebrity wearing my designs could put me on the map. For us designers, it's the dream. There's no better review for our work."

Wil shouts from the stage, "Mateo's here."

I clamber off the stool and drag myself over to the Wil and Mateo. On the edge of the stage are six boxes of microphones. "I don't know most of them. I have no clue what they sound like."

"Try them out." Mateo points to the stage. "You can keep whichever ones you like. My friend doesn't need them till the end of the month."

That's a lot of microphones to try.

I glance at Wil. "Help me?"

One side of his mouth tips up. "Are you asking me to sing with you?"

"Always."

"I can't say no to you."

Zoe sits in the nearest booth. "Front row seats for a WE concert." She pats the chair next to her. "Aren't we lucky."

Mateo goes over to the monitor sound board and turns on the power, hooking in the new mics and giving us a thumbs-up.

Backstage, I unlock the instrument closet and select a guitar.

"What shall we sing?" Wil jumps onstage and holds out a hand to help me up. "Do you remember *The Only One* by The Troops?"

I grin as I say, "One, two, three," into the mic. That's the song Wil and I first sang together on this stage. The one that won us the open mic contest. Wil takes the acoustic guitar and I hum the opening notes.

His smile is electric and I'm drawn to him like a magnet against steel. He bends and our foreheads touch. This time I have no trouble with the first line, the words pouring out of me like liquid honey. That thing that happened every night we sang on this stage takes over. The world slips away and it's just Wil and me and the music. The timbre of his voice feeds me and I reciprocate, losing myself to the feeling. Our tones blending here and now is better than oxygen.

Wil's every word resonates in my chest. Our voices weave together, our gazes latching, our souls entangling. Zoe's right. He's not Dillon. He'd never use me. The new clothes are just that. The person underneath is the same Wil. The boy I love. The man I want to spend the rest of my life with.

This, here, right now is what matters. This is where we belong.

We both hold the last note as if we don't want the song to end. Wil breaks first. I fling my arms around him and hold on tight. Hold on to my Wil.

Zoe claps and Mateo whistles. I release Wil. "WE still got it."

He beams, picking up on the pun. "WE sure do." He lifts and twirls me, just like he did the night we first met. Except this time when he stops he doesn't release me, but kisses me, soft and slow, his mouth is over mine, with the need to taste me or steal his name from my lips.

Wil's breath caresses my cheek. "You're amazing."

"We're ama—"

The ringtone of Wil's phone drowns out my voice. He sets me down and fishes his phone out. "Harper. What's up?"

My heart sinks as I watch him walk offstage, disappearing into the shadows of the wings.

"Those mics work," says Mateo. "How many more do you need?"

"At least four." I return to the box.

Twenty-Two

I LOVE MY WORK. I love my work. I love my work. I internally repeat my mantra, hoping it sinks in. The recording booth at Rocker Inc. is as high-tech as it gets and everything I've ever wanted is here, but I'm bristling. My stiff fingers slide the gain up, increasing the signal strength for the mic recording El's voice. Although they are in a soundproof recording studio, the speakers play the music for me so I can adjust the levels.

With the newest version of the first verse, Corbin rushes through the switch between the first and second line, merging them together into one sentence. The day I met El, the first time we sang together. It's all hidden in the words that are mine. Corbin doubles up on the second chorus, just like at The Devil's

Martini. I tap in rhythm with the catchy tune, the words rolling around in my mouth.

Going once, going twice.
It's in my head, it's in your eyes.
Going once, going twice.
It's in my head, it's in your eyes.

El echoes the lines of the third chorus and the meaning shifts. No longer a guy pining for a girl, but a reciprocated attraction. Two people. Two voices. The song that started as black ink on the pages of my journal comes alive in the studio.

My song.

But not my song.

In the sound booth, El asks the band to pause. "Lucian, can you come in a little faster on the second verse?" The bassist nods. "And Gideon, I know you want to drive to the chorus but try not to rush it. Corbin and I need time to . . . Wil? What's the word?"

I press the intercom button. "Immerse."

El snaps her fingers. "That's it. Immerse in the lyrics there. We need a few extra beats. To make the chorus really play off our voices."

Gideon nods and El hip checks Corbin. "Ready to try again?"

The lead singer, who has been putty in El's hands all morning, nods and stretches. El gives Gideon the go signal and counts in the band.

Corbin steps closer to her, serenading her like there is a stadium full of people watching. But it's only me. The thick glass separates us but they might as well be a continent away. El and Death Elbow in the room with the music. Me, blocked from the music, essentially only able to turn the sound up or down. Separate from, not part of the music. My throat burns.

El drinks in Corbin's performance, hanging on every word, and the fire sinks to my chest. The pressure to break through this glass, push Corbin away, and confess to El these words are about her, for her, to witness her reaction pushes me out of my chair.

Her voice freezes my hand on the soundproof door to the studio. I can't interrupt the recording. This take is good. It doesn't matter who wrote the words. I'll tell her later. I turn away from the sight, sink back into my chair, and flip a switch, killing the sound. I can't take the torture of watching or listening to them making music anymore.

The side door opens and Dad walks in, followed by Harper carrying two trays of coffee.

"I ordered from Blend," he says. "Thought you might need a break."

I push away from the soundboard. "Thanks."

Dad inches nearer the window. On the other side, El weaves her voice over Corbin's. "You know I've never actually seen El sing live." Dad presses a button and Corbin and El's vocals flood the room. The hairs on my arm rise, reacting to her. She always has an effect on me, but her voice was the first influence, maybe the strongest. The three of us watch the musicians in the other room create magic.

"She knows how to make the song burrow into your head." Harper looks up from her phone. "Guess she learned from the best."

"I wish." Dad sets his coffee on the table. "That's all her. I helped teach her guitar but this talent is all thanks to Matthew Vella. Every recording of his operas I've listened to is proof of how good he was. Why he became so famous so quickly." He crosses his arms. "El had classical voice lessons and sung popular songs around the house all the time as a kid, but that always felt, I don't know, like she was pretending." His mouth falls. "But she wasn't, was she?" He glances my way. "This is her passion."

I shrug, not knowing what to say.

His face brightens and he hands me a tall cup with my name on it. "And producing is yours. At least I got that one right."

I gulp the coffee, the hot liquid singeing my tongue and preventing me from answering. He's right. The plan was to get a sound engineering diploma and turn it into a lucrative job, something more stable than DJing or busking on the streets. Working with Dad makes that plan more solid. I'm lucky. I should be grateful for this opportunity.

Then why do I feel hollow? Like a husk with nothing but air keeping my heart pumping.

As Corbin takes the song to its conclusion, anger I've been stifling suddenly drops across my windpipe like an unspotted barbell. As he sings the last words, he falls down on his knees before El, like a worshipper praying before his muse. He says my words, how sometimes the unexpected is what you were waiting for even if none of it is what you've ever thought possible.

His chest heaves with emotion. El stares down at him, the concentration on her face lit with a smile.

The paper cup crunches in my hand.

On the other side of the glass, Corbin stands, picks up El, and swings her around in a circle. Coffee curdles in my gut. The words "that should be me" scream in my brain and I have to sit down so I don't vomit. I place my head in my hands. What is happening to me?

"Yup." Dad tosses his empty cup into the bin. "That one has Grammy written all over it."

He's right. This song has what it takes to win Corbin and Death Elbow Best Song of the Year. How could it not? It's about the love of my life.

Dad flicks the two-way switch so the people in the other room can hear him as well. "Great job, everyone."

I force myself to join in, congratulating them. Corbin struts like a peacock. Lucian and Xander high-five. Gideon taps a drumstick on one of the cymbals.

El beams.

I should be happy for her. Not . . .

"Does everyone have passports?" Harper interrupts the party, her normally calm and collected voice verging on boisterous.

Everyone turns to Corbin.

He smirks. "I drove to Vancouver to see Blatantly Subtle earlier this year. I have a passport."

"Why?" El pulls the headphones off her ears.

Harper tries to appear professional but can't hide her smile. "I have"—she clears her throat—"great news." She lifts her phone with the open email still on the screen and faces Dad. "I booked us a last-minute spot on *Beat Night*."

There's a whoop in the corner. "Bloody hell." Xander steps forward and slaps Lucian on the back. "When?"

"In three weeks," she says.

"What's *Beat Night*?" Corbin's confused face stands out in the room full of smiles.

Xander throws his head back. "If you got your head out of your ass, you'd know it's only the hottest music show in England, practically all of Europe. The Troops blew up after their interview."

Corbin snickers. "Tweens aren't exactly our vibe."

"Rocker loves that show." El nudges Corbin. "Along with millions of people. It's like our late-night shows and SNL all mixed in one. Audience members line up for hours to get a seat." She smiles through the glass partition at me. "You can't buy that kind exposure."

I hold El's gaze. This is the break I've been waiting for. Death Elbow on the world stage. In the spotlight the week their album drops. Why do I feel nothing? El tilts her head as if to ask, "Aren't you excited?" I force a grin on my face.

Lucian points to Xander. "But it's in England."

"They film in London." Xander raises his hands.

Harper taps her phone. "I'll book the flights."

"Are you coming?" Corbin turns to El.

The smile drops off her face and she steps back. "No. I have to get ready for the Grand Reopening."

"But you have to." He holds his hands wide. "You're practically a member of the band."

El's gaze flicks to me then back at Corbin. "I told you. I can do the recording, but you'll have to find someone else to perform live."

"We'll play a track of her voice for the show." I fiddle with a slider on the sound board before me. "It'll be just like having her there."

Xander lets out a low whistle. "I say we celebrate. Who wants to get drinks?"

The other band members cheer in agreement.

I wave El over. "We have plans early in the morning. Celebration of our own."

"Where are we going?" El's eyebrows lift.

"It's a surprise."

"I'll have a drink for you both," Corbin calls over his shoulder as he swings open the door of the sound booth.

"Let's go to The Devil's Martini." Lucian bounces after him. "El's grandmother made this cocktail with papaya juice and I want another." Gideon nods in agreement.

While the guys collect their phones from the tray on the desk, Dad puts his arm around me. "Good job, son. This song will put Death Elbow on the map."

Dad's praise should be everything. This is what I wanted. Isn't it?

El peers around in confusion. The low sun of the early morning surrounds the entrance to the terminal.

"Are we meeting someone? Is Hanna in LA already?"

I shake my head and point to the suitcases by my side. "I'm taking you on a date."

"That involves flying?"

I take out a travel folder and pass it to her. "And passports."

"Are we going to Germany?" She grasps the handle of her yellow suitcase. "And who packed my bag?"

"Not Germany, closer. And Zoe packed it. You can thank her later." I tug her behind me. "We have first-class seats and a direct flight."

"To?"

I take her to the Air Canada gate. "Canada. Toronto."

"I . . ." Her mouth moves but no words come out.

"I'll get you home tomorrow and you'll be back to start work at three on Wednesday as always." Without our family, Death

Elbow, or Rocker Inc. to intrude, this date is the most expensive one yet, but I don't care. "This date won't be interrupted."

"And a flight is the best thing you could come up with to get rid of possible interferences?"

"We get to watch movies. We get to eat food that's made by actual chefs, can ignore phone calls."

By the time we land in Toronto and go through customs it's late afternoon. The driver I prearranged hails us by the exit.

The car veers onto the highway. "One more country we can say we've been to together."

"We should go to Norway next." El crushes into me and I soak up the feel of her. "Mormor's house is amazing. And the food. And the nature. You'll love it."

"Dad insists Sylvia will make it there this Christmas. If only to get her out of the house."

El rests her head on my shoulder. "If they are going, you are going too."

The sky is blue and I can feel the heat of the humid day through the window. With the city on one side and the lake on the other, Toronto feels a bit like California.

The bellman whisks our suitcases away. We climb the steps and I take El's hand as we cross the two-story lobby, on full display. Nothing untoward happens. No cameras, professional or otherwise, snap our picture. No phones shoved in our faces. No nagging questions. We are just another couple. As Harper directed, we bypass the reception desk and head to the private elevators indicating Gold Level. Known for hosting celebrities, this hotel has a separate floor for private VIP check-ins. The ornate doors of the elevator glide together, shutting out the world. I whisper in El's ear, "Hopefully you like what Zoe packed, because I had very specific instructions for her."

El's cheeks turn pink. "I'm suddenly afraid."

"Trust me."

Her gaze holds mine. "I do."

The base of my skull fizzes like a cascade of tiny fireworks.

The Gold Level lives up to its name with saffron art deco geometric accents shimmering against textured walls. The hotel receptionist passes us two key cards. "Cocktails are being served in the Gold Lounge. Enjoy your stay."

I open the door to our room, where the luxury theme turns to gold and silver with soft gray carpets, a sleek slate sectional couch, and heavy curtains framing the wall. The view from the Royal York Hotel gives a picture of a city skyline, skyscrapers, and Scotiabank Arena.

"The plan is to change and then our date starts." I massage El's bicep and revel in her melting into me.

"Or we could just stay in. In bed. Alone."

I press my lips into El's hair. "There's something I've been longing to see you wear and today I finally get to do that."

Her grin is infectious. "Are you trying to compete with Rocker at how elaborate your surprises are?"

"Like father, like son I guess."

El wheels her suitcase through the double doors into the bedroom where the giant king-sized bed I requested awaits. Her idea of staying in and not going anywhere reenters my brain. She heads for the bathroom. "Do I have time to shower?"

"We're leaving in an hour," I say as she closes the door behind her. "Or would you like me to join you in the shower?"

Her head peaks around the door. "After the date. Definitely."

I cross the room. "We have time."

She holds up her hand. "Oh no. I don't want you to be the reason we miss this date."

It's impossible to stifle my glee as I open my suitcase. The tux Zoe gave me is black, the crisp white shirt fits perfectly. Zoe promised it's durable and that I shouldn't be concerned about ruining the fabric, but maybe this date idea was too much. I put in my custom cufflinks and slip on the black leather shoes.

There's a creak behind me and I spin, a flutter at the base of my throat. I've waited too long for this. Since that night she didn't make it to the Starlight Foundation Gala.

El emerges and I no longer question my elaborate plan. Because she's perfect.

I saw the dress hanging in Zoe's pool house the night El was supposed to wear it to Death Elbow's concert, but on her the dress transforms. The light blue highlights the deeper color of her eyes, causing my heart to stutter. Zoe is a genius. The airy fabric falls over one shoulder, leaving El's creamy skin bare on the other, and golden heels give El some extra inches. My gaze languishes at the slit over El's left leg that exposes most of her thigh, which is my downfall. My hands tremble.

"This was the only thing that wasn't lingerie." She lifts her gaze to mine. "Is this what you've been looking forward to?"

I swallow hard. "What I imagined isn't even a quarter of what you actually look like in this dress." I stride over to El and wrap my arms around her waist. "You are so damn beautiful. And mine." I press my forehead to hers and inhale her smell, smile, sighs. The room around us falls away and I sway to the music that comes alive when I'm with her. I hum the song we've been writing together and we turn in place. Her voice intertwines with mine.

Words and melody flow, and we riff and improvise on the song that's ours.

Our fingers weave together, our chests touching, our souls entangling. This is the life I want. Every moment doing this. El does too. Guaranteed. "Let's live together."

El stops, and her lips stretch. "You'd want that?"

My heart leaps at the concept. Waking up to the sight of her every morning. Going to bed with her every night. Cooking meals in our kitchen. Eating them at our table. A room filled with our guitars, maybe her harpsichord, a small recording studio. Her eyes peer up at me, glistening with happiness. No sneaking out of Carlee's house. Her being in the other room, not across a hidden pathway.

I kiss her forehead. "There is nothing." My mouth grazes her cheek. "I want." I place a feather-light kiss on her lips. "More."

"Nothing?" She mouths against my lips.

My fingers bunch in the material of her dress, yanking her closer, our lips crushing together. I kiss El with new hunger, my hand diving into the red bob of her hair, holding her to me. I give her my heart to do with as she pleases, because it's no longer mine. I kiss her with the lust of a future with this girl, this woman. I kiss her because I can.

Because no one is watching.

Because I want to share an apartment with her. A life with her. A forever.

We break apart, gasping for air.

"So that's a maybe?" I ask, one eyebrow up.

"That's a yes." Her grin shines brighter than the sun through the windows.

"Yes." I shout to the ceiling. "She said yes."

She buries her face in my shirt. "The other guests will hear."

"I don't care." I pull her closer. "We'll start the search for a place as soon as we get back."

She nods into my chest.

My plan to spoil El with Toronto's award-winning butter tarts slips away like melted butter. We don't eat at the Michelin-star restaurant I have reservations for. We don't check out the club Mateo got us VIP access to.

We don't make it out of the hotel room until it's time for our flight back to LA.

Twenty-Three

THE FLAKY SWEETNESS OF the last butter tart Wil flew in from Toronto for the third week in a row since our date barely masks the bitter taste in my mouth from another cookie-cutter song by the boy band I'm considering as a headliner in the fall.

Zoe's text breaks through the overproduced demo.

Zoe: Still on for tonight?

Me: Still not telling me what we're do-ing?

Zoe: I'm not going to spoil your surprise.

Zoe: I'll drop by early, catch the last set.

I have a suspicion that's code for "I'll make sure you're dressed appropriately for this adventure we're going on and do your makeup." It hasn't even been a month since my last surprise. I'm still living on the high of Wil and my date in Canada. I might want to live there someday. Access to butter tarts would be a bonus.

> Me: If I hate it, you promised we can leave early.

> Zoe: If you hate it, I'll make sure you don't have to suffer. But I know you and you'll thank me later.

A little thrill shoots up my spine. The only people who've known me longer than Zoe are my mother and Mormor. Not talking to Zoe for months was ripping holes in my heart. Mending them took hours of conversation, even after we cleared the air in Sven's bathroom. I thought we'd snap back to the Zoe and El of my childhood, but things are different.

My love for my cousin is the same, but I'm more conscious of what's going on in her life, not just blabbering about mine. We didn't come up with a contract of what our friendship will become going forward, but there is a new unspoken layer of care and openness to being in each other's lives. She does know me, and I know her.

> Me: See you soon.

"El."

I turn the screen of my phone off as Carlee strides across the floors Mr. Peters varnished to a high sheen. With new paint, new lights, and a new sound system, The Devil's Martini is hardly recognizable yet the same. Mr. Peters stripped the floor and somehow made it come across as both new and perfectly part of the classic character we're trying to maintain. The man is a hard worker, much like his grandson.

Carlee has her business face on. "We have a problem," she says, and my heart swoops. The insurance company confirmed they will cover the stolen microphones, and Carlee agreed with Sven to reinforce the back door and change the locks. What now? "Dasher's manager called." She perches on the bar stool. "Dasher has the flu that's going around. He thought he'd feel better, but his doctor forbids him from singing for several days."

"He won't be able to perform tonight?"

Carlee's reply is a sigh and a nod.

We cleared this day for Dasher. People are coming to see him and the updated space. I rub my eyes. A hole forms in the schedule I've meticulously managed, ensuring we had acts in place around the days we were closed for major renovations.

"Can the warm-up act play longer?" Carlee's eyes plead for a yes.

"The folk duo?" I shake my head. "Maybe an extra song, but they have a gig right after."

Carlee massages her temples.

I check my phone. Seven o'clock in big numbers shouts that I have less than an hour to find a replacement. "I can ask Wil if Death Elbow can come in." I twirl a strand of my hair. "But they played that concert in San Diego last night."

The reviews this morning raved about the event, calling it the concert of the summer. Death Elbow's six-song set even got a shout-out from Daniel Davison.

"They are doing some posh radio interview tonight." At the far end of the bar, Mr. Peters peels painter's tape off the mirror-backed shelves he stained and varnished yesterday. "Wil took them to see Harper for an extra media training session."

How does Mr. Peters know more than I do? I tap the heel of my shoe. It explains why Death Elbow and Wil were a no-show for rehearsals here today. I love the guy, but one fancy night together doesn't make up for how little I've seen him this month. My long hours and chaotic schedule haven't helped. No matter how much we text and call, I feel like I'm less and less a part of his life. I stuff my hair into a topknot, the elastic catching on my waves. We just need to get past the reopening and Death Elbow's trip to England and album release. Once we find a place together, I will get to see him every day.

I hope.

"Everyone I've called is busy or out of town." Carlee adjusts the gold and silver bangles on her wrist. "I don't see another choice." She groans. "I'll have to fill the spot."

I wag a finger. "You can't." My head joins the side-to-side motion of my hand. "Your health . . ." I try to find the right words to express my concern.

"I'm not that ill." Carlee eyes me like Mom does when Pickle tries to pull himself up using the kitchen stools. "I can still sing."

I pull on the sleeve of my shirt. "It's not that. Of course you can sing." This is awkward. I lower my voice so Mr. Peters can't hear me. "It's just that after the infusion of Ocrevus this morning, the doctor recommended bed rest. You're not even supposed to be here today."

"Good thing I am." She throws her hands in the air. "I can't start my new business venture as a musical venue owner by not having music for the audience." Carlee places an elbow on the part of the bar that's already varnished and dry. Mr. Peters even painted the dividers to match the black accents on the menu Mateo designed for Mormor's cocktails. "The show must go on."

The Grand Reopening is set for seventeen days from now. Despite Carlee's dismay at the Dasher article, we've had a good audience most nights when we have bands booked. If tonight holds to the trend, we might even hit capacity.

"We could push back the tables, play Dasher's new album, and turn it into a dance night."

Carlee's lips pinch. "This isn't a club. People come here ex-pecting live music." She sets her jaw. "If we set me up with a chair I can hold the guitar in my lap. That way if my leg gives out again, I'm already seated. I can play acoustic versions of old Blatantly Subtle songs."

I glance at the empty stage, the single spotlight illuminating the mic stand. I know Carlee's success depends on her reputation, but the tough act she's putting on is not a positive trait of her character. On tour I watched her almost pass out onstage, her perfectionism kicking in to give her fans the show they expected. The image of Carlee unable to pronounce the words to one of her songs, leaning on me for support, makes my chest constrict. That can't happen again.

"Can't El sing?" Mr. Peters butts in.

Carlee flattens her hand on the bar. "That's not part of our deal."

"But she sings beautifully. I've heard her and my Wil when they were busking in Bremen. I bet she's better than this Danger."

"Dasher," I correct.

I chew on the cuticle by my fresh blue nails, courtesy of Zoe's attempt to stop me from biting my nails.

Carlee's head tilts. "I can't ask that of you."

"Of course you can. You need a singer. El can sing. I don't see the problem."

Of course Mr. Peters doesn't. He's been in LA for only two months and the paparazzi haven't caught on that he's related to Wil. Mr. Peters lives in the bubble. The one I'm trying to maintain.

Mr. Peters's face scrunches. "Don't you want to help your friend?"

I can't let her get on that stage. The collar of my T-shirt pushes against my windpipe, and I tug at it. There's no one else that can help. My hands shake and I press my palm over the churning beneath my collarbone. I'm Carlee's right-hand woman. I have to fix this.

Carlee's head tilts. "I'm not asking you to do this."

I pace in front of Carlee's stool. "I have some covers ready, and if I add in a few songs of my originals, I should have enough for a full set." Carlee's gaze meets mine. I twist my fingers together. "I can sing."

"Are you sure?" Carlee sits up.

"Just this once. For you." I pull my lips into what I hope passes for a smile and glance around the much-improved venue. "For The Devil's Martini." I pull back my shoulders despite the quickening taps of my heart against my ribcage. "The show must go on." I belt Queen's famous line as if to prove I can sing.

Carlee's mouth transitions into a smile. "This means a lot." Carlee's fingers find mine, give them a tiny squeeze, and disappear as if I've imagined the tender gesture. "I appreciate your help. With The Devil's Martini, with my life, with making sure I don't crash and burn either of them."

The part inside of me that was unsure quiets and steals away, leaving the familiar feeling of pre-show jitters. Tonight, I don't hate it. I don't hate it at all. I text Wil.

Me: I'll be singing onstage tonight.

An hour, six texts, and no replies from Wil later, I hang up as my call to him goes to voicemail. I'm sitting in a chair in the green room, the warm-up folk duo on the small tv screen mounted to the wall. Their vocals blend well but this song would work better if they slowed it to andante. I wish Wil's voice would calm the nerves that are dancing across my scalp. But I can't rely on him all the time. This was my decision, and everything will be fine.

I watch my reflection in the mirror as Zoe applies the most dramatic smokey eye I've ever had. "I'm singing at The Devil's Martini, not performing *Tosca* at the Met."

Mormor tuts. "A splash of dramatic is always good for the soul." She runs the straightening iron along the bottom of my hair. No more wigs for my performances.

Zoe's full lips twist in a mischievous grin. "This look is hot right now. You need to embrace edginess. And I need your face to complement my design. For my socials. If your boyfriend won't wear my clothes in public anymore, I need a new brand ambassador."

I glance at the one-shoulder cut-out top hanging on the door. A braided green around the neckline and hem contrasts the trim-fit cream silk body made to match the tight tiny leather shorts Zoe's paired with the top. I rub my finger along the side seam of the well-worn jeans I rescued from my donation pile in my old walk-in closet at Rocker's. "Are you sure that isn't a bit . . . fancy?"

Zoe's head jerks. "Are you doubting my design?"

"Never." I nudge her shin. "It's just . . . I don't want to . . ."

"Make a big deal out of this?" Zoe snaps the eyeshadow case closed. "Sorry to tell you, El, your singing is always a big deal."

"I'm just covering for a no-show—"

Mormor interrupts me. "I know this is a 'one-time thing' tonight." I think this is the first time I have ever seen Mormor use air quotes, which stops my protest. "All the more reason to be your fabulous self." She puts some hair product on her hands. A gentle aroma of citrus surrounds me. Mormor runs her fingers along the part in my hair. "I finally get to hear you sing onstage."

My cheeks grow hot. This gig is turning into a much bigger deal than I intended.

Zoe spins the chair and almost dumps me on the floor. I touch the material of the top and even though the design is closer to that edgy feel Zoe seems to be pushing me into, the fabric is soft against my fingers, like it won't strangle me or make my skin itch mid-song. The leather shorts, however, aren't something I can imagine myself squeezing into. "I'll wear the top, but I keep the jeans."

Zoe makes a motion for me to twirl. "These are cute on you. I'll allow it." She hands me the platform shoes I've loved ever since she introduced them in her collection. "We'll wait for you outside."

Dressed, I open the door to the hallway off the green room.

"I knew it would make your eyes pop." Zoe aims her phone at me. Mormor smiles at both of us.

I smile back.

"Can I stay back here?" Mr. Peters is slumped on one of the benches he insisted on redoing. "I'm too old for that." He nods to the packed main room of The Devil's Martini.

"Nonsense." I take a seat beside him. "You've done half the work to renovate this place. You have more energy than most of the people out there." I bump my shoulder into his. "But you can watch from here." Just like Wil did the last time I stood on this stage alone. The night he arranged for my surprise video shoot, when I wasn't confident I could walk out there without him. But just like the first night I met Wil, he knew exactly what to do to infuse me with strength. Maybe Wil isn't just the Pickle whisperer. He's the El whisperer.

"These are the best seats in the whole venue." Mormor sits on Mr. Peters's other side. The arm's-length distance or more they've maintained ever since they met disappeared sometime over the last weeks. If I didn't witness the initial cat-and-dog bickering, I'd assume they are . . . friends? Seems Griffith Observatory worked its magic again.

I stand and pick up my guitar that Mormor brought for me from Carlee's. Applause starts as soon as the duo's song ends. I should invite these two again, maybe for the headliner spot.

"Well." Zoe squeezes my shoulder. "I guess that's my clue to join the audience." She shakes the phone in her hand. "And play official videographer. You'll have plenty of fodder for social media."

My pulse starts to hammer against my eardrums at the thought of what posting my performance might stir up. The paparazzi have been quiet lately. Just the way I like it.

Zoe flips her hair over her shoulder. "Kidding. I'm sure Wil will want to see this."

The panic subsides and I walk to the side of the stage. Every step I take strips the confidence my weeks of performing with Wil and months onstage with Blatantly Subtle equipped me with. I might as well be the Melodie of a year ago, a green newbie at my first open mic. But then I had Wil to get me out of the frozen zone. Without him? Doing this feels off. I shake out my wrists and give the folk song duo who are shuffling off the stage two thumbs-up.

"Now, as a special treat." Carlee glances at me and I see how grateful she is. "I'm pleased to introduce . . . El Vella!"

I put the strap of my guitar over my head and let my feet carry me onstage to the riotous applause of the audience. My blood pumps faster. The spotlight blinds me as I adjust the microphone to my height.

"Thank you for that warm welcome." This is not singing, but I am not frozen. I'm thawing into the familiar burn of anticipation. I move the mic stand closer to the ledge as if months haven't passed between now and my last public performance. "I know you were expecting Dasher tonight, but he asked me to stand in."

Out in the darkness, someone gives a disappointed aww.

"I know I'm not him, but here's my version of Dasher's hit." I launch into my rendition of the popular song. Sound carries differently in the packed room and I expand my voice until it fills every corner of The Devil's Martini. The crowd cheers me on and I lose myself to the coming-home feeling of my fingers pressing on strings, my guitar pick strumming an easy tempo, my voice flying through the changes in pitch, glissandos, and the cadence of each cover song of my set.

The crowd picks up the energy I send them and throws it back. I soak it in, lace my blood with its power, and slip into a life where I never abandoned this high, where I continue to fill this cup of mine song after song.

My planned set comes to an end. "I hope you didn't miss Dasher too much," I say, as disappointment that the time flew too fast surges through me.

"Play *Don't Give Me Comfort*," someone in the crowd calls out. A few cheers follow.

I don't stop to consider how long I've been onstage and launch into the first song Wil and I wrote together.

This feels amazing. Better than singing with Blatantly Subtle. I wouldn't trade that experience for anything. I was lucky Carlee picked me to join the band, but she was also right. Being on this stage as myself, playing what I want to play, how I want to play—it is exhilarating.

Even though I haven't sung it for months, I slip into the melody without missing a beat. Wil's words spill from me, familiar and urgent, weaving the story of how I felt before I met him. Lost and scared and desperate to prove myself, separate and different from my parents' fame.

I don't feel that way anymore. Not quite, anyway.

Like with Zoe, things have shifted. The old me who described these feelings to Wil doesn't exist anymore. She was afraid to stand on a stage by herself. Afraid to be recognized because of who her stepdad was but not be worthy of recognition for her own talents.

I'm not that girl anymore.

The desire to do things on my own is still there, but the urgency to prove myself has molded into just wanting to be happy with myself. It's not all or nothing anymore. I can earn money and accept Zoe's freebies. I can enjoy being onstage and helping my friends. I can work hard and spend time with my family. I can argue with my cousin and still have her love and support.

After the first verse I kick it up to the right tempo, the guitar and I playing together. I slow down the third chorus and end the song. Hollers and hoots erupt from the crowd. I don't move, too stunned by what just happened. The joy buzzing in my veins. I feel so alive.

At the edge of the stage, Carlee flags my attention, giving me the extend the set sign. I don't have any more covers to sing. So I sing *Orange*, and then the audience shouts, "More."

"Glad everyone liked that one." I take a deep breath, unsure what Wil will think of this. "Does anyone want to hear a new song?"

The applause is ferocious. "This is something my boyfriend and I have been working on."

In the void in front of me someone yells, "WE."

I grin into the spotlight. "Good memory. Our fans merged Wil and El into WE. We," My cheeks lift, "adopted the name. I wish he were here tonight with me, but I don't think he'll mind me giving you a sneak peek."

The melody I wake up to every morning flows from my guitar. I play the bridge I added. The words Wil and I crafted in Canada fit into the strums and the song morphs into a complete rendition I haven't sung with Wil yet. Several couples in the audience stand and sway in sync to the song about love.

Love conquers all the movies said

but when I'm lonely in my bed

I think of you

Tears well behind my eyes. Happy tears. Maybe the happiest tears I've shed in a while. I don't want the song to end, to walk off the stage. My voice cracks on the last chorus as I watch the audience wave their hands in the air. Our love that's been woven into every syllable and notes covers The Devil's Martini in a warm hug. One even I would welcome.

My hands still when I run out of notes and silence greets me.

A clap breaks the stillness, followed by another and another. I let go of my guitar and breathe. A cacophony of cheers surrounds me.

"Thank you, thank you all," I mumble into the mic and wave so hard that my hand hurts more than my cheeks from all the smiling. The song is good. Our song is good. Maybe better than good.

Carlee, Zoe, Mormor, and Mr. Peters meet me in the wings of the stage.

"That was amazing." Zoe gives me a side hug.

Mr. Peters rubs his chin. "My grandson wrote that with you?"

Mormor grips Zoe's and my hands. "My beautiful talented granddaughters."

I sit and set the guitar down on the bench, my knees not able to hold me anymore. I did it. I sang onstage by myself again.

And it felt right.

Carlee sits beside me. "Do you see it now? Why I couldn't choose you as my replacement for Blatantly Subtle?" She stares out on the stage. "You held that room in the palm of your hand." She grasps my shoulders and makes me face her. "You are a star."

Her eyes glisten with unshed tears and pride and encouragement. All those are for me and because of me. I wipe my cheeks and let her certainty sink in. The ball of emotions that sits in my gut unravels. My chest tingles with belief, hers and mine.

"I know you said this is a one-time thing, but I have to ask." Carlee takes my hands in hers. "Would you perform for me at the Grand Reopening of this place we've built together?" She squeezes my fingers with her trembling ones. "You don't have to answer now, but please consider it."

I take a deep breath. Do I want to step out on that stage again and sing?

I think I know the answer.

Twenty-Four

Wil

THE VIEW OPA ADMIRED when I gave him a tour of this apartment shows the beginning of a stunning LA sunset, azure melting into a soft pink that makes me think of El's lips. My abdominals tighten. She'll love this, I convince myself.

I climb off the ladder, push the bed into place, and admire my handiwork. Since the apartment was empty, moving in early was only a matter of paying Mateo's friend's rent and a bonus to Mateo to move out. Worth the extra money. So was paying the mattress store for the rush delivery of the one piece of furniture I need for tonight. After insisting I know nothing about thread count, Zoe brought over sheets and pillows earlier this afternoon and gave the place her stamp of approval.

She's the one who volunteered to get El here for the ultimate surprise. She'll drive El over after work tonight and I'll open the bottle of champagne chilling in the fridge for the two of us to toast our new home.

I smile at the California king dominating the room. No more squishing myself into El's single bed. I know this apartment is what El wants. A vein in my neck thrums. We just have to get past the money aspect.

I wash my hands over my face. Everything will be fine.

The rap on the door draws me into the living room.

"I brought beer." Mateo beams as he lifts the six-pack of Becks. "Met this guy in the lobby."

Sven towers over Mateo, face stoic as usual. The two men are polar opposites, Mateo dark and slim, Sven muscular and blond.

"Okay then." I point to the supplies in the corner that Opa helped me pick out this morning. "Are you ready to paint?"

Sven pushes up the sleeves of his Henley. "You promised cupcakes."

Sweets. The way to Sven's heart. Someday a lucky woman is going to discover the gentle giant's secret. I slap Sven on the back. "Blend is making a special delivery of a dozen. Thanks for helping me spruce this place up."

An hour later drop cloths, paint trays, and three rollers sit on the living room floor as I call the coffee shop that kept me fed on day-olds and awake on caffeine for months last year. We managed to paint two walls the soft silver tone Mateo insisted would go with anything El and I decide to put in here.

I groan. "They're not answering."

A muscle ticks in Sven's jaw.

"What?" I open the fridge and hand Mateo two beers. "The new manager swore they would deliver here."

Mateo unscrews the cap off and offers a beer to Sven.

"Not drinking today." Sven crosses his arm.

"Relax a little." Mateo wiggles a green bottle. "You're off duty."

I want to laugh at the concept of a relaxed Sven. I try Blend again while taking a swig. The cool liquid hits my tongue and I'm reminded of Bremen. My old home.

"I'm never off duty," says Sven.

"This is your first time in Wil's new place. We have to christen it." Mateo gives Sven the expression I've seen convince bouncers to let us into the club. "You wouldn't want to be rude."

Sven grabs the bottle, twists off the cap, and chugs half the liquid in one impressive gulp. How does Mateo persuade people to do what he wants so easily, and can I learn that trick?

I hang up on Blend. "How about pizza?"

Mateo pops the lid off the last beer as Sven annihilates the second half of his drink.

"And maybe some more beer," I say.

My phone buzzes in my hand.

Corbin: WTF?

My Corbin's-about-to cause-trouble radar blares.

Me: What's wrong?

Corbin: You got a new place?

A pit opens in me. How did he find out? Death Elbow, and particularly their lead singer, will not ruin this night for El and me.

Corbin: Rocker told your news after the interview.

A video call from Corbin comes in. I pinch the bridge of my nose but answer.

Corbin's cocky grin fills my screen. "You moved?" He's shouting like he's on speakerphone in Zoe's convertible.

"Moving."

Sven and Mateo pick up their paint rollers with a clank behind me.

Xander juts his head into frame. "Are you having a party?"

"No." I rub my chin. "Just a couple of friends helping me paint the place."

The phone screen skids to the right and Lucian's grin makes an appearance. "I love painting. Used to do it as a part-time job. It's so zen when you're in the zone."

Mateo peers up over my shoulder. "We could use your skills."

I elbow him.

"What?" He shrugs. "More hands, light work, or something like that."

Off-screen, Corbin laughs at someone else in the car. "Wil. Text us your address. We'll bring beer."

Mateo beams in an I-like-this way. "We do need more beer."

I glance at Sven, expecting him to give me an out.

"And cupcakes," says Sven.

I hang up, text the guys my address, and take a photo of the room. "Should I text it to El?"

"Surprise, remember?" Mateo goes for my phone, and I shove it into my pocket.

The pizza and Death Elbow arrive at the same time and I instruct the concierge to send them up. When I open the door, each member of the band has a girl on their arm. Or in Corbin's case, clinging to him like a spider monkey.

"Whoa." I hold up a hand. "I didn't say bring guests."

"Roan here gave us a lift." Xander jabs a thumb over his shoulder where a leggy brunette taller than Lucian holds a bottle of dark liquid so large it could be a mini keg. "The least we could do was offer her a thank you drink."

This is not at all what I needed tonight. I stand in the doorway, arms crossed.

"One drink?" Mateo shouts from behind. "We'll do a proper housewarming party later."

Exactly when did I become the guy who puts a stop to a good time? I used to be the life of the party. I roll my eyes and step away from the door. Whatever powers Mateo has apparently work on me too. I let the motley crew in. "One drink."

I tip the pizza delivery woman as everyone introduces themselves. Mateo tries his "kiss the girl's hand" move on the girl Lucian introduces as Lola and she blushes. Lucian tugs her closer and his perma-smiling face stills. Mateo nods and backs away. Sven and Gideon eye each other.

Sven tips his head an inch in greeting.

Gideon echoes the act with one of his own.

Sven opens the pizza box, retrieves a slice, and eases the container across the kitchen counter to Gideon, who takes a slice and wordlessly passes it back to Sven.

I wonder if Gideon likes to work out.

"Move over." Xander shoulders me away from the fridge door and shoves aside the champagne I had chilling for later to stuff the two cases of beer and a box of cupcakes they brought into the empty shelves. "Do you have glasses?"

I grind my teeth. Two champagne glasses, but they're for later. "Only coffee mugs." I know my girl and she'll need coffee tomorrow morning. The real reason I went to Blend earlier was for freshly ground coffee and a French press.

Lucian opens the cupboard over the sink. "That'll have to do."

I slap his hand away and retrieve the two cups I stowed in the cubby above the counter by the fridge.

"For Roan and Lola," says Lucian. I glance at Lola, who has drifted back to Mateo and is whispering in his ear.

The good humor on Lucian's face falls away as he follows my gaze. "Is he stealing my date?"

I wince. "I wouldn't put it past him."

Lucian grabs two mugs and a bottle that might be tequila and storms back to the smiling blond.

"Wil." Xander hands me a beer. "Is this the penthouse?"

I can handle my liquor but tonight I need to be clear-headed. One small gulp of the chilled beer helps cool the ire at this not party that is not occurring. "Technically."

Corbin tips back the bottle he brought and downs two mouthfuls. The two girls bracketing him watch his Adam's apple move up and down. Roan's hand slips into his barely buttoned shirt while the other girl no one introduced me to practically dry humps his left leg. Corbin slams the bottle down on the counter. "How many bedrooms in this place?"

Nope.

Not happening.

I tap my fingers against the solid granite. There is no way Corbin is having sex in my place before I do. Or ever. I push the can of beer away from him. No one will be throwing this through any windows. "Two. But no furniture yet. We'll convert one into a studio so El can record in there."

Corbin's mouth twists. "A room for her?" He rolls his eyes.

"Every room is for her." I snatch the bottle from him and want to take a gulp. But alcohol won't quell the burn in my throat from Corbin's insinuation. "We are moving in together."

An eyebrow rises on the lead singer's face. "Rash move."

Xander runs over, his shirt soaked in beer. "Do you have a towel?"

I hold up a finger. When I return from the bedroom with a towel Zoe brought with the linens, Dad's greatest hits blast across the room from someone's phone. Mateo now has Lola and a redhead I don't know the name of twirling in his hands while a foot away a shirtless Xander and a pouting Lucian have a line of crumpled beer empties. I pick up the cans and toss the towel at Xander who immediately uses it to slap Lucian across the rear.

In the kitchen, I dump the empties into a bag. Sven and Gideon are doing some kind of leg stretch, silently using beer cans as tiny dumbbells.

"Sven. Don't you have to work in the morning?" If anyone can shut down this party, it's the big guy.

"Nope." He balances another can on his thigh. Gideon mimics the move.

I turn away, choking down my disappointment. Looking for an escape, I see my front door is cracked and I dash for the hallway, expecting an angry mob of neighbors or police officers. Instead, I find Corbin, Roan, and three new people.

"Here he is." Corbin waves me over. "Wil, these are you new neighbors."

I nod at the trio. The smile I plaster on my face wouldn't convince anyone that I'm currently happy.

"Or I guess you're the new one here." Corbin takes a sip of the bottle in his hands. "I invited them to the party."

"It's—" I stop myself. It is a party. There's no denying that. But I'm putting a stop to it after the introductions. I hold out my hand. "It's nice to meet you."

"I told them we'd play a set. Personal concert to welcome you to the building."

I crack my knuckles. "I don't sing."

"But I saw you and El Vella play at The Devil's Martini last October." Roan attaches herself to Corbin again. "Is she coming?"

My chin lifts. "She'll be here later."

"Great." Corbin slaps me on the back. "Where's your guitar?" He doesn't wait for my answer, striding through what seems to have become the temporary dance floor. "Bet it's in one of the bedrooms."

I scramble to catch up with him, but he beats me to the door, barging in and somehow spilling beer on me in the process. Corbin lets out a slow whistle. "This is nice. I could see myself living here."

"Thanks." I open my closet to get a clean T-shirt. This one had paint on it anyhow. I whip it off and reach for the new one when Corbin pushes past me and snatches up my guitar case. "There it is." He tosses it on the bed. "Request, ladies?"

I spin around. "Put that back."

"Oh, please." Roan runs a hand along the rim of the case. "Just one song?"

I squeeze the back of my neck. "One song and then the party is over."

"Sure." Corbin plunks himself on the edge of the bed. "So what should we play?"

"Ooh. Do that one you and El sang." Roan snaps her fingers repeatedly. "It was a color I think."

"You mean *Orange*?"

Her finger flies in my direction. "That's it."

"Wouldn't you rather hear a Death Elbow song?" Corbin stretches back on his forearms. "Wil can play and I'll sing."

"No." Roan's voice is dreamy, like the darkening sky outside has her under a spell. "*Orange* is really good." She slurs a little at the end.

I bite the inside of my cheek not to grin. She's here because of Corbin, but she wants to hear me sing. I shake out my fingers, ignoring the way my pulse races. I put it down to nerves and pick up my guitar. "*Orange* it is."

The wood of the guitar is cool against the bare skin of my chest. I spend a few moments making sure the instrument is tuned and clear my throat. Roan slips to the floor and stares up at me like I'm her idol. The first few chords are rough. It's been far too long since I played this progression. El always sang the lyrics but I listened to her countless times, obsessed with how she turned this song into musical sunshine. I channel her now and launch into the first verse.

Twenty-Five

I ADJUST THE SILK scarf Zoe insisted I wrap over my eyes after we left The Devil's Martini. "Is this really necessary?"

"Yes." Her convertible comes to a halt. "It's all part of the surprise."

"Don't you think I've had enough surprises?" The buzz from my performance keeps my blood coursing faster than it had over the last six months. "Can't we do this another time?" The feel of singing to a live audience is one I can't quite explain to Zoe or Mormor but that Wil will understand, because he felt it. We felt it last year on the same stage. Why hasn't he still answered my texts? "I need to talk to Wil."

"Indulge me for a few more minutes." An E-flat chimes as she opens her car door. "I'm sure you'll be happy." Cool air brushes my face. "Now give me your hand and trust me."

Zoe assists me out of the car and we walk a few feet. There's a staccato B beep. Another door noise, followed by the sound of something that must be an elevator. The swooping sensation intensifies as we move up. The hum of the elevator's engine plays a rendition of a toddler playing Hot Cross Buns enough times on repeat to suggest we're going to a high floor.

The elevator bobs and when we step out muffled music fills my ears. "Zoe, I told you, I'm too tired to go to a club."

My cousin tugs me along, no longer careful. "It's not a club." There's a tightness in her voice. The music increases tenfold and Zoe yells, "What the hell?"

"Zoe?" There's no answer. I scrape the scarf off my face and blink into the bright lights of a hallway. The sconces appear familiar. The charge that hasn't stopped coursing in my veins electrifies my senses. I know this hallway. Number five still hangs on the door. This is the doorway to Mateo's apartment, the one he's housesitting.

I quicken my pace, now thrilled about my surprise. I walk through the doorway to find a group of strangers all jumping in the living room to the thrum of blasting music. I spot Mateo in the crowd. Is this another one of his infamous parties, like the HallowRade Wil and I played at last Halloween? My pulse speeds at the prospect of playing a set with Wil. Or two. We didn't get to finish our second set last time.

Mateo's glassy eyes meet mine and a slow grin takes over his face. "Elllllllll." He encases me in a bear hug before I can protest.

"What do you think?" He swings a hand around the place, nearly knocking out a smiling blond dancing at the edge of the improvised dance floor. "Now the party can truly start."

I step out of his clutches. "Where's Wil?

"He's waiting for you in the bedroom with"—Mateo winks—"his guitar."

Mateo laughs like he's told me the funniest joke and the blond woman snakes her arm around him, drawing him away from me. He sinks into the moving bodies of unsteady dancers.

I stretch up on my tiptoes to find the direction of the hall l but catch sight of a familiar hulking blond instead. Sven has a hip resting against the counter between the kitchen and the living room, a can of beer in one hand and a trail of icing down his completely naked torso. His abs are more ripped than the last time we ran together, and he is using his discarded T-shirt to mop off sweat. My head swims in confusion. Is this really happening?

As I approach him, a softer, slower tune starts.

"I don't understand," Sven says to the person on the other side of the counter. His voice is slow and slurred.

I place a hand on his forearm. "Sven?" Like he's moving through molasses, my quick-to-react friend swivels and slowly blinks. I squeeze his bicep. "Are you okay?"

"No." His face crumples. What is happening here? Is Sven going to . . . cry? He pitches forward, his forehead resting on my shoulder. "She has such pretty hair."

"Who? Carlee?"

Sven hiccups against my shoulder. "No. I mean sure, she has nice hair, but it's not the right color. Do you think she dyes it?"

"Carlee?"

"Nooooo," Sven whimpers like a lost dog. "Gretche—"

"Gretchen?"

"Nooooo." His head rolls wildly side to side. "Did you know she's her daughter?"

None of this makes sense. I pat him on the back like I've seen Mom do with Pickle when he's upset. What the heck am I supposed to do? "What did you drink?"

"Beer." Gideon, who's also without a T-shirt, nods like a bobblehead. Although much slimmer than Sven, Gideon also delivers in the abs department. Is there some no-shirt contest going on?

Sven straightens and takes a long drink from the can and then crushes it against the countertop. "I like beer."

"But you need water." The counter is littered with empty beer cans, a toppled champagne bottle, and a couple of dirty mugs. I search through the cupboards, but they are empty. How can Mateo live like this? I turn to Gideon. "I'm going to find Wil. Can you watch Sven?"

Gideon purses his lips and nods again. Another man of few words.

Down the hall, the bedroom door is open and Wil perches on a massive bed, guitar in hand.

Shirtless.

I stumble over my feet.

Two girls sit on the floor in front of him. The green-eyed monster I've rarely met roars to life in my chest. I charge into the room. "Wil?"

My boyfriend stops playing and blinks like he's coming out of a trance. His golden eyes ablaze, he squints then grins at me. "You're here." He stands and steps in my direction, arms held out. The jealousy diminishes with his look of adoration. I step into his embrace and he attempts to kiss me.

"Wait." Wil narrows his eyes. "Fuuuuck." He rubs his head. "What time is it?"

"Around eleven I think. A little late to play a set but I'm game if you are," I say.

He tilts his head. "No, El. This isn't—"

"Finally." Zoe burst into the room. "I've been searching for you everywhere." She spins on Wil. "Having people over was not part of the plan."

I squeeze against Wil. "It's okay Zoe. I don't mind."

Her head jerks back. "You don't?"

"OMG." The brunette on the floor stands up. "You're actually here." She turns to her friend. "This is her. El Vella."

The shorter girl takes out her phone and raises it. I stand in front of Wil. I don't want him to be recorded like this, the video sold to Daniel Davison and another fake story about him splashed across the internet.

Zoe slaps her phone down. "Nope. Not happening." She snatches the device away and the girl protests, but Zoe takes her by the arm. "Time to leave." She glares at Corbin and the tall girl. "You two as well."

Corbin drawls, "Bossy much?" as Zoe guides him through the door and glares at Wil.

"Zoe. I messed up." Wil puts his guitar into its case. "This wasn't supposed to happen. I had a plan."

I grin at him. "It's a great surprise. Us singing for Mateo's guests."

"Sing for Mateo's guests?" Wil shakes his head. "No. A plan to move in together."

"Right." I inch backward, not sure why he's bringing this up now. "Someday. When we find something affordable."

"No need to." Wil's opens his arms wide. "I rented the apartment. Surprise."

"What?" My shriek surprises even me.

"Mateo's friend gave me a discount and I thought, why wait?"

The wave of happiness I've been riding since stepping on the stage at the bar tonight crashes against my ribs and I try to make sense of his declaration. I glance around the room like the four walls can give me a clue as to what is happening. There's a massive bed, covered in a fluffy white duvet, and a half-naked Wil.

The picture doesn't add up. I press my hand into my abdomen to quell the nausea bubbling there.

"You said you liked it," he whispers.

My fingers itch to brush away the concern etched across Wil's face but I can't move. The Wil I know and love wouldn't do this to me. Wouldn't go behind my back and betray me like this. Wil is not Dillon. Dillon's text informing me he'd moved to London presses against my skull. I stumble out of Wil's embrace, the air in the room stifling. I pull on the material around my neck, the green braid choking me.

"El?" Wil brushes my arm. His touch, usually so calming, so gentle, scorches me and I jerk away.

"You rented this apartment?" The question spills from me, the words burning my tongue. I glare at him. "You rented this apartment for *us* without talking to *me*?"

Wil's fingers catch my wrist. "Wait. Let me explain."

"What's there to explain?" I yank free of his hold. "You wanted this place so you got it." I dial up my sarcasm. "Even though you know I can't afford to pay half of the rent."

"I can pay more. I have money."

Hot tears stain my cheeks. "Money? It's always about money."

"No." Wil runs a hand through his hair. "Well, yes. In this case."

"I thought you understood . . ." The words catch in my throat. He was supposed to be the person who got it. Got me. The boy who didn't obsess about money. Who cared about me, not fancy apartments. Wil blurs before me and I brush away the tears. "I can't do this." I force myself away from him and through the door.

My shoulder hits the wall as I stagger down the hall. The music is off and the living room is a scene from a zombie movie. There are crumbled napkins and beer cans on the counter and the floor. Bodies slowly shuffle through the exit, bottlenecking the door.

"That's it, people, keep moving." Zoe stands in the center of the room hands like an air traffic controller. "And no drinking and driving. Order a rideshare or the concierge can get you cabs."

Xander pauses in front of her. "Who are you?"

"Your worst nightmare." She taps the center of his chest. "Now get your ass out of here."

Mateo and the blond that was practically living off him are the last to file out, leaving only Zoe, Wil, me, and a leaning-against-the-wall Sven.

Sven stumbles forward.

"Whoa there, big guy." Zoe ducks under his enormous arm and props him up. "Time to get you home."

"She won't be there," he grumbles.

Zoe makes a quizzical face at me and I shrug. "Sveny needs some water and a good night's sleep." She pats him on his icing-covered naked chest. "You can tell me about this mystery woman when you sober up."

I step to the other side of Sven and balance out the load.

"El. Wait." Wil touches my shoulder. "Where are you going?"

"To Carlee's."

Wil glances at Zoe like he's desperate for backup.

She shakes her head. "You made this mess, you fix it."

"You have to believe me, I didn't mean for this to happen. Everything got out of hand." The crease between his eyebrows turns into a ravine. He points to the wall. "It was only supposed to be Sven and Mateo helping me paint so it'd be perfect for our first night here together."

Sven burps. A foghorn that lasts an eon. Zoe clutches her sides in a fit of laughter. I can't find it in me to smile. I want to go home. No, I want to go to Carlee's, because I don't even have a home.

"Please." Wil paces before us. "Don't leave. Don't leave me."

Tendons stand out on his neck and his hands are balled into fists. He stops before me and clutches his biceps. His wild eyes plead with me.

I halt. As upset as I am right now, I can't abandon him like this. My gaze slides to Zoe. "Do you need help getting Sven in the car?"

"Nah, we've got this." She shakes her head.

I slide out from Sven's bulk and make sure they get over the threshold.

Zoe rolls her eyes. "Text me."

I slam the door shut. "I'll help you clean up."

"Okay." Relief paints Wil's face.

I cross my arms. "Then I'm taking a rideshare home."

The shine in his eyes dulls.

He stuffs his hands into the pockets of his paint-splattered jeans. The old ones he wore when we first met. Memories of my hand resting on the soft, lived-in material as he held my hand through my doubts stir the questions I've been ignoring for a while. The Wil I fell in love with didn't care about brands or what people thought of his clothes. The jeans might appear the same, but the man wearing them . . . I peel the blue nail polish off my pinkie. He changed. I clench my jaw. I changed too.

Wil inches forward.

I walk around him, take an empty Blend bag, and shove the first crumpled beer can I see into it. How much change is too much?

TWENTY-SIX

I PICK THE CHAMPAGNE bottle off the floor covered in gray footprints and yank the dried-out paint tray and a semi-dry roller from under the bunched drop cloths. The hardwood is ruined. I mash my teeth and stack the two other paint trays next to the first one. Why did I have to mess up today of all days?

In the kitchen, El stuffs crushed cans into a garbage bag. Not looking at me. It's been at least fifteen minutes of her not looking at me.

I don't blame her.

I close the empty pizza boxes and add them to the pile I'll have to throw out whenever I figure out where the garbage chute is. I blame Mateo for suggesting Death Elbow should help paint.

I wipe up spilled alcohol from a tipped over mug. The mug I imagined El sipping coffee from in our bed tomorrow morning. I blame Opa for convincing me to go ahead with taking the apartment.

El pours beer out of partially empty bottles into the sink. I blame Corbin and that girl for making me play guitar. I curse under my breath. Why the bloody hell did I agree?

Everything is messed up because I gave in to the music. I lost track of time and now instead of impressing El with my surprise, I've pissed her off. I don't know what I would have done had she not stayed.

El rinses the sink, washes her hands, and splashes water on her face. "Didn't have this on my bingo card for tonight."

Me neither. "Can we talk?" I abandon the dirty mugs in the sink. "I can't stand the silence."

"You know what I couldn't stand?" She lifts her chin. "I couldn't stand not being able to get ahold of you. I wanted to tell you about the pretty amazing night I had." A few strands of hair cling to her skin. She gestures to the remains of the party. "Before I walked into this mess."

El's exaggerated eye shadow reminds me of the night I saw her coming offstage in Las Vegas after performing with Blatantly Subtle. I'm so used to her without much makeup. Her beauty takes me by surprise at times. "I was going to cancel plans with Zoe. To find you."

Damn it. I drag my hand through my hair. I don't even know where my phone is. Somewhere in this apartment surely. "El, I—"

She crosses her arms. "When I walked in I thought my surprise was that you and I would be singing together at Mateo's party." She throws her hands in the air. "Not you renting this apartment."

"I rented it for us."

"Us? Or you?"

I aim to catch her hand but she pulls out of reach. "Both."

"You know this is way out of my budget. What's going on with you? What were you thinking?"

"I was thinking I want to be alone with my girlfriend," I say, louder than I intended.

"This"—El makes a circle motion in the air—"was the opposite of alone."

My fingers clench. "This wasn't my intention."

"Oh, I suppose people just showed up with alcohol and music without your knowledge and turned this into a party in *your* apartment without *your* consent?"

"Yes, actually."

But El's not listening.

"And two girls wandered into your bedroom, tore your shirt off, and forced you to play guitar for them?"

El is jealous? My lips curl.

"This is not funny."

I capture her elbows. Her arms are stiff and it guts me. "It's not. I went in there to change my shirt, which was covered in paint, by the way, because I was trying to make this place nice for us to have an actual date. Then Corbin wanted to impress those girls but ended up spilling beer on me instead. They asked me to sing too and I lost track of time. You know how it goes. We've done it in the studio before."

I tear at my hair. "It was only supposed to be that one song. But the guitar felt so good in my hands." The music so right. I caved, got lost in the notes, the chords, the words. Like an addict. "I couldn't stop."

I have to stop.

Stop playing guitar.

Stop writing lyrics.

I'm working with the band, not playing in it. I have to keep the music separate. I release my hair. "It was just Corbin and me singing. I promise you. That's it."

El blinks at me. "Are you singing with Corbin?"

"This is not about Corbin." Her muscles under my grip tense. I suck in air. "This is about me. I screwed up. Mateo and Sven and *only* Mateo and Sven were invited over to paint and help set up our date. The band and their guests talked their way in." I hold up a hand before El can interrupt. "I know, it's an excuse. I'm sorry I screwed up."

I slide my hands down and entwine our fingers. I want her to listen to me, to understand I'm serious. "Hear me out. If you don't like what I have to say, I'll stay at Dad's, sublet this place until we can both afford it."

The lines around her mouth soften. "Okay. Talk."

"I know it's important to you to pay your own way, to be independent. I've always supported you and will always support you. I'm in this for the long haul." I lift her hand to my lips and kiss her wrist. "We are a team."

She nods. "I thought we were partners."

"I prefer team. In Uni I was on the rowing team. Our boat came together in the fall and worked all year. I was the stroke and set the pace. I loved that feeling that we *only* got when we all were exactly in time, when I led the rhythm but we all moved as one, when the cox had us perfectly aligned and knew how to push us to be greater as a team. But it took everyone working together, adjusting to each other's strengths and weaknesses. Pulling harder when another rower struggled or letting someone else take charge when the cox couldn't."

El's eyebrows knit together. "I understand how rowing works."

Maybe I should have used Opa's cooking dinner example. El loves to cook. I squeeze her fingers.

"When we first met, you were struggling to find the words for *Don't Give Me Comfort*. You knew what you wanted to say, and I helped you find the way to express them. When I had a few notes in my head, you took that melody, used your talents, and transformed my thoughts into the progression for an entire song, everything coming from these talented fingers." I press my thumb to her knuckles. "We don't split creating our songs into two equal tasks. We share the load."

El cocks her head.

"When you can't find the words, I step in. When I can't unearth the tune, you forge it for us. We learn and grow together and are better for it. Our relationship isn't a list of tasks that we split down the middle."

I stitch our hands together. "Right now, I have the ability to take the load of the rent for this place. There may be time in the future where the roles will reverse. I have no idea how to furnish this living room. Zoe gave me a lecture on thread count this morning. But you, you turned your bedroom at Dad's place into a space that was a reflection of you."

Her forehead crinkles. "You want to hire me as your interior decorator?"

"No. I want you to help us make this place ours. I want you to be comfortable here, to carry the parts of the load I'm not so good at. Let me take care of the rent."

"No. I can't." She pulls out of my grip.

I ball my hands into fists. "Why not? Why can't I take care of you?"

Her head snaps back. "Because I don't need to be taken care of. I'm not a child."

I pace away. I hate this woman's stubbornness. I sniff. I love this woman's stubbornness. I turn and come back. "How about this. We can keep track of what I pay each month and as you make more money, we put it in an account to save for a down payment on a house."

"You want to buy a house with me?"

"I want everything with you." I place her hands over my heart. "I want a lifetime with you where we're a team. You and me, supporting each other's dreams and hopes and wants and desires. Living the best possible life we can. Share this life with me," I plead with my words and my gaze. "Share this apartment. Share everything. Not an even split, but everything. One hundred percent. All in."

El studies my face. I'm afraid to move. I silently beg for understanding. She releases my grip and my heart stutters. But she doesn't walk away. Instead, she slides her hands up my chest and loops them around my neck. She pulls my forehead down to touch hers. "I'm all in too."

It hurts to swallow. All the promises I want to make clog my every breath. When she said "I love you too" at Griffith Observatory, I thought those were the most important words I would ever hear from her mouth. Her saying "I'm all in too" feels no less important. I let out a shuddering breath. "El."

"We'll be a team." The surety in her voice is a balm against my racing thoughts. "But from this point on, no more trying to take care of me without talking first."

I can't promise her that. It's my job to take care of her. It's why I rented this place. Why I have to set the music aside and stay at Rocker Inc. She is the reason I do this. I kiss the tender spot behind her ear and run my lips along her jaw. "I like taking care of you."

Her fingers massage my scalp. "Let's take care of each other," she whispers.

I scoop her up in my arms and head to the bedroom. "I do have one surprise that didn't get ruined."

"Pretty sure I've experienced that before."

I laugh. "Not that." I lay her gently on the bed. "Stay here." I dash to the door and flip off the light. The silhouette of El's figure on our big bed is bathed in a bluish-green neon glow.

She gasps and props herself up on her elbows, her gaze taking in the incandescent cutouts decorating the ceiling of our bedroom. "Stars."

"I know you love them." I climb onto the bed and lie down beside her, watching her soak up my handiwork. "I want you to have everything you love." I cup her cheek, my thumb tracing her chin. "Stars for my star."

"I already have everything I love." Her lips nip at mine. "I have you."

My breathing turns thin and reedy.

"I love you, Wil." Her voice caresses my name with gruff need. "I love you more than all the stars in the universe."

Twenty-Seven

A WARM WIL PRESSES against me in his . . . no, *our* luxurious bed. He bought this bed for us. With his money. The thought pulls me from the hazy aftereffects of the last few hours of testing out this mattress.

We're a team.

That certainty dulls the sharp barb. I'm lulled back into paradise with the soft touch of Wil's lips against my chin, collarbone, shoulder. Each gentle stamp spells "I love you" and sets off sparks of euphoria that shouldn't be possible with every muscle in my body limp and languid. But this is Wil. He makes the impossible possible.

The tips of his fingers tap an undiscovered rhythm along my ribcage and abdomen, and below my skin my heart adds an accompanying drum roll. My moan is faint as I resist the pull of sleep because I want more. Want more of him. He must too because his mouth lingers on mine in a delicate kiss that lasts millennia. We hold each other close, skin against skin, lips against lips, heart against heart. I feel safe and loved and un-afraid. Around and between us my love for Wil merges with his love for me, swishing and swirling like bells pealing at the end of Tchaikovsky's *1812 Overture*.

We're a team.

With a groan, his lips leave mine, but I chase after them, twisting our bodies using my weight to pin him to the sheets. It's my turn to explore, to mark my territory, to suck on his sun-kissed skin and elicit one of his low growls that turns my insides to molten lava. His muscles shudder under my lips as I kiss the hard line that divides his six-pack. His palm rests on the curve of my hip, holding me close.

Another growl. "I might want to marry this bed."

I giggle. "You said that about the bed in the guestroom at Rocker's."

"Did I? When?"

"Labor Day weekend, the night you stayed over." I rest my chin on his chest. Bathed in the blueish-green hue of the glowing stars above our bed, Wil has the appearance of a celestial being, the sharp line of his nose casting a shadow on his stubble-covered cheek. "When we wrote *Don't Give Me Comfort*."

He winces. "I wanted to tell you about Rocker being my dad that night." The tips of his fingers brush my hair behind my ear.

"Except I couldn't stand the thought of you not talking to me ever again." His grip tightens, like he doesn't want me to move, to be an inch away from him.

"Kick you out on your birthday?" I tap his chin to lighten the mood. "That goes against the perfect hostess code. I'd lose my membership."

The joke works and his eyebrows unknit. "Working in Dad's studio with you was a breakthrough. I love what we created."

I love hearing the word love from Wil. It's like now he's released the word into the world, the boy who doesn't do relationships has the freedom to express himself honestly. No more secrets hiding in the wings.

The kind generous boy who tries to take care of everyone. I pepper his chest with kisses. Who came to the States for money to help his mother. I run my tongue across his lower lip. The boy who organized the house renovation for her. The pictures of the updated kitchen are beautiful, a vast change from the dingy but loved room where I drank countless cups of tea and learned to bake stollen. Without his job, without Rocker, Wil couldn't have transformed his family's life. Helping his mother is at the center of the Wil I love.

I love Wil so much it hurts. My fingers trace the line of his jaw, the muscles contract under my touch. His grip on my hip tightens.

Wil wants this apartment. His first place of his own, where everything is new and shiny. Not used and worn out. I can't hold that against him. Can't mess up his life because he wants to enjoy things. Wants something different from me. Dillon wanted to be a producer, a professional, not Rocker's stepdaughter's boyfriend. That tore us apart. But I was selfish back then.

I'm not going to make that mistake again. Wil has the right to have good things. He's not the same boy who couldn't afford to eat anything except noodles every night, never mind pay rent. We're both growing and changing and that's okay.

We're a team.

We'll support each other. Tell each other everything.

I prop myself up on my hands. "I sang *Love Conquers All* at The Devil's Martini tonight."

"Wait." Wil grabs my shoulders. "You sang? Onstage?"

"I did." The giddiness of being onstage was such a high. I jam my teeth together to stop myself from smiling like a goof. There's no denying it and I'll always tell Wil the truth. I blow out a long breath and walk him through the evening, including how the audience responded to our song. "It was amazing."

Wil's lips on mine interrupt me. Gone is the lazy kiss of earlier. This is fierce and passionate and over as quick as it started. His hands bracket my face. "You were born to be onstage." Even in the darkness I can sense the electricity in his eyes.

I flop onto my back, the bed bouncing underneath me. "I think I might want to do it again."

"Sing onstage?" The mattress dips as he lays beside me, his head propped on one elbow.

I squeeze my eyes shut and replay the view of the audience from the stage and feel the emotions that trigger inside me.

Nerves, yes, but the good kind. The kind you get before the greatest surprise of your life.

"When I sang our song, I slowed down the third and fourth lines of the bridge, sort of Joni Mitchell style."

He sits up. "Wait." He reaches for his guitar, hesitates, then hands it to me. "Show me."

His strings are harder than mine, but I've played it so many times it's like exchanging a T-shirt for a hoodie. I settle in and find the portion of the bridge I modified. Wil stares at the space on the bed between us, a small dent between his eyebrows as he concentrates. I adore that look. My run-through of the chorus-bridge-verse sequence fades out.

I hug the guitar and sit still.

The corners of Wil's mouth curve. "It's beautiful."

Just like you. "I was thinking of you."

His eyes shine at me.

I nudge him with a foot. "Can we sing it together?"

Wil's eyes drop to his hands.

"Please?"

Those broad shoulders of his drop and he scoots closer, his knees pressed against mine, and I relax. His gaze flits to me and he smiles. "Always."

It's not like when I sang onstage earlier. The music is always better when Wil and I sing together. Different and better. These changes I like. He matches my pace without question and our voices blend. We fall into the past, where we're just a boy and a girl singing. No paparazzi, no brand endorsements. Where we sing doesn't matter. It's only him and me, doing what brought us together on a worn stage almost a year ago. Doing the thing that made him impossible not to love. Doing what we do best.

We make music.

Together.

We're a team.

Maybe I'm mostly the melody and maybe he is responsible for the words, but without him my melody would be only mixing notes. His words might not hold any meaning.

> Love conquers all, the movies said
> but when I'm lonely in my bed
> I think of you

My pulse picks up, not to match the tempo, but because of the tempo. Because like nothing else, this feels so right. We come to the final words and Wil raises his gaze to me. It's not possible that his eyes blaze golden fire, but they do, infused with an energy I know I'm responsible for. The air between us crackles. Tingles create paths across my arms and legs. I know that as long as I can see myself reflected in them, I'd lit up from inside as well.

> Maybe they were right,
> maybe they were wrong
> maybe I should just give up, give in and fall
> Maybe they were right,
> maybe they were wrong

maybe I should just give up, give in and fall for

. . . you

My gaze drops to his lips. His perfect, sweet lips. I taste them, pressing my own to his, to capture all he has to offer. My hands discard the guitar for his skin and I shift to straddle him, changing the angle of our kiss, deepening it. Fingers grip my waist as he adjusts our position and my tongue glides across his. I'm singing again, but in a different way.

There's my Wil. This doesn't change. This has been the same since our first real kiss. Right. All-consuming. Yet grounded. Our chests crash together as if our hearts are desperate to combine. This is us.

We need to stay here, hold on to this feeling as long as possible. Never let go.

I inch up his lap. It's not close enough. He reads my mind, scoops me up and lays us on the bed, his weight setting on me. Full body contact is better yet still not enough. It will never be enough with him.

Time slows as he skims his fingers along my stomach, my hipbone, like he wants to explore my skin. I squirm beneath him. I should let him set the pace but I need *my* Wil. Now.

I ask for more. Wil moans and I revel in that sound, almost as good as him singing our song. When there's no space left between us the bedroom becomes our concert hall. We orchestrate a symphony of leitmotifs until we still. I cling to him, refusing to let go until my fingers cramp and I'm forced to release.

His fingers trail up and down my skin like my arm is his piano and he can't stop playing.

I face Wil, his profile is in shadow. "Do you miss it? Singing like we used to at The Devil's Martini?"

The question pops out. I know Wil was really only singing onstage for my sake. He loves making the music, writing the words, mixing the sound board, producing the final product. Singing the same songs week after week in a set was never his thing. He didn't daydream for years of being on the stage.

More silence. I scoot forward and press my hand against his chest. "It's okay if you don't. I understand."

"I liked it more than I ever thought I would." A wrinkle of worry forms between his eyebrows. "I busked back home many times, but the goal was to make money to pay the heating bill or buy Mum a birthday present. I'd ham it up for the crowd, wink at the girls, all to get people to throw cash into my guitar case." His voice is low, like he's spilling secrets only I get to know. "Not until I played with you did I truly enjoy singing."

My heart swoons.

He covers my hand with his. "You add this dimension to making music that turns it from a task into an experience. Like going from jotting down a grocery list to cooking the food. I love you and that makes everything related to you more exciting. But the song thing we have, it's more than that. I love making music with you." His mouth hooks up at one side. "Last year I couldn't wait until Saturday night for you to walk through that stage door at The Devil's Martini. To live in that world with you, even if just for an hour."

I rub the heel of my hand over my eye. "I couldn't wait either."

His nose grazes mine. "If I could, I'd spend every moment performing with you."

We're a team.

A future of touring the country, playing theaters and stadiums, outdoor festivals and intimate venues flickers before me. In the past, in my dreams of stardom, I stood alone on the stage, but now I see Wil beside me. Low gnarly twists of heartache dig into my ribs.

"Why don't you?" The words spill so quietly I'm not sure Wil can hear them.

Silence hangs between us. Our chests rise and fall.

The sheets rustle as Wil rests his head on the pillow. "Death Elbow is about to break." His monotone deepens my sadness. "They'll be big, and I'll get ten percent of album sales, never mind the tours. That's royalties for as long as I work with them." Wil blows air through his nose. "Then there're the endorsement offers, which are almost free money for free stuff." He laces his fingers on top of his head and I watch the even up and down of his chest. "When I made the deal to work for Dad, I expected Rocker Inc. would be a vanity project, but I can see why he started the company."

The words come calm and sure, the cocky German who can amuse a crowd with his DJ sets, a producer who can get the project done through sheer determination. The air around him simmers with his passion and I'm sucked into his vortex, hanging on his every sentence.

"Being there at the beginning of everything, shaping the songs, mixing the tracks. It's what I always said I wanted." Another breath fans over his lips. "My dream."

The words snag on my heart. His dream is not my dream. He's never lied about this. Sound engineering brought him to the States when he earned a coveted spot in the Starlight Foundation competition. I've always known this.

"I'm glad you and Rocker are working together." It's what I wanted. Wil to get to know his dad. I berate myself for being selfish. If Wil and I toured he wouldn't see Rocker for months. They need time together to make up for what they lost.

"I wouldn't have this relationship with him if you didn't push me."

"C'mon." I nudge his knee with mine "You know Rocker well enough by now." I snort a quiet laugh. "The second he found out you're his son, there was no chance he was letting you out of his life."

Wil huffs. "True." There's another silence as Wil pulls me into him. "I'm happy I stayed."

"I'm happy you're happy." I snuggle into him, the blanket of sleep creeping over me. I drift between a world where I lie wrapped in Wil's arms on a soft bed and the one where he holds my hand at the edge of a stage, a darkened crowd chanting our name.

Touring with Wil is only that, a dream.

He should stay here, work for Rocker, make money. It's what he wants. I can't hold that against him. It's not a competition. This is part of life: we all change. I always love the first version of my melodies, but they change over time, morph into something better. I love the old Wil. I'll figure out how to love the new parts of this Wil too.

TWENTY-EIGHT

OUR LIMO CRAWLS DOWN Uxbridge Road toward the *Beat Night* studios. Being back in England is surreal. Not a single part of my trip resembles the languid days of going feral in the fields of Sussex. I tug on the lapel of my Antonia Ferelli suit jacket. The money she paid for me to wear her designs tonight will buy a couch for our new apartment.

The leather of Dad's jacket squeaks as he pulls out his cell. Tonight his outfit is not that of management like me or that of the father who barbeques in the backyard, but one hundred percent Rocker, the lead singer of a successful rock band. Head-to-toe black punctuated by steel chains and studs. Hair coiffed, stubble that resembles a five o'clock shadow yet was manicured by a barber an hour ago, eye makeup subtle but there. With Dad glammed up like this, I see how Corbin imitates him.

Death Elbow's mini performance and album signing at Banquet Records this morning had a line around the block. The band's social media account is flooded with tagged images of them meeting fans, Vatton water bottles on full display. I pause on one of Corbin, one foot on a chair, crooning at a trio of girls staring goo-goo eyed at him, and scroll through the comments.

Musicluvver: Can't believe I missed this

Corbinsmaingirl: Corbin 4evr

Dogguy103: When are they touring?

Dad nudges my elbow. "Look at these numbers." He tilts his phone my way and I scan the email from Harper tracking the streams and vinyl purchases of Death Elbow's album release. Dad's finger points out the Spotify plays of the song El sang backup on. "You're a success."

Something akin to jealousy flickers in my gut. "They are." I nod at the second limo behind us carrying the band.

"No, son." Dad grins at me. "They're only here because of your hard work. Don't think I haven't noticed the extra hours. You've managed to keep them rehearsing, out of trouble, in the studio, and talking to the press. Their success is your success."

The limo turns and we move away from the lackluster uniform streets and enter a spectacle of bright lights, jumping fans, and colorful banners with the face of the host of *Beat Night* blown up to twenty times its normal size. A thorny vine of unease bands my ribcage. I let out a resigned puff of air and force a smile onto my lips.

Dad pats my knee. "Time to put on a show."

The car door opens and Dad raises a hand, waving as he exits. The crowd explodes into rowdy cheers as flashes cascade around him like shooting stars. I climb out the other door and wait. Similar to the red carpet I attended with Zoe a few months ago, photographers and reporters line one side of the carpet, but this time the fans are above them in permanent stands. Dad poses in front of a wall of fake grass, the *Beat Night* logo shining neon purple in the background.

Behind me Death Elbow spills out of the second limo, Corbin leading the charge.

"Hell yeah." He whoops.

Xander flattens his hair while Lucian and Gideon pat each other on the back, grinning like a pair of Cheshire cats.

"Make sure you huddle so everyone is in the shot." I herd my band onto the red carpet where Dad is smiling for the paparazzi. "Mention Rocker Inc. if possible and eliminate the swearing so the press can get a good sound bite."

Corbin undoes one more button on his shirt, revealing his nipple piercing. "Lighten up and have a little fun." He turns to the first mass of fans. "We're rock and roll superstars."

The group cheers him on, iconic *Beat Night* placards flapping in excitement. Dad gestures for the band to join him. Photographers angle for shots as Corbin struts down the carpet with the confidence of someone who won awards, not just launched his first album. He and Lucian flank Dad on one side, Xander and Gideon on the other. I hang back, giving the cameras a chance to get the photos I want splashed across the internet.

"Are these boys your competition, Rocker?" a reporter shouts.

"Keep your competition close." Dad hooks a thumb in the belt loop of his distressed jeans. "Why do you think I signed them to my label?"

Corbin swings an arm around Dad's shoulders. "The OG legend, right here."

A million flashes flare, minting the image for eternity. I angle my phone and snap one of my own. I'll send it to El later.

"Which song are you performing on the show?" another reporter asks.

"All of them if I had my say." Corbin sweeps his arm toward the undulating rows of fans. "Give them a real concert."

The crowd in the rafters roars in appreciation.

I adjust my suit jacket again. It's too tight across the shoulders. I hate wearing this mass-produced mess, but it pays. I exhale a breath that doesn't bring any calm.

A smattering of flashes pops as other reporters vie for attention. "*Going Once* is really taking off. What inspired the lyrics?"

Corbin smirks. "The girl of my dreams."

I clench my fist. He's turning my lyrics into a cliché. *Going Once* is not about any girl; it's about El. Every line is inspired by what this last year of finding and being with El means to me. An emotion I can't quite name scrapes my solar plexus with every breath. The reporter is right. It's going to be a hit, and for the rest of my life the public will link Death Elbow with my words about El. No, with Corbin, the face of Death Elbow. The chicken sandwich I had for lunch sours in my stomach.

"What's it like working with Rocker's stepdaughter?" The hastily flung question is like a lash across my bare throat.

"She's a true professional," says Xander.

I drum my fingers against my thigh. These questions are a necessity, but I want the band off this red carpet and in the building, preparing for their performance and the subsequent interview.

Dad pulls out of Corbin's grasp and the four guys move down the carpet where an attendant is pointing for them to stand for the next photo op.

Another limo arrives and I step onto the red carpet to make room. I swallow thickly. Harper's instructions run through my mind. Pause. Smile. Move on. Don't react. I straighten my shoulders. Time to face the music.

It doesn't take long for the first reporter to spot me. "Wil. Are you excited to be here with your father?"

Dad halts and waits for me to catch up. I intend to keep moving but he turns me to the paparazzi. We stand side-by-side as the photographers snap away.

"Rocker. What do you think of your stepdaughter and your son dating?"

"They're great together." Dad squeezes my shoulder.

"Wil. Why isn't El here with you? Did you break up?"

A scowl creeps onto my lips.

Without dropping his grin, Dad speaks through his teeth. "Ignore them."

I strong-arm myself into resurrecting a pleasant expression on my face.

"Wil. Over here." I turn as if I can escape these asinine questions. Pressure on my back from Dad moves me down the carpet. "What do you think about El singing with Death Elbow?"

"Why hasn't El released any of her own music?"

We stop in front of the next group of paparazzi. "What are the perks of being Rocker's son?"

"Did he replace the new car you crashed?" Another shouts.

"Were you drunk that night?"

The back of my neck heats and the collar of the ridiculous jacket bites into my skin. What is happening? I get their morbid fascination with who my father and girlfriend are, but why aren't they asking me about album sales or what Death Elbow are performing? This should be about the music, the upcoming show, not stupid rumors.

Dad waves, his hand firm and reassuring on my shoulder.

"Is El cheating on you with Corbin?"

I trip over my own feet. "What?"

The question makes me angry. Ball-my-fists-and-join-a-bar-fight angry. Where would the paparazzi even get such a ludicrous idea? I glance at the other end of the carpet where Death Elbow are posed like my old rowing team before a heat. "She sang one track. That's all."

"Thanks guys." Dad strolls further down the carpet like the asshole with the microphone didn't just accuse El of cheating on me.

Dad's chest brushes my shoulder as he whispers. "Don't give them anything. Keep smiling."

Another pause and another volley of questions about what it's like to be Rocker's son, what does Sylvia think of my mum, and more creative wild assumptions about why El isn't with me. Nothing about the music, the band, the songs. Nothing about the reason I'm here tonight. To the paparazzi my accomplishments don't have enough merit to outshine the fact that I'm Rocker's son and El's boyfriend. I try to shrug this off, but the dizzying flashes and nauseating inquiries demolish any goodwill toward the press I started the event with.

This must be what it's been like for years for El. Dragged down every red carpet with these wankers slinging insults in the form of questions in an attempt to get a clickbait sound bite or photo.

I shove my hand in the too-tight pocket of my too-tight pants and smile at the camera. Apparently grin and bear is how I'll pay my dues in this business.

Twenty-Nine

I tap the fob to the lock above the door of the new apartment and walk into the fumes of paint that four days after Wil's painting party still sit heavy in the air. The garbage is gone and my steps echo in the empty room. It'll take us time to figure out and buy furniture, starting with somewhere to sit when we eat. I circle the stack of cardboard boxes forming a raft in the middle. Was spending part of my meager savings on barstools too reckless?

The knock at the door takes me out of my stress spiral. Mormor and Mr. Peters barely fit through the opening with the bags in their hands.

"I just needed something to open the boxes with," I say.

"I assumed you didn't have any kitchen towels." Mormor hangs one on the handle of the dishwasher and retrieves a lime green kitchen soap pump and matching scrubby thingy that she positions on the back of the sink.

Mr. Peters stacks bags by the kitchen counters and strides over to the sliding door to the balcony. "The floors are a mess but with some sanding and revarnishing, they'll be as good as new." Mr. Peters wipes his hands on his pants. "But that'll have to wait till after the reopening. I promised Carlee I'll spend today replacing the switch covers." Mr. Peters gives Mormor and me an awkward wave. "See you later?"

Mormor agrees and closes the door behind him. I feel lighter, seeing them together. Another change I can learn to love. Wil's grandfather and my Mormor are friends.

I slice the tape of the box on top and pull out the instructions. Stick figure people happily demonstrate the multi-step process of assembling the bar stools. Seems easy enough. Little to no reading is a good start.

Mormor shakes her head. "You are so much like your mother. Independent. Strong-willed."

"It's a family trait."

She snorts. "True." Mormor digs in one of the bags. "This isn't a housewarming gift." She sets a jewelry box on the counter and pulls out a pendant on a long silver chain. "It was given to me with several other pricey pieces by my mother-in-law, your great-grandmother. She wanted me to have some things I could sell in case of an emergency." She places the item in my hand and wraps my fingers around it. The edges poke into my skin. "Now it's yours." There's a twinkle in her eye.

Diamonds set in silver make the wings of a dragonfly. Emeralds create the segmented abdomen and a single blue stone is the head. "I can't take this."

"I gave a piece to each of my daughters. Aunt Nova paid part of her medical school tuition with her tiara. Patty used the pair of emerald bracelets to invest in Bob's first company. Your mom got the one with a giant ruby."

The necklace I used to bail Sven out of jail last Halloween. "That was from you?"

"That was her in-case-of-an-emergency. She used it well."

The blue stone in my palm is almost the same color as Mormor's eyes, and Mom's eyes, and mine. "I don't know what to say."

"No need to say anything. I want you to know that if you ever need money, you have something to fall back on. And don't think I've forgotten about the summer cash I always give you." Mormor pulls out an envelope.

"I don't need your money anymore. I get a paycheck." Not enough to afford half of the rent for this apartment, but something.

"That job is wrong for you. Just like working for Bill was." Her fingers tap against the counter. "You are a singer like your mother. I know it. She knows it. You know it. Everyone who has ever heard your music knows it."

I square my shoulders. "Everyone keeps telling me that. Can't I be happy just singing for myself?"

She cups my cheek. "Even though you aren't following your dreams?"

I open my mouth to say yes but I can't lie. I step away from Mormor and move to the other side of the counter. I want to tell her that *was* my dream, but my dream hasn't changed. I'm just not sure I can be brave enough to offer the sacrifice it requires. "I'm still singing. I'm a backup vocalist on one track with Death Elbow. I sang with Dasher. I sing with Wil all the time. I recorded a few cover songs this morning. My follower counts on social media grow every day."

"But is it enough?" She rips the cellophane from a bunch of white hydrangeas.

I groan.

"Don't moan at me. You practically came out of your mother's womb singing. You hummed before you talked." A smile tugs at her lips. "I get that you had a setback and you're frightened. Setbacks are a part of life." She uses shears I've never seen in this apartment to clip one stem. "Look at your mother. She practiced day and night and yet she didn't earn a spot in the Norwegian Academy of Music. She considered giving up too."

"Mom never told me this."

Mormor arches an eyebrow. "She tries to deny it now. But she moped around our place like the world had ended. But then you know what happened?"

I prop my elbows on the marble countertop. "What?"

Another stem gets snipped. "We went on a summer vacation to Italy. There we heard a performance by the students of the Venice Conservatory."

"Where Mom and Papa went?"

"Your Papa was one of the students who performed. They had coffee afterward and next thing we knew, he talked her into moving to Venice. We didn't want her to follow a boy, but she pawned her necklace, flew for an in-person audition, and got accepted."

I touch the base of my neck, where that large ruby necklace had sat as part of my Marie Antoinette costume. "But how did she get it back?"

Mormor clips the final stem and collects the flowers in her hands. "Your father. He tracked down the necklace after his first big solo." Mormor peeks at me from under her eyelashes. "See? If Sylvia had gone to school in Norway, she never would have met your father. And I wouldn't have such a wonderful granddaughter." Mormor offers a short smile. "The road of life is not always straight. The point is to not give up on the journey."

Another knock on the door interrupts us.

I'm grateful for the distraction. "Is Mr. Peters back?"

"Actually," Mormor starts as I open the door.

"Could you please hold him?" A pair of outstretched arms hands Pickle to me. I barely take him as Mom shouts down the open door to the stairway. "One more flight." She turns to me. "They couldn't fit it into the elevator."

Slobber covers Pickle's mouth and hands. His golden eyes stare at me. "Mom?" I peek into the hallway. "What's going on?"

Sweat rolls off the foreheads of two men in blue overalls trudging up the stairs, a cloth-covered rectangle in their hands.

"You will have to clear the way, ma'am," the man in front shouts, and Mom steps inside.

I back away from the door, careful not to fall over the disassembled stool parts.

Mom urgently shoves the parts I carefully laid out to match the stick figures and they end up in one messy pile. "I think it should go against the balcony wall."

I crane my neck to catch sight of what the men are carrying. "Did you buy me a couch?"

"Be careful," Mom orders as they undo the straps holding the protective material. It falls to the ground to reveal eight thin bowed legs and a double-stacked keyboard. Sunlight from the balcony illuminates the light-brown instrument. My harpsichord.

"Mom, you shouldn't have." I cover my mouth with my hand and Pickle slaps his palm over my mouth, maybe thinking it's a game.

I run my fingers along the top, gently lifting the lid to display the baroque pastoral scene in muted colors that reminds me of Papa.

"It's yours." Mom scans the place before dropping the ginormous diaper bag she's toting onto the kitchen counter. "I thought you'd love to have it in your own space." She puts her hand on my shoulder.

"Mom."

"The line was absolutely outrageous, but it's worth every new blister." Zoe freezes, one foot across the threshold. "Another party?" The tray with two coffees wavers in her hand.

"I didn't know they were coming."

She closes the door and steps out of the stilettoes that match the cross-body bag she's wearing. "Seems like you and Wil have another thing in common: being ambushed by parties. Why does this never happen to me?" She double-kisses Mormor and Mom and pinches Pickle's cheek. "Are you going to help us build the bar stools too? Are you?" She transitions into a baby voice with alarming speed.

"I can stay." Mom studies the implements laid out in neat rows inside the metal box, but I can feel that my answer is what she's most focused on.

"If you want to build stools." I smile.

Mom holds up a thick-handled object with what resembles a rubber meat tenderizer on the end. "It's never too late to do new things."

Mormor gives me a conspiratorial glance.

The non-meat tenderizer, called a mallet according to a quick internet search, is heavier than I anticipated. I hit the spot where the instructions tell me to lightly tap to align the joints.

"Do you have to do that right now?" Zoe continues to tighten the screws on her stool, her eyes glued to her phone propped on the counter, playing the end of the *Beat Night* interview. "They're about to sing. After that you can use the hammer to your heart's content."

I'm about to tell her it's a mallet, not a hammer, when *Going Once* bursts from Zoe's phone. I hum the chorus alongside Corbin's raspy rendition.

Mormor sips her latest cocktail concoction from the martini glasses she brought. "Since you are credited as a performer, if they do get a Grammy for the album, will you be an award-winning artist?"

"I don't think it works that way."

Mom turns the instructions upside down. "You may get a Grammy certificate, but with Wil as a producer and the song-writer, he would get a Grammy."

"Songwriter?" I face Mom. "Wil hasn't written any songs for Death Elbow."

"Bill said the song you recorded with them is all Wil's lyrics."

Mom must be confused. "Are you sure?"

"You can ask Bill, but I swear that's what I heard."

Her words are like an orchestra of instruments tuning before the concert. The sound is clear but there's no sense in them.

Pickle joins the applause that the studio audience dishes out for Death Elbow.

"Watch carefully, the bottom right corner." Zoe points to the spot and the camera quickly pans to Rocker and Wil clapping from their seats in the front row.

"I can't believe the questions they asked Bill on the red carpet," says Mom.

Zoe turns off her phone. "But consider how he turned it around. Stories about Wil and El as the *it* couple are popping up everywhere. A video montage of photos set to *Don't Give Me Comfort* is trending."

I roll my eyes. "Great, more press about me. Exactly what I don't want."

"Stop being afraid of the press." Zoe stands and brushes dust off her skirt.

"It's not the same for you."

She crosses her arms. "No. But you have things backward. They aren't in charge. You are."

"As if."

"Use them to amplify what you want." She points to her phone. "Meet them head-on. Like Rocker does."

It's true. Rocker has a good relationship with the press. Having a long-lost son could have been a scandal but he got in front of the story and turned it to his advantage. I grind my teeth. Once again, my cousin might be right.

I pull out my phone, go into the bedroom, and bring up the song credits for *Going Once*. Wil's name is the only one on the lyrics line.

Wil wrote a song and didn't tell me about it? The apartment, now the song. Whatever lightness I was feeling earlier disappears as a boulder of doubt rolls onto my chest. What else is he not telling me?

"Did I say something wrong?" Mom lingers on the threshold.

I shove the phone into my pocket. "It's not you."

Mom sits on the mattress next to me. "Something is bothering you. Should I not have come?" She gently strokes my back.

The confused emotions I've been carrying for months stir under her touch. I'm supposed to be independent, an adult. But being next to Mom unleashes the upset child within me. I curl into her, laying my head on her lap, and stare at the stars Wil put there for me. My chest aches. The epicenter of the tremors that rake my body is stuck in the middle of my throat.

Wil lied and I don't know what to do.

Mom doesn't press. She strokes my hair until the shaking stops. The same way she did after Papa's accident. My accident.

Out of all the questions churning in my head, one pushes through. "Carlee asked me again to sing at the Grand Reopening."

Mom's fingers slow. "What did you say?"

"I didn't say yes." I rub my nose. "But I didn't say no."

"What's stopping you?" She massages my shoulder blade. A soothing caress. A nudge. A silent promise?

I lift my head and stare at her. "You're not against me singing. Onstage?"

Her knuckles trace the line of my cheekbone. "I want you to do what you want to do. Work with Carlee. Move in with Wil." She lifts my chin. "Sing."

A cough of disbelief makes its way past the chaos in throat. "That's not what I've heard my whole life."

Mom lets out a long breath. "You're right. I've been overprotective, something I've been working on with my therapist." She fiddles with her diamond earring.

An incredible sense of relief spreads through me. Rocker listened to me. Mom listened to him. Maybe this is the start of a new phase of a relationship between Rocker, her, Pickle, and me. I can finally let go of the worry I've been carrying for Mom and for my little brother. My pulse steadies, a reassuring rhythm signaling hope.

"Even though my mind conjures these awful scenarios of what could go wrong, and there is nothing I wouldn't do to protect you, Pickle, and Bill, and Mormor, and now Wil. My sisters. Their families. Even Mr. Peters." Mom rubs her arms like she's cold. "That's what I want to do, but I won't. I'm not doing that anymore."

"Mom, I—"

She holds up a hand. "My heart knows that you are a smart and capable young woman and some part of me logically understands that you will make mistakes just like I did, no matter how many warnings I give you. Yet I'm constantly terrified. My therapist suggested the Comprehend, Cope, and Connect method. It's helping. Bill tries to help. Mor too." Mom tilts her head. "I'm aware I'm the real reason your grandmother finally decided to visit LA."

"Mom, I . . ." I try to come up with something that'll show her I'm here for her. Will be here for her. We used to be a team. I want us to be again.

"I love my mother for being here." Mom runs two fingers under each eye. "And I love you. I love you more every day and there will never be anything you do that would lessen my love for you." Her glassy eyes shine. "My worry has held you back for too long. If singing is your passion, if it's what you truly want, then Baby Girl, get on that stage and share your talent with the world."

I wrap my arms around my mother. "I won't let you down."

She grips me back. "You never do."

Thirty

MY HEAD BUZZES AS I push through the revolving doors of the skyscraper. I hope this breakfast meeting Dad requested has coffee in the form of an IV because I'm running on fumes. The *Beat Night* afterparty two days ago started the nightly celebrations trend which never really ended. Our final dinner in London yesterday turned into a pub crawl followed by an underground after-hours club.

The two-story lobby gleams with glass and high-end watches on the wrists of its patrons. Dad has left the rockstar persona behind, opting for causal jeans and a black T-shirt that reads, "I may be old, but I got to see all the cool bands," and I laugh. The stress relief feels good. Maybe a meal, just Dad and I, is what I need.

"I have the same shirt." I point to his chest. "But in your case, it's true."

He tugs at the hem. "Are you calling me old?"

"If the shoe fits." Never in a million years did I think I'd be joking with Bill Rockerby, the rock star, my dad. "Seriously, I wish I'd seen Queen perform live."

"I'm not that old."

I slap him on the back. "Where's the restaurant? I'm starving."

"About that." Dad's eyes shine. "I have a surprise first."

My caffeine-deprived brain groans. "West Ham's season is over."

His mouth quirks. "We'll catch a soccer match next time we're here." He guides me to the bank of six elevators housed in white marble. "This is much better."

The elevator zips us to the twenty-third floor so fast, my ears pop. Dad steps into an empty space with concrete floors and floor-to-ceiling windows offering a view of the Thames and a dreary London skyline. A metal desk sits off to the right, empty except for a picture frame.

I spin to Dad. "Am I missing something?"

He points to the picture and I inspect it closely. The white paper has the Rocker Inc. logo that dons the front of Dad's office and all the company's email signatures. Except this has one significant difference. Below the guitar, printed in thick, bold letters, is "London."

"Still not getting the joke," I say.

"It's no joke." Dad opens his arms wide. "Welcome to the new London offices of Rocker Inc."

The meaning of what I'm seeing is dripping slowly into my brain. "You're expanding?"

He scratches his chin. "I've been toying with the idea for a while now. Last year we officially maxed out on studio space and the choice was either a bigger place in LA or expand elsewhere. With Sylvia's family in Norway, I wanted an option that made travel a little easier. London is the perfect go-between, has a hot music scene, and gives us a foothold in the European market."

"That's fantastic." I glance around the space, envisioning it filled with artists lining up to sign with Dad's company.

His eyebrow lifts. "You made this possible."

I gape at him. "Me?"

The grin on his face is infectious. "I realize our deal is over. Hanna has completed the clinical trial and her health is remarkable." He touches his chest. "You're finished at UCLA for the year and with Death Elbow's album launch over, your internship could come to an end." He shrugs. "Time to plan for the future."

I tug my ear. Planning is all I seem to ever do. Except I didn't plan on this. I came to the States for a reason, first for Mum, then for El. I hadn't considered not staying because it's where El is. Los Angeles is my home. I just rented an apartment. At 4 a.m. London time El texted me a photo of four bar stools she assembled. I fortify myself with a deep breath. "You want to negotiate another deal?"

Dad's smile falls. The wrinkles around his eyes intensify. "That's the last thing I want. I want you to join Rocker Inc. permanently. Be part of the company."

The tired coils of my brain bring together the picture he is painting. My heart skips a beat.

"I thought I'd keep interning with Death Elbow. Arrange their tour, find collaborations, maybe have them sing on someone's album?"

"We'll hire a tour manager for that. You'll still manage the brand deals and sponsorship opportunities, but you have better things to do than babysit Death Elbow. Besides, touring is grueling. It's twenty-four-seven for months on end. I want my son around. Pickle will miss you."

Dad grins. I smile back.

"If you come here, be part of the London office, you can stay put, discover new bands as A&R or be a producer. If you'd like another role, we can discuss that. Harper is interested in making the move and we're scheduled to open in the New Year." His hand lands on my shoulder. "Of course, there're plenty of schools in London that would welcome you. Got to finish that degree."

I rub the freshly buzzed strip over my ear. "Right." I search the empty floor, assessing the massive amount of faith Dad has in me. This isn't just a job, it's a place in his organization. I square my shoulders and lift my chin. I'll be part of his business. This move means more stability. The slim steel bars outlining the window break up the panoramic views. But if El decides to tour again, I'll be tied down. I clench my teeth.

"Wherever you live, you aren't getting rid of me." Dad catches my gaze, misinterpreting my hesitation. "I'll be splitting my time between London and LA. Now that you and El are . . . out of the house, Sylvia and I want to travel. It's important to me that you stay in my life. But I know living with me in the US wasn't your life plan."

I glance at my feet. "I may have been . . . resistant but it worked out for the best." I scuff my shoe against the concrete. "I'm happy I took the deal."

His fingers graze my upper arm. "As am I. I do regret missing the first twenty years of your life, but these last few months have meant the world to me."

Dad continues. "So let's keep going. Be my eyes and ears over here. Someone I can trust to give me an honest opinion. And take care of the family business. Now I have you to help me, expanding is possible. Who knows, maybe someday Pickle will open our Seoul branch and we'll be worldwide."

The blood in my temples pumps faster. He trusts me. I take a deep breath to calm the jittery feeling in my head. We've come far. He's no longer the man who stood in a studio in LA accusing me of using his stepdaughter for financial gain. I'm no longer interested in him as a way to get money for my mum and my family. Warmth spreads through my chest and my stance relaxes. We know each other enough to like each other for who we are.

"There are other advantages to moving here. Think how close you'll be to Hanna and Mr. Peters. A flight to Bremen is only a little over an hour from here. You can visit them for dinner."

Not being torn between two worlds sounds bloody amazing. London is looking better and better. Yet a belt around my lungs cinches. "Can I talk to El about this first?"

Dad pushes off the desk. "I'd expect nothing less. This is a decision you should make together."

"Thanks for—" A lump clogs my throat. How do I express what his offer means? What having him in my life means? For twenty years I held a grudge against the man I used to refer to as the sperm donor. Now I can't imagine not having Dad in my life.

"You never have to thank me." He heads for the elevator and presses the call button. "C'mon, let's get some grub. I'm in the mood for a full English breakfast."

Delayed is the word of the day. If we can all get through customs quickly and our car is out front, I might just make it to The Devil's Martini to kiss El before she goes onstage.

I cannot miss this performance.

"Finally." Xander picks up his carry-on as the woman and her three children wave goodbye to the customs officer. Since

Xander has a British passport and mine is German, we have to take a different line than the other band members who are probably already waiting on the other side. Collecting our luggage, I hope.

"Passports." The officer doesn't glance at us. He types away, studies them, and then inspects our faces. "Anything to declare?"

Xander shuffles his feet. "No."

"I have a Beatles first-pressing vinyl for my girlfriend," I say.

The officer's big bushy eyebrows rise. "Do you have a certificate of authenticity?"

An alarm starts to build in my gut. "No. It's just an old record."

Those eyebrows merge and the customs officer's fingers fly over the keyboard again. I should've gotten El a mug with the Tower of London. She probably would've been equally happy.

"Is it in your luggage or in your carry-on?"

"Carry-on." I point to my backpack.

The officer lifts his hand in the air and waves over a woman dressed like him. "Escort these men to room B."

"Me too?" Xander gawks at the woman gesturing for us to follow. "I don't have any gifts."

"Please remain calm," she tells us and we follow her out of the main hall down a long corridor.

Every step is shaking something loose in me. This better be quick. I bought the record at a record shop. They didn't say anything about any documents. I don't need this right now. El's waiting for me.

The officer in the dark blue uniform holds the door open for us. "Turn off your cell phones."

"I need to call my father." Dad will know how to handle this situation. Or he can get someone to fix it.

She points to a sign showing an ancient phone with a line through it. "No phones."

I press the button and show her it's off. Xander does the same. There's no use fighting.

I attempt to swallow but my throat is too tight. My breaths don't quite fill my lungs. This situation is ridiculous. I plop down in one of the four vacant chairs and wait.

And wait.

My butt is taking the shape of the chair so I get up and pace. Ten steps to cross the room. Ten steps back. I tap every step on my thigh and count to five hundred.

"Come on Wil, take the brooding down a notch."

"I need to get out of here." I cross the room and bang on the door. "Hello. Is there anyone out there? We've been stuck in here for hours."

Xander inspects his watch. "It's been twenty-five minutes."

A marching band of tiny drummers parades through my brain. I'm definitely going to miss El going onstage. I promised to be there, and I can't call her and explain. I kick the chair. Pain radiates up my foot. "Bloody hell."

"You need to chill."

Chill. All I do is chill. I sit coolly in boardrooms negotiating a one percent difference on a payment schedule to have grown men walk around with magenta water bottles in their hands. I freeze my feelings to not reply to the paparazzi whose job it is apparently to get a rise out of me. I shove my disgust at watching another band record *my* music with *my* girlfriend in the deepest compartments of the refrigerator in my chest. I store the unpleasantness away under lock and key, numb and calm. Chill.

I slam my fists on the table. "I'm so damn sick of being locked up."

Xander grabs me by the shoulders. "Wil. What the hell?"

"I should be at The Devil's Martini watching El perform, not stuck in this windowless box."

"This isn't the end of the world." Xander lets go. "El will understand. That girl bloody loves you. What are you really angry about?"

The door to the refrigerator in my chest swings open and everything tumbles out. I cover my face with my hands and my teeth screech. This life I've been building for myself is wrong.

Yes, I was busking on the street to help Mum out, but I could've picked up extra work at Opa's construction site, I could've slung beer at the bar. I played and I sang and I experimented with music. Learning to be a sound engineer was a way to get a job with a paycheck and enough to support myself and my family, but DJing whenever I could, seeing the people's bodies respond to the music I dished out was the high. Singing with El at The Devil's Martini was to get to Dad and ask him for money, but it was the most fun I had in my life. The most alive. Heard. Seen. Enough.

What the hell am I doing here?

THIRTY-ONE

I ATTACH MY PHONE to the tripod and step away to the promotional background that spells The Devil's Martini in dozens of small splashes, a riff on the updated logo. The camera flashes and I return to the phone to see if that spot allows for a full height shot.

"Wil's friend is talented. I didn't know what to expect when he pitched this wall, but this is impressive." Over my shoulder, Carlee studies the photo of me pretend pouting.

"The influencers that are arriving an hour before we open will have photo ops with you here." I point to the illuminated backdrop Mr. Peters and I just finished installing. I run my hand down the wall and push on the hidden door in the pitchfork tail. "The VIPs will get their gift bags including new The Devil's Martini-branded bomber jackets, sunglasses, and martini glassware in here." She peeks into the coat room we've transformed for the event. "But for the regular tickets, they get the glow-in-the-dark pitchfork hats and shot glasses as take-homes."

"We're officially sold out." Carlee smiles as she scans The Devil's Martini interior. The bones and charm that I've always loved remain, but the feel is no longer tired and run-down. The whole place is upscale and inviting. "Can you believe we pulled it off?"

"I still need to run over the menu with the new bartender—"

"Your grandmother is taking care of that." Carlee beckons me to follow her onstage where a long row of tables is set up, microphones propped before each of the six seats.

From the stage all the big and small changes we worked on come together. A tingle runs up my spine.

Despite being brand-new, the deep red leather of the semicircle booths is the perfect level of luxe, like they've been here for generations. The bar Mr. Peters stripped and varnished sits strong and sturdy like him, the bottles Mormor stocked gleaming like precious jewels in the low light. Under our feet, the refinished floorboards creak a little less, and above our heads new lights shine.

"You think they'll like it?" Carlee's voice is barely above a whisper.

"The critics?" I whirl on her.

"The patrons." Carlee interlaces her fingers. "So many clubs in LA."

"The Devil's Martini has always been special." I focus on the collection of chairs set up for the reporters we've invited to attend this press conference. "And with the updated bar, the merch booth, the larger stage, new lighting, new bathrooms, the rigging that can hold the modern equipment—we're fully booked for three months and barely have any free spots for the rest of the year."

"Three more new venues just announced opening dates this year."

"And you had that accounted for in your business plan." I check the to-do list on my phone and for the first time in the last week the number of items on it doesn't require me to scroll. "Our ticket prices are competitive. With your name attached to the venue, people know to expect quality."

Carlee swishes her styled curls over one shoulder. Beneath the makeup I can see faint bluish circles under her eyes that are a tell-tell sign of her not sleeping. Or maybe it's a trick of the new lights.

"This was not the plan." She smooths out the tablecloth. "I imagined a quiet life, me with my production company where other musicians like you and I write songs together, but we're here instead."

"Sometimes plans change." I scrape my lower lip with my teeth. "Hopefully for the better."

Carlee meets my eye. "You're moving out."

"Wil rented this fancy apartment. I bought bar stools for it." I turn to face her "You helped me so much, I don't want to abandon you."

"I'm happy for you two." The tips of Carlee's fingers tap against the back of a chair. "Before you start protesting, the live-in housekeeper is moving in at the beginning of the month and my parents are coming to visit next Thursday. Pauline agreed to return as venue manager." She gives me a reassuring nod, expression soothing. "I'll be well taken care of."

My hand covers hers. "Promise to call if you need anything?"

There's a quick nod from her. "I know our deal was you work for me until we open the venue, but I hope you know, if you still want to be my assistant I'd be lucky to have you." Her hand lands on mine. "Or we can create a role for you that fits. Say, write some songs together?"

I study the woman who was first my idol, then my boss. Somehow between her not choosing me as her replacement as lead singer and today, Carlee has become my friend. I squeeze her fingers. "I think I might take you up on that offer."

She turns to me. "You're making the right decision, El. You belong on this stage. I'm grateful for your support. For being brave and performing tonight."

I twirl a strand of hair. "Let's see how brave I feel tomorrow morning when my name is dragged through the mud by Daniel Davison."

She catches my hand, stilling it. "For every Daniel Davison there are hundreds, if not thousands of people who will be touched by your music. Your music will play at someone's wedding, someone's funeral, on the soundtrack of a movie, on someone's driving playlist, as inspiration to write a novel." Her fingernails press against my skin. "It'll play in some little kid's bedroom as they dream of being a rock star. And someday they will come to you and call you their idol. Your songs will be woven into the fabric of life, be there to lift people up on the good days and hold them together on the bad ones. You can't imagine the impact your melodies and words will have on others."

I swallow. Will I still have Wil to write those with me?

"Don't let the petty words of the few stop you from becoming the best." Carlee indicates the empty booths that will be full of people tonight. Judging. Smiling. Forming opinions. "Give them enough to satisfy their craving and keep your private life to yourself. You can find a balance, I promise."

Balance. That sounds fair. It's not all or nothing with my fame. Maybe I can find my way with the paparazzi and still have a life. Like Zoe said—take control. I know I have to try. Because denying what I want to do is not working. I have to be truthful. If I can't lie to others, I probably should stop lying to myself.

Carlee claps her hands together. "Speaking of. Are we ready to let the wolves in?"

I suck in a breath and let it out slowly. "No time like the present."

"El, what does Rocker think of you singing at this bar?" Four questions into the press conference, and the reporters are already picking on me.

I scoot to the edge of my seat and lean toward the microphone. "My stepfather is a fan of The Devil's Martini and Carlee." Beside me Carlee tilts her head in thank you. "You can ask him yourself when he MCs the show tonight."

A woman in the back shouts, "What about your brother?"

"Pickle is a little too young to visit The Devil's Martini."

"Except on All Ages Night," Carlee interjects. "Tuesdays until ten p.m."

The woman stands up. "I meant your other brother. Wil."

A barrage of flashes momentarily blinds me.

"Oh, you mean my boyfriend." I make an exaggerated face. "He's flying back from England as we speak. The flight was delayed last time I checked. But I'm confident he will be here."

"Did you see the pictures of your boyfriend out on the town again in London?"

"Are the rumors true that he's out of control with his partying?"

I don't see who asked the question. I lift my chin and plaster on a smile. "Did your invite get lost in the mail?"

There's a small rumble of laughter from the group. "Seriously, my boyfriend is too busy these days. The band he's working with had their inaugural album launch party this week. Death Elbow. You may've heard of them?" I hold my hand up to the side of my face and fake whisper into the mic. "If not, you might want to see whose album is at the top of the charts as of this morning. Get on the bandwagon."

Another smattering of chuckles rolls over the group.

"Are you and Dasher going to sing together tonight?" I recognize Daniel Davison's cool tone. I find him in the crowd. My former nemesis respected my request and didn't print a word in his article about the duet he witnessed.

"Good question, Daniel." I turn to Dasher on my left. "What do you think? Shall we?"

He flashes a million-watt smile and every camera in the place scrambles to immortalize the image. "I wouldn't miss it for the world."

The next question is for Dasher and although I participate in some of the questions to the group, no one asks me anything else not related to music. We pose for photos in front of the step-and-repeat and everyone exits with a gift bag. Some ask if they can get tickets for tonight's performance and Carlee hands out the ones we reserved.

Daniel Davison is the last lingering reporter. He meets my eye. "Break a leg tonight." I hold my breath for the jab. Instead he offers me a small and maybe even honest smile. "I look forward to many new album interviews." He snatches his gift bag and strides out to the sunlit sidewalk.

I gape at his back. Was that a compliment?

Then it's done. I survived the press conference. All that remains is to sing.

My favorite part.

I straighten the dragonfly necklace and run through my vocal warm-up exercise. On the green room's monitor I can see Dasher swaying with the audience, but I have the sound turned off. Our duet opened his set to much applause. My last-minute yes landed me into the final spot of the evening, so I'm up next. I've waited all night, but I don't have the usual wings of dread flapping under my breastbone. Only a general humming throughout my body, like it's tuning itself.

I pace and re-read my last text to Wil.

> Me: I'm going onstage in ten. Where are you?

The message remains unread. No dancing dots. Just blank space.

At the door, Sven stands guard, and our gazes lock. I'm thrown back to the first night he brought me to The Devil's Martini. Me in my blond wig trying to fool the world that I wasn't Rocker's stepdaughter.

I walk to stand beside him. "I call you my personal Superman, but you're more like my fairy godmother."

His left eyebrow hitches.

"You know, you're kinda responsible for all this." I wave my hand at the walls. "My coconspirator in my mad plan to kick-start my singing career, sneaking me out of Mom and Rocker's house every Saturday night to sing here."

He shrugs.

"Without you I wouldn't have met Wil, sung at The Devil's Martini."

"Without me you would have had the money to make your video with Mr. Mustard."

"Astor." Yes, the money went to Sven's bail, but that's what friends do. "You gave me a place to stay when I had nowhere else to go. You watched over my boyfriend when I wasn't there."

"Things I regret."

I nudge his elbow. "Admit it, you two have a bromance."

"He's quite the upgrade from Dillon."

"That's an understatement." I roll my eyes. "I'm glad you're here."

A hint of a smile graces Sven's lips. "So am I."

Releasing a shaky breath, I lay a hand on his forearm. "My bodyguard." My cheeks are wet before I am aware of crying. "My friend."

A grin. And then a sober, heartwarming, "Your friend."

I crash into him. "Thank you."

His arms encircle my shoulders and his chin rests on the top of my head. We stay like that for two long inhales. He clears his throat. "Thank me by hiring my company to provide security on your world tour."

Mushy moment over. I glance up at him. "I wouldn't trust anyone else."

"Okay." Mom hustles down the hallway. "Sorry to interrupt but it's time."

I let go of Sven and straighten my The Devil's Martini bomber jacket. "Any word from Wil?"

"Bill's on the phone with the driver but no sign." My mother eyes the digital clock on the wall. "The plane landed late. Maybe they are stuck on the tarmac, or their luggage is delayed?"

I swallow my disappointment. This night, no, this day would be perfect if Wil were here. But he's not.

You'd think after weeks of either waiting for Wil to arrive or watching him abandon me to deal with work, I'd be used to his absence. The gaping hole in my heart argues otherwise. I want him here.

I lift my chin and take my mother's offered arm. "I wanted Wil to see me sing."

"He will. This is just the first of many performances." Mom's gaze is steady. "You'll have plenty of chances to show off to Wil. But we're all here. You can sing for us this time. Sing for me."

I roll my eyes up to stop more tears from escaping. "You're going to make me cry." My voice wobbles as we step into the wings of the stage. Dasher's final song is on its last chords.

"One more thing." Mom swipes a thumb under my eyelashes. "If you ever need my help, whether it's words of encouragement, a shoulder to cry on, or a hand to hold you through a difficult moment, you can always ask. I've made mistakes in the past, but please, trust me to just be there for you. I love you."

My nose waters and I sniffle because all I want to do is cry, but I slip my arms around Mom's waist and offer my best attempt at a hug. No longer crying on the outside but shedding an ocean of tears on the inside. "I love you too, Mom. I'm really sorry I didn't turn out to be the daughter you wanted."

Mum laughs into my hair. "You turned out to be better than I could've dreamt of."

I sniffle again and pry myself from the comfort of Mom as the applause for Dasher thunders.

"You are exactly who you are supposed to be." She picks up my guitar from the bench and hangs it on me. "Go show them who you are."

Rocker jumps onto the stage, shakes Dasher's hand, and turns to the crowd. "Our next guest is especially dear to me." He waves me over to join him.

A familiar buzz hums in my chest and I stroll onto the stage to stand by Rocker, who drapes his arm over my shoulders. I spent years trying to step out from under his shadow, but I'm grateful he's here.

"I met this wonderful person the same day I met her mother." Rocker smiles down at me and recites a shorter version of how he and Mom met at the Griffith Observatory. The audience laughs and awws and I search the rows and booths for Wil's face.

Rocker pats my back. "Today I'm proud to introduce her to you as a talented singer and songwriter. She's proven me wrong many times, and I can't wait to be proven wrong by her again and again. Be forewarned everyone, I'll be the one clapping the hardest." He steps away. "Please, welcome, El Vella!"

The whistles and applause eat up the sound of Rocker's retreat. I glide my left hand up the neck of my guitar and barge into the storm of a live performance. Elation crashes into my heart, my lungs and pushes tears of joy against the dam behind my eyes.

I adjust the microphone. "It's always been my—"

The mic doesn't work.

My chest constricts. I can't sing without the mic.

Rocker runs across the stage, replacing the microphone. He taps on it to ensure it's working and gives me a thumbs-up.

"Seems The Devil's Martini has a new stagehand," I say as I reset the microphone and myself. The audience laughs. "As I was saying. It's always been my dream to sing." More whistles from the audience. "With two opera singers for parents and a rock star for a stepdad some might say I was doomed. Or blessed. Depending on how you look at it." I strum a chord. The perfectly tuned guitar comes to life, but something is off. "Over the years, I've changed my mind many times, but music has been my constant." I search the room for a glimpse of Wil's mop of dark hair, amber eyes, or his lopsided grin. I play another chord, but the guitar is not the issue. I smile at the crowd. I can't stall much longer. "I was going to start with a song by Dasher." I glance offstage in the direction Dasher exited by. "But he already beat me to the punch."

Of the few laughs my joke receives, I hear Zoe's the clearest. My cousin did always get me.

I've stalled as long as I can. My left hand, the one I injured last summer, twinges like it wishes Wil was onstage with me. I scan the audience one last time but there's no cocky German in sight.

I resign myself to the reality that Wil is not going to make it. He won't see me sing. A spike jabs into my side but I press my guitar against the wound and the ache subsides. No matter what, I will always have music.

As they say, the show must go on. Nothing is going to stop me from performing.

THIRTY-TWO

My heart pounds in my chest, still charged after the taxi ride from LAX and now heightened by the sight of El standing onstage at The Devil's Martini. A lone spotlight illuminates her red hair, her smiling mouth close to the microphone.

Not since the night Nick, Sarah, Mateo, and I filmed the video for the song she's now singing have I seen her like this. Owning the stage by herself. She's enchanting, a siren, luring everyone into her gravitational pull.

Corbin and Gideon flank me on either side. Corbin gawks. "Holy—"

"Shh." I slap his chest.

The packed audience sits on the edge of their seats, eyes and phones glued to the singer and her guitar. That *something* the talent shows and A&R and agents hunt for, she has in spades. She always has. I got to stand beside her and witness the marvel up close and personal.

The swooping sensation below my ribs is the certainty of what's to come: bigger venues, grander opportunities. This concert will be a badge of honor for those here today. Pride rises in my heart, but I was the first to know. Before we won the open mic, before her video blew up, before Carlee invited her on tour. I knew when she started singing a year ago, when I pressed my forehead against hers and willed her to.

Looking back at that day, there is one thing I can confess: I was already whipped. If Blatantly Subtle had chosen El as their new lead, I would've spent my days following her around on tour and been her number one cheerleader.

El makes eye contact with audience members as she strums the opening chords of her next song. I press my hand against my chest, recognizing our song. The one we started working on only a few months ago but were composing since the day we met. Our lyrics and melodies, how it was always meant to be.

My stammering breaths cover something I don't want to confess. Why do I want to ruin everything I've created, take the guitar from El's hands, and be a part of the spectacle happening onstage? To be a team there too?

Onstage, El sings the first line.

> Love conquers all the movies said
> but when I'm lonely in my bed

I think of you

Jealousy roars in my throat, leaving a bitter taste on my tongue. Not jealousy over El's talent. Jealousy of her standing on that stage. Performing.

Without me.

Music has been a thread in my life but never a career option. When Dad and Sylvia told El that music is a fickle and unstable business, internally I agreed with them, because for people like me it's true. Not for El though. She's different. She was born to be on that stage. I've never wanted to be that. Stability, money, certainty are what I sought since I earned my first euro.

Until I met her.

El's gaze snags on me and I swallow my envy. I grin and mouth, "I love you." It's so easy to be happy for her. So natural. My heart brims with warmth.

Onstage, El's voice ceases and her guitar falls silent. Hairs rise on the back of my neck. She holds my gaze, commanding my attention. "I'm sorry. I can't do this."

The beats of my heart thud against my temples so hard I'm sure everyone around me can hear them in the deafening silence. My forehead burns.

Gideon nudges me. "Is this part of the act?"

I ignore him, willing El to continue.

Her eyes shine brighter. "Because this song doesn't belong just to me. So if you don't mind, I'd like to invite someone else onstage with me today."

A few members of the audience follow her line of sight, necks craning to the back of the room.

Corbin points to his head and asks, "Me?"

The hairs that were standing up in fear now feel like the needles of a hedgehog along my collar. There's a round of applause. Of course she wants to sing with Corbin. This is all my fault. Corbin unzips his leather jacket, shoves it into Lucian's hands, and struts toward the stage.

El holds up a hand. "It was great collaborating with you, but I have someone better in mind." She stares at me. "Wil, would you please join me?"

My hand shakes and I clutch the collar of my shirt, opening the first button as if that'll help me breathe easier, as if my heart will stop ratcheting up from my chest into my throat. My brain screams the familiar no. It shouts that I have to be responsible, that I can't disappoint Dad. I have to earn money. Have savings in case Mum gets sick again. The excuses roar into a crescendo. I have to pay for the apartment. I have to take care of El. Give her a safe place to live where no one can hurt her.

Yet my heart wars with my head, shouting wants.

I want to be on that stage with El.

I want to perform with my girlfriend. My heart slams each desire like morse code.

I want our voices to blend. I want to create songs with her, argue over lyrics, obsess over the perfect note, word, instrument to make the ideas and feelings in our heads build the emotions in the people who listen to us.

The future I want is with her.

My heart drums wildly.

I want to sing.

The truth surges in me like a sonic boom blasting away my resignation, my doubts, my jealousy, all the negativity that's been swelling inside and poisoning me. Whether El's just missing me or reading my mind, whether this is an invitation for one night or forever, I'll gladly be by her side.

I want to sing.

I propel myself through the crowd, weave between the tables, pass one with Opa and Mum and another with Zoe, Mateo, Sarah, and Nick. The crowd claps and cheers. I avoid the table with Dad and Sylvia, pull myself up on the ledge of the stage as if it's the side of a pool, and take two quick strides to El.

She bounces on her heels, whispers a playful, "You're late," and kisses me on the cheek. The crowd is a chorus of awws and catcalls.

Her eyes sparkle as she positions me in front of the mic. "I have a very important question for you."

I glance from her to the audience and give them a cheeky grin. "The answer will probably be yes." They laugh and my limbs feel lighter.

"Wil Peters . . ." She pauses as if for dramatic effect. "Will you . . ." In the crowd someone hoots. She turns to the audience. "No, not that." Her attention turns to me. "Will you sing this song with me?"

There's an odd wobble in her voice and I search her face for a sign of nerves, but find nothing. El tucks a white strand behind her ear and slides her eyes to the audience in a "they're waiting" gesture.

I float on the joy and rightness of her request and turn to the crowd.

"I did warn you." I shrug. "I can't say no to her." Unable to resist touching El, I cup her cheek and peer into the ocean of her eyes. "Yes." I press my forehead against hers and my blood zings. "I'd love to sing this song with you."

Under my touch, her face breaks into a grin. She squeezes my hand, backs away, and turns to the crowd.

"He said yes," she exclaims in a giddy voice.

Zoe and Mateo's distinct whoops reach me, and I know my face is flushed. Even though we haven't rehearsed this, and there are probably hundreds of cameras trained on us, I feel more relaxed than since I kissed El goodbye the afternoon I hoped on a plane for England. She adjusts the guitar and strums a chord.

"Usually Wil plays guitar when we're up here, but if it's okay with you, I'll do the honors." We beam at her reference to our first night on this stage.

She restarts our song and I don't even need to warm up. Like every time I sing with El, the certainty of us hits me as if standing here beside El onstage has always been inevitable.

The melody weaves around us, pulling our voices together, and she leads the way with the first verse. There's no need to question where she will end and I will pick up, we share the mic and the stage and the song. Never breaking eye contact, I feed off her insatiable happiness and she eats up mine. We play the version we adjusted in our new apartment. She launches into "Maybe they were wrong" with the right amount of crescendo and I weave the riffs on "you" to fill out sound. We balance.

This is what I want: sharing our lives on- and offstage. Not watching the music happen. Making it happen.

For months I've pushed El to return to music, to use her talents, while denying my own.

Maybe I was made to perform as well.

Maybe I can take a chance.

Maybe I should take a chance.

Our love song ends and the applause begins. A standing ovation.

I suck in maybe the first easy breath I've taken since the car accident. I hold El's hand and soak in this moment, in case it's my last.

El swings her guitar over to her back and thanks the audience.

Mateo whoops and there's another round of applause.

Dad crosses the stage and squeezes himself between us, and I lose contact with El. "I hope someone recorded that." The audience laughs. "I told you my stepdaughter was talented. She's a featured artist on Death Elbow's song *Going Once*, which you can now download on all streaming services." He kisses El on the forehead. "Maybe Wil might even produce on one of El's songs?" Dad grabs my shoulder. "Wil has been an asset at Rocker Inc. and I hope one day will lead the company."

My smiles slips but I pull it back. Back to reality. I try to catch El's gaze, know what she's thinking, but she doesn't meet my eyes. Her hand creeps up and clutches the colorless strands of her hair.

The bottom drops out of my world.

THIRTY-THREE

CARLEE WAVES GOODBYE TO Dasher from the front hall of her mansion and whirls my way. "Go relax."

I enter the notes of their conversation into my phone. "I can stay."

"I can handle it." A group of Hollywood producers who want to rent The Devil's Martini for a promo event head our way. They are the final guests apart from Wil and my family, who are lingering at the afterparty that was supposed to be over thirty minutes ago.

"Forward me their information and I'll send them the booking agreement myself." Carlee lightly pushes me in the direction of the backyard.

The balls of my feet are numb from standing and my mouth is dry from all the talking. I'll get a glass of water, kiss Pickle goodnight, and come back to check on Carlee, I promise myself as I step outside.

The mostly empty side patio is designed for the parties, after-parties, and small events Asher Menken's parents hosted here every year since Rocker, Mom, and I moved next door. The event planner Zoe recommended staged the deck with cocktail tables covered in white cloth. The lights flickering in electric candles and the Eddison bulbs strung around the perimeter of the glass fence set the mood.

Cater-waiters flow between the tables and pick up the empty plates that have leftover tiny food offerings and mostly empty glass champagne flutes. Tucked in the corner by the pool featuring red and white floating candles is the open bar. Two bartenders are packing up the liquor they used to serve the same cocktails as Mormor created for The Devil's Martini. The live performances are done but a recording of the reopening show plays on a screen.

I search for Wil but don't find him. I should not have dragged him onstage. It's not his thing. He told me that but I was selfish again. I wanted him there with me. When I saw him I didn't think. How could he have said no in front of all those people?

I take off my shoes and enjoy the feel of grass between my toes as I make it to the bar where my family is having a great time, judging by their relaxed smiles and intermittent bursts of laughter.

"Didn't think I'd get to talk to you tonight." Rocker is the first to greet me.

"Just doing my job." I drop my shoes by one of the chairs. "We booked three more events and had a dozen inquiries." I reach for a bottle of water swimming in the bucket of mostly melted ice. "You rocked it as MC." I point to the screen where Bill Rockerby introduces Dasher.

Rocker chuckles. "Pun intended?"

"Very much so." I scan the patio. Hanna is showing something on her phone to Mom, who's bouncing with Pickle in her arms. "Where's Wil?"

"He and Zoe are showing Estelle and Wilhelm the secret gate." Mom nods her head in the direction of their house and points to the phone in Hanna's hands. "Have you seen the renovations to Hanna's place?"

"Aren't they beautiful? I can't wait until we can bake in that new kitchen together when I'm in Europe for New Year's."

"Wil said yes?" Rocker's lips pull into a smile.

"We couldn't say no." I inspect Hanna's face. She loved having us last Christmas so much that I had to say yes to visiting her for New Year's. Plus we'll be a lot more comfortable with the Murphy bed Wil and Mr. Peters added to the exercise room/guest bedroom. I give Mom a pleading glance. "But I promise to be where you are for Christmas. Norway. Here. Wherever. I'm not spending another Christmas away. Maybe Hanna and Mr. Peters can join us too?"

"I've always wanted to be somewhere with real snow on Christmas." Hanna's smiling face is tired but glowing. "Especially with my son and this cutie." She tickles Pickle who proudly sits in Mom's arms. "He's grown so much since I last saw him."

"He's supposed to be asleep but after his first time with a babysitter, he needed some time with me." Mom kisses the baby's head. "Or I needed some time with him."

Rocker emits a sigh of relief. "Good to know everyone is on board. I thought you might be against Wil moving to London."

"Moving to London?" Hanna tilts her head.

Mine swims. The déjà vu is startling. I heard Rocker wrong. Wil didn't mention anything about moving to London. My hands go clammy. Then again, neither did Dillon. No, after Rocker sent him to London, all I got was a text from my no-longer-boyfriend telling me we were over. One minute I had a boyfriend, the next he's in another country, leaving me behind.

I blink to steady myself. This isn't the same. Wil is not Dillon.

"I don't understand," says Hanna.

Neither do I.

"Wil's going to spearhead the new office I'm opening. He'll be closer to Bremen." Rocker beams at Hanna like this is a good thing.

My mind stutters. Water gurgles from the water bottle and I loosen my grip. Wil is not Dillon. The four words play on a loop in my head. But a tiny voice asks if I put my trust into the wrong man. Again. "And Wil said yes?"

"What did I say yes to?" Wil's arms wrap around my waist and pull my back into his chest.

Rocker's gaze ping-pongs between Wil and me. "Working in London?"

Wil's skin blazes against my bare arms.

"London? I want to go this time." Zoe joins our huddle and scans my face. "Is it another video shoot? I want creative control of the costumes."

"What video?" Mom settles into one of the bar stools.

My heart thuds against my ribcage. I never told Mom the real reason I was in London last June.

"The one she flew to England for last year?" Zoe says slowly.

Mom turns to Rocker for confirmation. "You said she went there to see Dillon."

I stare at Rocker. Guess that secret is out.

"Wait." Hanna turns to Rocker as well, eyebrows drawn. "Did you say you asked Wil to move countries?" She lays a hand on Wil's forearm. "And you didn't tell me?"

Wil's body tenses behind me, his fingers digging into my hip. I'd move away but I'm frozen in place by Mom's piercing gaze and Zoe's apologetic pout.

"Wil and I discussed the offer, and I approved." Mr. Peters steps around the corner of the pool, Mormor trailing behind him. "We needed money for your treatment. You can blame me."

Is Mr. Peters talking about Wil moving to LA? What does that have to do with London?

Hanna spins on her father. "You approved the move to London because of money?" Her normally serene face crumples. "Dad, I don't need any more treatment. And I certainly don't need Wil to pay for anything."

Wil, Rocker, and Mormor all talk across each other while I try to keep up, not sure which information I should be explaining.

"Can we please pause." All conversations halt and we focus on Mom, who hands Pickle to Mormor. "Zoe, what video are you talking about?"

"The video for *Don't Give Me Comfort*?" Zoe fiddles with the tassel on her dress.

Mom rubs her forehead. "Didn't Wil shoot it for her here with his friends?"

"Yes, the second one, after they gigged at The Devil's Martini." Zoe crosses her arms.

"There's a new video? What was wrong with the old one?" asks Mom.

"No, Mom, Zoe means last summer, when I escaped to London and you thought I went to see Dillon?" Mom nods. "I was really there to film a music video."

As much as I didn't want my mother to find out this way, my heart is pounding for a completely different reason. Wil is not Dillon. I twist in Wil's embrace.

"Are you moving to London?" I will it not to be true.

Wil does a sweep of my face. "It's a good offer."

I shrink from his hold. Goosebumps cover me head to toe. That's not a denial. He didn't say he doesn't want to move to London. An invisible fist takes hold of my throat. I whirl away.

Mom grabs my elbow and pushes blond strands from her face. "What else didn't I know?"

"When I went to London last year, Dillon and I were over. I let you believe it was for him because you were less angry if I did something for a guy than for my music." I rejoin the sharing circle. "I was there because I paid Leonard Astor to shoot the video for *Don't Give Me Comfort*. At least the version I had then. When Rocker took me home and you banned me from singing, I signed up for an open mic night at The Devil's Martini to prove I was a worthy singer. Wil was at the bar that night. Because my fingers were in a cast and my original guitarist fell through, I had to accept Wil's offer to play for me. That's how we met. Not at the Blend coffee shop like I told you." I glance at Wil, who hasn't moved.

"Did you know Wil was Bill's son?" Mom's lower lip trembles.

"No." Wil comes to stand beside me. "At least not then. She found out in November when she overhead me tell Dad."

Silent tears fall out of Mom's eyes. "In November?" She glares at Rocker. "Why didn't you tell me that either?"

"I didn't believe him." Rocker steps toward his wife. "You know how often people claim to be related to me. Not until I came to Bremen to rescue El after we saw her busking and recognized Hanna, and found out Wil was her son, did I make the connection."

Mom slowly bobs her head like she's processing all this new information. Wil tries to take my hand but I inch away. The "Wil is not Dillon" refrain in my head doesn't feel as comforting.

"Stop." Mormor sets Pickle on the deck and waves her hands in the air. "Everyone stop this."

I halt in my tracks, my need to run, to flee blocked by loyalty to my grandmother.

"We are a family and it appears we've all been hiding things. That's not how this family works. So let me be the matriarch I should be. Out with the secrets and the lies now. Let's clear the air and be done with it."

I turn to Wil expecting an explanation. He shoves his hands in his pockets and stares at his feet. My mind races, thoughts swirling like a storm as I search his face for answers.

Mr. Peters takes a big breath and turns to Hanna. "I should tell you that I was the reason Wil went to the United States the first time. It was my idea for him to find Rocker and ask for money."

"I kinda guessed," says Hanna.

"It gets worse." He shuffles his feet. "Even after Rocker came to Bremen, I couldn't forgive him, couldn't let go of the grudge I held on to all these years. So I insisted Wil go to Los Angeles and Rocker pay you back for the time you spent caring for his child, by covering the cost of your treatments."

Mom gasps at Rocker. "You were paying for Hanna's treatments? What else haven't you told me?"

Rocker mirrors Wil, hands crammed into his pockets. "You were about to give birth to our son, stressed about being estranged from El, we'd just found out Wil was my son, and I'd asked him to move here without consulting you. There was so much going on. I didn't think a nominal amount of money was worth disturbing you over. I was taking care of my family." Rocker rubs his collarbone.

"Is that everything?" Mom crosses her arms on her chest. "Or are you all going to protect me from more things by keeping me in the dark about your lives?"

Everyone starts talking at once. Zoe confesses to Mormor that she sold the necklace she gave her to invest in her clothing brand. Hanna insists to Mr. Peters that she can fend for herself. Wil avoids my glare while Rocker grasps Wil's shoulders, saying something about London.

I open my mouth to apologize for running away and depriving Rocker of time with Wil, for dragging him onstage with me over and over again to cover my terror of doing it on my own. A splash behind me drowns out all the voices. I turn to make sure nothing has blown into the pool.

Air locks in my chest. At the edge of the pool, Pickle is sinking under the surface. I feel lightheaded. Unsteady. My heart gives a giant thump. The need to scream for help, drag Wil to the pool wars with my feet rushing forward as Pickle's limbs jerk under the water. I jump into the pool next to my brother's tiny body.

The water is warm, instead of cold like Lake Como. My brain time-travels to that afternoon and my limbs threaten to go slack. I could let the water rattle me, give into the urge to stand still. In every nightmare, Papa told me everything was going to be fine, but it wasn't. I let Papa go when he needed my help. Pickle needs help. My help. Instead of giving in, letting the panic take me, I push against the hysteria, dragging my legs, moving my arms. Chlorine stings my eyes and the fabric of my dress clings to my legs, urging me to give up, but I can't. I have to get to Pickle.

Ahead of me the baby comes up to the surface, rolls onto his back, and floats. I'm almost within reach when he opens his eyes. My fingers find skin and I jerk him out of the water, clutching him to my chest. My every nerve ending fires and I don't know if I should cry or laugh or faint. The little guy grins at me, his hair wet, and shoves one of the electric candles floating around us into his mouth.

"Baby." More splashes sound around me. "El." The shouts come in and out of my consciousness. "Should I call 911?"

Mom's face appears next to the baby's, her fair hair dripping. "Are you okay?" Her gaze snaps between him and me. She wraps her arms around both of us as she keeps saying, "Are you okay? Are you okay?"

"He's fine, Mom." Pickle babbles his own sentiment.

Mom unwraps herself from us. "I can see that." She strokes my soaking hair. "How about you?"

A quavering gasp comes out of me. Someone's hands close on my shoulders. The sounds surrounding us rush in all at once.

Splashing water, shouting cater-waiters. I put one hand to the surface of the pool. The spot I'm in is shallow enough that I'm standing waist-deep, but I'm in the water. Adrenaline shivers along my spine. My nemesis is around me and I'm okay. I feel dizzy and weak in the knees, but okay. My silk dress is ruined, but I'm okay. My face is wet but I'm not sure if it's pool water, or tears, or all of the above. I kiss Pickle's chubby hand. "I'm okay, Mom."

Rocker joins our trio. I assure him I'm fine. Along with anyone one else in the pool, which seems to be everyone. Even Mormor and Mr. Peters are in the water with us. Zoe's clutching Mormor's hand. Wil's fingers squeeze my shoulder and I find his hand, squeezing back.

Rocker takes Pickle and everyone coos over him. He gurgles with delight and hits the water, apparently loving the attention.

"There's one more secret to spill." Mom's voice brings my attention to her puffy eyes. "Well, Bill knows, I couldn't have done it without him." She raises her voice. "Everyone."

A hush falls over the pool.

Mom pushes sopping hair from her face. "When Bill and I found out we were having a boy we decided to call him William. The idea was to honor his father, the man who wanted nothing more than a family of his own. But another Wil came into our life." Mom reaches for Wil and squeezes his hand. "Then Mr. Peters joined the family." Mormor threads an arm through the crook of his.

"It seemed like there was an ocean of Wils." The group of wet spectators agrees. "We thought we'd continue another family tradition." She glances at Mormor. "The star names that run in the Nelson family. Estelle, Nova, Halley, who ended up Bailey." Mormor snorts. "Pickle seemed the last chance to represent this generation. The constellation of Archer is one of my favorites." Mom sucks in her lips. "Let me introduce you to Archer William Rockerby."

All eyes are on Pickle.

"Archer Rockerby," I say. "Sounds like a perfect name for a singer."

Mom's eyebrows shoot up.

"If he wants to be one." I hold up my hands. "That's another way for him to keep his family legacy. To make his mom and dad proud."

Mom steps close to me and takes my face into her hands.

"I am proud of you. Your Papa is proud, Baby Girl." She squeezes my cheeks. "If he were here today, he'd hug you until you giggled with joy."

I laugh with Mom. "He gave the best hugs."

"That he did."

Now I know the wetness on my face is tears because they mirror the ones on Mom's. I sob. She brings my forehead into her chest and we sob together surrounded by water, the thing that ruined our lives many years ago. But I'm no longer afraid of it, or of telling my mother who I am or what I am going after. I trust myself. I trust her.

"This is great and all, but can we get out of the water now?" Zoe plucks at the fabric of her skirt. "I'm sure chlorine is not good for silk."

Everyone agrees and we help each other out of the water. My hand in his, Wil pulls me up the last step, his wet hair flopping over a concerned face. "Can we talk?"

"Not here." I drag him to the secret gate.

THIRTY-FOUR

I LOCK THE SECRET gate behind us and my waterlogged shoes schlep down the path to Dad's house. El pulls the towel tighter around her shoulders ahead of me and I regret not grabbing one. My wet jeans restrain my every move, heavier than my lies of omission. The buoyancy of being onstage mere hours ago has dissipated and uncertainty has settled in the crevices of my bones.

El jerks open the door into the basement and heads opposite the stairs. She reaches the end of the corridor and turns the lights on in Dad's home studio as I follow her in. "No one will hear us here." She pats the foam egg-carton padding on the walls and locks the door. "Or interrupt us."

Both sound reasons for us to be here. This is not a date, but we don't need to fill another square on the "Reasons to interrupt us bingo card." As a small puddle forms beneath my feet, I'm not sure of my next move. El drapes the towel she had over her shoulders across one of the leather chairs and points for me to sit. I step out of my shoes, peel off my socks, and pad across the carpet to the spot she indicated. My pants squelch as I sit down. "El—"

She stops me with her raised hand. "I'm upset."

Her lips press into a thin line and she paces across the room. I can't stand the distance so I get up to move closer. She revolves away from the wall, stares at me, and points at the seat I just vacated. I've never seen her like this.

With no other good option, I sit my butt down. "This London thing it's—"

"You of all people know trust is very important to me." She tilts her head. "If I can't trust you, how can we be together?"

I shake my head and pop out of my seat. "You can trust me."

"Can I?" She completes another loop, stops before me. "You didn't lie exactly, but you didn't tell me things either."

"I was going to tell you about London."

"It's not only London. Mom told me you wrote the lyrics for *Going Once*."

My back crawls with pins and needles and I collapse into my seat. "It just happened. I didn't think it was important."

"Not important." Her eyes widen. "Everything about you is important, especially you writing lyrics. It's huge. You know how much I love your words. That's why singing that song worked for me, even though it was with Death Elbow and not you."

"You made that song into a hit—"

"Oh, don't try to distract me." The pacing starts again but this time she's shaking her hands. "Let me say this first, because if I don't, I might say something I'll regret and that's the last thing I want to do to you."

I clamp my mouth shut and force my body to stay seated.

"I thought I loved my first boyfriend, but Dillon kept things from me. First it was little things, like not showing up on a date and promising the next one would be better. But the omissions, as you'd call them, got bigger and bigger, until the worst one blindsided me." Tears shine in El's eyes. "Rocker offered him a job in England in order to separate us. Dillon chose money over me and didn't tell me until he had already moved to London."

That's too much. I knew her ex was a wanker, but not that he moved because Dad offered him money. My teeth clench and a low, gruff string of sadness vibrates through me at the thought El felt this way for even a second. I jump up and grip El's shoulders. "That's not what Dad's offer is about. He's not trying to separate us. He has this concept of turning Rocker Inc. into a family business. He wants me in London as his eyes and ears."

She rubs at her eyes, mascara painting darker circles around them. "But I didn't know that." Her voice cracks. "You should've called me, texted me, anything but wait until I had to hear it from someone else."

I squeeze her shoulder. "I couldn't. Dad surprised me with the offer and I didn't want to burden you before your performance. It seemed too much. I told Dad I needed to talk to you first. But I didn't want to do it over video. I promised you that we'd make all the decisions together. That I won't make you do something you don't want to."

She bites her lip. "About tonight." Her fingers wrap around my wrist. "I'm sorry."

I blink. "Sorry? For what?"

"For dragging you onstage today. I saw you there, in the back of The Devil's Martini, and I was so happy you made it. All day I'd been waiting for you and asking you to join me just slipped out. I didn't mean to pressure you into coming up on that stage."

My shoulders drop.

"I never meant to do that to you. I know you don't want to be involved in performances." Her eyes tear to the side and her mouth droops. "That you like the money your job brings."

"El, I—"

"I know I haven't been supportive and I'm sorry. I didn't understand what it meant to you. But if that's what you want, I'll learn to love it."

I stare at her. "Learn?"

"Yeah. Each time you were pulled away because of work or missed our dates, I struggled. Thought I was being selfish because I miss the old days, when it was just you and me. But I know things can't stay that way. Things change. Just don't exclude me."

My heart halts halfway through a beat. "I didn't know you felt this way."

"We can move to London if it's important. I don't want to be what stands between you and Rocker."

"You could never." I bend my knees to get to her eye level. "Besides, I don't even think I want to go."

Her eyebrows scrunch. "You don't want to move to London?"

"It's not about London. It's about Dad. He needs me. After twenty years of not having a father, now that I've found him and know he's a good guy, I want to be in his life as well. I can't let him down. Yet."

She presses closer. "Yet?"

I loosen my grasp on her and do my own pacing. "Seeing you back onstage and then singing with you turned everything upside down."

"So you didn't want to sing with me," she squeaks.

I stop in front of her. "The exact opposite. And that's the problem."

"You didn't have to come join me if you didn't want to."

"Don't you see? I did want to. When you asked me to sing with you, I realized the truth." I suck in air. "I wanted to sing with you more than working with Death Elbow, who might be the next big band, or opening a new office for Dad in London and scouting the next ten bands that might break." I rub the hollow below my throat. "I watched you on that stage and wanted to throw it all away." I stop pacing. "Be irresponsible."

I snicker. "I've always loved Mum and Opa, cared for my rowing team, but getting close to anyone else was not an option, because with closeness comes responsibility. I was always scared if I cared for someone, I'd want to be able to be there for them financially, emotionally, physically, and I already was failing with just Opa and Mum."

El crosses her arms, the hurt expression on her face morphing to one of anger. "You don't need to take care of me."

I bracket her face. "But I want to. I love taking care of you. But that is not the problem. The problem is that I can't do that and choose music. If I work for Dad, open his new office, I get what I've always wanted: money and stability. That is logical. I can take care of everyone." Her skin is soft where my thumbs gently massage circles. "But when you asked me to sing with you onstage, I couldn't deny what *I* wanted. Your simple request obliterated all logic."

"I didn't think. I just couldn't sing our song without you."

"I'm so proud of you, El. Unlike Corbin, you didn't step on that stage tonight to earn money or gain fame. You sing because it's your passion. You are willing to take risks, like accepting jobs well below your talent level, like being a backup singer for Blatantly Subtle when you are clearly lead singer material. But you took the chance because it meant you could do what you love." My heart pounds. "That is so much braver than I can be."

"It was just The Devil's Martini, not Sphere in Vegas."

"But it could be one day." I release her face and stuff my hands in my pockets. "You are going to give singing a real go, right?" I don't want to hear any answer but yes.

El rubs the heel of her palm between her eyebrows. "I'd like to, but there are so many things to think about. You say I'm not onstage for the money, but I do need to make a living. Carlee asked me to stay on as her assistant, and I'm trying to see how I can fit that in and sing. I don't know how that will work if my opportunities to play clubs at night and on weekends overlap with The Devil's Martini schedule. I'll need something that has more flexible hours." Her chin wobbles. "Maybe I try songwriting, or teaching kids how to sing, or ask Sven if he wants to hire me back as an assistant."

I wash down the disappointment. "If you need more flexibility, I can say yes to Dad's offer. We can move to London, the music scene is spectacular there, and you can do the night gigs, and we can rent a place there. I'll support you while you work on getting to a place where your gigs pay enough."

"And what if they won't? What if two, five years from now I cannot support myself with singing?"

I take hold of her hands. "But what if you do? I believe in you. Your parents believe in you."

"That's family. It doesn't count."

"Carlee believes in you." I shake our joined hands. "Death Elbow was blown away by you. Dasher can't wait for another collaboration. It's not a matter of if, but when. You should do it."

El's chin lifts. "Then you should do it with me."

"We can't both be starving artists. It's your dream, not mine."

"It may not have been your dream originally, but you just said you wanted to be on that stage with me." She grips my hand tighter. "So do it. Sing with me. Write music with me. When you are next to me the music is better. I'm better."

"You don't need me as a crutch. You are great on your own."

"Yes, I can sing on my own. But I want to sing with *you*. Dreams can change. I never considered being part of a duo. I thought I had to do everything by myself. You taught me that isn't true." El pulls me closer. "You say I'm brave. Let me teach you to be brave too. Give us a chance, Wil. Give WE a chance."

The hope in her eyes ransacks my gut. I focus on the gleaming surface of the sound board across the room. "It's not logical. I'd have a good job if I work for Dad."

"Maybe you can have a good life if you choose us." El's fingernail presses against my chin, asking to draw my attention back to her. "You said we're a team. Do you still believe that?"

"More than ever."

"And being a part of a team means sometimes one person supports the other when they need it." I nod. "It's not about equal shares, but about what the other needs. You supported me when I needed time to find myself. When I took the job with Carlee because you knew music is where I need to be and that was the path I had to take." Her palm nestles into the side of my neck. "Let me support you." Her thumb traces my jaw line. "Let me carry some of the fears about money and disappointing Rocker and whether we can make it or not. Be on my team."

A version of my life rolls out before me in a vision of images and sounds. We'll support each other, give each other space to retreat and space to take charge. The ebb and flow of trusting that the other person has your best interest at heart, and you have theirs.

We blend. We breathe. We balance.

We sing and perform and as long as we have each other, everything will be fine.

"I want to." My throat bobs. "But I can't disappoint Dad."

El digs the pads of her fingers into my scalp, the pressure reassuring and solid. "You can't disappoint *you*."

I inhale the assertion. The last time I did something for myself, was honest, I stood upstairs in El's room after months of lying to her about who I was and lying to myself that I didn't care for her, afraid I was losing her. I asked her why I couldn't be the type of guy she'd fall for. And she answered me with a kiss. With her honesty. Because El can't lie. I don't want to lie to her anymore. Or to myself. Being on that stage with her tonight felt good. Felt right. I didn't have to deny any part of me or hold myself back. I was truthful and I was the Wil who felt free.

The pit of my stomach churns, each realization leaving me feeling raw and exposed. I don't want to lie any more. Can I do this, or is it just a dream? "I don't know."

"Let me help." Her touch drops away and she steps back. "You said onstage at The Devil's Martini that you can't say no to me. Is that still true?"

A chill skims across my skin. I chase the connection to her, desperate for contact. "Please don't ask me this."

"I don't want you to say yes to please me." She stays out of reach. "I adore that you care enough to put my needs first. But for once, think about yourself. Don't analyze or weigh the pros and cons. Close your eyes and answer my questions from your gut, your truest self. We can use our brains to figure out the rest later. Can you do that?"

I nod and close my eyes.

"You promise?"

"I promise."

"Wil Peters, do you want to be half of WE with me?"

The answer is desperate to escape my lips. This isn't a yes for her. This is a yes for me. If it becomes a yes for us, I'm not going to complain. "Yes."

El squeals and I breathe in a future full of possibility. Saying yes to myself is hard, but I don't want to take it back. The hardest thing is ahead: figuring out how to make it a reality, and how to tell my family.

Three weeks after the Grand Reopening, El and my apartment is full of people again. This time we actually invited every single person who is chitchatting loudly in our living room. I might've wanted to delay this "party" but it's past due. Even with the secondhand love seat and four stools, there's not enough room for everyone to sit. Sylvia and Dad are on the floor next to a rectangular contraption that functions as a miniature baby prison and keeps Pickle from crawling away and potentially hurting himself.

Opa, Estelle, and Mum stand in the kitchen with partially cut fruit and pitchers of Estelle's latest creation splayed around the counter.

Zoe and Mateo are consuming cocktails at such an alarming rate, I'm not certain they'll be able to understand what El and I are going to present them with today. Sven and Carlee are on the love seat and I hope they are not discussing anything business related again.

"Thank you everyone for coming today." El takes a sip from our beat-up water bottle and the W&E she retraced with a marker on the bottle is just another sign that we are on the right path. "Wil and I have an announcement for you."

"Are you pregnant?" says Opa.

"Wilhelm, we've talked about it. You can't ask women these questions." Estelle turns to us. "Are you?"

"No." We shake our heads.

"Let's try this again." El lifts her chin. "Wil and I would like to share something with you. We have our minds made up but we'd like your support as we go into this new stage of our lives. That doesn't include babies."

I place my hand on the small of El's back. Someday there might be little Els for me to teach guitar to, but not anytime soon. We have bigger plans.

"We are young and we understand that all of you in your unique way want us to be happy." She smiles at Zoe. "To succeed." She nods at Sven. "To do well in life." She meets Dad's gaze. "To not to repeat your mistakes." She glance at Sylvia. "To take care of ourselves." She winks at Estelle. "To follow our dreams." She waves at Carlee. "But also have a backup plan." Her gaze lands on Opa.

Our guests nod.

"This is our way to show that we've heard you, but that we've also heard ourselves and we'd like you to hear us too."

I turn on the TV to a photo of El and me singing onstage at the Grand Reopening. "We have decided to make W&E, the singing and songwriting duo, official."

Dad stares at me. "Are you quitting?"

I shake my head. "Not yet. We agreed that I will work for Rocker Inc. for another year. Here in LA and then in London as we establish our social media presence and play on different stages, make connections in the business, and cut our first album." I meet Dad's gaze. "That way I won't completely abandon you. I can help you establish the London office, get things up and running, and get my degree before I leave."

"You will still have plenty of time with Wil." El bounces on the balls of her feet. "I'm not stealing him away."

Dad slowly rises and I feel El bristle. I brush her fingers with mine, giving her a physical, "Everything will be fine."

Dad takes me by the shoulders. "Is this what you want to do? To perform with El as a duo?"

I plaster my hands to my sides in an attempt to still the itch to tap. "I do. I know it's not—"

"But it's what you want?"

I nod.

"Then you have my support." Dad shakes me gently. "Seems the apple doesn't fall far from the tree after all." His grin lights up the room. "I'm here for you. Even if that is only standing in the front row at your concert cheering."

The anticipation that was twisting my heart disappears. Time for El's part of the plan. She steps forward. "If you'd still like to write songs with me, Carlee, I'd love to do that for the next year and see where that takes us."

Carlee smiles. "I'll ask my lawyers to come up with contracts as soon as possible."

Zoe pushes away from the wall. "Maybe this is how I get famous. You two megastars wearing my outfits will have all the celebrities clamoring for my designs."

Mateo stands. "I assume I get to handle your merch. I'll give you a great deal."

Sven steps forward. "Does this mean you're moving back in with me?"

I turn to El. "No, we have the money from the Death Elbow endorsement deals to cover rent for the next six months. But maybe keep the couch open for us?"

"I don't have any music industry talents," says Opa. "But you know I'm here for you two."

"As am I." Estelle clutches Opa's elbow.

Mum comes over and moves the hair off my forehead. "You taking a chance on yourself is what I've always wanted for you." She takes El's hand. "Wil was always the world to me, now, the world will get to meet him."

El breaks away from Mum and finds Sylvia's still figure. "So? What do you think?"

Sylvia stands and brushes the creases out of her pants. "I think if anyone can make it, you and Wil can."

I hug El into my chest and memorize the smiles on the faces of the people we love.

Maybe love does conquer all.

Epilogue

Wil

EVERYTHING HAS GONE according to plan. The two days of the video shoot for *Love Conquers All* with Leonard Astor were better than any of my stays in London.

A smattering of paparazzi in front of the marble staircase turns our way the moment the taxi pulls up to the Four Seasons. I button the suit Zoe finished in time for our trip here.

"Are you ready?" I say to El.

The familiar flash of cameras surrounds us as we exit, hand in hand. Shouts of "Wil, El, over here" greet us.

"Can we have a kiss?" One photographer calls.

El grins at me and nods. I know what to do. I slide my hands around her waist and touch my lips to hers. The world around us lights up. I linger long enough for the shouts to subside and we start up the steps to the wrought iron doors of the hotel.

Inside the lobby, it's quiet and calm.

"Wil." I hear my name ring across the gleaming two-story lobby.

I smile wide. "Dad?"

I glance over to the plush maroon couches arranged in a semi-circle, and sure enough, there's Bill Rockerby. My dad. Archer jumps on his knees, his London beanie almost covering his eyes.

"What are you doing here?" I stumble over my words.

"The better question is, how did the final day of the shoot go?" His voice is low and curious.

"I—" I don't know where to start.

"We did the whole reverse recording thing," El rushes in. "Leonard used glitter to coat the ceiling of the final room, but the best part was the rig the car was on when we pretended to drive."

"So not fun at all." Dad shakes his head and stands. "You'll have to repeat everything for your mothers, they're waiting to get on a group video call." He corrals us toward the elevator and presses the call button.

"Excuse me." A teenager with braces pulls a phone from her bag. "Can I get a photo with you?"

"Sure." Dad sits Archer on the floor and stretches one arm to the side for her to come closer.

The girl turns on her phone and gives it to him. "Take them in portrait mode, not landscape," she says as she moves between El and me.

"You want the picture with us?" El's eyes go wide.

"You're W&E, aren't you?"

We smile up at the camera and enjoy another photo with a fan.

If we succeed in this business, fame will follow us everywhere. But with El by my side, we can make it work. It is all about balance.

Thank you for reading Wil & El's romance.

Enjoyed their story? Spread the word.

Honest reviews persuade other readers to click on The Falling for the Rockstar's Daughter Trilogy and are a powerful way to support authors.

If Wil & El entertained you, we would be grateful if you'd spend five minutes of your time leaving a review.

Your review can be a few words or a few sentences.

GOING ONCE
(Lyrics)

Verse 1

Saw you first, heard second

Beneath deceptions of our first impressions

I hid the truth when you chose to confess

Devil winds they beckoned

Stranded in the valley of bad intentions

Spent nights awake your heartbeat in my chest

Chorus 1

Going once, going twice

It's in my head, it's in your eyes.

Going once, going twice

It's in my head, it's in your eyes.

Verse 2

Crying lips, words pierce

Chased you away no longer tethered

Without you my soul is stuck on mute

Always sweet yet fierce

Your voice, my guitar in the dark, together

Our moans spell out the truth we can't refute

Chorus 2

Going once, going twice

It's in my head is in your eyes

Going once, going twice

It's in my head is in your eyes.

Bridge

My heart was first to realize,

the real truth behind the lies,

Not everything is as it seems

Sometimes

the unexpected is what you were waiting for and it's far beyond

my dreams

Chorus 3

Going once, going twice

It's in my head, it's in your eyes.

Going once, going twice

It's in my head, it's in your eyes.

Going once, going twice

It's in my head, it's in your eyes.

Going once, going twice

It's in my head, it's in your eyes.

LOVE CONQUERS ALL
(Lyrics)

Verse 1

Love conquers all the movies said

but when I'm lonely in my bed

I think of you

My fingers flex my memories fade

and on this day, I can relate

I think of you

Chorus 1

Maybe they were right,

maybe they were wrong

maybe I should just give up, give in and fall for . . .

you–you–you

Verse 2

I wanna see you, know your thoughts,

your lips on mine full fever hot

I think of you

Bow of your spine, my palm on yours

Your tears seep into my pores

I think of you

Chorus 2

Maybe they were right,

maybe they were wrong

maybe I should just give up, give in and fall for . . .

you–you–you

Bridge

What if we'd never met, our paths didn't cross?

And that day I'd said hell no, what a loss

What if you ran away and I didn't follow

Endless todays . . . but no tomorrow

Verse 3

Love conquers all the movies said

but when I'm lonely in my bed

I think of you

Chorus 3

Maybe they were right,

maybe they were wrong

maybe I should just give up, give in and fall

Maybe they were right,

maybe they were wrong

maybe I should just give up, give in and fall for . . .

you

Turn the page for a sneak peek of
the first book in the And Us Series.

Watch movies and real life collide with Sarah and Nick in a right person/wrong time, hidden identity, new adult romance.

One night to bring them together
One lie to tear them apart
Five holidays to fall in love

NICK

The truth is—I tell lies all the time. What's one more?

I twirl the fake ID my friends gave me for my birthday. It's my face all right, but according to the black block letters on this driver's license, my name isn't Nick, it's Shawn. The address is also not mine, nor the age. I'm newly nineteen, and Shawn's twenty-one. Old enough to drink but not too old for those inclined to question.

I catch the bartender's eye for the third time. A tingle travels down my neck.

She reaches over in front of a woman my mom's age, lays a snowflake-shaped coaster on the bar to my right, and places a fancy pink cocktail with a paper umbrella on it. Glossy green leaves frame the name tag on the pocket of her white resort uniform. The sprig of ivy is the only nod to Christmas Eve. The tag hangs down at an angle, making it hard to read her name, but it begins with an S.

"And what can I get for you?" She hands a glass of sparkling water to a server who appears and disappears to my left. Her voice rings over the smooth jazz. My pulse beats in my ears and dampens the chatter of a couple dozen patrons scattered around the small dimly lit bar.

"Old Fashioned." Dad's been ordering them at every place we've been to this week. This whole trip turned into him show-ing off that he's landed on his feet. He spends every day trying to get back into Mom's good graces. Bonding time with me doesn't appear to be on the agenda anymore.

"Is that your ID?"

I slide the laminated card her way, and she flicks her eyes between the photo and me. The one-corner-of-the-mouth smile I learned from my brother plus the direct eye contact should project enough confidence to calm any suspicions. I vibrate like she raised the bass in my chest to high but don't lift my eyebrow or move into full-on flirting. That'd be too much.

"Visiting from Chicago?"

"Yep."

One of those preppy professional-service smiles reveals white teeth that amplify the glow of her sun-kissed face. Lots of hours spent at the tanning booth to get that shade, I bet.

She beams even wider, and I see that one of her canines on top is crooked. You have to pay attention to notice, but now that I do, her whole image changes, and the film of affluence the resort transferred onto her disappears. The tightly wound string inside slackens.

The bartender hands my fake back. Her fingers are cold and . . . damp? I run my thumb over the ID to remove what I hope is water and slide the card into the pocket of my jacket.

"Sorry." She catches my gesture and wipes her fingers off on a bar towel, reinforcing the humanity behind the uniform. I relax into my seat. "Buffalo Trace or Woodford Reserve?"

What the hell are those? I flip my phone over. Me, Nick, has no idea what she's asking about, but the twenty-one-year-old Shawn should have an answer.

"Whatever you think's best." Another thing I picked up from Dad. He's been throwing the phrase around, and Mom thinks he's matured. I hope he did. For her sake.

The bartender nods and turns around. While the bulky shirt doesn't reveal much of her body, the black pants hug her butt, and she'd get much better tips displaying that thing to the customers. More of a boob man myself, but I don't discriminate. She stands on her tiptoes to get a bottle with amber liquor from the glass shelf. I should stop staring at how cute her nose looks in profile, or wondering what she would look like in a less bulky top, or looking at her pants. I shift in my seat and try to ignore the flare of heat at the base of my spine. Definitely not looking at those. It's a slippery slope.

I force my eyes away from the perky backside that matches her whole sunny persona and survey the rows of bottles. The bar has no Christmas trees or Santas, going with a snow theme instead. Along the shelves with multi-colored jewel cases containing alcohol lies white fluffy material pretending to be the snow that doesn't exist in LA. A string of large snowflake-shaped lights glows above the top of the bar.

There aren't many things I'll miss about Chicago, but snow on Christmas might be one. I'd have to get used to people walking around in shorts, flip flops, and light sweaters. No matter how festive it is, nothing screams "Christmas" to me in LA.

The blond ponytail above the bartender's shoulders bounces when she moves to get a short tumbler with a line design cut across the bottom. Something James Bond would use. Many steps above the red plastic cups I drink cheap beer out of back home.

She grabs three bottles and sets them next to the glass. It's like I'm watching Mom's favorite British baking show, wondering what's next. I lean in. First, a bit of clear liquid goes in, then water, some dark stuff from a small container with a yellow cap, and a dash from an even tinier one with an orange label. The text on them is too small for me to read to find out what they are. I assumed cocktails could be convoluted, but this looks a bit like my chemistry class. She stirs the mixture with a silver spoon that has a long skinny handle, places one gigantic baseball sized ice cube into the glass, and pours Woodford Reserve over the ice.

Everything she does is self-assured and practiced. She shaves a bit of orange and lemon peel, folds them, runs them around the rim of the glass, squeezes a twist of mist over the whole thing, and places them in next to the ice. The scent of citrus hits my nostrils and sends me back to Yaya slicing lemons from her garden for Psari Plaki. The bartender's tan fingers match my drink but it's her crisp uniform, the glass, and the garnish that make this scene look like everything I'd expected from an overpriced bar at a high-end resort.

"Enjoy." I almost believe she means it. I bite the inside of my cheek as she moves the glass my way.

Ah, here it is. This would be the money shot: her hand setting the drink down as if it's in front of the viewer. The bar top can't be wood. I'd change it to something more reflective, maybe acrylic, so I could play with the lights and reflections.

I narrow my eyes and see the camera moving in as her hand pushes forward with the drink. The contrast of the amber liquid, tan skin, white cuff of the shirt, and touch of yellow and orange from the fruit peels work together to make the shot dramatic. I could underscore this scene with some sick beats as the glass comes toward us, and then something slow as we pan to it.

"Something wrong with the drink?" She leans closer and the foliage moves on the tag, revealing her name. Sarah C.

"Sarah, right? All good, thank you."

Another trick of Dad's. "Call them by their names," he told me yesterday, "the staff appreciates it." The staff. My stomach churns. People like him who come to places like this have staff, listen to smooth jazz, and order drinks you need a degree in mixology to make. He forgets Mom is the staff.

She's been cutting people's hair for the last ten years.

How do I drink this? I take a deep breath and rotate the glass. I've come too far to disappoint Sarah. Am I supposed to sniff it, like Mom does with her wine? I can't remember if Dad did anything special with his. I raise the drink to my lips.

The liquid burns my throat, but I think I hide it well. Lying's always come naturally to me. I get that from Dad, too.

I take another gulp. Pretending. One more gulp. Fibbing.

Sometimes I forget who the real Nick is.

And another one. It burns less with every swig, but I hate the taste. Bitterness coats my tongue. I can't drink any more. The glass, however, I love. Maybe I'll buy one like it for myself one day and drink beer out of it.

Why didn't I order a beer and enjoy something I liked instead of pretending I'm sophisticated? For the sake of who? The middle-aged crowd around me? The sunny Sarah, with her big grin and bright blue eyes? Eyes that are checking me out. No. I shake my head. Checking the fancy, Old Fashioned-drinking Shawn out.

Would she like me if I didn't pretend? If, for once, I was just me?

The fake ID can shield the real Nick from potential fallout yet let me be...well, me. Minus the right name. I straighten, my brain lighting up at the idea. The little piece of plastic, the small lie offers a chance to not be afraid to be Nick. Be myself.

"Sarah?" I begin my experiment.

From this point on, I vow to only tell the truth.

To this girl.

For this one night.

My heartbeat tries to outrun the tapping of my foot. Bartenders are like shrinks—they're supposed to listen and keep your secrets. Right?

Sarah

And I thought tonight would be boring.

Pull a double on Christmas Eve, compliment a few drunk lonely men, and make some good tips so I can pay off my overdue cell phone bill. Maybe get back to the apartment and the swinging Christmas Eve party my roommates are holding before someone starts having sex in my bedroom. The plan was simple.

Enter this guy. He's a plot twist in the film noir that was supposed to be my evening. He's all sorts of tall, dark, and handsome dressed in a black jacket and a red T-shirt that's calling to me like a beacon in this sea of winter white.

I swish the martini shaker and watch out of the corner of my eye as Shawn takes a sip of his drink. Did he notice I put a little extra bourbon in? Probably not. Months of bartending to figure out how to pour the perfect shot, but no one notices. They just want to name drop when ordering their fancy drinks. The silver cylinder almost flies out of my grasp, I rattle it so hard. I grit my teeth and restore my customer satisfaction smile. Sometimes I wonder if they even know what it is they're drinking, or if it's just the latest fad.

Shawn rubs the condensation off the smooth tumbler of his Old Fashioned. Up and down. His strong fingers wrap around the crystal. Lucky glass.

Really, Sarah? It's been a bit of a dry spell but c'mon. It's just fingers. And who under forty orders an Old Fashioned?

Old Fashioneds aren't in right now. It's all about gin these days. Thanks, Ryan Reynolds and your millions of Instagram followers. But maybe I should change my lead character's drink from a rum and coke to an Old Fashioned? Make Wesley seem more worldly. Hmmm. Need to think about that.

Sure. I've been *thinking* about Wesley and my opus for two months now. How about writing for a change? That screenplay isn't going to finish itself.

Unlike this martini. I can make 'em in my sleep. Plop, swish, pour.

I turn on my signature smile and focus on delivering a perfect martini to the next customer. In return, I get the glassy-eyed response from the woman sitting next to Shawn. Seeing me, but not seeing me. To her, I'm just another California blonde. That's me, your sweet, valley-girl bartender, here to listen to your woes, offer a kind nod or encouraging word as you spend your evening getting pickled at this swanky resort my poor broke ass couldn't afford to eat at, never mind stay.

Except I'm not sweet or from the valley. No one here notices or cares that I grew up far away in the great white north, as Californians like to joke. No, really, never heard that one before. It was like a daily mantra when I first got here and people remarked on my accent, or rather lack thereof. It's plain Canada to me, where the maple syrup is sweet and people can't look you in the eye when they lie to you. Not like here.

But Shawn's brown eyes didn't look away. The sparkle I see there almost makes me believe he cares enough to know my name.

"Sarah?"

Shawn *did* want to know my name. I sway his way. "Yes, Mr. Old Fashioned."

He swings his head, and I watch his dark hair flop over his forehead. "You're never going to let that go, are you?"

"Well, I call 'em as I see 'em and you . . . you dug your own hole, Mister." I bite my lip.

"Seriously, what can I do to change my reputation here? I'm desperate. Give a guy a break." His puppy-dog eyes urge me to give him anything he wants. I grin.

Holy crap. What is wrong with me?

"Fine. Give me something to work with here." I roll my eyes but flash him my real smile. Will he even notice the difference? Wow. Did he just raise an eyebrow at me? I'm seeing things now. "What's your favorite song?"

It's like he struck gold. Or I did. He sits up straight, and I have to look up. The skin on my neck heats. Wow, he is tall. I like tall.

Evens out my short. One side of Shawn's mouth curls. Cute. So cute.

"That's a big question. I mean, one song for all time? Too many options." His gaze locks on mine, and his pupils grow as we enter a staring match. "You have to narrow down the playing field a bit. You can't put my latest fave and the Beatles in the same category."

I laugh. I actually laugh. Air rushes into my chest, and I'm giddy. Where did this guy come from?

I place my arms on the bar and lean toward him, waiting to see if he checks out my cleavage. I'm pretty sure he was eyeballing it earlier. They all check out my chest. It's in their DNA. Maybe I should give him the benefit of the doubt and chalk it up to an attempt to read my nametag. Yeah, right.

Shawn's eyes never leave mine. Okay. The bar behind him falls out of focus. I might need to sit down. "Okay, then. Favorite Christmas song."

Now he laughs. Crinkles form at the corner of his eyes, and the sparkle is back. "Oh, I asked for that, didn't I?'

"Yup." Who am I to disagree?

Tapping his finger—the one previously feeling up his glass—against his bottom lip, Shawn makes a face like he's concentrating hard. Goosebumps rush across my clavicle. I love that he's taking this seriously. He's taking *me* seriously.

"Well, you know, I like the classics. I'm gonna stay in my lane. *Little Drummer Boy,* wait for it"— his grin is infectious—"*Peace on Earth* by Bowie and Bing." He slaps his hand on the bar, pleased with himself. "Two geniuses of their genres coming together to create magic. That's Christmas to me."

"Who are you?" My mouth takes over.

The light in his eyes dims. No, no, we were having fun. Ignore my stupid question, keep talking about Bowie. I clutch the edge of the bar. My brain scrambles, trying to bring back the sun. "I love Bowie too."

"Just a k . . . guy from Chicago here for the holidays visiting my dad." He rubs the fine layer of stubble on his chin. Would the short hairs be soft, or scratch my fingers? "I'm waiting for him to finish up a meeting."

"The windy city, eh? Enjoying the warm weather?"

"I guess. Doesn't feel like Christmas, though."

"Where I grew up, we always had a white Christmas. We'd go skating on Boxing Day."

Shawn scrunches his nose. "Boxing Day?"

He's peering at me like I have two heads.

"Keep forgetting you Americans don't celebrate Boxing Day. In Canada, where I'm from"—I point at my chest, but his eyes don't stray— "it's the day after Christmas. You get to lounge around stuffing yourself with leftovers, watching movies, or, if you're like my mom, you throw your kids out into the snow to burn off the sugar we inhaled. I think she wanted some peace and quiet."

Why am I still talking? I pick at a snowflake-shaped coaster. I just shared more with Shawn in two minutes than I did the first six months I lived with my roommates. And I'm pouring the liquor, not drinking it. Yet. One of the perks of this job is sampling new products our boss acquires so we can recommend them. The new Japanese and Belgian beers I'm bringing to the "so you're alone on Christmas too" celebration—the impromptu party my friends Siobhan and Claudia are throwing for out-of-towners—looked promising. Is there even such a thing as a local in LA?

"I can roll with that. Not the sugar, it's not my thing, but the movie part, for sure. I'm either watching one or filming one."

"Well, you're in the right town." I wince at the vinegar in my voice. Really, Sarah, you gotta get over this. It was one bad move. How were you supposed to know it was a scam? Not everyone in Tinseltown is a liar or a crook. Newbies, like Shawn here, start off decent, straightforward, and honest, and he might even stay that way. I shrug. For most of us, this town eventually chews us up and spits us out like yesterday's trash.

"That's my plan. Move here."

Should I burst his bubble? Warn him? Nah, not my place. Shawn has family here. They'll look out for him.

"Hey, Sarah, where d'you want this?" Ryan's holding another box of the wine I asked him to bring from the storeroom. Is it number eight or nine? I'm losing count. I massage my temples. Hope we have enough to last the rest of the night.

"There is fine." I point to the other end of the bar, where the last unopened bottle sits.

"What else do you need help with?" Patience has never been Ryan's virtue. The man can't seem to sit still. "I need to get back to the floor. The VIP group needs attention."

Shit. I survey the dwindling crowd. Standing here just chatting with this Shawn guy isn't good for my tips.

"On my way," I shout to Ryan over my shoulder and give Shawn my best apology smile.

I top off the guy whose attempts at flirting irritated me before Shawn showed up but are ridiculous at this point. He's drinking Veuve like it's water, which is great for the bar, but my skin crawls as he licks his lips while not so subtly staring down the open collar of my uniform. My stomach rolls. I pull the material closed and hoof it down to Ryan to help him unpack the box.

This Icellars Winery's red is popular lately. Glad something from my hometown can make it in LA. I leave two bottles on the bar as my coworker stacks the rest underneath.

"Got a live one there?" Ryan turns his stoned smirk on me.

"What?"

"The hot kid." My partner for the evening nods in Shawn's direction.

"Him? He's not a kid." Not with that five o'clock shadow.

Ryan narrows his eyes at me like he's got a secret. "Only guy here under fifty. Besides me."

"What's your point, Ryan?" He's a little too aware of my LA loser streak. You could say, he got the ball rolling. We had a thing when I first started—another one of my mistakes. I was so green when I moved out here. All bright-eyed and bushy tailed. Good thing the thick skin grew quickly.

Still, unlike every other aspect of his life, Ryan is pretty mature about being friends. I think. He doesn't seem to mind that I'm basically his boss.

"All I'm saying, I've seen that look before." His eyes dart down the bar to Shawn. "Is he eligible to join the Sarah Club?"

I follow Ryan's gaze. Shawn's honey brown hair flops over his eyes as he studies the half-empty glass he's no longer drinking. Flutters dance at the base of my throat. Good taste in music. Check. Doesn't take himself too seriously. Check. Hands big enough to wrap around my waist. Check.

"Why not?" I scrunch my nose. "Could be fun."

"Attagirl." Ryan grins at me. The same grin that got me in trouble the first time. Good thing it holds no power over me anymore. "Get back on that horse. Ride, baby, ride."

I punch Ryan lightly in the stomach as I turn and saunter toward my target.

"Hey, Shawn." He doesn't react. I reach over and touch his hand. He startles, tugs on a red cord, and takes out an earbud.

"Talking to me?"

The whirl spreads to my diaphragm. "Yes. My shift's ending. Wanna ditch these old folks and hang with some people our age?" The offer is out of my mouth before I have a chance to overthink it.

He pulls the other earbud out and lowers his head, looking at me. The whir falters. Why isn't he saying anything? Should've buttered him up first. He must have plans already.

"Got something in mind?" Shawn asks.

He's interested. My stomach does a little flip. Maybe this Christmas won't suck after all.

"Yeah, my roommates are having a party. The more the merrier." Please don't say no. Please don't say no.

"Sure."

And just like that, I won't be the only single girl at the party tonight. Of course, he's only coming because it's better than hanging out with this crowd all evening. But still. My lungs expand.

"Great. Give me ten to finish up and change."

"Okay. I'll wait here."

As I turn to go, Shawn scans my body with another raised eyebrow, and I can tell he likes what he sees.

END OF SNEAK PEEK OF

Kisses, Lies, & Us

THE AND US SERIES

One night to bring them together.
One lie to tear them apart.
Five holidays to fall in love.

Watch movies and real life collide with Sarah and Nick in a right person/wrong time, hidden identity, new adult romance. One year, five parts, six major holidays, many twists.

Kisses, Lies, & Us
Passions, Hopes, & Us
Distance, Love, & Us

or

The Complete Series

with bonus scenes and an additional epilogue

Turn the page for a sneak peek of
the first book in the Falling for the Movie Star Series.

If you like an age gap, brother's best friend romance featuring
LA's red-carpet glamor, Irish charm, and a reunion written in
the stars, Siobhan and Asher's story is for you.

Siobhan

A CARDBOARD TUBE WITH a shred of toilet paper mocks me. Of course, I end up in the bathroom stall that's missing the key element. My parents ran out of Irish luck when they had me: I'm the only member of the Casey clan born on US soil.

"Can't open the flippin' holder." My best friend isn't her usual happy-go-lucky self. She's nervous for a reason. Months of hard work, and the possibility of writing for a big Hollywood movie comes down to tonight.

"Don't break your new nails. Just shove a bunch under the divider."

The coveted wad of white toilet paper and Sarah's undamaged red nails appear beside the spike of my stiletto.

"Got it." My voice sounds strangled, because I'm holding the bottom of my floor-length sequined dress between my chin and my chest.

"Good. Now hurry. We don't want to miss the opening number," says Sarah. "I hope we'll be celebrating more than just your birthday tonight."

The best birthday present would be hearing, "And the Starlight award goes to Sarah Connor." Ever since I met her two years ago when she moved to LA, Sarah's been the one with a plan: become a screenwriter. May have hit a few bumps (okay, craters) on the road, but my girl is making her dreams come true.

The shapewear I have on at the insistence of Mrs. Marino, my boss who lent me this elaborate golden gown worth a year of my salary, doesn't want to go back up. How do people spend all night in these things?

"We were so sorry to hear about you and Leyla," the interviewer says on the TV in the lounge part of the restroom.

My ears perk up. I'm not sorry at all. I've been obsessing over my favorite romantic star's newfound freedom for weeks now.

"Well," Asher Menken's deep baritone loses its smoothness, "all I can say is—"

"Ladies and Gentlemen"—the TV switches from the pre-recorded interview to the real-time coverage of the awards ceremony—"welcome to the Fifth Annual Starlight Foundation Gala."

For feck's sake. The world is dying to know Asher's take on his ex. Okay, I'm dying to know. Even if I get a chance to see him, it's not like I could ask him myself.

"How much longer?" Sarah can't hide her impatience. "I don't want to miss anything."

"Just go." I wave my free hand at the closed door as if Sarah can see me. "I'll be in as soon as I can wrangle this tiny torture device back onto my crotch."

"You sure?"

"Aye, go already. Nick's waiting." Probably cursing me. Boyo is also nervous tonight, and we don't get along at the best of times. "Enjoy yourself. You've worked so hard for tonight."

A few clicks of her high heels plus the sound of the door closing, and I'm left alone with my tight beige nemesis.

I tuck the bottom of the dress into my décolleté. This is bollocks. I peel the undergarment off my thighs and balance on one, then the other silver strappy sandal as I struggle to free myself. Dress righted, I take my first deep breath of the night, ball up the offending material, toss it into the bin, give it the finger, and exit the stall.

A quick check of my stomach in the mirror shows it's as flat as it was with the awful contraption. I wash my hands and ensure my hair survived the battle of the bulge. The aquamarine dye I've been using this summer is starting to bore me. Might be time for a change.

The blue corner of the tattoo on the inside of my wrist is showing. I tug the long sleeves of the dress down, causing the neckline to plunge even more. Gotta make sure I cover up my body art tonight. While highly unlikely, Mum and Da might see pictures. They don't exactly know about this version of my artwork. My tastes run more towards black ink than gold sequins, but I do rock this dress. I blow myself a kiss in the mirror. Time to get this show on the road.

I reach for the door handle when the painted wood panel flies open and smashes into my shoulder. For a moment I teeter on my heels, sure I can save myself, but this battle I don't win. I land hard on the solid tiles of the bathroom floor.

"Bloody hell," I yelp.

The door slams shut, then opens again, and a tuxedo-clad figure enters the room. "Damn it, sorry, I didn't mean to . . . didn't know . . . are you hurt?" The crisp black silk of men's trousers crinkles as the offender crouches down and stretches his hand my way.

I blink. Then blink again. Wide pools the color of whiskey I've drooled over during movie nights with the girls peer at me.

"Are you okay?" An expression worthy of an Oscar nomination graces Asher Menken's face as he scans my body for broken bits.

I wiggle my toes, rub my shoulder, and swivel my head around. "All in one piece, no thanks to you." I've wanted to approach him since I first saw Ash on the red carpet a couple of feet ahead of us, but he was in the middle of an interview, probably the one I'd just been listening to. He and my big brother Owen are still best friends, but over a decade has passed since the superstar and I have been in the same room together.

"What can I do?" There is no spark of recognition in his eyes despite the fact that other than the long hair, I'm a mini copy of my brother. I wait to see if anything clicks, but his focus is not on my face. Rather, he gawks at my naked leg, exposed in all its glory thanks to the thigh-high slit in this fancy dress. His gaze travels up my leg and I follow, until we get to where the lace of my aquamarine thong is visible, no longer shielded by the Spanx. He looks at my hair, then my thong, and swallows.

"I still like matching things," I say.

"Sorry?"

"My hair matches my thong. Like my hair bows used to match my clothes, remember?"

His eyes narrow, and he tilts his head. "I think you might've hit your head."

"I'm Siobhan." I lift the sleeve off my left wrist and show him the tiny star, my very first tattoo. I got the memento as soon as I moved here seven years ago: my design, based on the one I drew for Ash a lifetime ago. "Réiltín?"

Another sweep of his eyes takes in more of my face as he scans me up and down, or left to right, or however the horizontal plane is looked at. "Owen's little sister?" His eyebrow rises.

"Aye."

"Unbelievable." He reaches inside his jacket, pulls out his wallet, and takes out a piece of paper. Ash sits next to me on the icy floor as I tug at the dress in a too-late attempt to cover up. He gives the paper to me. "My good luck charm."

I stare. In my hand is a faded copy of what I now have on my wrist. The original little star I drew for him when I was nine.

"You . . . kept this?"

Asher casts his eyes to the floor, and my pulse takes off. I mean, I've seen the expression before, both on and off the screen, yet up close and personal like this he's . . . gorgeous. Yes, the teeth are perfect, the chin is chiseled, and the hair—oh, how I want to run my hands through his hair to test if those strands are as tuggable as they appear. But this is more than the good looks. He's lit up from within.

I hand the piece of paper from the past back to him and will my heart to slow.

"Owen did say you lived here." Ash tucks the drawing carefully back in his wallet and puts it away. "Of all places to run into you." He smiles, and there's the "I'm sorry" smile that got him out of a trip to the police when he bumped into a car in front of us. The lady who owned the Peugeot let him go with, "What's one more scratch on this old heap of metal?" She would've berated any of my brothers for doing the same thing.

"I promised my friends not to get starstruck, but I didn't think they meant literally." I smile back. "Howeyeh, Ash? Can I still call you that?"

He nods, giving me the once over again. "Can't call you Little Star anymore. You're no longer . . . little."

My turn to swallow. The way he said *little* sends a shiver through me that I can't blame on the chill of the tile floor. My name is a puzzle for most people in LA. At work I heard a million attempts at my name until I came up with "she-Vaughn." Sarah shortens it to just Sio, "she." Back in Ireland my family calls me Shiv, and Mum insists on Baby Girl. But Asher's nickname for me, Réiltín, which means Little Star, might be my favorite. "I don't mind." He can call me anything.

"Réiltín it is, then." He runs his hand through the thick light brown strands he inherited from his movie star mother and rests his fingers on the nape of his neck. "We should probably get off this floor." He jumps to his feet, wraps his fingers around my wrist, and lifts me up. I wince in pain.

"Did I hurt you?"

"The shoulder is a bit tender." I lower the neckline and see a red line across my skin. Ash's thumb traces the mark from the door. His touch doesn't make the pain go away, but I'm both nervous and more secure with his skin on mine. His presence has always had this effect on me. The thrill and the comfort at the same time.

The first time I met him, my nine-year-old self didn't know what to think about Ash. He wasn't a famous Hollywood star then, just the nineteen-year-old friend my brother brought home for Christmas break because Ash had no family in Ireland to spend the holiday with. A breath of fresh air all the way from California to light up our middle-of-nowhere in County Kerry.

I fix my dress. "We should get going. My friend Sarah must be wondering where I am."

"Sure you're okay?"

"I'm tougher than I seem."

"You look"—he pauses—"great in this dress. All grown-up." His eyes stray to my cleavage.

"Yup." I straighten and push my chest forward. "Got me big girl boobs and everything."

"I didn't mean to . . ." His "I'm sorry" smile is back. "This isn't what I—"

"Just having a laugh." I tap him on the arm, like we're old pals. "Great way to start my next quarter century."

"Today?"

"'Tis."

"Well, happy birthday to you." He purses his lips, and his eyes brighten. "We could have a drink after the gala? Celebrate? Catch up?"

"Bang on." I don't jump up and down like I used to when I got to spend time with him, but I flash him my "thank you for a great tip" smile. Asher Menken wants to have drinks with me. I ain't saying no.

"Great. But"—he rubs the wrinkles between his eyebrows—"a favor? Could you check if there is a guy in a red velvet tuxedo hanging around by any chance? If he is, I'll stay here a while longer."

"Aye." I peek out of the door and see empty hallways. "The coast is clear."

Siobhan Casey.

I can't believe Owen's baby sister scared my bathroom stalker off with foul language worthy of an R-rated movie. The creep thought he was clever hiding around the corner, ready to accost Siobhan and me on our way to the ceremony. Her vocabulary, among other things, has grown. In fact, there isn't much left of the little girl with a short bob, matching hair accessories, and hand-me-down outfits from her brothers. Although the eyes, those sometimes green, sometimes blue, sometimes gray eyes of hers, and Owen's, and their Ma's. I should've recognized those eyes.

When my publicist Jackson asked me to be part of tonight's ceremony, I almost said no. I hate these types of affairs. The fakeness. The shallowness. The constant vying for attention. I never dreamed my night would be like this.

I glance out into the sea of creativity, and the rush of youthful exuberance hits me like a tidal wave. My partnership with the Starlight Foundation was the right decision. This is the perfect project to kickstart my new production company. I already got the green light for two TV shows, and this movie, with the proper amount of press, will give me the cachet to do more.

Still, the best part is the opportunity to give back, do something worthwhile with the fame I've been lucky enough to achieve. And when the tall kid accepts his Best Director award, he's genuinely ecstatic. I can't help grinning like a fool along with him.

"That's Nick." Siobhan sits down after she finishes clapping her hands raw. An empty seat next to me had been an open invitation for the opportunists looking to pitch, but now I'm glad the organizers assumed I would bring a date. "He's been in LA less than six months, and look at him. I'm here seven years and keep slinging drinks."

"You want to be in the movie business?"

"God, no. Owen is the one with the acting bug in our family."

"Why LA then?" Owen refused to tell me the full story.

"Farthest place I could escape to with my American passport that met my criteria."

"Which were?"

"Far from Ireland, fun, sunny, and not an island." She winks at me. Good to see she hasn't lost her spunky attitude. "Had a string of jobs. Let's see, I was the Belgian waffle girl at Disneyland first. Girl's gotta start somewhere. Graduated to waitressing at a fifties themed diner. Gawd, that was horrible. They put that yellow American plastic they call cheese on everything. Who puts cheese on pie?"

Siobhan has the right to judge. Her family's cheese is the best I've ever tasted. Of course, I've had the privilege of stealing the stuff fresh from the cheese fridge when no one was looking. As a teenager I preferred to ask for forgiveness rather than permission. The bonus of performing in Dublin was that in three hours I could be at the Casey farm indulging in unlimited quantities of first-rate cheese. Well, and pretending I'm part of their large warm family. Owen is so lucky.

"Anyhow, now I work at a swanky resort bartending with my girl Sarah over there"—she swings her champagne glass in the direction of a group of young people, of which Sarah could be any one of three girls—"but the hours give me time to play artist."

"Well, lucky me. You saved me from being cornered by overeager fans and wannabe writers." And she saved me before. The first Christmas I spent at her family's farm, she saw me struggle to memorize my part for *The Little Prince*. I was ready to throw in the towel. Maybe the acting gene skipped a generation, maybe the tabloids were right and my good looks and family connections were the only reasons Trinity's theatre program accepted me.

Siobhan didn't let me give up. She ran lines with me, jumped up and down every time I got one right, and even drew me a picture of a little star, a réiltín, for good luck. The folded piece of paper with her design was in my pocket when I first went on stage and has been with me ever since, calming me when I'm nervous. And being back in the States has me super nervous tonight.

"He deserved the tongue-lashing. Shoving his script at you in the middle of the event is the worst way to get your attention."

"Hollywood is hard, I get it. But he was going to stuff the flash drive inside my jacket if you didn't interfere. I should've just shoved him off, but that'd end up in the papers with me as the unreasonable superstar, too stuck-up to talk to his fans." I take another sip from the flute the server keeps refilling. "The guy's face matched his red suit after you told him off. You're more effective than my bodyguards."

She laughs. Not the polite tut-tut of reporters reacting to my lame jokes or the light tinkle that warmed my heart when I managed to get Leyla to break character. No, this is a roaring, full-bodied, full-of-life laugh.

And I'm laughing along with her, feeling lighter than I've felt in months. No, years.

My real smile hasn't graced my face in forever. The world thinks Leyla and I broke up a few weeks ago. In reality, we've been apart for over a year. Our publicists timed the news for maximum impact, every step calculated to advance our careers. Well, her career. It's always been about her career. Every fight, a tug of war between her need to shoot for the stars and mine to settle down. In the end, our marriage came down to one thing: I can't wait to have kids, and she didn't want any.

"Gotta stand up for myself and those I care about," Siobhan says. "You know my older brothers; add waitressing in LA, and there's no better verbal self-defense school." She curls her arm and almost spills champagne onto herself. I catch the glass in time. "I know how to punch, too, if it comes to it. Owen made sure to teach me. And I always keep my thumb out."

She puts her glass down and demonstrates the proper fist technique. "Brothers." Her eyes widen. "Oh." She holds out her hand. "Give me your phone. Let's send Owen a selfie. It'll freak him out."

I like nothing more than pulling pranks on my best friend. My phone in hand, Siobhan leans in, her shoulder brushing against mine, and I inhale a mixture of honey and something spicy. "Smile," she instructs.

Easily done.

She plucks my cell from my fingers, her thumbs fly over the screen, and in a second, she flashes our smiling faces at me. "Check out who I bumped into," is written underneath our picture.

"Bumped into, huh." I chuckle at her play on how we met in the bathroom. She sends the text.

Siobhan opens my jacket, the gesture she berated the guy in the red suit for. "Done."

My body shrunk away from the rando's touch, but with my grown-up réiltín, I savor the contact. She puts my phone in the inside pocket and adjusts my sky-blue tie. Her eyes narrow, and she runs her fingers against the dots on the smooth silk.

"This tie, doesn't it remind you of the *Infinity* exhibit Yayoi Kusama did with the mirrors at The Broad a few years ago?"

I nod. "Like being inside a kaleidoscope." I took Leyla on a private tour of the immersive art installation at The Broad Modern Art Museum. We spent the evening lost in the multi-reflective rooms.

"Exactly." She smooths my tie one more time. The touch of her hand on my chest does things to me it should not. "Wasn't it deadly? Blows you only got five minutes in each room."

She's deadly. Real and beautiful. And alluring.

Gone is the little girl who doodled on anything she could get her hands on. Before me sits this vivacious, gorgeous woman. Her green—or are they blue—eyes twinkle in the low light of the reception hall.

"Did you study art?"

"I take classes when I can, but nothing official. I love to explore—oils, watercolors, sculpture, loom, pottery, print—tried them all. I even thought about costume design. But I think skin is my favorite canvas." She looks down at the star on her wrist.

This woman is a bright star in the dark night that has been my life lately. I can't look away; I won't, not when there's so much to see.

Even her dress teases by covering up practically everything yet accentuating her body in a way no garment should be allowed to. But I've glimpsed the secrets the fabric hides. Thinking about her long leg and how I'd run my hand up the curves to . . . I feel a twitch I haven't felt in a long time.

What am I doing? How can I be thinking like this? What would Owen say if he saw me ogling his sister?

Hey, boyo, don't even think about touching her.

Which is exactly what I'm doing. Thinking. And that's where I'll be stopping.

"So, you've traveled the world?" Siobhan reaches for another glass from the server walking by and our hands brush.

There it is again, the little electric shock like when I touched her in the bathroom. What is she doing to me? Am I having any effect on her? It's so hard for me to tell these days, reality and fiction always blurring. Is a woman truly interested in me, or is she just caught up in my fame and fortune?

It was easy when I met Leyla. We were both unknowns at the time, just starting out in the business. When our movie hit number one at the box office everything changed overnight. I was used to my parents' fame and seeing my face on the cover of tabloids wasn't new, but with my own fame, the frenzy reached a whole different level. Leyla and I relied on each other, bonded in the fire of chaos.

Siobhan is different. She knows me and doesn't have the starstruck expression my fans get. Talking to her brings the instant comfort I associate with my visits to her family farm. She taps her glass to mine, and I enjoy another brush of our fingers.

Her skin is cool. No, comfort isn't the right word. Connection? There's something here. We're on our third glass and I should be feeling the haziness of the alcohol, but instead, everything is crystal clear. For the first time in a long time, I'm alert and aware.

Four delicate fingers brush over the back of my hand, as if she's painting me with invisible watercolors. Her pupils dilate, and I'm sure mine do too. A slender index finger wraps around my thumb and slides up, down, and up again. If I'm reading her right, my year of celibacy is ending tonight.

She touches a sensitive part at the base of my thumb. "Wanna get out of here?" Siobhan's eyes confirm her invitation.

"Yes" escapes my lips before I even think about consequences.

"Give me a minute."

As she walks away, I text my security detail to let them know I'm ready to leave and there's going to be a plus one. Hopefully, we can slip out the back door and not get noticed.

Across the room, Siobhan's talking to a short blonde in an even shorter silver dress. They hug, and my little star's walking back toward me. Her slender hips swing with the movement, glittering gold. My body reacts with more than a twitch this time.

"Where to, sir?" asks the limo driver.

"The hotel," says Siobhan.

"How'd you—"

"Know? Figured you'd be staying with your parents since you just got back. Their house is in Malibu, right? A tad too far for tonight."

She's too smart for me.

The hotel is only a short ride from the venue, and in no time we're in the underground garage. I hop out of the car hoping to open the door for Siobhan, but she's too quick for me too. Leyla would've waited, expecting a grand gesture from me in case there were any cameras around. Always a show with that woman.

This girl—woman—however, pinches my security guard's arm. "Oh, you're a tough one." The guard sticks out his chest and eyes Siobhan up and down. "Spend every day at the gym, do we?"

I feel a pang in my chest. Jealousy? I jut out my arm. "Shall we?" Siobhan slinks hers through and leans into me. My temperature rises with the contact of her warm body as we make our way to the private elevator.

The metal doors slide together and once again we're alone.

"What is it about elevators?" she asks, a hand running down my arm.

"What d'you mean?"

"They're just so damn sexy."

"You think?"

She reaches up and tugs on my tie, giving me a low, breathy, "Yes."

I'm done for. Reason, propriety, and resistance are out the window. My lips collide with hers, one hand circling her waist to pull her closer, the other finally getting to touch the soft skin of the long lean leg she's hooked over my hip. My palm travels up her thigh and cups her butt.

The sequins of her dress scratch against my thin shirt as if they are clawing to get at me. She's amazing, and so alive. Her taste, her scent, her heat invade me, send currents through my body, and light me up like no other. The twitch is now a throb.

I don't have enough hands. I need to touch more of her, but there's no way I'm letting go of this luscious ass. I tear my mouth from hers and explore her chin, her neck. I pause, pressing my lips against her pulsing artery, the thump matching my own racing heartbeat.

The soft ding of the elevator indicates we've hit my floor, but I don't want to leave our little cocoon. Siobhan has other ideas and starts backing out of the elevator, my tie still clutched in her hand. I'm happy to follow, as long as I get to keep kissing those amazing lips.

We move down the hall, and I reluctantly break the kiss. "Wait."

"What? Bored already?"

"Not in the slightest." More like alive for the first time. "My room is this way." I clutch her arm and haul her down the hallway in the opposite direction, searching for my hotel room key with my free hand. I jam the card into the reader, the light goes green, and we burst into my suite.

Before the door closes, her fingers are undoing my belt.

"Careful of the gown. It's not mine."

The first time I roll a condom on, she doesn't even take her dress off.

END OF SNEAK PEEK OF

Star Struck

THE FALLING FOR THE MOVIE STAR SERIES

If you like an age gap, brother's best friend romance featuring LA's red-carpet glamor, Irish charm, and a reunion written in the stars, Siobhan and Asher's story is for you.

Acknowledgements

Well, the final note has been sung in Wil & El's swan song and we have so may people to thank.

Our editors helped us bring the melody to life. Thanks Kia, Victoria, and Laura for keeping us from creating a twelve-minute song with the word cheek repeated 49 times. (The first version had 49 cheeks. There are only 35 chapters in this book!)

Our fellow writer friends helped us out of plot holes and no third act break ups. Shout out to fellow slow burn romance author KG Fletcher for the brainstorm session that cracked Wil's character arc and answering last minute panicked emails about what could cause a band to be kicked out of a venue.

Our Discord Channel Willa Drew Readers helped us with important things like naming the band members of Death Elbow. Tanya M, we are a little in love with Lucian and Gideon, the polar opposite brothers and readers can thank Ashley M. for the suggestion of Xander.

Our Street and ARC teams helped us keep us going when we doubt ourselves, hype us up and steer us in the right direction when they read our early drafts and thoughts. We also enjoy chatting with them about other romance books, pets, our days, jewelry, and things we all get as a team.

Our book cover artists helped us by bringing together the visuals to showcase this love story. Thank you Books and Moods for pulling all three of the covers together and to María Peña for bringing three different scenes from Wil & El's story to life. Fun fact: We created the cover image for WE Balance before we wrote the book but wanted to have El in her beautiful blue dress. However, the first draft of WE Balance didn't have a place for her to wear the dress. So if you liked the date in Toronto, you can thank the cover for inspiring us.

Our PA Cece helped us by keeping the ball rolling with many admin tasks so we can concentrate on the writing stuff.

Our families helped us in ways that we can never repay. They are our first fans, our support network, and our sounding board. We wouldn't be able to do this without them. We can write about love because they show us what love is.

Our readers helped us because they remind us to share our stories with the world. From the bottom of our heart, we thank you for reading our books.

Our obsession with music helped us get through the many days that we spent brining Wil and El's trilogy to life. It tamed our savage souls when we were having a bad moments (or week) and reflected our joy when we were high on things going well. It brought us together. Music is a thread in both of our lives and this trilogy is our tiny homage to our love of music.

As an encore, we encourage you to head over to Spotify to listen to the two original songs written for this book. We not only wrote the lyrics for the songs in this book, Gala, with the help of a few professional singers and producers, came up with music and gave voice to Wil and El's love songs. Enjoy!

Join our newsletter mailing list for updates
and follow Willa Drew at
www.willadrew.com

If you like this book, please consider giving it a review, so others
can enjoy it as well.

SERIES BY WILLA DREW

SECOND CHANCE BILLIONAIRES

The Second Chance Billionaires series follows five lifelong friends—a grumpy CEO, a charming playboy, a retiring hockey pro, a British aristocrat, and a sci-fi author—from college roommates to billionaire boardrooms as they each get one more shot at love.

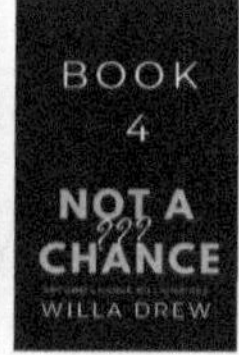

AND US

Watch movies and real life collide with Sarah and Nick in a right person/wrong time, hidden identity, new adult romance. One year, five parts, six major holidays, many twists.

Kisses, Lies, & Us

Passions, Hopes, & Us

Distance, Love, & Us

or binge the complete series with bonus scenes in

Friendzoned By My Crush

FALLING FOR THE ROCKSTAR'S DAUGHTER

An upper young adult, friends-to-lovers, slow burn romance

featuring a reluctant collaboration between two musicians.

WE Blend

WE Breathe

WE Balance

ANDERS INVESTIGATIONS

Meet the men of Anders Investigations, a new contemporary

romance series with a romantic suspense element.

Taming the Grumpy Bodyguard

Loving the Grumpy Bodyguard

Two authors. Two countries. One obsession with love stories.

Willa Drew's contemporary slow-burn romances are full of feels, playful banter, and high-stakes emotions. Their globe-trotting characters fight for love as they discover who they are and where they belong.

Willa, a proud Canadian and devoted Leafs hockey fan, and Drew, a Russian-American with a lifelong love of languages, always search for the perfect words to capture heartbreak and connection.

Their books guarantee swoon-worthy kisses and happily ever afters.

Come hang out with them
@willadrewauthor
willadrew.com